The Hemlock Falls Mysteries
1 pretty little town in upstate New York
1 picturesque inn overlooking Hemlock Gorge
2 talented sisters better at solving crimes
than they are at their day jobs
1 (or more) murders

A WINNING RECIPE FOR MYSTERY LOVERS
Don't miss these Hemlock Falls Mysteries . . .

A Carol for a Corpse . . .

Having the Inn featured in a magazine and on a television show chases away the holiday blues for Meg and Quill—until a slope-side slayer strikes . . .

Ground to a Halt . . .

Murder doesn't stop the Inn's pet food conventioneers from fighting like cats and dogs—but it does bring business to a grinding halt.

A Dinner to Die For . . .

Less-than-friendly professional competition. A serious case of cold feet. And, oh yes, a local murder. Could things go worse on Meg's wedding day?

Buried by Breakfast . . .

The leader of a raucous group of protestors turns up dead—and the Quilliams must quell fears and catch a killer before another local VIP is greeted with an untimely R.I.P.

A Puree of Poison . . .

While residents celebrate the 133rd anniversary of the Battle of Hemlock Falls, the Quilliam sisters investigate the deaths of three people who dined at the Inn before checking out.

continued . . .

Fried by Jury . . .

Two rival fried chicken restaurants are about to set up shop in Hemlock Falls—and the Quilliams have to turn up the heat when the competition turns deadly.

Just Desserts . . .

There's a meteorologist convention coming to the Inn, and it's up to Quill and Meg to make sure an elusive killer doesn't make murder part of the forecast.

Marinade for Murder . . .

The Quilliams' plans for the future of the Inn may end up on the cutting room floor when a group of TV cartoon writers checks in—and the producer checks out.

A Steak in Murder . . .

While trying to sell the locals on the idea of raising their own herds, a visiting Texas cattleman gets sent to that big trail drive in the sky. The Quilliams set out to catch the culprit and reclaim their precious Inn . . . without getting stampeded themselves!

A Touch of the Grape . . .

Five women jewelry makers are a welcome change from the tourist slump the Inn is having. All that changes when two of the ladies end up dead, and the Quilliams are on the hunt for a crafty killer.

Death Dines Out . . .

While working for a charity in Palm Beach, the Quilliam sisters uncover a vengeful plot that has a wealthy socialite out to humiliate her husband. Now the sleuths must convince the couple to bury the hatchet—before they bury each other!

Murder Well-Done . . .

When the Inn hosts the wedding rehearsal dinner for an ex-senator, someone begins cutting down the guest list in a most deadly way. And Quill and Meg have to catch a killer before the rehearsal dinner ends up being someone's last meal.

A Pinch of Poison . . .

Hendrick Conway is a nosy newsman who thinks something funny is going on at a local development project. But when two of his relatives are killed, the Quilliam sisters race against a deadline of their own.

A Dash of Death . . .

Quill and Meg are on the trail of the murderer of two local women who won a design contest. Helena Houndswood, a noted expert of stylish living, was furious when she lost. But mad enough to kill?

A Taste for Murder . . .

The annual History Days festival takes a deadly turn when a reenactment of a seventeenth-century witch trial leads to twentieth-century murder. Since the victim is a paying guest, the least Quill and Meg could do is investigate.

A PLATEFUL
OF MURDER

CLAUDIA
BISHOP

BERKLEY PRIME CRIME, NEW YORK

THE BERKLEY PUBLISHING GROUP
Published by the Penguin Group
Penguin Group (USA) Inc.
375 Hudson Street, New York, New York 10014, USA
Penguin Group (Canada), 90 Eglinton Avenue East, Suite 700, Toronto, Ontario M4P 2Y3, Canada
(a division of Pearson Penguin Canada Inc.)
Penguin Books Ltd., 80 Strand, London WC2R 0RL, England
Penguin Group Ireland, 25 St. Stephen's Green, Dublin 2, Ireland
(a division of Penguin Books Ltd.)
Penguin Group (Australia), 250 Camberwell Road, Camberwell, Victoria 3124, Australia
(a division of Pearson Australia Group Pty. Ltd.)
Penguin Books India Pvt. Ltd., 11 Community Centre, Panchsheel Park, New Delhi—110 017, India
Penguin Group (NZ), 67 Apollo Drive, Rosedale, North Shore 0632, New Zealand
(a division of Pearson New Zealand Ltd.)
Penguin Books (South Africa) (Pty.) Ltd., 24 Sturdee Avenue, Rosebank, Johannesburg 2196,
South Africa

Penguin Books Ltd., Registered Offices: 80 Strand, London WC2R 0RL, England

This is a work of fiction. Names, characters, places, and incidents either are the product of the author's imagination or are used fictitiously, and any resemblance to actual persons, living or dead, business establishments, events, or locales is entirely coincidental. The publisher does not have any control over and does not assume any responsibility for author or third-party websites or their content.

PUBLISHER'S NOTE: The recipes contained in this book are to be followed exactly as written. The publisher is not responsible for your specific health or allergy needs that may require medical supervision. The publisher is not responsible for any adverse reactions to the recipes contained in this book.

PRINTING HISTORY
Berkley Prime Crime trade paperback edition / October 2009

Library of Congress Cataloging-in-Publication Data

Bishop, Claudia, 1947–
    A plateful of murder / Claudia Bishop.
        p. cm.
    ISBN 978-0-425-22985-9
    1. Quilliam, Meg (Fictitious character)—Fiction.   2. Quilliam, Quill (Fictitious character)—
Fiction.   3. Sisters—Fiction.   4. Restaurateurs—Fiction.   5. Murder—Investigation—
Fiction.   6. Hemlock Falls (N.Y. : Imaginary place)—Fiction.   I. Bishop, Claudia, 1947–
Taste for murder.   II. Bishop, Claudia, 1947– Dash of death.   III. Title.
    PS3552.I75955P63 2009
    813'.54—dc22
                                                                            2009025634

PRINTED IN THE UNITED STATES OF AMERICA

10   9   8   7   6   5   4   3   2   1

CONTENTS

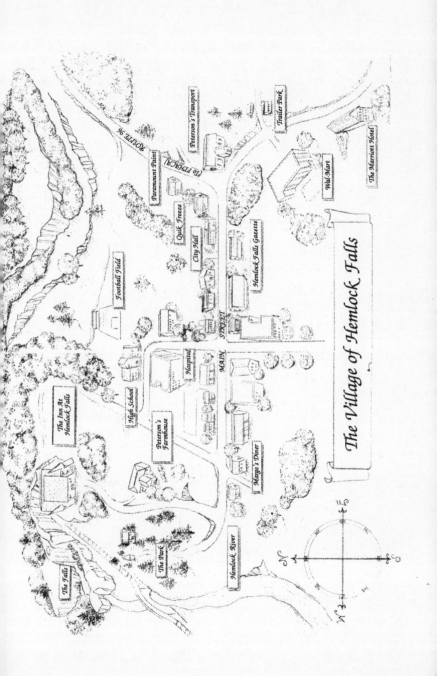

The Village of Hemlock Falls

A TASTE FOR MURDER

For Robert, with love

ACKNOWLEDGMENTS

This novel was supported by my good friends Nancy Kress, Miriam Monfredo, and Patricia Trunzo. My sister Whit supplied information on menus, recipes, and culinary technique. She is a far better cook than my interpretation would suggest.

THE CAST OF CHARACTERS

THE INN AT HEMLOCK FALLS
the staff

Sarah Quilliam	the owner
Margaret Quilliam	her sister, the chef
John Raintree	the manager
Doreen Muxworthy	head housekeeper
Peter Williams	assistant manager
Frank Torelli	a *sous* chef
Bjorn Hjalsted	a *sous* chef
Kathleen Kiddermeister	a waitress
Julie Offenbach	a waitress
Dina Muir	the receptionist
Nate	the bartender
Mike	the groundskeeper

(Also part-time waitresses, bartenders, and housemaids)

the guests

Amelia Hallenbeck	a widow
Mavis Collinwood	her companion
Keith Baumer	a bachelor
Edward Lancashire	a bachelor
The Reverend Willy Max	an evangelist

MEMBERS OF THE CHAMBER OF COMMERCE

Elmer Henry	the mayor
Gil Gilmeister	a car dealer
Tom Peterson	his business partner
Christopher Croh	a bar owner
Nadine Gilmeister	Gil's wife

Harvey Bozzel	advertising agency owner
Howie Murchison	town justice and local lawyer
Mark Anthony Jefferson	a banker
Esther West	dress shop owner
Marge Schmidt	diner owner
Betty Hall	Marge's partner
Ralph Lorenzo	newspaper publisher
Norm Pasquale	high school band director
The Right Reverend Dookie Shuttleworth	a minister
Harland Peterson	farmer, and president of the Agway cooperative
Freddie Bellini	a mortician
Miriam Doncaster	a librarian

THE SHERIFF'S DEPARTMENT

Myles McHale	the sheriff
Dave Kiddermeister	a deputy

CHAPTER 1

Elmer Henry, mayor of Hemlock Falls, swallowed the last spoonful of zabaglione, disposed of the crystallized mint leaf with a loud crunch, and burped in satisfaction. He whacked the Hemlock Falls Chamber of Commerce official gavel and rose to his feet. This familiar signal jerked Sarah Quilliam out of a daydream involving rum punch, Caribbean beaches, and a lifeguard. She grabbed her notebook, scrawled "HFCOC Minutes," and tried to look attentive.

Elmer looked down the length of the banquet table with a somewhat bovine expression of pleasure. Twenty of the twenty-four members of the Chamber looked placidly back. The imminence of the annual celebration of Hemlock History Days brought the members out in force. The corps of regulars—Quill, the mayor, Marge Schmidt, Tom Peterson, and Gilbert Gilmeister among them—were swelled considerably; like Easter, Hemlock History Days offered unbelievers a chance to hedge their bets.

Oblivious to the command of the gavel, Marge Schmidt and Betty Hall held a *sotto voce* conversation concerning their mutually expressed preference to die rather than consume one more bite of suspect foreign substances such as the Italian pudding just served them. Quill rejected various witty rejoinders in defense of her sister's cooking and opted for a dignified silence.

Elmer rapped the gavel with increasingly louder thwacks until Marge and Betty shut up and settled into their seats. "This meeting is called to order," Elmer said. He nodded to Dookie Shuttleworth, minister of the Hemlock Falls Word of God Reform Church.

Dookie was thin, rather shabbily dressed, and had a gentle, bemused expression; under stress, input frequently vanished altogether from Dookie's hard drive, a circumstance wholly unrelated to his vocation and met with tolerance by his parishioners.

He wiped his napkin firmly across his mouth and stood up for the invocation. "Lord, bless this gathering of our weekly session, and all its members." He paused, looked thoughtful, and suppressed a belch. "Most especially, the management of the Hemlock Falls Inn, Meg and Sarah Quilliam, for this fine repast."

Quill smiled and murmured an acknowledgment, which Dookie ignored in his earnest pursuit of the Lord's attention. "Lord, if you see fit, please send us fine weather and generous folks for the celebration of Hemlock Falls History Days next week. May these men and women seek you out, Lord, particularly in Your house here at Hemlock Falls. When the collection plate is passed, may they open their hearts and more, in Your service. As you know, Lord, the church checking account . . ."

Elmer Henry cleared his throat.

Dookie concluded hastily, "All these things we ask in Jesus' name. Amen."

"Amen," echoed the assembled members.

"Hadn't you ought to ask the good Lord for blessings on our stummicks so we don't end up in the hospital after eatin' this pudding?" Marge Schmidt demanded. A principal in the only other restaurant in town, Marge's German heritage was evident in her fair hair, ruddy complexion, and blue eyes. The protuberance of those eyes, the double chin, and the belligerence were all her own.

Quill straightened in indignation.

Marge continued blandly, "Made with raw eggs, this stuff. What d'ya call it? Zabyig-something."

"Zabaglione," said Quill. She pushed back her mass of red hair with one slim hand and said mendaciously, "It's one of Meg's eggless varieties."

"It's made with raw eggs everywheres else," said Marge. "You won't find raw eggs in good old American food. Strictly against the New York State Department of Health instructions. Din't you and your sister get that notice they sent out last week? Got one down to the diner if you need a copy."

"Salmonella," interjected Marge's companion and business partner, Betty Hall. "All of us in the restaurant business got that notice. Maybe that sister of yours can't read."

Quill reflected that nobody, including the patrons of the Hemlock Hometown Diner (Family Food! And Fast!), got along with Marge and Betty, and a response would invite acrimony. The first law of successful innkeeping was to maintain neutrality, if not outright peace. "I can't imagine anyone getting sick on Hemlock Falls cooking, Marge," she said diplomatically. "Yours *or* ours."

Marge rocked back in her chair, to the potential danger of the oak. "Me, either. No, ma'am. But that's something different from bein' in violation of the American law with weird Italian food. Betty and me stick to pizza. And this-here pudding is a clear violation of the law. Right, Sheriff McHale?"

Myles McHale nodded expressionlessly and dropped a wink in Quill's direction. He was looking especially heroic this afternoon, and Quill made a mental note to ask him if he'd ever been a lifeguard. With that chest, it was certainly likely.

Myles said, "Why don't I just go ahead and arrest both Meg and Quill, Marge? Been wanting to do it anyhow. Locking Quill up may be the only way I'll get her to marry me. And I'd have Meg's cooking all to myself."

"Ha, ha." Marge adjusted her blue nylon bowling jacket with a sniff and subsided, muttering, "Eggless, my ass."

"Let's get to the agenda," Elmer said. "First off, Quill, will you read the minutes from the last meeting?"

"Shall I move to dispense with everything but the agenda for today?" Quill asked. She hadn't translated her scrawled shorthand and wasn't at all sure she could read last week's notes out loud.

"She can't do that," said Marge. "She's the secretary. The secretary can't move not to read the minutes."

"Then I'll so move," said Myles.

"Let's just get to the agenda for today," said Elmer. "History Days is less than seventy-two hours away, unless everyone's forgotten. What's the status as of last week, Quill?"

Quill squinted at her notes. "Booths. Four *P*'s," she read uncertainly.

There was an expectant silence.

Four *P*'s. Quill tugged at her lower lip. Four *P*'s . . . "Parade. Play. Parking . . ." She tugged harder. "Promotion!" She smiled triumphantly. "We need a report on the status of the booths, on the parade, and on the rehearsals for the play . . ."

Elmer deciphered the remaining *P* with no trouble; Quill had been Chamber secretary for five years. Promotion was adman Harvey Bozzel's job. "So the first thing is the booths. How many we got registered, Howie?"

Howie Murchison, local attorney and justice of the peace, paged methodically through a manila folder drawn from his briefcase. "One hundred and twenty-two, as of yesterday." He peered deliberately at Quill over his wire-rimmed glasses. "I'll go slowly so you can get the information *into* the minutes. Twenty-three home-crafts. Sixteen jewelry. Fifty-eight assorted pottery and painting. Six food. Seven habadashery, that is to say, T-shirts, straw hats, and other clothing items. Eleven miscellaneous, such as used books, something referred to as 'collectibles,' and Gil's display of the new line of Buicks. Forty-three percent of the registration fees have been prepaid for a total of six hundred and fifty-nine dollars and forty-six cents."

Quill scrawled: 101. 23 ditz. 16 ? ? ? ? $659, 46 is 47%. Then, after a moment's thought: Re. NYS memo: Meg.

"And the parade report?" Elmer turned to Norm Pasquale, principal of the high school.

Norm bounced to his feet. "The varsity band's been rehearsing all week. They sound just terrific. The Four-H club has fourteen kids on horses signed up to ride. We've got eight floats, down one from last year because Chet's Hardware went out of business after the Wal-Mart moved in." He sat down.

Elmer nodded matter-of-factly. "I told Chet he'd never get a dollar and a half a pound for roofing nails. What about the play, Esther? Rehearsals going okay there?"

Esther West owned the only dress shop (West's Best) in Hemlock Falls. She was director of the re-creation of the Hemlock Falls seventeenth-century witch trial, *The Trial of Goody Martin*, a popular feature of History Days. She frowned and adjusted the bodice of her floral print dress, then patted a stiff auburn curl into place over her ear. "I do believe that the Clarissa's sickening for flu."

A murmur of dismay greeted this statement.

"Who's playing Clarissa Martin this year?" asked Quill.

"Julie Offenbach, Craig's girl."

"Oh, my." Quill knew her. A wannabe Winona Ryder, Julie

spent the summers between high-school semesters waitressing at the Inn. "She'll be crushed."

"You got that right!" hooted Gil Gilmeister. Even Quill, a relative newcomer to Hemlock Falls, knew Gil had been a star quarterback for the high school twenty years before; like Rabbit Angstrom, he'd gone into that quintessential small-town American business—car sales. Unlike his fictional counterpart, he was filled by more *Sturm* than *Angst*, with a boisterous enthusiasm for Buicks, Marge Schmidt, and town activities not unrelated to his days on the football field. "Go-o-o-o *Clarissa*!" he shouted now, thumping a ham-sized fist on the table. "Splat! Splat! Splat!"

The witch trial dramatized the real seventeenth-century Clarissa's death by pressing. Most pre-Colonial American villages burned, hanged, or drowned their witches, and Hemlockians were inordinately proud of their ancestors' unique style of execution—Hemlock Falls witches had been pressed to death. Although any large flat surface would have done, Hemlock Falls citizens of bygone days dropped a barn door on the condemned, then piled stones on the door until the victim succumbed to hemorrhaging, suffocation, or a myocardial infarction. Julie, as Clarissa Martin, would be replaced by a hooded dummy at the critical moment, but there was a wonderful bit of histrionics as "Clarissa" was driven off to await her fate. Julie had rehearsed with enormous relish for weeks.

"Doesn't Julie have an understudy or something?" asked Betty Hall. "No?" She jerked her head at her partner. "Marge here. She could do it. She's a real quick study. Memorizes the specials at the diner every night, just like that." She snapped her fingers.

Elmer, perhaps thinking of the size of the barn door required to squash a dummy of Marge-like proportions, not to mention the creation of a new, more elephantine dummy to replace the one traditionally used for years, said sharply, "Budget," which puzzled everyone but Quill, whose thoughts had been running along the same lines but in a much less practical way.

"Marge'd be terrific," said Gil Gilmeister earnestly. Since almost everyone at the table—with the possible exception of Dookie Shuttleworth—knew that Marge and Gil had been a hot item for several years, Gil's support was discounted without any discussion.

"Although," Esther whispered to Quill, "if Nadine Gilmeister could get herself out of those Syracuse malls long enough to do right by the poor man so he didn't have to spend his nights over to the diner, maybe more people would listen to him." Elmer rapped the gavel loudly, and Esther jerked to attention.

"What do you want to do then, Esther? Appoint an understudy?"

"It should be somebody stageworthy. Somebody with presence. And good-looking. The execution is the highlight of *The Trial of Goody Martin*. It's what everyone comes to see." Esther's eyes glinted behind her elaborately designed glasses. "When the actors pile the stones on the barn door, the audience should be moved to enthusiasm as Clarissa's blood spews out. Most years, as you've observed, the tourists join in."

"Well, they'll more likely laugh if fat ol' Marge is supposed to be under there," said Harland Peterson, the president of the farmer's co-op. A large, weatherbeaten man, Harland drove the sledge that carried "Clarissa Martin" from the pavilion stage to the site of the execution. "No offense, Marge," he said, in hasty response to her outraged grunt. "Now, the ducking stool—that's gonna be just fine. That ol' tractor of mine'll lift you into that pond, no problem. But we get a dummy your size under that barn door, it's gonna stick out a mile. What about Quill, there? She'd be great."

Harvey (The Ad Agency That Adds Value!) Bozzel cleared his throat. "I'd have to agree." His tanned cheeks creased in a golf-pro grin. "Try this one on, folks. 'Quill fills the bill.'"

Quill, who so far had managed to avert Harvey's advertising plans for the Inn (No Whine, Just Fine Wine When You Dine!), said feebly, "I don't really think . . ."

"I'm not sure that Julie's vomiting is going to continue through next week," said Esther thoughtfully, "but you never know. And of course, the costume is black, and just shows everything."

Myles said, "I move to nominate Sarah Quilliam as understudy for julie Offenbach."

Quill glared at him.

"I second," said Harland Peterson.

"All in favor?" said Elmer, sweeping the assembly with a glance. "Against?" He registered Marge's, Betty's, and Gil's upraised hands without a blink. "Carried. Quill takes Julie's place as Clarissa Martin, if necessary."

Quill experienced a strong desire to bang her head against the solid edge of the banquet table. This was followed by an even stronger desire to bang Myles McHale's head against the banquet table, since he'd started the whole mess in the first place. She took a deep breath and was preparing to argue, when the Hemlock Inn's business manager, John Raintree, appeared at the door to the Banquet Room.

"Yo, John!" said Gil. "Mighty glad to see you. Sorry I missed our meeting last night. I figured you and Tom could handle any stuff that needed to be decided anyways, and I had some things come up at home."

Esther looked significantly at Quill and mouthed, "Nadine!" Then more audibly, "Poor Gil."

"No problem, Gil," said John easily, "but I won't be able to get the audit to you until next week."

"That's okay with you, innit, Mark?" Gil wiped a handkerchief over his sweaty neck. "It's not gonna hold up the loan or anything?"

Mark Anthony Jefferson, vice-president of the Hemlock Falls Savings and Loan, tightened his lips. "Why don't we discuss this later, Gil? Your partner should be present anyway, and John's on Quill's time, now."

"Oh, I don't mind," said Quill. "John's moonlighting has never interfered with our business." She looked hopefully at him. "Do you need me, John?"

"Yep."

Quill sprang out of her chair with relief. "I'll be right there. Would you all excuse me? Esther, could you take over the minutes? I'd appreciate it."

Quill made her way swiftly into the hall and closed the door behind her. "Just in the nick of time. I was about to be forced into taking Julie Offenbach's star turn. I have no desire to be dunked and squashed in front of two hundred gawking tourists." She frowned at his glum expression. "Any problems?"

John claimed three-quarters Onondaga blood, whose heritage gave him skin the color of a bronze medallion and hair as thickly black as charred toast. He had an erratic, whimsical sense of humor that Quill found very un-Indian. Not, Quill thought, that she knew all that much about Indians, John in particular. He'd been with them less than a year, and for the first time, the Inn was showing a profit. Despite the money he made between his job at the Inn and his small accounting business, John lived modestly, driving an old car, wearing carefully cleaned suits that were years out of date. He refused to touch alcohol, for reasons tacitly understood between them, and never discussed his personal life. He nodded. "Guest complaint. And one of the waitresses called in sick for the three to eleven shift. Doreen's on vacation this week; otherwise she could pinch-hit. So that means we're short two staff for the dinner trade."

"Did you try the backup list?"

John nodded Yes to the phone calls and No to the results. "Exam week for summer session," he said briefly.

"Damn." Most of the summer season help came from nearby Cornell University. "All right. I'll take the shift myself. Unless Meg's short-handed in the kitchen?"

"Not so far."

"And the guest complaint?" She swallowed nervously. "No digestive problems or anything like that? Meg had Caesar salad on the menu for lunch, and she just refuses to omit the raw egg."

"Not food poisoning, no. But we'd better comply with the raw egg ban, Quill. We're liable to a fine if we don't."

"I know." Quill bit her thumb. "*You* tell Meg, will you, John? I mean, I should take care of this guest problem."

"Tell your sister she can't use raw eggs anymore? Not me, Quill. No way. I'd walk three miles over hot coals for you, shave my head bald for you, but I will not tell your sister how to cook."

"John," said Quill, with far more decisiveness than she felt, "you can't be afraid of my sister. She's all of five feet two and a hundred pounds, dripping wet. That makes her a *third* your size, probably."

"You're half again as tall as she is, and *you're* afraid of your sister."

"Then you're fired."

"You can't fire me. I quit."

They grinned at each other.

"I'll flip you for it," said Quill.

John pulled a nickel from his pocket and sent it spinning with a quick snap of his thumb. "Call it."

"Heads."

"Tails." John caught the coin and showed her an Indian-head nickel, tail-up. "My lucky coin. Came to me from my grandfather, the Chief. I told you about the Chief before. You want to keep this in your pocket while you tell her no more raw eggs?"

"I'll take care of the guest first. Is it a him or a her?"

"Her."

"Perennial?" This was house code for the retired couples who flooded the Inn in the spring, disappeared in autumn, and reappeared with the early crocus. In general, Quill liked them. They tended to be good guests, rarely, if ever, stiffing the management, and except for a universal disinclination to tip the help more than ten percent, treated the support staff well. This was in marked contrast to traveling businessmen who left used condoms rolled under the beds—which sent Doreen, their obsessive-compulsive housekeeper, into fits—or businesswomen demanding big-city amenities like valet services, a gym, and pool boys.

"It's an older woman," said John. He paused reflectively. "Kind of mean."

"I'm good with mean." She glanced at her watch; fifteen minutes before the start of the afternoon shift. She'd just make it if John's complainer didn't have a real problem. "The wine shipment's due at four. The bill of lading is . . . um . . . somewhere on my desk."

"I'll find it. My grandfather, the Chief . . ."

"Was a tracker," Quill finished for him. "I'd like to meet your grandfather. I'd like to meet your grandmother, too, as a matter of fact—" She stopped, aware that the flippant conversation was heading into dangerous waters. John's quiet, lonely existence was his business. "Never mind. Where is she?"

"Lobby." He grinned, teeth white in his dark face. "Good luck."

Quill took the steps up to the lobby with a practiced smile firmly in place. She and Meg had bought the twenty-seven-room Inn two years before with the combined proceeds of her last art show and

Meg's early and wholly unexpected widowhood. Driving through Central New York on a short vacation, Meg and Quill had come upon the Inn unexpectedly. They came back. Shouldered between the granite ridges left by glaciers, on land too thin for farming, Inn and village were fragrant in spring, lush in summer, brilliant with color in the fall. Even the winters weren't too bad, for those tolerant of heavy snowfall, and Hemlockians resigned themselves to a partial dependence on tourists in search of peak season vacations. The Inn had always attracted travelers; as a commercial property, it proved easy to sell and less easy to manage. It had passed from hand to hand over the years. New owners bought and sold with depressing regularity, most defeated by the difficulty of targeting exactly the right customer market. The relationships among longtime residents of Hemlock Falls were so labyrinthine, it was a year before Quill realized that Marge Schmidt and Tom Peterson, Gil Gilmeister's partner, had owned the Inn some years before. Marge had made a stab at modernizing. She installed wall-to-wall Astro-turf indoors ("Wears good," said Marge some months after Quill removed it. "Whattaya, stupid?") and plywood trolls in the garden.

The reception-lobby was all that remained of the original eighteenth-century Inn, and the low ceilings and leaded windows had a lot to do with Quill's final decision to buy it. Guests were in search of an authentic historical experience, as long as it was accompanied by heated towel racks, outstanding mattresses, and her sister's terrific food. If they could restore the Inn with the right degree of twentieth-century luxury, people would come in busloads.

Quill had stripped layers of paint and wallpaper from the plaster-and-lathe walls, replaced vinyl-backed draperies with simple valances of Scottish lace, and tore up the Astro-turf carpeting. The sisters had refinished the floors and wainscoting to a honeyed pine, and landscaped the grounds.

The leaded windows in the lobby framed a view of the long sweep of lawn and gardens to the lip of Hemlock Gorge. Creamy wool rugs, overwoven in florals of peach, celadon, taupe, and sky blue, lightened the effect of the low ceiling. Two massive Japanese urns flanked the reception desk where Dina Muir checked guests in. Mike the groundskeeper filled the urns every other morning with flowers from the Inn's extensive perennial gardens. As usual this early in July, they held Queen Elizabeth roses, Oriental lilies of gold, peach, and white, and spars of purple heather.

The lobby was welcoming and peaceful. Quill smiled at Dina, the daytime receptionist, and raised an inquiring eyebrow. Dina made an expressive face, and jerked her head slightly in the direction of the fireplace.

An elderly woman with a fierce frown sat on the pale leather couch in front of the cobblestone hearth. A woman at least thirty years her junior stood behind the chair. The younger one had a submissive, tentative air for all the world like that anachronism, the companion. Quill's painter's eye registered almost automatically the lush figure behind the modestly buttoned shirtwaist. She could have used a little makeup, Quill thought, besides the slash of red lipstick she allowed herself. Something in the attitude of the two women made her revise that thought; the elder one clearly dominated her attendant and just as clearly disapproved of excess.

"I'm Sarah Quilliam," she said, her hand extended in welcome.

"I'm Mavis Collinwood?" said the younger woman in a Southern drawl that seemed to question it. Her brown hair was lacquered like a Chinese table and back-combed into a tightly restrained knot. "Mrs. Hallenbeck doesn't shake hands," Mavis said, in a voice both assured and respectful. "Her arthritis is a little painful this time of year."

Only the glaucous clouding of Mrs. Hallenbeck's blue eyes and the gnarled hands told Quill that she must be over eighty. Her skin was smooth, shadowed by a fine net of wrinkles at eye and mouth. She sat rigidly upright, chin high to avoid the sagging of throat and jowl. Her figure was slim rather than gaunt, and Quill took in the expensive watch and the elegant Chanel suit.

Mrs. Hallenbeck fixed Quill with a basilisk glare. "I wish to speak to the owner."

"You are," said Quill cheerfully. "What can I do for you?"

"Our reservations were not in order." The old lady was clearly displeased.

"I'm very sorry," said Quill, going to the ledger. "You weren't recorded in the book? I'll arrange a room for you immediately."

"We were in the book. I had requested the third-floor suite. The one overlooking the gorge, with that marvelous balcony that makes you feel as though you were flying." She paused, and the clouded blue eyes teared up a little. "My husband and I stayed here, years ago. I am retracing our days together."

Quill's look expressed sympathy.

"That girl of yours. She put us into two rooms on the second floor. It overlooks the back lawn. It is not a suite. It is not what I require. I demanded to see the owner, and John Raintree said that these arrangements had been made and could not be changed."

"Let me see what we can do." Quill checked the booking: *Hallenbeck, Amelia, and Collinwood, Mavis*. The reservation had been made three months ago, by one of the gilt-edged travel agencies in South Carolina. Paid for in advance with an American Express Gold card. There it was: *Requested Suite 312–314*. And just as clearly marked in John's handwriting were their current rooms: *Confirmed 101 and 104*. "Did Mr. Raintree say anything at all about why the rooms were booked this way? He's a wonderful help to us, Mrs. Hallenbeck, and rarely makes mistakes. It's not like him to make a change like this without a reason."

"He did not say one word." The tones were decisive. If she'd had a whip, she would have cracked it.

Quill suppressed a grin. "I'm certain that no one's in three-fourteen. Shall we go up and see if it's suitable for you?"

Mrs. Hallenbeck nodded regally. The three of them went up the stairs. Any notion that John may have booked them into first-floor rooms due to Mrs. Hallenbeck's arthritis was quickly dispelled; she took the steps with a lot less effort than Mavis Collinwood, who began to breathe heavily at the second-floor landing. Quill unlocked the door to the suite and stepped aside to let them enter.

Quill loved all twenty-seven rooms at the Inn, but 314 was one of her favorites. A white Adams-style fireplace dominated the wall opposite the balcony. The carpeting was crisp navy blue. The couch and occasional chairs were covered in blue-and-yellow chintz, the colors of Provence. French doors opened out onto a white-painted iron balcony cantilevered over the lip of Hemlock Gorge, giving 314 a panoramic view of the Falls.

Quill stepped out and watched the cascade of water over granite.

Bird calls came from the pines and joined the water's rush. Sweet smells from the gardens and the hemlock groves mingled with the daffodil-scent of fresh water. Mrs. Hallenbeck followed Quill onto the balcony, her chin jutting imperiously. She inhaled. "Dogwood," she stated precisely, "and one of the scented roses."

"Scented Cloud," said Quill. "It's a lovely rose, too. We grow it out back."

"This," Mrs. Hallenbeck said, "is what I asked for. I will walk in the hemlock glade after dinner."

"I'm sorry about the confusion, Mrs. Hallenbeck." Quill drew her inside the suite. "I'll see that your luggage is brought up here. Would you like some tea? I can have it brought to you, or you can have it in the dining room."

"An English tea? I believe your brochure described an English tea."

"Yes. A traditional high tea, with scones, Devonshire cream, and watercress sandwiches."

"Perhaps there will be no charge for that, since I have been seriously inconvenienced."

Quill, slightly taken aback, swallowed a laugh. "I'll be sure that there isn't."

"Then we shall be down after Mavis unpacks us." She nodded dismissal. Quill meekly took the hint, and went back to the Chamber meeting. She took the stairs slowly, not, she told herself, because she wasn't anxious to get back to the meeting, but because it was a beautiful July day, the Inn was booked solid for the week of History Days, and a relaxed country environment was one of the many reasons she'd left her career as an artist to move to Central New York.

"There you are," said Esther West, as Quill stepped into the lobby. "We're taking a bit of a break before we go back and vote."

"Somebody else volunteered to take Julie Offenbach's place?" Quill said with hope. "I've got a couple of ideas for you, Esther. What about Miriam Doncaster? You know, the librarian. She's a heck of a swimmer. I couldn't swim to the side of the pond as gracefully as she could after being dunked in the ducking stool."

"No. Everyone agrees you'd be the best Clarissa. Marge wants us to vote on whether or not the monthly Chamber meetings should be held at the Hemlock Home Diner instead of here."

"Oh," said Quill.

"But we all decided to take a bio break before we voted, and anyhow, Myles and Howie both thought that you'd probably want to be there for the discussion part."

"You bet I would," said Quill. "That monthly Chamber lunch is a good piece of business. John'll have my guts for garters if I lose it. Maybe I'd better have him sit in." An increasingly noisy argument from the lobby succeeded in drawing her attention. "Excuse me a second, Esther. Dina seems to need help."

Dina, one of the Cornell Hotel School graduate students on whom the Inn depended for much of its staff, was scowling ferociously at a middle-aged man at the counter. An elegantly dressed man in his thirties stood behind him, watching with interest.

"Can I give you a hand here, Dina?"

"I've been trying to tell this guy that we're booked for the week. He said the Marriott called and made reservations for him this morning." She scowled even harder. "Then he said well maybe the Marriott forgot to call, but that places 'like this' always hold back a room in case of emergencies, and he wants it."

"Keith Baumer," said the middle-aged man. He extended his hand. Quill took it. He grinned and wiggled his fingers suggestively in her palm. "You the manager, or what?"

Quill freed herself. "I'm really sorry, Mr. Baumer, but Dina's right, of course. We're booked for the week."

"Come on, kiddo, I need some help here. I've got a sales convention at the Marriott, and the bastards overbooked. I hear this is the only decent place to get a room. I know you guys; you're always holding something in reserve. Whyn't you check the reservations book yourself? I'm here for the week. I don't mind paying top dollar." He grinned and edged closer to her.

Quill took two steps back, hit the counter, and repeated, "I'm sorry, Mr. Baumer. We simply don't have a room available." The phone shrilled twice, and Dina picked it up as Quill continued, "We'll be happy to call a few nearby places for you—"

"Quill?" said Dina.

"—but I'm afraid you're going to have a rough time if you want to stay close to your sales meeting. This is the height of the tourist season . . ."

"Quill!" Dina tugged at her sleeve. "We just got a cancellation. Couple that was booked for the week for their honeymoon, Mr. and Mrs. Sands. Only it's Mrs. Sands that just called, and she said they had a fight at the wedding and the whole thing's *off*! Isn't that sad?"

"There," said Baumer. "Not that I believe that phony phone call for one little minute. What? Ya got a button down there?"

Quill counted to ten. "Would you check him in please, Dina? Enjoy your stay with us, Mr. Baumer."

He cocked his head, swept a look from her ankles to her chin, gave her a thumbs-up sign of approval, then leered at Dina. "Okay, dolly. You take American Express Traveler's Cheques?"

Quill looked longingly at the Japanese urn nearest Baumer's thick neck.

"Too heavy," said the man who'd been waiting behind Baumer. "Now, that replica of the Han funeral horse on the coffee table? Just the right size for a good whack."

Quill choked back a laugh. "Are you here to check in? Let me help you over here." He was, thought Quill, one of the best-looking men she'd ever seen, with thick black hair attractively sprinkled with gray. He wore a beautifully tailored sports coat.

"Quill," Esther called, "we're going back to vote now."

"I don't mind waiting for young Dina, there," he said. "I'm Edward Lancashire, by the way."

"We're looking forward to having you at the Inn, Mr. Lancashire."

"You go ahead to your vote. I'll be just fine."

Quill went back to the conference room and sat down, a little breathless.

"Who was *that*?" hissed Esther. "The second one, I mean. The first one sounded horrible."

"The first one *was* horrible. Speaking of horrible, where's Marge?"

"In the kitchen." Quill froze. Esther looked at her watch. "This darn meeting's got to get over soon; I've got way too much to do on the costumes."

"The kitchen? Marge is in Meg's kitchen?"

"She was headed that way."

"Oh, God," said Quill. "I'll be right back."

Quill pushed open the kitchen door to silence, which meant one of two things: either Meg had discovered Marge among her recipe books and had killed her, or nobody was there.

The flagstone floor was clean and polished. The cobblestone fireplace in the corner, where Meg had a Maine grill to do her lobsters, crackled quietly behind the Thermo Glass doors that kept the heat from the rest of the kitchen. Meg's precious copper bowls and pans hung undisturbed in shiny rows from the pot hanger. No sign of either Marge or, for that matter, her sister. Quill pulled at her lower lip, went to Meg's recipe cabinet, pulled out the lowest drawer, and flipped through the Z's. *Zuppa d'Inglese*, zucchini, zarda, zabaglione. She edged the zabaglione card carefully out of the file. Was that a greasy thumbprint? It was. But was it Marge's or Meg's? And if it were Marge's, did that mean she was going to place a phone call to the Board of Health? She read the recipe gloomily. There it was in Meg's elegant script: four raw eggs per serving. She closed the file drawer and marched determinedly back to the conference room.

It was empty, except for Myles.

"Where'd they all go?" Quill demanded. "Did they vote on whether or not to move the meetings to Marge's diner?"

"Since neither you nor Marge were here, Howie voted to table. Esther asked for an adjournment because she's still sewing costumes. I waited for you to see what you wanted to do tonight. Would you like to go to supper? Can you get away about eight-thirty?"

"Myles, can you take a fingerprint from a recipe card?"

"Yes, Quill," Myles said patiently. "Do you want to go to supper? I thought I'd make a stir-fry at my place."

"Where was Marge, when I wasn't here?"

"I don't know. She came back in here grinning and said she had to make a phone call. Why?"

Quill gazed at him thoughtfully. Myles had strong views on law and order. He had an annoying tendency to spout phrases like "due process" and "probable cause." Those gray eyes would get even icier if she asked him to arrest Marge for snooping. That strong jaw would set like an antilock brake at the merest suggestion of a phone tap on the Hemlock Home Diner. There was no way he'd test a recipe card for fingerprints without uncomfortable questions regarding the existence of an eggless zabaglione.

She decided to answer his first question, and solve the Marge problem herself. "Why don't you come by the kitchen for dinner about eleven, after we close? You made dinner last night. It's my turn."

"Fine." He kissed her on the temple. Quill wasn't fooled for a minute. This was a man who'd lock her in stir the instant she whacked Marge up the side of the head with Meg's skillet.

Halfway out the door, Myles turned to look at her. "You sure nothing's wrong? You're not coming down with anything, are you?" His eyes narrowed. "Wait. I know that look. You're fulminating."

"No," said Quill absently. "One of the waitresses is, though." She gasped and glanced at her watch. "The second shift! It's after three o'clock! Damn!" She sprinted past him and ran down the hall.

CHAPTER 2

Quill dashed through the lobby to the locker room at the back of the kitchen. The fresh odor of Meg's private stock of coffee filled the air, but there was no sign of her sister, just two assistants scrubbing pots at the triple sink. Quill grabbed a clean uniform and looked at her watch: three-ten. No time to go to her own quarters and change into more comfortable shoes. She changed her silk blouse and challis skirt for a freshly laundered uniform and swung into the dining room. Three tables were already occupied for tea. John stood at the opposite end, carefully polishing the silver tea urn.

"John, where's Meg?"

"Supervising the fish delivery in the back. Red fish in lime for the special tonight."

"I think Marge Schmidt went through the recipe file and found we use raw eggs in the zabaglione."

"Yeah?"

"Yeah. Thing is, I told her Meg had an eggless version."

"Even Marge isn't going to believe in eggless zabaglione." He thought for a moment. "Dookie Shuttleworth might."

"Did you see Marge in the kitchen?"

"No. That what's-her-name—Mavis Collinwood—went through on her way out back." He rubbed harder at the tea urn, his lips tight. "Said she wanted to explore."

"Don't you think we ought to do something?"

"Like what?"

Quill wrapped a strand of hair around her finger and pulled on it.

"I don't know," she confessed. She let the curl spring back. "Why did you book Mrs. Hallenbeck on the second floor when she'd asked for the best suite in the house three months in advance?"

John rubbed at a spot on the handle and didn't reply.

"And she's not mean," Quill continued. "Rather sweet, as a matter of fact. In terrific shape for her age. She's a little bossy, but God, at that age, that's allowed."

John shook his head. "Move them both to the first floor."

"Why?"

"Bad feeling."

"Oh." John's bad feelings were not to be taken lightly. "About what exactly? Isn't her credit good? She's paying for both of them. Should I check with American Express? I *hate* doing that."

John shrugged. "It's not money."

"What then, John?"

"Remember the guy from IBM?"

Quill took a deep breath. "Of course I remember the guy from IBM. Who around here doesn't?"

"Had a bad feeling about that, too."

"He was drunk. And high on coke. He fell over that balcony into the gorge by accident. I can't see Mrs. Hallenbeck stoned on a gallon of Rusty Nails smuggled into her room in a Thermos bottle, which is what that guy did."

"You're the boss." Quill knew that attitude: polite, courteous retreat. He looked at the open archway. "More guests. I'll seat them."

Quill's intention to grab a quick look at the script for Clarissa's speech, probe John for the real reason behind his discomfort with the widow and her companion, and finally, talk to Meg about the raw egg ban and the threat posed by Marge, got lost in the rush of the next six hours. The tea trade was followed by the Early Birds, patrons who took advantage of reduced-cost meals before seven o'clock, then the regular evening trade, and finally, at ten o'clock, a few late diners, Mrs. Hallenbeck and Mavis among them.

They ordered a dinner as enormous as their tea had been. Mavis requested a single glass of the house white, which she sipped all through the meal, and Mrs. Hallenbeck no liquor at all. On one of her trips to the kitchen, Quill hissed to John in passing, "They're both sober as judges."

Just after ten-thirty, Quill stopped to take a rapid survey of the tables. Mrs. Hallenbeck and Mavis were at table two by the big windows that overlooked the gardens. The man in his fifties at table seven was Keith Baumer, who'd said he was part of the overflow crowd from the sales convention at the Marriott on Route 15. Baumer slumped over the menu, smoking a cigarette and flicking the ashes onto the rug. Table twelve held another sole diner—the dark, good-looking Edward Lancashire. After careful deliberation, he'd ordered some of the specialties that had made Meg's reputation: Caesar salad, Steak Tartare, Game Hen à la Quilliam. He finished his Caesar salad with a thoughtful expression, writing briefly in a notebook by his plate. Quill hesitated, alarmed. He looked awfully well-dressed to be a Department of Health inspector, who tended to be weedy, with thin lips and polyester sports coats. The suit on the guy seated at twelve was an Armani. Could Department of Health inspectors afford Armani?

Quill went to Baumer to take his order, one eye mistrustfully on table twelve.

"Quill," Baumer purred, reaching up to lift her name tag away from her breast pocket. He let it fall back with a smirk. "Let me guess. The hair. Hair that red and curly has gotta be the reason. Looks soft, though, not prickly like porcupine quills."

Quill moved the ashtray nearer his cigarette with a pointed thump. She was tired. Her feet hurt. If Edward Lancashire *was* from the Department of Health, the Inn could be in trouble. She had Marge to fence with and Clarissa's stupid speech to memorize. It'd be another three hours before she could even think of going to bed. If this turkey pushed it, he was going to find out just how prickly she could be. She'd admired Mrs. Hallenbeck's beady stare. She tried it. Baumer jumped a little in his chair. She said politely, "Are you ready to order, sir? I can recommend the Red Fish in Lime, or the Ginger Soy Tenderloin. Either is delicious."

Baumer dropped the menu onto the table, knocking his knife and fork onto the floor. Quill bent over to pick them up. He slipped his hand past her knee up her thigh. She disengaged with the ease of long practice, took the place setting from table six, and laid fresh silverware next to his plate.

Baumer closed the leather-covered menu with an exaggerated pursing of his lips. "Hemlock Inn," he mused. He looked arch. Quill braced herself, then lip-synched silently with him, "Sure I can trust the chef?"

"We're named for the Hemlock Groves, Mr. Baumer, not the poisonous herb. You must have noticed the trees when driving in. A lot of our guests like to walk the path to the foot of the gorge at this time of year. The hemlocks are in full bloom."

She deflected the invitation to join him in a walk after dinner, with gritted teeth, and took his order for the New York strip, medium, no veg, extra sour cream and butter on the baked potato. She cheered up. That meal and the two Manhattans preceding it forecast a short life of waitress-harassing. She crossed the mauve carpeting toward the kitchen, and stopped at the Hallenbeck table. Mavis had teased her hair into a big bubble. The scent of hairspray fought with the perfume of the scarlet lilies in the middle of the table. "How is everything, Mavis, Mrs. Hallenbeck? Are you comfortable? Was your dinner all right?"

"It's just lovely here," said Mavis, "and the room is wonderful. The food! Why, it's just the best I've ever had."

"I am having hot water and lemon after my meal," pronounced Mrs. Hallenbeck. "It's a habit I acquired while traveling abroad with my husband." She lifted her chin. "We prefer England. Although this place is quite English, for an American restaurant." She paused and fixed Quill with a modified version of The Glare. "I assume there is no charge for the hot water?"

"No," said Quill. Then as she reflected on the probability of Mrs. Hallenbeck's next question, "Just for the meal itself."

"Mavis," said Mrs. Hallenbeck disapprovingly, "had the tournedos. Quite the most expensive thing on the menu."

Mavis blushed, and Quill said curiously, "Have you and Mavis been together very long, Mrs. Hallenbeck?"

"Mavis is my companion. We are both impoverished widows." She waved a gnarled hand at Quill. The third finger of her left hand held a diamond the size of an ice rink. "We are companions in loss, on an adventure. I assume that we are eligible for a senior citizen's discount?"

Quill ignored the latter half of this statement and said warmly, "I hope you both find adventure. You're going to stay for the whole week of Hemlock's History Days? Admission is free."

"We will consider it," said Mrs. Hallenbeck regally. She sat up straighter, if that were possible, and said, "Move, please. You are blocking my view of the entrance." Quill stepped sideways. "Mavis! I recognize that person. What is her name?"

Quill turned around and groaned. Marge Schmidt stumped in. She'd exchanged her blue bowling jacket for a pink one, which did nothing to soften her resemblance to an animated tank. Marge's turret eyes swung in their direction.

"Marge!" squealed Mavis. "Coo-ee!" She waved energetically.

"Mavis!" Marge bellowed. She marched up to the table. "So you made it okay!" Mavis got up. The two women embraced. Mavis squealed again. Marge thumped her back with bluff good humor.

"This is a friend of yours, Mavis?" said Mrs. Hallenbeck sternly. "She is dressed abominably. She is too fat."

Quill warmed to Mrs. Hallenbeck.

"You remember Marge Schmidt, Amelia. She ran the Northeast region for a couple of years before she quit to come home here. She runs a restaurant now."

"Northeast region of what?" said Quill.

"Brought that D.O.H. order for you, Quill," Marge said loudly. "'Bout the salmonella? You din't eat the Italian puddin', did you, Mave?"

"No, not yet," said Mavis, sounding alarmed.

"Nasty," said Marge with satisfaction. "Very nasty."

"Marge," said Quill, "dammit . . ."

"This food is bad?" said Mrs. Hallenbeck. "I don't believe we should pay for a meal if the food is bad."

"Here!" Marge rummaged in the pocket of her bowling jacket and thrust a creased paper at Quill.

Quill took it and said, "Marge, we are well aware . . ."

Marge grabbed it back. "I'll read it to you." Her lips moved and she muttered, "Shipment of beef tainted with E. coli, that ain't it. Here! Wait!" She took a deep breath, preparatory to another bellow.

Quill grabbed the memo, scanned it, and translated the governmentese which boiled down to John's statement of that afternoon: no more raw egg. "Now look, Marge . . ."

"I am ready to go up, Mavis." Mrs. Hallenbeck rapped the tabletop imperatively. "This person is loud. I am tired."

"Now you got the memo, you got no excuse, Quill," said Marge.

"MAVIS!" said Mrs. Hallenbeck loudly.

"All right, all right," Mavis replied, flustered. "Marge. I cain't take time to talk to you now, but I'll see you soon, you hear?"

"Right." Marge nodded ponderously. "We got old times to talk about."

"Northeast manager of what?" said Quill, hoping to divert Marge's attention from further bellicose thunderings about salmonella.

"You got some more damn fools wantin' to eat here," said Marge. "C'mon, Mave, I'll walk out with you."

Quill turned a distracted glance to the maître d' station. Tom Peterson was waiting there patiently. John was nowhere in sight.

"'Lo, Tom," said Marge as she walked by. "Stay away from the Italian puddin'." Marge disappeared in the direction of the front door. Mavis supported the miffed Mrs. Hallenbeck up the stairs. Quill wondered if she'd actually serve time if she gave Marge a fat lip.

"I should have made reservations," said Tom Peterson. "Is the kitchen still open?"

"Oh, sure, Tom." Quill picked up a menu. "How many in your party?"

"Just one other. He's looking at the mural in the men's room. He'll be out in a moment."

Quill took another menu. "Would you like to sit near the

window?" Tom followed her to the table next to Edward Lancashire. The Petersons had lived in Hemlock Falls for close to three hundred years, their fortunes fluctuating with the business competency of each generation. A shrewd nineteenth-century Peterson had boosted the family fortune for some considerable period of time through investments in railroads. Tom, whose pale eyes and attenuated frame were a diluted version of his richer ancestor, had stuck with the transportation business after his brief excursion into the hotel with Marge; Gil's Buick partnership was part of Tom's larger trucking firm.

Quill seated Tom, then banged into the kitchen with Baumer's order in one hand. "Hey!" she said to her sister. "I quit."

Meg stood at the Aga. She'd inherited their father's rich dark hair and gray eyes, along with his volatile Welsh temper. Quill was an expert at reading her sister's moods; Meg's hair stood on end, which meant that the cooking was going well.

"The sauces are really behaving," said Meg, ignoring the familiar imperative. "I think it's the weather. I wasn't sure about the dessert for the Chamber lunch, though. Damn mint leaves kept wilting. Got the sugar syrup too hot, I guess."

"The food was great. The meeting was kind of a pain in the rear."

Meg raised an eyebrow in question.

"Myles nominated guess who to be squashed artistically under a barn door. Under the current circumstances, that's a consummation to be wished for devoutly. Probably because of the consummation devoutly wished for by the jerk at table seven."

"Uh-oh," said Meg. She grinned, shook her head, and skillfully ladled three perfect brandied orange slices over a crisply browned game hen. "Don't tell me you got hooked into playing Clarissa this year."

"Julie Offenbach is sick," said Quill gloomily. She sighed and consulted her order pad. "We've got one more order. One medium-rare New York marinated in fungicide. No veg. Double cholesterol on the potato. Table seven."

"Mr. Baumer?"

"Yes indeedy. He almost forced me to break my number one rule."

"I thought the number one rule was don't hit the help."

"That's number two. Number one is don't piss off the patrons." Quill flopped into the rocking chair by the fireplace. "It's been a long day. I've still got to pay bills and go over the accounting with John before I go to bed. And my feet hurt." She glanced at her sister, wondering how and when to bring up the raw egg ban.

Meg, indifferent to the business side of the Inn, sniffed appreciatively at the copper pot filled with orange sauce on the stove. Her brown hair was shoved back from her forehead by a bright yellow sweatband. She liked to be comfortable when she cooked, and wore her usual chef's gear—a tattered Duke University sweatshirt, leggings, and a well-worn pair of sneakers. She looked at her sister's elegant feet. "It's those shoes, kiddo. Handmade Italian leather is the worst possible thing for your disposition. Want to borrow a pair of sneakers?"

"I want to borrow a life." Quill pushed the rocker in motion and closed her eyes. "Preferably on a beach somewhere. In the Caribbean. With a gorgeous twenty-year-old lifeguard and an endless supply of rum punch."

"Umm. I've heard *that* song before. And what about Myles? Face it. You love it here." Meg piped potato rosettes around the base of the bird, added two rings of spiced apple to the brandied orange slices, and presented the platter. "Ta dah! For table twelve. Bless his little heart. Ordered *all* my specialties, including game hen stuffed with The Sausage that made us famous."

Quill got up and took the platter. "Meg. About table twelve . . ."

Meg placed a silver dome over the bird. "You said he was cute."

"Very cute. The sort that could take us both away from all this."

"Rich? Single? Got a yacht?"

"No, the sort that could take us away from all this because I think he might be from the D.O.H."

Meg scowled. "What are you saying?"

"I'm not sure. But he was scribbling notes. And he ordered the Caesar salad and the Steak Tartare"—Quill took a deep breath—"and I wouldn't put it past Marge Schmidt and her creepy pal to have called them after that memo about the salmonella came out. She showed up here with the memo not ten minutes ago. Although

I don't see how he could have gotten here so fast. Meg, you'll have to stop with the raw eggs. Just temporarily."

Meg slammed down her wooden spoon, marched to the swinging doors to the dining room, pushed them open, and peered through. She looked back at her sister. "That's an Armani, or I'm a short-order cook. People from the D.O.H. wear polyester."

"Yes, but is he taking notes?"

Meg peered out the door again. "How should I know? He's holding the Merlot by the stem. He's swirling the wine. He's inhaling it." She shrieked suddenly. "Quill! He's taking notes!"

"I *told* you he was taking notes." She looked over Meg's head into the dining room. "Oh, damn. There's Tom Peterson ready to order. Where's John!"

Meg let the doors close and said tensely, "*L'Aperitif*! You know, 'The Magazine to Read Before You Dine.'"

"I know *L'Aperitif*, Meg." Quill patted her sister's shoulder soothingly. "Forget it. I'll just go out and get Peterson set up."

Meg tore her sweatband from her hair and wound it around both hands. "I'm going to scream."

"Meg . . ."

"It's been eighteen months since we were last reviewed, Quill. Oh, God. And that managing editor hates me. She hates me. You know what they said in that article?"

"They love you, Meg. You're the only three-star . . ."

"My tournedos were dry! That's what they said. That I overcook my beef!" She grabbed the game hen out of Quill's hands, stamped to the stove, and ladled more brandied orange juice over the hen, drenching the potatoes. "There! That'll teach the sons of bitches to call my cooking dry!"

"Meg!" Quill grabbed the platter back. "You have absolutely no proof that this guy's a food critic."

"Well, you thought he was from the Department of Health! In an Armani suit!" She shoved Quill toward the dining room. "You go out there. You find out what kind of review he's going to give me. If he dares even *hint* that that bird is dry, I'll personally shove the rest of his bloody meal down his bloody throat!"

Table twelve faced the window overlooking the gorge. Edward

Lancashire's eyes crinkled at the corners when he smiled. They crinkled as Quill set the game hen in front of him. "Looks great."

"Thank you."

He looked around the dining room. Quill noticed his wedding ring, and discarded the possibility of a nice flirtation with Meg. "Not bad for a Thursday night," he said. "You must do pretty well."

"We do. Is there anything else I can get for you, Mr. Lancashire?"

He forked a piece of the game hen. His eyes widened. "This is terrific. That's tarragon. Maybe a touch of Italian parsley? And mint. Excellent." He swallowed, and waved his fork at the chair opposite. "Dining room closes at ten-thirty, doesn't it? It's past that now. Have a seat."

"The owners don't care for the help fraternizing with guests." He looked up, his eyes shrewd. She smiled. "What? Do I have a sign that says 'Owner-Manager'?"

"No. But there's a bronze plaque in the front that reads 'Your hosts, Sarah and Margaret Quilliam.' And your name tag says 'Quill'."

"I might be their impoverished cousin from Des Moines, living on the bounty of relatives, pinch-hitting as manager and eking out a bare existence as a waitress."

"The uniform doesn't fit," he continued unperturbed, "and a woman wearing a three-hundred-dollar pair of shoes wouldn't voluntarily wear a dress that was too big across the hips and too tight across—" He stopped, as Quill frowned indignantly. "Sorry. You had enough of that this afternoon." He nodded toward Baumer, happily swigging down a final Manhattan. "Besides, I saw your show in New York a few years ago. Your picture was on the poster."

"Oh. That."

"Yes. You aren't painting anymore?"

"Some," she said, deliberately vague. "I don't have much time during the season. Are you staying with us long?"

"Depends on the food." He smiled, and Quill's heart gave an excited thump. He was asking enough questions to qualify as a food critic. Although he was awfully thin. Quill worried about the skinny part. But Meg was skinny, and she was the greatest chef in the state.

"Then you're not here for History Days?" He raised an interrogative eyebrow. "Hemlock Falls' biggest tourist attraction. Featuring Central New York's only three-star gourmet restaurant. Among other attractions."

He laughed a little. "Other attractions?"

"Craft booths and everybody in town dressed up like the Empress Josephine and Napoleonic soldiers. It's the wrong century of course, but the Ladies Auxiliary decided a long time ago that Empire costumes are prettier than Colonial." She cleared her throat a little self-consciously. "I may be prejudiced, but I think the reputation of the Inn has a lot to do with History Days' success. We're booked a year in advance for the whole week. We were even written up in the *Times* last year in the Sunday travel section. Maybe you saw it?" She leaned forward anxiously. "How's the sausage stuffing in the game hen?"

"Fine."

"Just fine?" she said worriedly. "It's my sister's recipe, you know. Margaret Quilliam. *L'Aperitif* wrote an article about her when we opened up two years ago. Maybe you saw that, too. 'Engorged at the Gorge'? Meg received Central New York's only three-star rating. Some people think it's time she was given a four. She's terrific, don't you think?"

"I'm not much of a gourmet," he said apologetically, "tastes great to me."

Quill calmed down. She'd pushed him too far. "Anything you need, just ask us."

"Coffee would be nice."

"Coffee. I'll have it here in a minute. Freshly brewed, of course."

Quill signaled to Kathleen Kiddermeister, who was clearing the Hallenbeck table, to take the Peterson order, and swept back into the kitchen. Meg sat nervously in the rocker, her feet up, smoking a forbidden cigarette. She jumped up and demanded, "Well?"

"It's *L'Aperitif.*"

Meg turned pale.

"He registered as Edward Lancashire. I've never seen an Edward Lancashire byline in *L'Aperitif*. Probably a pseudonym."

"Now? Now!? The week of History Days. Oh, God."

"Meg! I'm not positively sure it's *L'Aperitif* . . ."

"Oh, God."

". . . but we are overdue for a review."

"Oh, God."

"And he's asking *very* gourmet-type questions. He wants coffee. I'll make sure the whipped cream is fresh . . . and the cinnamon sticks . . . fill the bowl of cinnamon sticks."

"Why not the week after next? Oh, God."

"I'll tell Kathleen to make sure the orange juice is fresh-squeezed tomorrow morning. What's the room service breakfast?"

"Blueberry muffins. It's July, remember? Oh, God."

"Take a deep breath."

Meg took a deep breath and let it out in a long sigh.

Quill patted her back. "We've survived Health Department notices, cranky widows, horny businessmen, drunks, even that kitchen fire last year—and the quality of your cooking's *never* dropped! Right?"

"Right."

"So!" Quill smiled affectionately at her. "What could happen that the two of us can't handle? You, the cooking genius. Me, the business genius."

John Raintree came through the door. He looked at Quill, his face grim. "That woman that checked in with the widow? The one with the stiff hair?"

"Yes, John. Mavis Collinwood. I moved both of them to three-fourteen."

"I've called the police. She's gone over the edge of the balcony in three-fourteen. To the gorge."

CHAPTER 3

"I just don't have the littlest idea what happened!" Mavis slumped plaintively on the yellow-and-blue couch in front of the fireplace in Suite 314.

Mavis had been found dangling over the lip of the gorge, like a baby in a stork's beak. Her patent leather belt had caught on one of the joists which fixed the balcony to the side of the building. Mrs. Hallenbeck, with great presence of mind, had taken a sheet from one of the beds, wrapped it around Mavis' stomach, then tied the other end to the handle of the French door. Mavis' wildly swinging hands had scratched her cheek.

The volunteer firemen found Mavis' predicament hilarious. Herbie Minstead and his crew winched Mavis off the balcony with the fire truck ladder, and shaking their heads, left for the Croh Bar and a restorative glass of beer at Quill's expense. Myles and two of his uniformed officers were exploring the balcony. Mrs. Hallenbeck sat upright and disapproving by the open French doors. Meg jigged from one foot to the other in a corner with John Raintree. Doc Bishop, the young internist who treated most of Hemlock Falls, bent over Mavis. Clearly suppressing his amusement, he straightened up and wiped a bit of blood off his surgical gloves with one of the expensive peach towels from the bathroom.

"Is she going to be all right?" asked Quill.

"Scrapes and bruises; that's about it. No evidence of oxygen deprivation. She wasn't high enough." He grinned. Quill looked at him in exasperation; his expression sobered. "Sorry, Quill. It could have been a real tragedy. If her belt hadn't caught onto the joist like it did, she could have gone into the river, but it *is* ten feet deep there. She would have floated like, a cork down to the sluiceway and been able to climb out."

Quill dropped to her knees beside Mavis. Her knees were

scraped and bloody, the torn pantyhose gritty with concrete dust from the balcony. Her cheeks were scratched, her makeup smeared, and her expression furious.

"Can you talk about it?" asked Quill gently.

"I done *tol'* you," Mavis snapped, her Southern accent deepening to incomprehensibility. "I went out for some fresh air. I leaned against that old railing. Next thang I knew, I *pitched* into the air."

"You eat too much," said Mrs. Hallenbeck, and whether this was referring to Mavis' expensive dinner or her general size, Quill wasn't too sure. Mavis gave her employer a furious glare.

"And then Mrs. Hallenbeck came out and tied you to the balcony with a sheet."

"I like to *choked*, she tied that sheet so tight."

"You may have saved her life, Mrs. Hallenbeck," said Quill, stretching the truth in pursuit of making everyone feel better. "You were very brave. Very quick thinking."

Mrs. Hallenbeck lifted her chin and smiled complacently. "I have often been complimented on my presence of mind."

"I can *swim*," Mavis muttered. "I told her just to lemme *go!*"

There was more to Mavis, Quill decided, than had previously met the eye.

Quill wondered if she should send John downstairs for a brandy for everyone. They all looked as though they needed it.

Myles prowled in from the balcony and drew Andy Bishop to one side. He shook hands with Doc Bishop, then came over and sat next to Mavis. "You had just the glass of white wine for dinner, Mrs. Collinwood?"

"I am not in the habit of overindulgence, Sheriff."

"Huh!" said Mrs. Hallenbeck. "She's forty pounds overweight if she's ten, and *that* is a result of overindulgence. At, I may add, my expense." She lifted her chin again and fixed Myles with The Glare. Quill, admiring, noticed he was totally unaffected. "I believe, Sheriff, that we need to discuss the negligence in this case. I may have to call my lawyer in the morning."

Quill glanced at John and raised both eyebrows. He nodded with quick understanding, then moved unobtrusively around the room. Just one small Thermos bottle filled with Rusty Nails, thought Quill, preferably a large one.

"You were in the bathroom, Mrs. Hallenbeck?" asked Myles.

Mrs. Hallenbeck nodded. "That is correct. I was brushing my teeth. I heard a rumbling sound, then a squall like a scalded cat. I rushed from the bathroom to the balcony. Poor Mavis was swaying over the gorge. I tugged at her to help her back onto what was left of the balcony. I myself was beginning to slip." She closed her eyes momentarily, her face pale. "If *I* had slipped! Sometimes I think that God has taken a personal interest in me, Sheriff, and as you see, I did not. Well, I quickly saw that I was far too frail to pull that great creature up myself . . ."

"Not quick enough," Mavis muttered. "I was out there *hours*."

". . . so I stripped the sheet from that bed, tied it around her waist, and called the front desk."

"A tragedy averted," said Andy Bishop, solemn now; he had finished repacking his little black bag, and may have been regretting his earlier lightheartedness. He scribbled for a moment on his prescription pad, tore off two sheets, and held out the prescription and a small box of pills to Mavis. "I'm giving you both some Valium. These are samples to take until you can get to the pharmacy tomorrow. You're going to be stiff tomorrow, Mrs. Collinwood. And so will you, Mrs. Hallenbeck, after those exertions."

"I never take drugs," said Mrs. Hallenbeck, "nor do my employees."

Mavis tucked the samples into her purse and said, "Thank you, Doctor. I believe I will take advantage of your kind offer."

Andy Bishop picked up his bag. "I'll leave you ladies now. Stop by my office, Mrs. Collinwood, if you feel the need." He gave Quill a brief hug, nodded to Myles, and walked to the door opening onto the hallway.

"Doctor!" commanded Mrs. Hallenbeck. "You will send your bill to Ms. Quilliam. This entire affair is the responsibility of the Inn."

Quill glanced quickly at John. He nodded reluctantly. "Of course, Andy," she said. "I'm so sorry this happened, Mavis."

Myles, who had been leaning against the mantel with a thoughtful expression, said, "Sarah, maybe you and John could move Mrs. Hallenbeck and Mrs. Collinwood to a different room."

"Why?" Quill asked. "Myles, the Inn is booked to the gills in two days for History Week. There isn't any place we can put them but here, after Sunday."

"I'm going to seal off the room until the investigation is completed."

"Maybe they'll be gone by then," said John, surprisingly ungracious. "Come on, Sarah. Mrs. Hallenbeck, we'll take you down to two-fourteen. I'll see that your luggage is packed up and brought down."

"Where we began," said Mrs. Hallenbeck. "I am assuming the rest of our stay will be free of charge. And we do intend, Mr. Raintree, to stay the entire week."

Quill, distracted, watched them go. "Myles—how long is this going to take? And what kind of investigation? I'll have to have the insurance company in to look at it, of course, but it's just the balcony, for Pete's sake."

"I want to show you something."

Quill looked at her watch; after midnight. She yawned suddenly. "Can't we do this in the morning, Myles?"

"Now."

Quill followed him out to the balcony. The July night was soft, the moon a silvery half crescent over the Falls. The northwest edge of the balcony gaped, bent and broken, just as it had when she'd looked at it before.

"Look at this." Using his handkerchief to protect the wrought-iron surface, Myles gently rocked one of the posts free from the edge of the concrete.

Quill peered at it in the half-light from the suite behind them. "The mortar's all crumbled away," she said. "What do you think the insurance company's going to want me to do? Should I call the architect?"

"Look at it, Quill."

She reached out to touch the mortar. Myles caught her hand gently and moved it aside. "It's *eaten* away," she said.

"My guess is acid. Do you have any here?"

"Sulfuric," said Quill, suddenly wide-awake. "Doreen insists that a solution of sulfuric acid and water is the only thing that gets the mold off the concrete. She uses it once every six months."

Myles crumbled a few bits of mortar in his handkerchief and

sniffed it. "Undiluted, is my guess. It's been poured around these five posts here. How much have you got on hand?"

Quill's thoughts scattered, then regrouped. She stood up slowly. "A fifty-gallon drum, at least. John orders it in bulk. It doesn't decay or lose its potency or anything." She stared at him. "But *who*? And *why*?"

"Who has access to it?"

"It's in the storeroom. We lock it at night, but during the day—anyone, I guess."

"I'll send someone down to check it. What did those two do today?"

"They checked in about noon. Mavis went for a walk. Mrs. Hallenbeck stayed in her room until teatime. They both came down for tea at four o'clock. They ate a huge one. Then Mrs. Hallenbeck went up to her room for a nap, I think. That was about five o'clock. I guess Mavis went with her. They came back down to dinner about nine-thirty. They'd changed clothes after washing up, I guess."

"How many guests did you have for tea?"

"Four tables. Two tables were people passing through on their way to Syracuse. The fourth table was a guest that checked in about two o'clock, Keith Baumer. He—"

"Wait a minute." Myles wrote in his notebook. "And after nine-thirty? Who was at the Inn?"

"The regular kitchen staff. Meg, me, John, Kathleen Kiddermeister. We were short a waitress, which is why I was waiting tables. Other than the guests, just Tom Peterson and some customer of his, I think. They came in around ten-thirty. Oh! And Marge showed up."

"And the guests?"

Quill ran over the roster of the guests. "Excluding Hallenbeck and Collinwood—we've just got six others. There's a family in three twenty-six and three twenty-seven. An orthodontist, his wife, and two kids taking a tour of the Finger Lakes Region. They're due to check out tomorrow, and they were hiking all day today. And—oh, Myles! The most awful thing! We think the food critic for *L'Aperitif* is here incognito. He's calling himself Edward Lancashire. Meg's fit to be tied. But that last one—" Quill broke off.

"What about the last one?"

"The most disgusting human being. Keith Baumer. Eyes like sweaty little hands. Ugh."

"Do any of the guests smoke?"

"Keith Baumer does. He's a sloppy smoker. Why?"

Myles reached into his shirt pocket and took out a plastic evidence bag. It contained a matchbook.

"That's one of ours," said Quill.

"Notice how it's folded?"

Quill examined it through the clear plastic. The cover had been folded over three times, exposing the matches. The book was full.

"Have you seen a matchbook folded like this before?"

Quill shook her head. "Is it a clue?"

"Beats me."

"This doesn't make any sense, Myles."

"Not at the moment it doesn't." He rubbed the back of his neck. "Why don't you get some sleep? It's been a long day. I want to go back to the station and think about this a little bit."

"You think this was just a stupid prank?"

"Beats . . ."

". . . me," Quill finished for him.

"I'll do some background checks. On all of them. I want to get the state lab boys in here tomorrow to run some tests on the balcony." He put his arm around Quill, and she burrowed gratefully into his chest. He smelled faintly of aftershave and clean male sweat. "I don't want to think about this any more tonight. I want to think about the way you smell. I like the way you smell."

"Quill." Myles tipped her head back. The moonlight shone into her eyes, and his face was a dark shadow behind it. "There's a third option."

"Yippee," said Quill, thinking delightfully lewd thoughts.

"Malice."

"Malice?"

"Someone could be out to put you and Meg out of business."

CHAPTER 4

Quill snatched a few hours' sleep, dreaming of Mavis bobbing along the duck pond like a fat cork, Mrs. Hallenbeck yelling, "No charge for the swim!" and Marge Schmidt nailing a "For Sale" sign to the Inn's front door.

She overslept the alarm and woke groggily to sunshine, bird-song, and a distinct feeling of unease.

She threw open the bedroom windows and looked crossly at the scene below. French lavender grew directly under her windows. Mike the groundskeeper grew them as annuals; they were a lot of trouble, but worth it, he said, for the scent. Quill inhaled, held her breath, then let it out sharply. She ran vigorously in place for a few minutes. Neither lavender nor exercise cleared her brain enough to make sense of Myles's offhand comment of the night before.

Had Marge Schmidt and Betty Hall advanced from verbal slings and arrows to outright war? The more she thought about it, the madder she got at Myles, who had no business second-guessing without facts. Intuition, thought Quill virtuously, was a rotten character trait in a sheriff. How often had he lectured her about leaping to conclusions? Now here he was, driving her bats with supposition.

Harvey Bozzel had left the new brochure copy for the Inn's advertising campaign with her a week ago. Quill went into her small living room and pulled it out of the desk. She'd already blue-penciled Harvey's tag line extolling the Inn's customer service: "No Whine, Just Fine Wine When You Dine!" But his description of Meg's cooking wasn't too bad.

Meg's art was at its peak with the breads, terrines, pâtés, and *charcuterie* of Country French cooking; for the past year, she'd been making increasingly successful forays into French haute cui-sine, perhaps as a reaction to *L'Aperitif*'s first review. "Quilliam's coarsely ground sausages are exceptional," *L'Aperitif* had commented in the review that awarded her the coveted three stars. "A celestial blend of local pork, freshly picked herbs, and the crumbs of her excellent peasant breads. Her efforts at the more sophisticated levels of classic French cooking are reliable."

The local pork came from Hogg's Heaven, a pig farm three miles upwind of Hemlock Falls. The herbs came from the gardens maintained by Mike the groundskeeper. The breads were made by a series of apprentice *sous* chefs under Meg's supervision. Meg herself was rebuilding the ramparts of "reliable" into "exceptional."

The ad copy described all this in prose only slightly less purple than the lavender below her window. Quill scowled furiously at the copy, then stuffed it back into the desk. Who would want to put such a great cook out of business? She glanced at the clock. It was obviously running fast; it couldn't be past eight already. She dressed hastily and went downstairs.

Her mood was not improved after an encounter with Keith Baumer at table eight, who stopped her rush to the kitchen with a smarmy suggestion involving the length of her skirt (short) and a repulsive summation of his ideal wake-up call.

Quill held on to her temper. The Cornell Hotel School offered a night course in Customer Relations, and Quill had dutifully attended CR 101 and CR 102. "I'm sure you'll agree your suggestions are inappropriate, Mr. Baumer," she said. "May I take your food order, please?" She kept a prudent distance from his sweaty hands, then stalked self-consciously into the kitchen.

Meg, humming an off-key version of "The Gambler," was folding shiitake mushrooms into an omelette with one hand and stirring a béarnaise sauce with the other. She looked up as her sister came into the room. "Lancashire's ordered the works. French omelette in a bird's nest of cr-r-r-isply fried potatoes, and of course, The Sausage."

"I didn't see him in the dining room."

"How could you miss him? Those good looks fly across the room." She switched to an equally off-key rendition of "Some Enchanted Evening."

"That's because I was contemplating unique *Tortures of the World*. You can order a videotape from Time-Life Books, I think."

"Not Baumer again."

"Baumer. Had a suggestion having to do with short-skirted uniforms and appropriate poses for waitresses over the right table height."

"Ugh!" shrieked Meg. "That foul, grungy pig!" She took the saucepan off the Aga and regarded it thoughtfully for a moment. "What'd he order?"

Quill looked at the slip. "Stuffed tomatoes, scrambled eggs, bacon."

John came softly into the kitchen carrying a room service order. "Two orders of Eggs Benedict, grilled grapefruit with brown sugar, blueberries with whipped cream, German pancakes, and two orders of Smithfield ham."

"That doesn't sound like the orthodontist," said Quill with trepidation.

"Mrs. Hallenbeck." John's tone was curt. "Is all this on the house?"

"For now."

"That's a forty-dollar breakfast," said John.

"I know." She explained briefly what Myles had discovered the previous evening. "We'll wait until the lab results are in, but we don't know anything yet. If it's vandalism, we're responsible."

"I think you should talk to them about keeping costs within reason."

Quill grimaced.

"I'll talk to them, then," said John insistently. "We can't afford this kind of cash drain, Quill."

"John, if we *are* liable for this accident, it's just going to annoy them to insist that they watch it."

"I warned you about those two when they checked in."

"Yes, you did," Quill admitted.

"Did you check the supply of sulfuric acid?"

"No, I don't have any idea of what was there before. Doreen might, but she's not back from vacation until this afternoon."

"I saw her out here yesterday. Mavis Collinwood, I mean. She passed right by the storeroom."

"John, you think *they* staged the accident? Come on! We can afford this, can't we? You said last week this is the first year we're going to show a profit."

"Maybe," he said gloomily. "If you don't keep buying food and drink for the whole town. I can't wait to get the bill from the Croh Bar. Half those guys on the volunteer firemen should be in A.A."

"They may have saved Mavis' life," said Quill. "Meg! What are you doing to that tomato?"

"The one for salesman-creep Baumer?" Meg gleefully shook baking soda into the chopped parsley, sausage, and onion dressing that composed the usual stuffing.

"No." Quill took the orange box from Meg's hand and replaced it in the cupboard.

"Yes!" said Meg. Her face reddened, always a sign of rising temper. Then her hair seemed to flatten, which indicated it had risen. Quill could never figure how she accomplished the trick with her hair. Meg retrieved the baking soda and sprinkled a bit more on the tomato.

"Why don't we suggest that they curb the spending, at least until we establish the cause of the accident?" said John.

"Okay, okay, okay." Quill lifted her hands in a gesture of defeat. "I'll do it."

"When?"

"In a bit. I've got to memorize that stupid speech for *The Trial of Goody Martin*. The dress rehearsal's this afternoon at the duck pond."

"No time like the present," said John. "They're waiting for you in two-fourteen. I said you'd be along to speak to them. Kathleen will bring their breakfast up."

Quill sighed. "Okay. Okay. I'm going. See this? It's Quill, going to do her duty."

Meg was singing ". . . when I am dead and gone, dear, sing no sad songs for me" to her omelette as Quill left the kitchen.

It was shaping up to be a hell of a week.

Two-fourteen and two-sixteen were two separate bedrooms connected by an interior door. Quill didn't particularly like the decor, having given way to a brief infatuation with grape-and-ivy chintz for the bedspreads and drapes.

Mrs. Hallenbeck opened the door to her knock, dressed in a red double-knit suit that screamed "designer." Quill's painter's eye recoiled from the clash with the purple and green.

"I very much dislike this room," said Mrs. Hallenbeck, by way of greeting.

"So do I," said Quill frankly. "You must have a nice sense of color, Mrs. Hallenbeck. Would you like to move to the rooms below? They're a little more soothing to the eye."

"Perhaps that would settle Mavis down," Mrs. Hallenbeck admitted.

"Coo-ee!" Mavis waved at her from the bed. Quill, momentarily speechless, didn't respond at first.

"Dr. Bishop's Valium samples seemed to have loosened Mavis' more obvious inhibitions," said Mrs. Hallenbeck dryly. Mavis' generous breasts spilled over the top of a lacy nightgown. Her makeup had been applied with a lavish hand. Her hair, released from its tight bun, spilled over her shoulders. Chewing gum with enthusiasm, she waved again, and said, "This is just so *lovely*!"

"Please sit down, Ms. Quilliam." Mrs. Hallenbeck sat stiffly, though with elegance, at the tea table fronting the windows. "I take it you have come to discuss a settlement with us. I am prepared to listen to any reasonable offer."

Quill sat in the chair opposite and took a deep breath.

"Where's that breakfast?" caroled Mavis. "I swear, I could eat a hog whole."

Quill took a second deep breath. A double knock on the door acted as a brief reprieve. She opened it, took the tray from Kathleen Kiddermeister, and set it on the tea table. Mrs. Hallenbeck examined the tray with disdain. Mavis hauled herself out of bed with a whoop, parked the wad of chewing gum on the bedpost, and settled herself at the table. She and Mrs. Hallenbeck had a brief, sharp discussion over who had ordered the grapefruit. Mrs. Hallenbeck won and took the blueberries mounded with whipped cream.

"Would you care for coffee?" asked Mrs. Hallenbeck, after a moment's more-or-less silent chewing. "It's quite decent. I discovered yesterday that one has to insist on the chef's private stock, or else you are served a brew that is quite ordinary."

Quill pinched her own knee hard. She was awake. She was part owner of this Inn. She was in charge. She had to talk to the widows with the direct yet tactful charm that had never failed her, and convince the widows that costs should be kept down for all their sakes.

"It looks as though sulfuric acid was poured on the mortar around the balcony," she blurted. "The sheriff has sent samples off for tests to confirm it."

The widows stopped eating. Mavis looked at Mrs. Hallenbeck, her mouth open. Mrs. Hallenbeck looked out the window. Her mouth was firmly closed.

"Tests?" said Mrs. Hallenbeck. "Who in the *world* would want to make that balcony unsafe?"

"I don't know," said Quill carefully. "But until we do, I thought you might want to . . . to . . . be as careful about your expenses as you have been in the past."

"Vandals!" said Mavis. "My God. Are we safe in our beds here, Amelia?"

"You seemed to think so when you talked me into coming here, Mavis," said Mrs. Hallenbeck tartly.

"I thought you and your husband had been here before," said Quill.

"Yes, of course. Mavis reminded me of it when we were planning our trip this summer. She did *not*, however, tell me that we would be fair game for malicious tricks."

"I don't know how this happened," said Quill. "But until we know who will have to pay for the repairs to the balcony, we won't know who will be responsible for your hotel bill. We are delighted to have you as guests, of course, but you must understand that we're running a business."

Mavis broke into shrill laughter that stopped as suddenly as it started. Mrs. Hallenbeck shot her a venomous glance, then nodded benignly at Quill. "We will be happy to accommodate you, Sarah." She picked up Mavis' plate of Eggs Benedict and the Smithfield ham. "You may return these to the kitchen and remove them from our room service charge. Mavis does not require that much for breakfast."

"I certainly do!" said Mavis. She snatched the plates back. "I'm sure Miss Quill and the sheriff don't want us to starve while we are waitin' to hear what's what." She picked up a slice of ham in her fingers and rapidly chewed it.

Quill murmured her goodbyes and left them to it.

Going downstairs to her office, Quill had a moment's feeling of control. She fervently hoped it was not illusory. It lasted through the staff meeting (all the waitresses showed up for work) and the business meeting with John (the Inn was booked solid for History Days). She even found time for a quick glance at Clarissa Martin's two big speeches, one before being ducked in the duck pond, the other as she was sentenced to being pressed to death. The feelings of competency even lasted through the lunch trade and Meg's excited report that Edward Lancashire had *come to the kitchen* to compliment her on the omelette. This was offset somewhat by Quill's receipt of a customer-satisfaction card, unsigned, that complained bitterly about the baking soda in the scrambled eggs. Quill, looking ahead to the month's receipts, decided to let it go.

She lost the glow at the Chamber meeting that afternoon. Since the Chamber budget allowed only for a once-a-month lunch in the conference room, supernumerary sessions were held in the Inn's Lounge. Quill donated coffee and soft drinks at these sessions, and she came into the Lounge early to make sure of the preparations.

Esther bustled in behind her, clipboard in hand. "Julie Offenbach is sicker than a *dog*," reported Esther in glum satisfaction, "so you'll just have to rehearse with us, Quill."

"Has Andy Bishop seen her?" asked Quill, with slowly extinguishing hope. "They've got all kinds of miracle drugs these days."

"It's just *flu*!" said Esther. "She'll be maybe better by Wednesday. First performance is day after tomorrow, so there you are. You'll do *fine*, Quill."

"Oh, dear," said Quill. "Esther, I'm just not good at this kind of thing."

"But you're so pretty!" Esther said unenviously. "It's for the good of the town, you know. You have been practicing, dear, haven't you?"

"You bet," said Quill firmly, "I'll just take a minute to . . . to look at it one more time." She escaped into the hallway, only to be swept back into the Lounge by an ebullient Mayor Henry and Gil Gilmeister. Marge Schmidt and Mavis Collinwood were right on their heels, and Marge yelled, "You got that part memorized, Mave?"

Quill turned around. Mavis, in a modest print dress much like the one from the day before, shrieked, "It's just *adorable*. I'm going to love it!"

Quill studied her for a moment. The effect of the Valium had carried over into the afternoon. The big patent-leather belt was cinched two notches tighter. The top of the print dress was unbuttoned. Her hair was loose, and the makeup laid on with a trowel.

"Goings-on!" sniffed a dire voice at Quill's elbow. "Dressed like the scarlet woman of big cities. Detroit, for instance."

"Oh, hi, Doreen!" Quill gave the housekeeper a hug. "So glad you're back from vacation. Did you have a good time?"

Doreen's beady brown eyes bored into hers. "Praise be that I went when I did, Miz Quill. Praise be, for I found the Lord."

Nobody knew how old Doreen was. Meg guessed late fifties, Myles late forties, with a hard life behind her. She'd shown up truculent and bellicose at the Inn's back door one January afternoon, and Quill had hired her on a temporary basis. That was two years ago. Except for a tendency to fierce, short-lived enthusiasms, Doreen was the most loyal, hardest-working employee they had. There was no one at the Inn Quill liked or trusted more. Except, Quill thought, for John Raintree and Meg.

"In Boca Raton? At your nephew's?"

Doreen nodded. "Just in time, too."

"For what?"

Doreen folded her arms, leaned against the wall, and paused dramatically. Quill braced herself. Doreen had run afoul of Quill's erratically enforced guest-courtesy standards before. Cigarette dangling, skinny, and a frequent victim of the Hemlock Hall of Beauty's experiments in permanent waves, Doreen had profanely terrorized more than one unsuspecting visitor. Checkout was a favorite arena: "You inspect that sumabitch's goddam suitcase for towels and ashtrays? I'm missin' towels and ashtrays." Quill had a brief, happy vision of a kindlier, Christianized Doreen accosting visitors with reassuring Bible verses instead of fiercely wielded mops.

"Just in time for what, Doreen?"

"Day of Judgment is at hand," said Doreen darkly. "Those who have not been brought howling in repentance to the throne of the Lord will be damned in the Pit forever."

Quill found the regret in her voice spurious, given the glee in her eye.

"Now, Doreen—" began Quill.

"People!" Esther waved her hands imperiously in the air. "Dress rehearsal, people! Just one day to the Real Thing. Chop, chop!"

"—I'd like to discuss this religion thing with you—"

"Quill!" Esther cried. "Come on! We can't do without our star!"

"—but not right now," Quill finished hastily.

"What's that old bat Esther want with you?" asked Doreen suspiciously.

"Julie Offenbach's got the flu."

"So you're gonna be Clarissa?" She shook her head. "You ain't never been in a play in your life. I better pray for you."

"Pray for rain instead. A thunderstorm, even. I don't want to do this, Doreen."

"You'll be fine." Doreen gave her hand a rough, affectionate squeeze. "You can do anything you set your mind to. But I'll pray for a disaster, if you want." Her face lit up. "One to demonstrate His power."

"Great. After the rooms are done, though."

Esther, thorough as always, had left a stack of scripts by the coffee table in the Lounge, and Quill thumbed glumly through a copy as the Chamber members settled into their seats. Myles walked into the room and Quill greeted him with a swift, intimate smile.

"Everyone seated!" Esther said. "Clarissa? Are you ready?"

Quill waved the script feebly at Esther, and settled across the table from Myles and Gil Gilmeister. "Any results from the lab yet, Myles?" she asked hopefully.

He shook his head. "Not until Monday or Tuesday. It's not exactly a priority problem."

"Maybe it was just a prank," said Quill, "or an accident. Doreen was gone on vacation and one of the temporaries could have spilled it."

"Full strength?" said Myles. "I doubt it."

"Accident," said Quill stubbornly. "Maybe you should just drop the investigation."

"We need to get to the bottom of it," Myles said. "You've got to be tougher than that, Quill."

"I'll say." Gil, his attention drawn by the latter part of this comment, leaned back in his chair and took an overlarge bite of the beignets Meg had set out with the coffee. Sugar dribbled down his chin. He licked it off reflectively. "You got to be tough all over. That darn Mark Anthony Jefferson at the bank? Well, I had to get tough with him this morning. Wants to call in that loan I got right this minute." He looked at Myles. "He can't do that can he, Sheriff? I mean, it's gotta be against some law or other. I've been paying on the note right along."

"Can't help you there, Gil."

"Well, it's not right," Gil said again. "I have to find some cash somewhere. Thing is, people just aren't buying cars. Got any rich widows here at the Inn, Quill? One that might want to invest in one of the best little businesses in Hemlock Falls?"

"Sorry, Gil. It's been a tough year for everyone. But things are getting better, don't you think? Business looks great for us for the rest of the summer."

Gil gave her a cheerful smile. "You might be right. Now, I'll tell you who's got money. Marge Schmidt. That diner business is all cash, if you know what I mean, and she's not paying half the taxes I have to. 'Course, she doesn't have my expenses, either."

Quill, who knew how frequently Gil's wife, Nadine, went to Syracuse with Gil's charge cards, murmured sympathetically.

"Where *is* Marge, anyway?" asked Gil. "She's supposed to have my judge's costume with her."

"Right here!" boomed Marge. "And guess who I have with me!" She stumped into the Lounge towing Mavis behind her. "Everybody? I wanna introduce you to an old pal of mine, Mavis Collinwood. Mavis, this is the cast of the play I was telling you about. That's Gil Gilmeister." She winked at the car salesman and waved heartily. "Gil's the judge in the play. Next to him is Myles McHale, our sheriff. He's here 'cause of the traffic control and on account of we use some equipment that's gotta be safe. Then there's Howie Murchison, Tom Peterson, Mayor Elmer Henry. They're all witnesses to the witch, and say the things she's done. And Reverend Shuttleworth plays the minister who condemns the witch. Esther's our director. And Norm Pasquale directs the high-school band. You know, they play that Funeral March as the witch is dragged off in the sledge." Marge paused for breath.

Mavis waved at the crowd, and spoke in a low voice to Marge.

"Hah? That there's Betty Hall. She's my business partner. No *way* she could play the part."

Betty, unclear as to the nature of the discussion, clearly heard an insult implicit in Marge's dismissal of her, and said, "What the hell?"

"No," Marge said, again in response to a question from Mavis, "Clarissa's usually played by some girl from the high school. Miss Sarah poison-your-guts Quilliam's supposed to play it this year." She gestured in Quill's direction.

"Marge!" said Esther. "For heaven's sake! This is a *private* rehearsal. As director, I must insist that your guest wait outside while we finish."

"You've met before?" said Betty icily.

"Met before?" said Mavis breathlessly. "Why, we worked together for this age!"

"Doggone good dogs," said Marge cryptically.

"*Doggone* good dogs," responded Mavis, and both women went off into gusts of laughter.

"The fast-food chain," said Tom Peterson. "It's out of Syracuse. You wouldn't know this, Quill, but they do quite a bit of recruiting from the high school." He blinked his pale eyes slowly—rather, Quill thought, like a lizard in the sun.

"Yeah," said Norm Pasquale. "Hot dogs and paint are the only jobs our graduates get unless they go to college. It's not like the old days, when all the kids went back to the farm."

"So what's your point, Marge?" said Elmer impatiently.

"Point is that Mavis here is a hell of an actress. She can do this part better'n anyone here."

"Then she'll have to audition," said Esther.

"*She* din't." Marge threw a large thumb in Quill's direction.

"Yes, she did," said Esther. "I auditioned her. I'm the director, and I say who auditions and who doesn't."

"Quiet!" said Elmer. "Whyn't you tell us your experience, Ms. Collinwood. What exactly did you do at Doggone Good Dogs?"

John Raintree came into the room and settled unobtrusively in a chair. Doreen tiptoed in behind him. Quill drummed her fingers in irritation and wondered who else from the staff was coming to watch her debut as an actress.

"Best hot dogs in the South," said Mavis.

"Best in the whole damn country!" said Marge. "Good plain American food."

"I never knew you worked for somebody else before," said Betty Hall stiffly.

"Oh, yeah. Managed a whole chain of 'em down to Atlanta," said Marge. "Mavis was in the Mid-Atlantic region. She was Human Resources Coordinator and—"

"That's just fine, Marge," said Elmer Henry impatiently, "but we've got to get on with this rehearsal."

"Let me finish," said Marge, "*and* the best damn actress in the whole chain."

"Oh, I don't know about that," said Mavis modestly.

"Do they have actors in fast-food places?" asked Esther, in genuine bewilderment.

"Of course," said Marge scornfully. "We had an employee talent show every year and Mavis got the cash prize every time. Sang "The Doggone Good Dog" theme song. Go on, sing it for 'em, Mavis. She done a little dance, too," she said in a helpful aside.

"I don't have my costume or anything." Mavis sent a brilliant smile around the room.

Quill, acutely sympathetic to the agonies of performing in front of crowds, and still somewhat nettled over the "poisoned-guts" remark said, "Honestly, Marge. Let the poor woman sit down," surprising herself. If she kept this up, she could handle a dozen Mrs. Hallenbecks in a week.

"Go *on*, Mavis," said Marge.

"Well." Mavis cleared her throat and said confidently, "Now, y'all are going to have to do some *imagining*, and pretend I'm dressed as a hot dog." She winked at Dookie Shuttleworth, whose eyebrows rose in alarm. "The hot dog comes out in front of me, and out back—I'm in the middle of the bun." Then she sang, in a contralto:

> *"You can slather me with mustard*
> *and a dilly pickle, too.*
> *Tickle me with onions,*
> *I'll be doggone good for you.*
> *I'm a plump and juicy red-hot*
> *In a toasted whole wheat bun.*
> *For less than two and fifty*
> *We can have a lot of fun."*

She and Marge locked arms and swayed together in a lockstep.

> *"Hot-Hot-Hot dog*
> *Doggone Doggone good.*
> *Bet you'd love our hot dogs*
> *Anyway you could."*

Harvey Bozzel broke the silence. "Could use a *leetle* bit of editing, but it's good. Pretty good."

"Sing it again," said Gil Gilmeister huskily. "You looked great, Mavis. You, too, Marge."

Mavis tossed her head, and dimpled. Her dangling earrings clicked. She reminded Quill of someone: a chubby Vivien Leigh as Scarlett O'Hara. Quill cleared her throat and stood up. "This is a wonderful opportunity, don't you think? I mean, we practically have a professional right here. We'd be crazy not to take advantage of it. If you don't mind, Mavis, I think you'd make a wonderful Clarissa."

"We voted on Quill and we should stick with her," said Betty Hall. "Some newcomer just swanking on in here, even if she is a famous actress—I don't know how the town is going to feel about that."

"She's not a famous actress, Betty," Esther snapped. "She's a Human Resources Director."

"Whatever." Resentment was in every line of Betty's bowling jacket.

"Marge, you have the best judgment of anybody in the Chamber I know of," said Gil earnestly. "And I think this is a prime example of it."

"We gotta talk about that loan, Gil," said Marge jovially. "What d'ya think?"

"I move to have Mavis Collinwood take on the role of Clarissa in the History Days play," said Quill immediately. She ignored Myles's sardonic grin with the restrained dignity appropriate to an innkeeper rescued from public humiliation at the last minute.

"Second," said Gil.

Elmer called for a vote. Esther and Betty abstained, with what Quill identified as darkling glances, but the motion passed. Quill entertained a fleeting thought about the efficacy of Doreen's new commitment to prayer; she decided she was inclined to leniency in the matter of religious fervor. This was much more satisfactory than a tornado.

"I suppose we'll discover just how quick a study you are, Miss Collinwood?" Esther said stiffly. "Come, people, we're running behind schedule. Everybody at the pond in ten minutes."

Quill stopped John in the hall during the general exodus. "Do your plans include watching the rehearsal?"

He smiled faintly. "Not if you're a member of the audience rather than the cast."

"Thank you so much."

He glanced at her out of the corner of his eye. "Did you talk to the widows?"

"Yes."

"Is Myles going to continue with the background checks?"

"I'm not sure. John, Mrs. Hallenbeck's sitting by herself by the fireplace." Quill looked back at the chattering crowd leaving the Inn. Mavis, expansive, was in the center. "I'll just speak to her."

She crossed the lobby and sat next to Mrs. Hallenbeck. "Did you get a chance to walk in the gardens today, Mrs. Hallenbeck?"

"Not yet. Mavis and I were going to go this afternoon, but she appears to be busy. Perhaps we'll go tomorrow." She folded her hands. "I'll wait until she is finished with her friends. The old are boring to you youngsters."

Quill was quiet a moment. It was pathetic, this small confession. "Would you like to walk down to the rehearsal with me? Only part of the cast will be in costume, but it might be kind of fun. I can't stay for the whole thing, but you're more than welcome to. There's always a crowd watching. Mostly townspeople."

"I'd like that very much."

It was one of those July afternoons that made Quill glad to be in Central New York in summer. The sky was a Breughel blue, the sun a clear glancing light that made Quill's hands itch for her acrylics. As they came to the edge of Falls Park and the small man-made pond that had been formed from the river water, Edward Lancashire picked his way over the grass to them.

"I'd call this a paintable day," he said by way of greeting.

"Do you paint, Sarah?" asked Mrs. Hallenbeck.

"I used to. Not much anymore."

"She was becoming quite well-known when she quit," said Lancashire. His dark eyes narrowed against the bright sun, he smiled down at Quill.

"A painter," said Mrs. Hallenbeck with satisfaction. "I knew you were quite out of the ordinary, my dear. I should like to see your work."

"My sister's work is more impressive," said Quill. "Are you finding the food to your liking, Mr. Lancashire?"

"Call me Edward. And the food's terrific."

"And what do you do?" asked Mrs. Hallenbeck.

"Oh. Reporting, mostly," he said vaguely. "What's going on down there?"

"This is the part of the play that's the witch test."

"The witch test?"

"Yes. When a person was accused of witchcraft, there was sort of a preliminary cut made of witches and non-witches. A real witch could swim. Innocent victims couldn't. So many American villages used the ducking stool as a test. The real witches swam to shore and were tried and convicted at a later trial."

"And the innocent victims?" asked Mrs. Hallenbeck.

"Drowned," said Quill.

"My goodness!" With a certain degree of ceremony, Mrs. Hallenbeck took a pair of glasses from her purse, fitted them on carefully, and peered at the makeshift stage by the ducking stool.

With the steadily increasing popularity of Hemlock History Week, the town had turned the area adjacent to the ducking pond into a twenty-acre municipal park some years before. An asphalt parking lot lay at the north edge, and half a dozen picnic tables surrounded

the pavilion. The pavilion itself consisted of a large bandstand surrounded by enough wooden benches to seat two hundred spectators.
The entire park fronted the Hemlock River; the Falls that formed
such a unique backdrop to Meg and Quill's inn rushed gently into the
river at the south of the park. The ducking pond was edged with concrete. A sluiceway was lowered to fill the pond in spring, and lifted to
empty it in winter. A ten-foot fence of treated lumber stood at right
angles to the pond's edge, where Harland Peterson parked his ancient
John Deere farm tractor every year to power the ducking stool into
the water. A chorus of cheers greeted him as the John Deere chugged
into place behind the fence. He hopped out of the cab, waved his
baseball hat to the crowd, and began hooking the ropes attached to
the ducking stool to the metal arms on the front loader.

"That thing is old," Edward observed. "Fifty-six or fifty-seven
at least."

"The Petersons are pretty thrifty," said Quill. She avoided Mrs.
Hallenbeck's eye. Harland jumped back into the cab and raced the
motor. Belching black smoke, the tractor jerked the front loader
aloft. The ducking stool dangled freely in the breeze from the
river.

"I thought a ducking stool was sort of a teeter-totter," said
Edward. "The judge or whoever sat on one end, the accused witch
on the other, and then the judge got up."

"Yes," said Quill.

"That's a lot simpler than using a tractor, isn't it?"

"Yes," said Quill.

"So why . . ."

"Harland Peterson wanted to be part of the play. But he refused
to dress up in a costume."

"And!"

"The Petersons have owned most of the town for generations.
See that nice house there, over by the pavilion? Tom Peterson lives
there. He's Harland's cousin. Harland donated the land for the
park. And he owns a tractor."

"Ah." A look of ineffable pleasure crossed Edward's face. "I'm
going to enjoy this."

Howie Murchison, Tom Peterson, and Elmer Henry ranged
themselves in front of the stool. Esther dragged Mavis unceremoni-

ously in front of them, shoved her head forward into a bowed and penitent attitude, then spoke earnestly to her. She stepped back, raised both arms, and dropped them.

"Take One!" she shouted.

"Are they filming this?" said Edward.

"Oh, no," said Quill cheerfully. "Esther sent away for a PBS video-tape on directors' techniques. The Chamber argued for months about paying for it."

"Did they pay?" asked Edward, clearly fascinated.

"No. Marge said she'd tell Esther what to do for free."

"I ACCUSE!" roared Elmer Henry suddenly.

Mrs. Hallenbeck jumped.

"It's just the play," said Quill. "There's a whole bunch of 'accuses.'"

"I ACCUSE GOODY MARTIN OF THESE WILLFUL AND SATANIC ACTS!" Elmer hollered again. "THE DEATH OF MY GOOD MILCH COW! THE SICKENING AND DISEASE OF MY FLOCK OF HENS!"

"Crowd!" demanded Esther authoritatively. "The chorus, please!"

The crowd consisted of the eighteen Chamber members who didn't have major speaking parts. Quill noticed Keith Baumer had insinuated himself into the group.

Mumblings indicated the crowd was confused. Esther circulated briefly, issuing instructions, then stepped aside. "Take Two!"

"I ACCUSE!" roared Elmer, and recounted the death of several chickens, ducks, and sundry hogs.

"Crowd!" shouted Esther imperatively.

"Sink or swim! Sink or swim!" the crowd roared.

Mavis flung her hands over her head and fell to the ground with a thud. "As God is my witness! I'll never be hungry again!" Mavis shrieked dramatically.

Esther threw her script to the ground, hauled Mavis up by the collar of the print dress, and shook her finger in her face. "Take Three!" she said in loud disgust.

Elmer, Tom, and Howie declaimed in turn about the demise of their livestock. The crowd yelled "Sink or swim" until it was hoarse. With a defiant shake of her head at Esther, Mavis prostrated herself in front of her accusers and cried, "As God is my witness . . . I am innocent!"

"She got the line right this time," said Quill.

The "judge"—Gil in a black cloak, a tricorne hat, and a ruffled shirt—handed Mavis over for trial.

"Of course," Edward observed with a mischievous glance at Quill. "The French costumes. So much more attractive than those staid Pilgrims."

Screaming enthusiastically, Mavis was dragged to the ducking stool, roped in, and swung aloft. The front loader flipped forward, and Mavis slid into the pond. She emerged and swam to shore to loud applause.

"They go to the pavilion and have the trial next," said Quill.

"What happens there?" asked Edward.

"Well, she's tried. Convicted. There's this speech. Elmer comes out from behind the fence with a horse-drawn sledge and she's drawn off on it just long enough to substitute a dummy. The sledge comes back with a hooded dummy on it—they believed witches could hypnotize you to hell with their eyes. There's a procession to the foot of that statue of General Hemlock, and then a bunch of guys lower a barn door onto the dummy and the crowd piles stones on it."

"My goodness!" said Mrs. Hallenbeck. "The violence of these Pilgrims."

"Straight out of a Shirley Jackson story," muttered Edward.

Gil, his arm around a laughing Mavis, broke away from the crowd at the pond and headed toward them. Keith Baumer and Marge followed them like hopeful puppies.

"You're soaking wet, Mavis," said Mrs. Hallenbeck. "You should change."

"Don't worry your little ol' head about me," said Mavis with a broad smile. "So. What d'yall think?"

"You were marvelous," said Quill promptly. "It's going beautifully. If you don't mind, I'm going to take Mrs. Hallenbeck back to the Inn. I've got a lot of work backed up."

"Oh, we'll take care of Mrs. Hallenbeck," said Gil. He swept his tricorne off his head with a flourish. "Ma'am? Mavis has told me all about you. I'm eager to make your acquaintance. Mavis here suggested we take you down to the pavilion so you can watch the rest of the play. Then we're going along to Marge's diner for a bite of supper—Keith, Marge, Mavis, and me."

Mavis batted her eyelashes at Edward. "Why don't you come along, too?" She smoothed her print dress over her hips. "I am just dyin' to hear what you think of the rest of it. And Amelia? You're going to love Gil, here. I have to tell you he reminds me a lot of your late husband, good man that he was." She smiled even more broadly at Quill. "Now, what's that worried frown for? I've been taking care of this lady for a good many years now. She's in good hands, Miss Quilliam."

Quill, walking back to the Inn alone, had begun to doubt that very much.

"It's not that I have anything to go on other than this feeling, Myles," she said to him over a late dinner. "There's just something odd about Mavis."

"What, exactly?"

"The first day she was here, she was—I don't know. I thought. This poor woman is completely under Mrs. Hallenbeck's thumb. I even thought how awful her life must be, at this dreadful old woman's beck and call. But now . . ." She moved the salt and pepper shakers a little closer to the sugar bowl, then back again. The dining room was quiet. Most of the staff had gone home.

"Now, what?"

"Mrs. Hallenbeck isn't dreadful—just pathetic and lonely. And I don't think it's the Valium that's making Mavis so . . ."

"Slutty?" suggested Myles.

". . . she's just *like* that!"

"Sheriff?" Davey Kiddermeister rapped at the dining room door and walked in. The youngest of the uniformed officers on Myles's force, his normally ruddy face was pale. "Sheriff? Gil Gilmeister's dead. They found him drowned over to the duck pond. Where the play was on this afternoon. He and Marge and a couple of guests from the Inn were at the Croh Bar. Guess they were getting into the booze pretty good."

"Dammit!" said Myles. He rose in a single powerful movement. "Quill. You *stay here*, understand me? I don't want you meddling."

Quill, a little numb with shock, followed them out the door.

CHAPTER 5

Davey raced ahead to set up the floodlights. Following Myles to the duck pond, Quill saw that the moon was a ghostly galleon riding the wine-dark sea. Bess, the landlord's daughter, she told herself in justification, would have been a lot better off if she'd *done* something rather than hanging out the Inn window fiddling with her hair.

"Myles."

Myles didn't bother to turn around, but threw over his shoulder, "Back to the Inn, Quill."

"T-lot t-lot to you, too," she muttered, jogging behind him. Then aloud, "If nothing else, I can see that the rescue team gets coffee."

The red lights of the ambulance spun wildly, bouncing off the cars and pickup trucks already jamming the small parking lot. Most of the onlookers were patrons-in-residence at the Croh Bar. Situated directly across from the Volunteer Firemens' garage, the bar acted as a kind of holding pen for rubberneckers.

There was a shout. The floodlights switched on. Quill stopped, dismayed. Gil's body lay facedown on the grass beside the pond, the ducking stool twisting slowly above him. Mavis and Marge, both soaking wet, huddled near the body. Keith Baumer was nowhere in sight. There was a short silence as Myles approached, then a babble of voices.

"Who pulled him out?" asked Myles.

Davey jerked his thumb at Marge.

"Andy Bishop here?" Myles crouched by the body.

"He's on his way, Sheriff," somebody called from the crowd.

Myles took a pen from his shirt pocket and pushed Gil's rucked-up shirt collar aside. Quill peered over his shoulder. There was a gash in the back of Gil's head. The water had washed it clean, and the purple lips gaped at Quill.

"Davey, I need a hand here." Myles grasped the body's shoulders, Davey the feet, and the two men turned Gil over.

Quill had never seen a drowning before; one look at the blue face, the foam at nostrils and mouth, and she turned quickly away. Myles cleared the area around the body with a few sharp words. Quill backed up, then walked around the fence that concealed Harland Peterson's John Deere tractor. It crouched like a metal Arnold Schwarzenegger, arms holding the front loader extending over the top of the fence. The front loader itself hung at a sharp angle, one end dangling free of the metal arm. Quill stood on tiptoe. The heavy shovel had worked loose. Partially dried blood glistened on the edge. Quill squinted at it in the glare of the floodlights. Blood, hair, and what may have been a bit of bone.

"Gotta close this off, Ms. Quill," said Davey.

"Where's the bolt?" asked Quill.

"Ma'am?"

"The bolt that held the front loader to the tractor arm."

Davey shrugged. "Into the river, maybe? It'd be swept away for sure. Sheriff wants to know if you could see to Mrs. Collinwood and Marge."

Marge and Mavis huddled under a blanket marked "Hemlock Falls Volunteer Ambulance." Quill sat down in the grass next to them and folded her arms around her knees. "You guys all right?" she asked. "Can I get you some hot coffee or anything?"

Marge snorted.

"What happened?"

Mavis began to cry. Marge herself was weeping silently, and impulsively, Quill put her arm around her.

"We were just practicin'," wailed Mavis, "for the play. Just foolin' around. I swear I never dreamed this was gonna happen."

"And Gil sat in the ducking stool?"

Mavis gave a gigantic sniff. "He was saying my lines. Jus' jokin'. Hopped in the stool, and the next thing happened was that big ol' shovel came right down on his head. He fell into the pond and we went to drag him out, but we couldn't *find* him. Marge here kept going under water and pokin' around"—a convulsive shudder shook her—"and his *arm* or somethin' brushed my leg and I screamed."

"Was Keith Baumer with you?" asked Quill.

"*Him*," said Marge with contempt. "Took off like a scalded cat. I pulled Gil out, tried CPR. Didn't work. Mavis here called the ambulance from the pay phone."

A brand-new white Corvette screamed into the parking lot and came to a screeching halt. The passenger door slammed, and a tall, skinny woman with bleached blond hair walked toward the body. Tom Peterson got out from the driver's side.

"Shit," said Marge. "Tom Peterson's brought ol' Nadine."

"Nadine is Gil's wife," said Quill in response to Mavis' bewilderment, "and Tom's her brother." *And Marge is Gil's girlfriend*, she said silently. "Maybe you two ought to come back to the Inn with me."

"Too late," said Marge practically. "Here she comes, and Tom with her."

Years of up-and-down dieting, combined with a permanent, free-floating discontent, had not been especially kind to Nadine Gilmeister's face. Quill noted with interest that her makeup was freshly applied, and her hair as elaborately styled as ever. It was after midnight, at a time when only innkeepers and late-night partiers were in street clothes, but Nadine had taken the time to put on a newly dry-cleaned jumpsuit. Although, Quill saw, at least she'd been upset enough to forget to remove the cleaner's tag from the collar.

Tom held Nadine's arm, greeted Quill with a nicely balanced degree of calm and concern, then said, "I was watching a videotape when I saw the ambulance light. I walked over here, and thought I'd better go get Nadine."

"Susan isn't home?" asked Quill.

"No. It's her bridge night. I think I can handle Nadine—but I may need to call on you, Quill."

"So this supposed rehearsal and business meeting was with you, Marge Schmidt," Nadine said.

"You know darn well it was, Nadine. We was both there when he called you."

"Both?"

Marge indicated the sodden Mavis. "Mavis. This is Gil's wife, Mavis."

Mavis, still crying, said, "The one runnin' the poor soul into debt?"

"How dare you!" shrieked Nadine. "And my poor Gil lying there dead as a doornail."

Tom looked nervously at Quill.

"A pretty well-insured doornail," said Marge. "Which is good for you, on account of he owes me a pile of money."

"Can you *believe* this woman?" Nadine addressed the stars. "I am standing right here and I cannot believe my ears. The man's not yet cold."

Marge glared up at her, then rose menacingly. "He'll never be as cold dead as you are living, Nadine Gilmeister." She took a deep breath.

Gil's relationship with Marge, as yet unacknowledged by either wife or girlfriend, appeared to be the next item on the agenda. Quill, sensing ill will, if not the potential for outright violence, stepped forward to take a hand.

"What is this dreadful noise!" demanded a familiar voice. "What has happened here? Mavis! Why in the world are you dressed in those wet clothes?" Mrs. Hallenbeck trotted out of the darkness, well-wrapped against the evening air in a plaid Pendleton bathrobe.

"What're you doin' here, Amelia?" asked Mavis sourly.

"If I may remind you, both our rooms overlook this view. The emergency vehicle lights wakened me. I knocked on your door. There was no answer. I deduced that you must be down here. What has happened?"

"Mrs. Hallenbeck." The authority in her own voice surprised Quill. She would have to practice more. "I want you and Mavis to come with me. Marge, I think you should check with the sheriff to see if you can go home now. Nadine, I am so very sorry for your loss."

"Let's go, Nadine," said Tom. "You'll want to ride with . . . er . . . to the hospital."

Nadine glared at Marge. "The ambulance's waiting on me," she said. "I'll leave you to later, Marge Schmidt."

Marge took herself glumly off. Quill walked Mavis and Mrs. Hallenbeck back to the Inn.

Most of the Inn's guests had crowded into the lobby, and when

Quill shepherded the widows in the front door, they volleyed questions. Meg, John, and Doreen were dressed, all three prepared to offer assistance. "But John said to stay here in case we had to evacuate or save the silver or something," said Meg. "What happened?"

Quill explained there'd been a drowning. The orthodontist's wife clutched her youngest offspring, an unprepossessing ten-year-old, and wanted to know if the Inn was all that safe for children. The orthodontist cleared his throat portentiously and said, as a medical man, he'd be glad to help if the accident had anything to do with teeth, gums specifically. Quill, engulfed in waves of tiredness from a second disturbed night's sleep, told everybody to please go to bed, and that breakfast in the morning would be on the house.

Keith Baumer, who'd apparently headed straight for the safety of the Inn's bar, volunteered to take the widows to their rooms. Edward Lancashire offered instead. Mavis, dimpling at them, said, "I swan!" with what she clearly thought was a delightful giggle. Mrs. Hallenbeck clutched Quill's arm and demanded that Quill see her to her room. "You must have some tea sent up, my dear, and we can have a nice, long talk."

"Quill's got an inn to run," said John. "I'll take you up, Mrs. Hallenbeck."

"Absolutely not!" said Mrs. Hallenbeck. "That is an intolerable suggestion! Quill, you will come up to my room at once."

"I'm sorry, Mrs. Hallenbeck," said Quill, "but I have my responsibilities here."

Keith Baumer, loud in confused explanations of why he had left the scene of the accident, escorted Mavis and Mrs. Hallenbeck upstairs.

Meg, after a close look at her sister's face, marched her into the kitchen and poured her a double brandy. John and Doreen trailed after them.

"What I don't understand is why the heck it took so long to pull Gil out of the pond," said Meg. "It's not that deep."

"Drink is the opiate of the masses," said Doreen, apropos of nothing.

"You're mixing up Marx with the Victorians," said Meg briskly. "And what do you mean, 'drink'? If this religious stuff you've come back from vacation with is teetotal, you can just forget it. Nobody wants you charging the bar and whacking the boozers with your mop."

"If Jesus turned water into wine for the Kennedys, then he blesses those that take a nip, on occasion," said Doreen loftily. She poured a hefty belt from the brandy bottle into a coffee cup. "What I meant is, those three was down to Croh's after eatin' at Marge's."

"*Real*-ly?" said Meg with interest. "Probably to help them forget what they'd had for dinner. But were they soused, you think?"

"I saw them," John volunteered. "I'd say half the town did. They were knocking them back."

"You were at Croh's?" said Meg. "Is that what you do on your nights off? I've never seen you take a drink here, John—not in all the months you've been here."

"Meg," warned Quill, "give it a rest."

"Eternal rest," mused Doreen, "rocked in the Everlasting arms."

"Poor Gil," said Meg. "Better everlasting arms than Nadine, though."

Quill choked on her brandy, and raised a hand in protest.

"So that shovel just whacked him on the back of the head and those two ladies were too smashed to pull him out of the water," Meg continued sunnily. "What a lousy accident."

"If it was an accident," said Quill. "And you didn't actually see it, Meg, so let's not joke about it, okay?"

"What do you mean, 'if it was an accident'?" said John.

"The bolt that attaches the payloader to the support was missing," said Quill. "Now, admittedly, that's an old tractor. A fifty-six or fifty-seven, somebody said. And the Petersons don't spend a lot on maintenance. But if it fell out, where was it? I investigated and I didn't find it."

"*You* investigated!" hooted Meg. "I should have sold all your Nancy Drews to Bernie Hofstedder in the sixth grade."

"Couldn't it have fallen into the river?" said John.

"It's not likely," said Quill crossly. "There's an enclosure there, remember? The bolt would have fallen inside the fence. I looked, and it wasn't there."

"It depends on *when* it came off," John persisted. "If it snapped under the tension of Gil's weight in the ducking stool, it could have flown quite a distance."

"Not that far," Quill said. "I looked at the one that was still in place on the other side of the tractor. That bolt has to weigh a pound at least. I just can't see something that heavy flying over the fence into the river."

"But who'd want to kill Gil Gilmeister?" said Meg. "I mean, other than the poor shmucks who bought cars from him. And how could anybody know that Gil and those two were going down to the duck pond for a drunken 'rehearsal'? More than that, how could this supposed murderer be sure that *Gil* was going to sit in the thing? The only person scheduled to use it was Mavis."

"The Devil's abroad tonight," said Doreen.

"Oh, it is not," said Meg. "Honestly, Doreen, just leave it to Myles. He'll do his usual bang-up investigation and clear it up in no time."

"Thorough, is he?" asked John.

"You haven't been with us long enough to see him in action," said Meg, "but he's just terrific. He was a senior-grade detective with the New York City police force before he moved here."

"He's too young to have retired," said John.

"He didn't retire, he quit," said Meg. "Just got fed to the back teeth. Said he was losing his sense of proportion. Thing is, he's got all kinds of great connections from his days on the force. What crime there is around here gets solved really fast."

"You didn't know about Myles, John?" asked Quill.

"Come to think of it, you two don't see much of each other," said Meg, "but you'll see him in action now. If Quill doesn't solve it first." She rolled her eyes at her sister.

John's face softened with what might have been a smile. "I wish you luck, Quill. Here—" He dug his hand into his jeans pocket and dropped his Indian-head nickel into her palm. "Maybe this will help."

"From your grandfather, the Chief?" She wrapped her fingers around the coin. "Did you inherit any of his tracking skills? If we pooled our talents, we could solve this before Super Sheriff even files a report."

John was silent a moment. "I'll leave it to the experts. Good night, Quill, Meg." He touched Doreen briefly on the shoulder, an unusual gesture for him, and padded silently from the kitchen.

"Well, Hawkshaw, what now?" said Meg. "Shall we haul out the magnifying glass, the scene-of-the-crime kit, and the rubber hose?"

"The only thing I'm going to solve now is my fatigue. It's after one o'clock. I'm going to lock up and go to bed."

"I'll do it," said Doreen. "You look bushed. You too, Meg." She shook her head dourly, the omnipresent cigarette dripping ashes on Meg's wooden counter. "The Devil's presence is here tonight. Just like the Revrund Willy Max warned us in Boca Raton. I shall seek Satan out in the dark corners of this place."

"Be quiet about it," advised Meg, "or you'll wake up the guests."

"Maybe some of 'em should be woke up," said Doreen, smacking her lips. "See the signs for their ownselves."

"The only sign I want to see is the face of my alarm clock at six A.M. tomorrow," said Meg.

Quill, agreeing, went upstairs to bed, and fell into an exhausted sleep. She was awakened by the shrilling of the house phone.

"Miss Quilliam? Sarah?"

Groggy with sleep, Quill blinked at the bedside clock. "It's eight o'clock!" she said into the phone. "Damn!" She shook the clock. The alarm, which had been set for six, burst into the morning silence like a chain saw. Quill smacked it against the night table and the ringing stopped.

"Miss Quilliam? It's me, Dina. You know, at the front desk. I'm sorry to get you up."

"It's way past time to get up," said Quill. Her thoughts soggy, she said belatedly, "Why are you whispering?"

"It's the guests."

"What?"

Dina raised her voice. There was a suspicion of a shriek in it. "The guests! They're milling around here like . . . like . . . hornets."

"They're angry? What hap—Never mind. I'll be right down."

She grabbed the first clothes at hand, a denim skirt and a navy blue T-shirt, hastily dressed, and headed for the lobby. The orthodontist, his wife, their little boy, Mavis Collinwood, and Keith

Baumer were clotted in front of Dina. They did resemble hornets after prey. They broke into a buzzing whine of exclamations as Quill descended the staircase.

"Here she is!" Dina said. Relief washed over her like water over a thirsty prospector. "Miss Quilliam, there's this sort of problem . . ." She trailed off helplessly.

"Why don't you go into my office, Dina, and take care of the phones. Have you called John?"

"Yes, but he didn't answer."

"Call the kitchen and ask Meg to get someone to find him. Now—" She turned to the orthodontist, who seemed to have the lowest level of agitation. "How can I help you?"

"It's downright disgustin'!" interrupted Mavis Collinwood.

"Calm down, Mave," said Keith Baumer.

"Dr. Bolt, maybe you could explain?" said Quill.

"It's these messages. Little scraps of paper pushed under our doors." He held out a piece of paper. Printed in large block letters at the top of the page was: CALL 1-800-222-PRAY! Beneath it, Quill read aloud, "The Lord sees all evil! The Lord hears all evil! Thou shalt not steal!"

The orthodontist's ten-year-old son burst into noisy wails.

"Adrian," said his mother. She shook his shoulder imperatively. "Stop that!"

Dr. Bolt avoided Quill's questioning look. "We were due to check out this morning, as you know. We packed our suitcases and went down for an early breakfast. When we came back, the room had been cleaned, and we find this message." His chest swelled with indignation. "Now, look here, Miss Quilliam. I do not condone Adrian's appropriation of towels and ashtrays as souvenirs. My wife and I have already discussed this with him. On the other hand, I must register a serious complaint about your housekeeping staff going through my little boy's belongings."

"Oh, dear," said Quill.

"And on my bathroom mirror?" said Mavis indignantly. "I jus' stepped out this mornin' for a walk with Mr. Baumer, and when I came back . . . well, I don' want to even repeat what was written on my bathroom mirror. In soap!"

"It didn't say anything about Detroit, did it?" said Quill.

"Don't you get smart with me, Miss High-and-Mighty," said Mavis. "I scrubbed that mirror clean. The ol' bat sees it, I'm out of a job."

"Where is Mrs. Hallenbeck?" asked Quill.

"Out for a walk," said Mavis sullenly. "Says she's been complimented frequently on her complexion and a walk helps. Lord!"

Quill apologized to the orthodontist, the orthodontist's wife, and gave a souvenir ashtray to the little boy, who stopped wailing and demanded a towel, too. She couldn't bring herself to apologize to Baumer. She took ten percent off the orthodontist's bill. She soothed Mavis, who flounced upstairs to see to Mrs. Hallenbeck, who may or may not have returned from her walk, and advised her to destroy any messages that may have been shoved under the old lady's door.

When the lobby was clear of guests, she took the master key, went up to Baumer's room, and let herself in. A slip fluttered from beneath the door: AND HE CURSED THEM WITH MANY CURSES! THE PLAGUES OF EGYPT ARE UPON HIM! After a moment's thought, she checked the dresser drawers (clear of noxious items), the bathtub (ditto), and then stripped the bed. She removed two dead grasshoppers, a garden slug, and a lively cricket from between the sheets.

She marched to the kitchen. Meg was busy with a cheese soufflé, an apprentice holding a large whisk, and a copper bowl. Doreen, she said in response to her sister's evenly worded questions, had left for a Bible class or something. "No! The egg whites have to peak before you fold in the yolks or the damn thing'll be flatter than my chest!" She turned her attention to Quill, who had reiterated her desire to see Doreen. "Can't this wait?"

Quill began an explanation.

"Hand it over to John," Meg interrupted. "He's pretty good with her."

"Where is he?"

"I don't know!" said Meg. "Quill, will you get out of the kitchen? Whatever she did can wait until after the breakfast crowd leaves."

Quill sat in the dining room. She ate an omelette *aux fines herbes*, grapefruit broiled in brown sugar, and a scone. She drank two cups of coffee. She decided that she wouldn't string Doreen up by her thumbs. She even began to find the messages funny. The second cup of coffee convinced her that all Doreen needed was a new enthusiasm. Maybe she could suggest cross-stitch.

By nine, John still hadn't shown up, and she went to look for him. None of the staff had seen him. She knocked on the door of his rooms and received no answer. She went outside, thinking that perhaps he'd gone down to see Mike the groundskeeper, but Mike was trimming the boxwood, and admitted he hadn't seen John at all that morning.

It was a glorious morning. The air was soft, the sun benign. The display of dahlias by the drive proved irresistible. Feeling a bit guilty, Quill took some secateurs from the gardening shed and spent a contented hour clipping dead heads, weeding, and aerating roots.

The mindless and beneficial calm that overtakes the dedicated gardener was interrupted by Dina. Quill sat back on her heels and smiled happily at her. "John show up?"

"No." Dina, who was affecting the seventies look this year, chewed at the ends of her long brown hair.

"Not more Old Testament doom, death, and disaster? Doreen isn't even here."

"No. Can you come to the office?"

Quill stored the secateurs, the trowel, and the gloves, and followed Dina back to the Inn.

"I heard about last night, and the night before that," she said, "and I thought, well, I'll just let her garden peacefully for a bit. But, Quill, this is a real mess. Maybe I should have come to get you before this."

"What's a real mess?"

"These cancellations!" The phone buzzed angrily. Dina groaned. Puzzled, Quill picked up the phone and answered, "Hemlock Inn, may I help you?"

An outraged woman demanded the manager.

"I'm one of the partners in the Inn," said Quill. "Can I help you?"

Why, demanded the voice, had her tour group received a last-minute cancellation notice this morning? Did she, Quill, have any idea how disruptive this was? Did she, Quill, have any idea of the contortions required to find a last-minute booking elsewhere? As far as Golden Years Tours was concerned, the Hemlock Falls

Inn was off their promotional literature. Forever. And everybody else in the tour business was going to hear about it. Immediately.

Quill hung up the phone.

"Another one?" said Dina. "That'll be the fourth."

"Have you seen John this morning?"

"Nope."

"Do you have the bookings ledger?"

"Couldn't find it. It's not behind the front desk, where I usually keep it, and it's not in the desk here. I *know* I had it this morning. It was on the counter, because all those people were checking out."

"There's a copy on disk in the computer," said Quill carefully. "Dina, I know you worked last night, but before you go, could you help me pull up the records on the PC and call everyone that's booked for this week? Just let them know that a . . . prank of some kind has been pulled. Tell them to disregard any phone calls they may have had. Tell them you're calling to confirm the reservations. If we split the list up, we can maybe salvage the week."

By noon, Quill thanked the exhausted Dina, sent her home, and totaled up the losses for the next business quarter. The caller had been busy; a dozen calls to the major revenue-producing tours had been made between eight-thirty and ten. The message in each case had been brief: the Inn was calling for John Raintree, to cancel confirmed reservations. Very sorry, but there's been a major problem. The Inn was closed. To those few customers who'd been loyal enough to inquire when the Inn would reopen, the message was curt: the Inn would not reopen.

CHAPTER 6

At first baffled, Quill searched the grounds, talked to the staff, and made phone calls to a few of John's accounting clients. By two o'clock, Quill's concern for John's whereabouts had escalated to irritation.

Quill went to the first-floor rooms John had occupied for the past year. She knocked, received no answer, then used her master key. She'd been in the rooms no more than two or three times, and each time wondered at the Spartan quality of John's personal life. Three suits hung in the closet: one winter, two summer. Two sports coats. A modest number of white shirts, a handful of ties, and other necessities barely filled the bureau drawer and the bathroom cabinet.

A photograph of a pretty Indian girl leaning on the hood of a car stood on the night stand; the print had faded a little. The car was a 1978 Olds Delta 88. John's diploma awarding him an MBA from the Rochester Institute of Technology was propped on the small desk. There were books on the shelf under the TV. *Aztec*, by Gary Jennings; *Beggars in Spain*, by Nancy Kress; dozens of science fiction and historical novels. There were perhaps half a dozen self-help books: all of them dealt with alcoholism.

Quill addressed the photograph. "I do not believe that this man did this," she said. "There is no way that I will ever believe John did this." The dark eyes stared back at her. "We've got three questions to answer," Quill told her. "First one is, Where the hell is John? The second is, How did he get there? The third is, Who tried to pull the unfunniest joke in hotel history and blame it on him? Marge Schmidt? She wasn't even *near* the place this morning. Keith Baumer, playing tricks on his morning walk? Maybe Mavis—out of revenge for her fall from the balcony? When I get those answers, there won't be any more questions . . . just a major whack up the side of the head for whoever gets in my way."

Quill slammed outside to the gardens in a highly satisfying rage. She collared a clearly startled Mike the groundskeeper, who said, No, he hadn't seen John; his car was gone, but he hadn't seen John leave. Balked, Quill went to find her sister.

"You're kidding!" said Meg. She was in the storeroom, stacking fresh vegetables in the wire bins. "Would you look at those Vidalias I got this morning? God, they're gorgeous! I'm putting French onion soup on the specials tonight."

"You can't, Meg," said Quill, momentarily distracted. "You use raw egg in the stock."

"So? Makes it richer. Did the Buffalo Gourmet Club cancel?

That's an oxymoron if I've ever heard one. Remember last year when they had that food fight in the bar?"

"That was the Kiwanis from Schenectady. Are you listening to me?"

Meg breathed on a tomato, polished it with the bottom of her T-shirt, and set it on the shelf. "Yes, sweetie. I'm listening to you. John's gone. About thirty percent of the business is gone because somebody pulled a jerky joke. But the bank hasn't called the mortgage or anything, has it? The business will come back. And we can get another hotel manager—the Cornell School's filled with wannabees. I mean, look at the luck I've had with the *sous* chefs from there."

"And salmonella hasn't poisoned anybody—yet."

Meg grinned and bit her lip. "Okay. I'll make onion soufflé. Or maybe just chop it up fresh with these beefsteak tomatoes. They're the most beautiful tomato in the world, these beefsteaks."

Quill sat on a hundred-pound sack of rice and put her chin in her hands. "So what do you think I should do?"

"What can you do? Myles is right, don't fuss so much, Quill. John will come back with a perfectly logical explanation, and if he doesn't—done's done."

"And those phone calls?"

"That foul Baumer is capable of anything, if you ask me. You turned down his gallant advances yesterday morning, didn't you? Well, in my vast experience of disappointed harassers, it'd be right up his mean, spiteful alley."

"You don't think it was Marge?"

"The bookings ledger was here this morning, and Marge wasn't. It would have taken her an hour to copy all those names and numbers. She wasn't here long enough last night to do it."

"And that missing bolt?"

"What possible connection could poor Gil's accident have with John running off on a toot, most likely, and a series of malicious phone calls?"

"I don't know," Quill said, "but by God, there is one."

Sitting at her desk, contemplating the display of Apricot Nectar roses outside her office window, Quill failed to find any connection at all.

She shuffled through her phone messages: nothing from Myles; one from Esther reading "The show must go on! Rehearsal at the Inn 4:00 P.M."; a few from tour directors wanting a chance to discuss the practical joke, which she set aside for Monday during business hours; and one scrawled on a piece of the wrapper for the paper towels the Inn bought in bulk: AND WORMS SHALL CRAWL THROUGH HER NOSE. "Doreen!" said Quill. "Dammit, *whose* nose?"

"Whose nose?" she repeated when she found the housekeeper scrubbing the toilets in 218. Doreen had listened stolidly to Quill's succinct summary of why she was *not* to impose her beliefs on the guests.

"That scarlet woman," said Doreen, "that whore of Babylon."

"I thought it was the whore of Detroit"

"Don't you laugh at me, missy. I need a little Bible study is all." She sat back on her heels and contemplated the gleaming porcelain with satisfaction. "I joined the Reverend Shuttleworth's Bible classes this morning. Learn me a bit more."

"Let's get back to this wormy person," suggested Quill. "You haven't whacked the orthodontist's wife, have you?"

"They checked out. Nope. It's that Miss Prissy butter-wouldn't-melt-in-her mouth friend of the widow lady. Mrs. Hallenbeck's companion. A righteous woman, that Mrs. Hallenbeck, to my way of thinking. She shouldn't have to put up with a person bound for the Pit."

"You mean Mavis Collinwood? Where is she?"

"Bar. Acting no better than she should with that skirt-chasing salesman."

"Doreen, I've just finished telling you that the guests' behavior is no business of ours."

Doreen got up from the tile floor with a groan, and attacked the tub. "Will be if that poor Mrs. Hallenbeck has a heart attack from the sheer cussedness of that woman."

Quill, mindful of the alarming changes in Mavis' personality after her ingestion of Andy Bishop's Valium samples, went to the bar. The mystery of John's whereabouts would have to be put on hold. Besides, she could tackle Baumer about the phone calls. Meg was probably right.

Called The Tavern in their brochures, the bar was the most popular spot at the Inn, occupying an entire quarter of the first floor. The bar's floor and ceiling were of polished mahogany. Floor-to-ceiling windows took up the south and east walls. Quill had painted the north and west walls teal, and Meg had persuaded her to hang a half dozen of her larger acrylics on the jewel-toned walls.

When Quill left her career as an artist, she'd been heralded as the successor to Georgia O'Keeffe. "A small stride forward in the school of magic realism," wrote the critic in *Art Review*. The brilliance of the yellows, oranges, and scarlets of her Flower Series leaped out from the walls with exuberance.

Some weeks, when Quill longed for the rush of her old studio in Manhattan, she avoided The Tavern altogether; at other times, she sat in the bar and took a guilty pleasure in her work.

It was early for the bar trade, but the tourists had started arriving for History Days, and the room was full. At first, Quill didn't see Mavis and Baumer. When she did, she wondered how she could have missed them.

Mavis had bloomed like the last rose of summer. Gone were the prim collars, the below-the-knee print skirts, the spray-stiffened hair. Mavis' full bosom spilled out of a black T-shirt with an illuminated teddy bear on the front. Quill couldn't imagine where Mavis had tucked the batteries. The T-shirt was pulled over a pair of black stirrup pants. Mavis' high-heeled shoes were a screaming red suede with bows at the ankles.

"Coo-ee!" Mavis called, waving her hand at Quill. Nate, the bartender, gave Quill a wry grin and a shrug. Quill leaned over the marble bartop and whispered, "How long have they been here?"

"Through two Manhattans for the gentleman and two mint—"

"Don't say it!" groaned Quill.

"—juleps for the lady."

"Nobody drinks mint juleps, Nate. Not willingly, anyway."

"That's one dedicated Southerner, I guess."

"As far as I know, she's still taking that Valium Doc Bishop prescribed for her," said Quill. "Keep an eye on them, will you?"

"Hard not to," said Nate. "I can short the drinks, if you want."

"If you do, short the bar tab, too." Quill threaded her way

through the tables and sat down next to Keith Baumer. "Did you and Mrs. Hallenbeck get a decent night's sleep, Mavis?"

"I did, I guess. I don't know about the old bat. She was up walking around awful early, I can tell you that."

"Best part of the day," said Baumer genially. "I'm up at six and out for a walk every morning. Get a head start on my work."

"Does your business include a lot of out-of-town phone calls?" Quill asked coolly.

Baumer showed his teeth in what might have been a grin. "Lots." He raised his hand and shouted, "Barkeep! Another round for us. And I'd like to buy you a drink, Ms. Quilliam. What's your poison?"

"Nate will bring me a cup of coffee. Mavis, about last night—"

"Wasn't it awful?" Mavis' eyes filled with ready tears. "That poor, poor man. I'd only met him that day. But he was such a friendly soul. So open, so candid in his needs. I declare, it was like seeing a dear friend pass."

Baumer gripped her knee with a proprietary air. "Comfort is what you need, Mave. And I've got just the ticket."

Mavis dimpled at him.

Nate set drinks and a plate of hors d'oeuvres on the table, a signal he had shorted the liquor in at least Mavis' mint julep. "Compliments of the house, Mr. Baumer."

"Hold it, hold it, my man. Let's see what we have here." Baumer poked disparagingly through the food. "Stuffed mushrooms, for God's sake. You'd think a place with this kind of reputation would be a little more creative, eh? And what the hell is this? Liverwurst?" He wiggled his eyebrows at Quill.

"Meg's Country Pâté," said Quill. "And that's pork rillette, and anchovy paste on sourdough."

Baumer stuffed a mushroom in his mouth, chewed, and grunted, "Not bad. I've had better. But not bad. Here, kiddo, sink your teeth into this." He offered Mavis a pork rillette.

Quill, contemplating Mavis, remembered that John had seen them at the Croh Bar. Was there any connection between John's disappearance and Gil's drowning last night? Her palms went cold. "I wasn't very clear on what did happen last night, Mavis. Was Mrs. Hallenbeck with you all evening?"

Mavis scowled. "Pretty near. We went down to Marge's for dinner. It war a business meeting, you know, whatever that Nadine person thought. Gil wanted to talk with Amelia about investing in his business."

"She doesn't act like she has that kind of money."

"Who? Amelia?" Mavis snorted, leaving a significant portion of the pork rillette on her chin. "You've got to be kidding. She's loaded."

Quill, hoping for more information, raised a skeptical eyebrow.

"Well, she is. She held practically all of the stock in Doggone Good Dogs. Made out like a bandit when the company was sold."

"She did?" said Quill.

"Well, sure. Her husband must have left her a packet, although she sure acts like she's broke. Penny-pinching ol' thing." Mavis giggled uncertainly. Her eyes were glazed. Baumer solicitously helped her to the rest of her mint julep.

"So that's how you met her? You worked for her husband?"

"Who says so?" demanded Mavis suddenly. "Who says I worked for him? It's a damn lie!" She swayed a little in her chair, the teddy bear on her T-shirt blinking furiously.

Quill was going to have to sober her up before asking about John. And she sure didn't want to ask any more questions in front of the rude and inquisitive Baumer. "Are you sure you don't want to lie down, Mavis?" said Quill. "You know, Dr. Bishop thought you should take it easy for a few days."

Mavis got to her feet. She swayed a little, her face pale. "I declare, I do feel jus' a little bit woozy."

"Why don't you come and lie down in my room," said Baumer. "I can give you a back rub or something, help you sleep."

"I'll give her a hand, Mr. Baumer," said Quill coldly. "Come on, Mavis. Alley-oop."

"Alley-oop!"

Quill propelled Mavis firmly through the bar and up the short flight of stairs to two-sixteen. She knocked briefly on the door; when no answer came from Mrs. Hallenbeck, she used her master key and pulled Mavis inside. The rooms were dark, the drapes drawn.

"Who's there?" called a timid voice.

"It's me, Mrs. Hallenbeck. I've brought Mavis up for a nap." Quill eased Mavis, by now half-asleep, onto the bed. The connecting door opened, and Mrs. Hallenbeck peered fearfully into the room.

"She is not drunk again, is she?"

Quill pulled the bedspread over the blinking T-shirt. Mavis looked up blearily. "Amelia? I'm sorry, sugar. Guess I had a li'l too much to drink. We'll go for your walk in a bit. I jus' need a snooze." She closed her eyes, then popped them open again. "Amelia? You're not an ol' bat." She sighed, "I'm the ol' bat," and began to snore.

Even die-hard aging Southern belles look vulnerable in sleep.

Quill decided John couldn't possibly be involved with this woman, or what had happened last night. She knew, abruptly, that what she most wanted was the Inn back the way it was before Mavis' catastrophic transformation into Southern sex kitten of the year. And the key to that was Mrs. Hallenbeck.

"Mrs. Hallenbeck? Could I talk to you a minute?"

"Of course, dear. Please come in."

Quill followed her into 214, closing the door behind her. "Would you like me to open the drapes? It's a beautiful day outside." She pulled the drape cord, and sunshine flooded into the room.

Mrs. Hallenbeck was dressed for walking in a beige trouser suit. She sat down at the little tea table. Her face was stern. "So many terrible things have been happening, Sarah. I was just sitting here in the dark, thinking about them. What's going to happen next? That dreadful accident last night. That Gil person. And Mavis behaving so oddly." Her lips trembled. "Sometimes I think I want to go home. But then I think, what would I do without you, my dear, and your lovely paintings, and your wonderful care of me, and I know we're doing the right thing by staying here."

"As a practical matter, I'm afraid Mavis doesn't have much choice. She'll have to testify at the inquest. But right afterward, you and Mavis can go on with your vacation."

"Oh, no," said Mrs. Hallenbeck firmly. "Mavis has behaved in a wholly unacceptable manner. I would like you to come with me, dear. That would be wonderful. We could have a very good time together."

"I have the Inn to run, and my sister to take care of," said Quill gently. "But surely you don't want to abandon Mavis after all you've been through together?"

"Mavis? I'm through with Mavis." Mrs. Hallenbeck shuddered. "Her friends make me suspicious. Sometimes I think she's going mad."

"Hardly that," said Quill. "But I do think she's not quite herself." Quill experienced a flash of doubt. What if Mavis *was* a con artist, out to bilk an old lady?

"Have you had these kinds of problems before in your travels? I mean, Mavis introducing you to"—Quill searched for the right, unalarming words—"potential investors?"

Mrs. Hallenbeck sent her a sudden, shrewd look. "You do not get to my age and stage, Sarah, by handing over large checks to boobs like that car salesman. That is not the problem, although Mavis would certainly like me to buy her friends for her. No. The problem is finding someone sympathetic to be with when you're old. Do you know . . ." Her lips worked, and the large blue eyes filled with tears. "I loathe it. How did I get to be eighty-three? Why, I look in the mirror, and I expect to see the girl I was at seventeen. Instead . . . this." She swept her hand in front of her face.

"You have a beautiful face," said Quill. "There is a great dignity in your age. We're all going to get there, Amelia. I just hope that when I do, I look like you."

Mrs. Hallenbeck looked at her. "Mavis used to say such things to me. When we agreed to be companions in our adventures, I thought that she cared for me. And now, everything has changed."

"She's been through quite a bit in the last few days. I think," said Quill carefully, "that she's one of those people who just reacts to the situation at hand. Do you know what I mean? Impulsive. That she'll be fine once the inquest is over and the two of you can leave. Things will be the same as they were before." The Cornell University evening course in Interactive Skills training had emphasized something called Identification as a "tool for change." Tools for change, Quill realized, were not tire irons, but nice, tactful lies that made people want to behave better. "Identification" was a lie that made people behave by telling them you did something you didn't, so they'd feel better about changing their ways.

Quill decided to try Identification. "You know, my sister Meg and I—we fight quite a bit. We say things we don't mean." Quill hesitated, searching for the most appropriate lie. "I'm the older sister. Sort of like you're the older sister to Mavis. And I know sometimes I get very bossy. You know, telling Meg what to wear, how to behave. I even yank on her salary once in a while, if she's not cooking exactly the things I think the guests want. But then I remember that Meg has her own needs and her own life, and that I have to let her be herself. And we get along just fine."

"You think I'm too hard on Mavis?"

Mrs. Hallenbeck, Quill realized, was very good at what the professor had called "cutting the crap." Quill patted her hand. "I should have known you'd be shrewd enough to handle poor Mavis. I should think," Quill said expansively, "that what Mavis is really looking for is guidance. She needs you, Mrs. Hallenbeck. One advantage of being your age is that you've had so much experience with people."

"Possibly you're right. I mean, about comparing this to you and your sister." She sat taller in her chair. "I shall take care of things. You know, Mavis and I have been together for many years. I shall reflect on ways and means."

Quill left Mrs. Hallenbeck and marched triumphantly to the kitchen. Meg was scowling hideously at the Specials blackboard, chalk smeared on her face.

"I am so good!" Quill said. She threw herself into the chair by the fireplace and rocked contentedly.

"What d'ya think goes best with the French onion soup?"

Quill stopped rocking. "Um. You mean the onion soup you weren't going to make because of the raw egg ban?"

"The soufflé's a bust. It's too humid for it. I know!" She scribbled furiously for a moment. "Potted rabbit."

"In this heat? Don't you think something lighter is better for July?"

"Lancashire's booked a party of two for dinner. And I've got fresh rabbit."

Quill rose majestically to her feet. Perhaps the improvised management tactics she'd presented to Mrs. Hallenbeck had been an inspiration; she'd never tried a firm hand with her sister before.

"Meg, if you do not stop using raw egg in the food, I will dock your salary."

"You will, huh?" said Meg, unimpressed. Meg put the chalk down and looked consideringly at her sister. "I just might remind Doreen that you spend every Saturday night—*all night*—with a certain good-looking sheriff. She'll want to put worms up your nose, I expect."

"You wouldn't!"

"It'd be nothing less than my duty," said Meg with an air of conscious virtue. She gave her sister an affectionate grin. "So what are you good at? Not this detective stuff?"

Quill sighed. "No. Not this detective stuff."

"You agree that John's probably gone off on a toot? Poor guy, after being sober all these years, and what're you looking at me like that for? You think it's a secret? Everyone knows John goes to A.A. on Thursdays. You know that Gil's accident was just that. And you can bet that creep Baumer was *probably* the one who made those phone calls, out of sheer despair at your rejection of his uncouth advances."

"Ye-e-es," said Quill reluctantly.

"I thought you were going to make a courtesy call on Nadine Gilmeister," Meg said briskly. "One of us has to. And you're *very* good at that."

"I suppose you're right."

"So take a couple of brioches as a tribute to the funeral; get out of my kitchen and do it. Oh, Quill?"

Quill looked back.

"Stop by Tom Peterson's, will you? I stuck some of yesterday's delivery in your car. The meat's tainted."

"The meat?"

"Yes! The meat. It stinks. I can't serve it. Something must be wrong with those refrigeration units. Tell him I want fresh good stuff in the cooler *now*. Make him eat that stuff if he won't."

"Okay," said Quill meekly.

Gil's ostentatious white Colonial was in the town's only suburb, about four miles from the Inn. The street where the now-widowed Nadine lived was lined with cars, and Quill parked her battered Olds half a block away. Hemlock Falls citizens were conscientious about funerals and calling hours. Friends of the deceased rallied around the family, dropping by with a continuous stream of food.

The front door was partly open and she slipped in quietly. She set the brioches in the kitchen between a huge home-cooked ham from the Hogg's Heaven Farms, and a chocolate banana cream pie—Betty Hall's specialty dessert for Saturdays.

She was unsurprised to see Nadine dressed completely in black, something that was Not Done in Hemlock Falls, because it was considered a waste of hard-earned cash. ("So whattya gonna do with a black outfit anyways?" Marge Schmidt had been heard to opine. "Only place to wear it is up to Ms. Barf-your-guts-out-Quilliam's, and after a meal there, you don't have enough left to pay for the dress.")

Marge was, of course, conspicuously absent, but most of the Chamber was there, in force. Quill said hello to Mayor Henry, who nodded gravely, and waved at Howie Murchison, who was in close discussion with Andy Bishop.

A large poster featuring a close-up of Gil's grinning face usually stood by the showroom door at his dealership. Some thoughtful soul had brought it to the house, and it now stood in state by the fireplace, a black-ribboned wreath surmounting the legend "Drowned, But Not Forgotten."

"Not real creative," said Harvey Bozzel, a thick piece of brioche in one hand. "But God! What'd you expect on such short notice? And I've decided not to send a bill. Although the printer double charged for the overtime." Mementos of Gil lay scattered on a table underneath the poster. "Nice touch, don't you think?" said Harvey. "His wallet, his Chamber membership, stuff like that. I think Nadine's going to bury it with him. Except for the credit cards."

"Is all this from . . . ?"

"The body? Some of it," said Harvey. "Quill, now that we have a chance to talk, what about that ad campaign? I've come up with some really exciting ideas."

"Harvey, this just isn't the right time to discuss it."

"Monday, then? I could drop by around ten o'clock."

"Sure." said Quill.

"I'll bring some roughs for you. It's gonna be great."

"Excuse me," said Quill. She edged over to Esther West, who was standing by an impromptu bar set up on the credenza.

"So where do you think she got that?" said Esther bitterly, with a gesture toward the widow.

"The dress?" Quill peered at it. "Looks like DKNY."

"You'd think she'd have the manners to shop at home at a time like this," said Esther. "I have the nicest little black-and-white suit that's been in the window for ages that would have been perfect. Purchased in the hope of just such an occasion." Esther belted back a slug of what smelled like gin. "Now, where's she going to wear that thing after this funeral?"

Quill said she didn't know.

"Mayor asked me to write a short piece in Gil's memory," said Esther. "You know, after the opening ceremonies tomorrow." She adjusted her earring. It was mother-of-pearl, at least two inches wide. "Taste. That's what the mayor's after. I kind of like what Harvey wrote, you know? 'Drowned, but not forgotten.' But we can't just say that. I thought maybe something from *Hamlet* might go over well."

"*Hamlet*?" said Quill. "You mean *Hamlet*?"

"That play by William Shakespeare. There's a scene from it on my director's video. This Queen Gertrude is very upset over a drowning. She runs into the palace and has some very nice lines about a drowning. Very nice."

"The ones about Ophelia?" Howie Murchison, occupied with refilling his Scotch, winked at Quill. "'Too much of water has thou, poor Ophelia; and therefore, I forbid my tears'?"

"You know that play, Howie? I think it's nice. And of course, that's what happened to Gil. Too much water. What do you think, Harvey?" Esther inquired of the ad man, who'd also come to the credenza for a refill.

"Well, Gil was bashed on the head first," said Harvey. "I don't know how creatively appropriate that drowning speech would be. I mean he *drowned*, yes. Too much water, yes. But he was hit on the head first."

"The rest of this play *Hamlet* seems to be people dead of sword wounds," said Esther critically, "and I don't suppose that would do."

"There's always 'Cudgel thy brains no more about it,'" offered Howie.

"Oh, no," said Quill involuntarily. She was afraid to look at

Howie; she bit her lower lip so hard it hurt. "I'll just say something to Nadine. Excuse me again, Harvey."

A space around Nadine had cleared, and Quill went over to see her. "I'm awfully sorry, Nadine," she said soberly. "Is there anything I can do for you? Do you need someone to stay with you?"

"Thank you, no," she said. "I called Gil Junior, of course, and he's driving up from Alfred. He'll be here sometime this afternoon." The two women were silent for a moment. Abruptly, Nadine said, "He was a bad husband, Quill. He ran around on me, and never came home, and caroused too much, and I spent like a drunken sailor to spite him. And now everyone in the town thinks I'm awful. And I was, Quill, I was." Suddenly, she began to sob. The low murmuring in the room stopped. Quill put her arm around Nadine. Elmer Henry proffered a handkerchief. "I'll take her," said Betty Hall with rough kindness, and she led Nadine away.

Quill sighed, turned, and knocked over the table that held Gil's final effects. With an exclamation of chagrin, she bent to sort through the items that had fallen to the floor. Gil's wallet, still damp from the duck pond, had opened and its contents lay scattered. Quill picked up his driver's license (credit cards were conspicuously absent) and a few family pictures. She tucked several of Gil Junior back into the wallet, and flipped over a picture that had been folded in half. She smoothed it out.

A pretty Indian girl stared back at her. The girl in the picture on the night stand in John Raintree's room at the Inn.

CHAPTER 7

Quill smoothed the photograph flat. The girl was dressed in a pink waitress's uniform, leaning across a diner counter. She smiled into the camera, black hair long and shining, dark eyes bright. Was this a girl John had loved? What would a picture of John's girlfriend be doing at the scene of Gil's drowning? Quill took a deep breath.

There had to be another explanation. John couldn't be involved with this. Could she have been a waitress at Marge Schmidt's diner? Could John or Gil have met her there? If that were true, this picture might belong to Marge, and not to Gil at all. No. Marge was Hemlock Falls' most notorious employer, running through waitresses and busboys, with the speed of a rural Mario Andretti. And anyone who'd tuck her aged mother into a nursing home on Christmas Eve, as Marge had done, was not someone you could accuse of sentimentality. Marge wouldn't carry a keepsake of a favorite waitress. If she carried photographs at all, they'd be of cream pies she had known and loved.

Mavis and Keith Baumer were from out of town and had never met John before. Could the picture have belonged to either of them? Was there any connection between John and Mavis? What possible connection could John have with the companion to an elderly and wealthy widow?

That left Gil himself. Gil and John were business acquaintances, hardly friends. But John, a loner, had few friends.

Quill carried the photograph into the kitchen. Nadine stood at the sink, staring out the back window.

"Nadine, I just wanted to say goodbye. If there's anything at all that you need, please call me."

"Thanks for coming, Quill. I've been telling everyone I don't know when the funeral's going to be held. Myles said maybe a week or two."

"That long?"

"He wants to complete the investigation. There'll have to be an autopsy. Howie Murchison says that's standard in an accidental death. He won't be able to probate the will until the inquest is done, so I hope Myles is quick about it."

"Will you be . . . all right . . . until then?"

This was local code for money matters. Wealthy farmers were said to be doing "all right." Marge Schmidt was said to do "all right" out of the diner. Betty Hall, a junior partner, was held to be doing not so well.

"Things weren't going so well," Nadine said, confirming the commonly held belief that Gil's money troubles were real and not the grousing of a Hemlock businessman who felt it unlucky to look too successful. "Mark Jefferson at the bank said there's a couple of outstanding loans that have to be paid off, but Gil had a lot of life insurance. That's the one thing he kept up. Now Marge Schmidt"—spite made Nadine ugly—"had better have some damn good proof that Gil borrowed money from her. If she doesn't, she can whistle for it."

"Meg and I could probably find something to tide you over," said Quill.

"Thanks. But I can always call on Tom. He's been a good brother, by and large. Been supporting Gil for all these years."

Quill shifted uncomfortably. "By the way, Nadine, I found this dropped on the floor of the living room. Is it yours or Gil's?"

Nadine glanced at the photograph. Her expression froze. "My sister-in-law," she said shortly.

"Your sister-in-law?"

"John Raintree's sister, yes. She was married to my brother Jack. We don't talk about her or him, so just forget it, okay?"

"Sorry," said Quill. "I didn't know."

"You didn't?" Nadine lit a cigarette and slitted her eyes through the smoke. "John never told you?"

"No!"

"Then *I'm* not about to." Nadine crushed the cigarette into a used coffee filter in the sink.

Quill went back to the living room. She made idle conversation with the remaining townspeople, but the visitors were clearing out. She wondered if she'd ever know all the town's secrets, or if she'd always be treated like a flatland foreigner.

Quill looked at her watch. She needed to get back to the Inn and she still had Tom Peterson to tackle about the meat. Perhaps he might tell her about John's sister. She fingered the photograph. She should either leave the photograph here, or take it to Myles as evidence in the case. And if she did that, she'd have betrayed John, perhaps, to the inexorable machinery of the law. If she could just talk to John first, show him the picture.

Her bad angel, a handy scapegoat for childhood crimes and misdemeanors, and little-used until now, whispered, "Swipe it!" She did.

After a hurried exit from the Gilmeister living room, she drove to

Peterson's Transport, wondering if the penalty for theft increased relative to the viability of the victim. "He's dead, *he* won't care," sounded like a practical, if graceless, defense. On the other hand, phrases like "impeding an official investigation" had an ominous ring to them. So did, "concealing the evidence in a crime."

I am hunted, beleaguered, and driven by time, Quill thought as she turned onto Route 96. It was four-thirty; she had to be back at the Inn before six for the Chamber dinner. Maybe she could just toss the spoiled meat in a convenient Dumpster rather than talking face to face with Tom Peterson. But Meg would have a fit. Peterson would want to send the meat back to the supplier, who in turn would dispose of it, and process, thought Quill, will be process.

Petersons had owned much of Hemlock Falls at one time or another; as the family's fortunes declined, bits and pieces of their property had been sold off. Tom had leased the parcel on the corner of Route 96 and Falls River Road to Gil when they had gone into the car dealership together. The land abutted the warehouses and dispatch offices from which Tom ran his trucking business, a location convenient to Syracuse, Ithaca, and Rochester. Gil's hopes of a customer base far beyond Hemlock Falls had never materialized, but the dealership managed somehow from year to year. Quill wondered who, if anyone, would take it over now that Gil had passed on.

Quill pulled into the driveway to the dealership. The Buick flags were at half-mast, and a black-bordered sign had been posted on the glass doors: CLOSED OUT OF RESPECT FOR GIL, which Quill thought had a better ring to it than "Drowned, but not forgotten."

She drove the car around to the converted house trailer that served as a dispatch office for Peterson Transport. It was placed outside the chain-link fence that surrounded the warehouse. She parked the car, got out, took the smelly cardboard box from the trunk, and carried it to the trailer door. Freddie Allbright, whom Quill knew from his occasional appearances at Chamber meetings as a substitute for Gil and Tom, opened the door partway and greeted her with a laconic snap of his gum.

"Hi, Freddie. Is Tom in?"

Freddie jerked his head toward the inside of the trailer. "Mr. Peterson!" he shouted, not taking his eyes from Quill. "Compn'y."

"Quill." Tom rose from his desk and came forward to welcome her. "Come in. Sit down."

Quill sat down in one of the plastic chairs that served for office furniture and set the cardboard box on the floor next to it. The scent of raw meat filled the air. Freddie hulked in the doorway, snapping his gum.

Tom stared at him. "Freddie, I want you to go out and find that dog."

"Just dig hisself out again."

"Then find him and chain him up," said Tom deliberately. "He's the best security system we've got." Freddie slouched out of the trailer. Tom shook his head. "You never seem to have trouble keeping good help, Quill. Want to pass along your secret?" Since this didn't seem to be anything more than a rhetorical question, Quill didn't reply. Tom settled himself behind his desk and smiled. "What can I do for you?"

"Two things. One's kind of a pain in the neck, the other's more of a question."

"Bad news first," said Tom. "Then we can end on a positive note."

"This last shipment of beef was spoiled," Quill said apologetically. "I haven't brought the whole side, of course, just the fillets."

Tom blinked his pale eyes at her. "It's been awfully warm, Quill. Are you sure your cooler's working properly?"

"This was delivered yesterday," said Quill, "and your guys are great, Tom, they always bring it straight into the cooler. Meg takes the beef out to let it get to room temperature about three hours before the dinner crowd shows up. Anything that isn't used is disposed of that night. She said this stuff is tainted." Quill rummaged in the box and unwrapped a pair of fillets. "See the graininess at the edges?"

Tom raised his eyebrows and gave the beef a cursory glance.

"Meg and I both thought you might want to check the whole shipment."

Tom nodded. His hands fiddled impatiently with a piece of paper on his desk. Quill, exasperated at Tom's indifference, said tartly, "Can you give us credit for this, Tom? And we're going to need another delivery."

"I've got one coming in from the Chicago slaughterhouse in about twenty minutes. We'll have it up there within the hour."

"That'll be fine."

He smiled at her. "And the second request?"

"Oh." Quill, not entirely sure why she was uncomfortable, demurred a bit. "I just wanted to tell you how sorry I am that Gil's gone."

"Yes," Tom nodded. "Nice guy. Lousy business partner. That it?" He rose, clearly prepared to show her out. The piece of paper he'd been playing with fell to the floor. It was a matchbook. A full one. The cover was folded in threes.

Quill picked it up.

"Nervous habit," said Tom, "ever since I quit smoking."

"I'd like to have a pack with me. Just in case." Quill slipped the matchbook into her skirt pocket. "There *was* one thing I wanted to ask you, about your brother's wife?"

"Jack's wife?" Tom's eyes narrowed. With his thin lips and prominent nose, he looked more like a lizard than ever. "She's no longer with us, I'm afraid."

"They divorced?" said Quill sympathetically. "I'm sorry to hear that."

"Jack's dead," said Tom. "I don't know where that little bitch is, and I don't care."

Quill's face went hot with embarrassment, "I didn't mean to intrude," she said, "but . . ."

"None of your business, Quill. The past is past. Now, if you'll excuse me, I've got to check on Freddie. He's supposed to retrieve that damn German shepherd and plug the hole in the chain-link fence where it dug out. Has trouble remembering orders. I have to keep tabs on him every minute." Still talking easily, Tom had her out the door and in front of her car before she knew it. He opened the driver's door and waited for her to get in. "Any more trouble with the deliveries, you call me directly, Quill. See you tonight at the meeting."

Quill drove back to the Inn, the matchbook and the photograph safely in her purse. Something, she told herself darkly, was definitely afoot.

She parked in her usual spot by the back door to the kitchen, turned the ignition off, and thought through the events of the past few days.

John, the ready recipient of all her confidences over the past year, her true partner in the sometimes harrowing responsibilities of innkeeping, had to be protected somehow. Quill knew there was an explanation of the picture, of Tom Peterson's matchbook, of Gil's death, if she could just buy a little time for John. She had to talk to him.

But first she had to find him.

The dashboard clock said six-seventeen. The Chamber was in the middle of a costume rehearsal, followed by dinner at six-thirty. She and Myles had a standing date Saturday nights—subject to various Tompkins County or Hemlock Inn emergencies—which started about ten. The rest of the evening left very little time to search John's room for further clues—such as, a nasty voice whispered in her head, the bolt from Peterson's John Deere tractor. Quill bit her lip hard, and pushed the thought away.

She couldn't talk to Meg; the presence of *L'Aperitif*'s critic coinciding with a dining room oversold to History Days tourists would already have her bouncing off the walls. As it was, with John still missing and unable to serve as *sommelier*, Quill would have to scrape her off the ceiling.

Myles could help, of course—with an All Points Bulletin. But exposure to official questions raised by the presence of that photograph in the wallet of a drowning victim could only endanger John, at least until she knew the facts.

No, Myles was out of the question. Besides, she'd interfered with his investigations before. The wrath of Moses on discovering the defalcations of the Israelites was nothing to it. She would just have to handle this herself. There was one advantage to half of Hemlock Falls stuffing the Inn tonight—somebody must have seen John. If she kept her inquiries discreet, she might find him before anyone other than she and Meg knew he'd gone missing.

"Did John show up yet?" Meg thrust her head in the open car window. "Did he tell you where he'd been? Is he sober? Did you get the meat? And what the heck are you doing sitting in here doing absolutely nothing! Do you know what's *happening*?" Meg raked her hair forward in irritable bursts.

"What's happening?" asked Quill, calmly getting out of the car. "Are the *sous* chefs all here?"

"Yes!"

"And the wine and fruit deliveries okay?"

"Yes! Yes! Yes!"

"And the Inn's not on fire." Quill steered her sister back to the kitchen.

"No! Don't be such a smartass, Quill. We need John! Look!" Quill pushed the right half of the dining room door open and peered around it. Edward Lancashire, dressed in an elegant charcoal-gray suit, was talking to an equally elegant blonde by the windows overlooking the gorge. His wife, Quill bet. The dining room was filled with chattering tourists for the Early Bird specials. Quill squinted at a tuxedoed figure seating guests. Not John, but Peter Williams, the young graduate student who worked as headwaiter on weekends. Peter circled the room, quietly observant of the quality of service. Quill let out a small sigh of relief; Peter could pinch-hit as *sommelier* cum maître d'. All she had to do was distract Meg long enough to get her back to the kitchen. Once absorbed in her cooking, Meg would be oblivious to Armageddon and stop plaguing her with questions she couldn't answer.

"I've seen the woman with Edward somewhere before," Quill said mendaciously. "Is that one of the editors, do you think?"

"Oh, God," breathed Meg. "I'll bet it is! Where's *John*, dammit. They'll need an aperitif."

"I'll tell Peter to take care of them."

"Don't tell him they're from *L'Aperitif.* They're supposed to be incognito."

"And you go back into the kitchen."

"Right."

"And cook like hell."

"Right." Face as tense as any Assyrian coming down like a wolf on the oblivious Sennacherib, Meg flexed her hands and returned to the Aga.

Quill looked at her watch and dashed to her room to change. One of these days she'd get organized enough to leave time for a real bath, but two years at the Inn had honed her fast-shower technique. The desire for a leisurely soak fell prey to necessity more and more often.

Quill's rooms were simply decorated, designed as a refuge from the demands of her day. Natural muslin curtains hung at the windows. A cream damask-stripe chair and couch sat under the mullioned south window. A cherry desk and armoire stood in the corner. Beige Berber carpet covered the pine floor. The egg-shell walls held two paintings, both by friends from New York, and a few pen-and-ink sketches she'd done as a student. Her easel stood in the southwest window, a half-finished study of roses and iris glowing in the subdued light. She spared the roses a perplexed frown, then showered quickly, subdued her curly red hair into a knot at the top of her head, and slipped into a teal silk dress with a handkerchief hem. The Saturday night before the start of History Days was traditionally fancy dress. The costume rehearsal was an excuse for the actors to parade their elaborate outfits for the admiration of the tourists and those citizens unlucky enough to be merely bystanders.

By the time Quill clattered down to the dress rehearsal, the Inn was filled with the low hum of guests.

Quill slipped into the conference room unnoticed. Two of the salespeople from Esther's store had spent the afternoon cataloging and tagging the costumes in the conference room and Quill walked into a room transformed. Portable clothes racks filled with gold silks, pink taffetas, green velvets, and enough ecru lace to choke the entire flock of Marvin Finstedder's goat farm lined the walls. All twenty-four cast members of *The Trial of Goody Martin* (eighteen whose participation was limited to the repetition of the phrase "Sink or swim!") squeezed together cheek by jowl. Esther laced Betty Hall into a fuschia chiffon townswoman's costume; Elmer Henry stood in front of a full-length mirror on wheels adjusting the gold lace on his cuffs; Howie Murchison paced gravely around the room, and flipped the lapel of his skirted coat forward to reveal a hand-lettered button that read "Colonial Intelligence Agency" at anyone who'd stop long enough to read it.

"What do you think?" he asked Quill.

"It's just as nifty as the Empire costumes," she said diplomatically. The confusion would be an excellent cover for a few discreet questions concerning John's whereabouts. Howie was as good a person to start with as anyone else. "John had to run to Ithaca, and said he was going to drop off some stuff he picked up from the drugstore for me at your office, rather than take the time to come back here. Did he get there?"

"Haven't seen him all day," said Howie. "Sorry. Do you want me to call Anne and see if she can pick it up for you?"

"Oh no, Howie. Thanks. It'll keep until Monday."

All Quill learned in the next twenty minutes was that practically everybody in Hemlock Falls would be happy to send somebody else to the drugstore for her, which made Quill grateful for the neighborliness exhibited, but left her unenlightened as to John's whereabouts.

Nobody had seen him all day.

Quill surveyed the crowded room and wondered what to do next. Pointed questions of both Mavis and Marge concerning their activities last night would give her a better grip on what had happened. Had they seen John after they left the Croh Bar? Was he driving or walking? Was anyone with him?

Mavis, face pink with excitement—and, Quill hoped, nothing else—was being stuffed into her costume with the aid of a heavy-breathing Keith Baumer. Any interruption there would be fruitless. Marge was busy organizing the removal of the clothes racks to Esther's van outside with a verve to rival General Patton's drive to Berlin. Mrs. Hallenbeck stood proudly in the corner, dressed in the black cloak and broad-brimmed hat of A Member of the Crowd. "I have practiced 'Sink or swim,'" she said when Quill stopped to admire her costume. "Miss West seemed to feel that I would add verisimilitude to the mob scene. I shall shake my walking stick, like this."

"You were at dinner with Mavis and Marge last night, Mrs. Hallenbeck. What time did you come back to the Inn?"

"About nine-thirty. I retire every evening promptly at ten, and I insisted that they bring me back here well before that time."

"Everyone came with you?"

"Mavis had to go see Gil's partner, Tom Peterson. Keith Baumer, Marge, and Gil took me home. I left them at the lobby entrance. I believe Marge said something about going to a place called the Croh Bar afterward."

"You didn't see my manager, John Raintree, with them at all?"

"The Indian? No. I did not. Do you think he could be involved with the accident last night?"

"No," said Quill firmly.

"Well, I'm sure you know best, my dear. You seem to have such an excellent head on your shoulders." She leaned forward and lowered her voice. "I am taking your advice. Regarding Mavis."

With the exit of the cast members in full costume to the dining room at six-thirty, Quill knew she should check the front desk, see to the wine cellar, and finally, beard the chaos in the kitchen. Instead, she went to John's room with the picture from Gil's wallet tucked in her pocket. She switched on the overhead light. The room was as she'd left it earlier in the day: silent, the clothes hanging neatly in the closet, the books and papers in the same places. The picture stood on the night stand where she had left it. Quill picked it up and turned it over. The cardboard backing was loose. She drew it carefully out of the frame. The picture from her pocket fitted the back. When she replaced the cardboard backing, it fit perfectly.

She held the frame in her hands, concentrating hard. It was all too obvious that both pictures had been kept here, in this frame. How had the one picture gotten from the frame to the duck pond, and from the duck pond to Gil's wallet? And why? Did John carry it with him, as a reminder of his sister? If he didn't, who took the picture from the frame? Had John or someone else dropped it at the duck pond while drawing the bolt to set a trap for . . . whom?

"Find anything interesting?"

The frame jumped in her hands. "Myles!"

He came into the room with that infuriatingly silent walk. "Let me see that."

"It's . . . just a photograph, Myles. Of John's sister."

"John's sister? I found this picture at the pond. Nadine said it was her sister-in-law. Gil was going to put it in the family album." He looked sharply at Quill. "It agitated her."

Quill bit her lip. Myles took both photographs and put them in his shirt pocket.

Myles set the frame back on the night stand. "I'd like to talk with him, Quill. Is he here?"

"How did you know I was here?"

He nodded at the uncurtained window. "I've been waiting for him."

"And you saw the light go on. Of all the sneaky—"

"This is serious business, Quill. We need to question him."

" 'We'? 'Question'? What the hell are you talking about?"

He looked at her silently for a long moment. "You'll know eventually, so you might as well know now. The computer's turned up a record on John."

"What kind of a record?"

"I don't want you involved in this, Quill."

"Well, I am involved, Myles. Not only is he the real manager of this Inn, but he's a friend. A good friend. And I think it stinks that there's some stupid accident in that damn duck pond with a bunch of drunks horsing around, and the first thing you think of is—'Oh! Must be that Indian up to the Inn.' " Her mockery of local speech patterns nettled him, but she went recklessly on. "And *of course* you go to that blasted database and ask, not for Gil Gilmeister's jail record, or Marge Schmidt's, or that fuzzy-headed Mavis', but John's."

"Tom Peterson saw him at the pond earlier that evening," Myles said levelly.

Quill was momentarily caught off stride. Then she said, "Of *course* he would. He probably did it! I was at Peterson's today. Look at this matchbook." She pulled it out of her skirt pocket and waved it at him.

Myles took it, his face grim.

"Tom Peterson was up in Mavis and Mrs. Hallenbeck's room," said Quill, recklessly. "*He's* the person you should be investigating. Not John. And everyone knows that Mavis was the one person who was supposed to sit in the ducking stool. You should be looking for Tom's motives!"

"Quill, I've told you before to stay out of this."

"But why pick on John?"

"He served eighteen months in Attica for manslaughter. He was released last year, just before he came to work for you."

She sat down on the bed. She knew her face was pale.

Myles sat down beside her and took her hand in his. "Is there anything else you want to tell me?"

She stood up to avoid the touch of his arm against hers; physical proximity to Myles always weakened her resolve. "Do you know the details?"

"Of John's case? No. I'm going to Ithaca to pull the files Monday. All I've got now is the computer record of the sentencing and time served."

"Will you tell me when you find out?"

"Will you tell me when John shows up?"

She glared at him, mouth a stubborn line.

Myles eased himself to his feet. "This could be a case of murder. Or it could simply be an accident. I don't have enough information. And without information, I won't know if it's murder or accident."

"What does your gut-feel tell you?"

"My gut-feel tells me I want to talk to everyone in the vicinity of the accident. And John was in the vicinity."

"That's not enough of a reason and you know it," Quill said.

"Quill!" Myles stopped, exasperated. "Listen to me. I'm going to tell you one more thing. And if I tell you, you've got to promise me that you'll let this alone. You agree?"

Quill put her hand behind her back and crossed her fingers. "Yes," she said.

"A couple of the boys down at the Croh Bar said John and Gil got into an argument about ten-fifteen."

"An argument? What kind of an argument? Over what?"

"It wasn't over what, it was a *who.*" A reluctant grin crossed his face. "Mavis seems to be getting around quite a bit."

"John got into an argument with Gil over Mavis? I don't believe it." She hesitated. "Was he drinking?"

"Not according to the bartender."

Quill hadn't realized how tense she'd been until she relaxed. "I'll tell you what it was. I'll bet he saw how much Mavis was drinking on top of that Valium and tried to get her to go home."

"That sounds more like John," Myles admitted. "But no one seems to know what the argument was about."

"What does Mavis say?"

"That she doesn't want to talk without a lawyer."

"Can't you do something about that, Myles?" said Quill anxiously.

"Of course I can do something about that, if I can find a judge on a Saturday night in Tompkins County in the middle of July. Davey's gone to Ithaca to try and get the summons."

"Marge must have been a—what d'ya call it—a material witness. What does she say?"

"That she was in the ladies room, and missed the whole thing. Given the amount of beer they were drinking, it's not unreasonable. Now, I've told you more than I should. And you're going to butt out, right?"

"Mm," said Quill, nodding.

Myles narrowed his eyes at her. "I'll see you at ten unless Davey's back with that summons."

Quill gave him her most innocent smile.

Quill made John's rounds of the Inn before joining the Chamber members at dinner. The Inn's lares and penates, perhaps in sympathy with the stresses of the past forty-eight hours, were being merciful tonight—and, thought Quill, it was about bloody time. Everything was in order at the front desk. Guests who were booked to check in had checked in; those who were scheduled to leave had left, without noticeable depredations to the supply of ashtrays, towels, or shower curtains. All the staff that was supposed to had shown up on time, and the line waiting for tables was satisfyingly long but not intolerable; even the bar hummed with relaxed, not drunken, voices.

Nate poured her a half glass of Montrachet. Guiltily, she decided to hide out in her office and drink it slowly and alone.

A breeze blew in the open window, carrying the scent of lilies. She sorted through the events of the past two days. There were questions to be answered, all right. Mavis might refuse to talk to Myles without a lawyer, but she might talk to Quill, given the right investigative technique. She needed Mavis. And Myles. She finished the wine. She'd weasel information about John's prison time out of him, no matter what. Undeterred by the fact that she'd never once been able to get information out of Myles he didn't want to deliver, she went in search of Mavis Collinwood.

Saturday night at the Hemlock Inn dining room with an overflow crowd was a scene to bring joy to a banker's heart. As a rule, Quill didn't much care for bankers, whose affable smiles and neatly pressed suits hid hearts of steel when it came to matters of cash flow and lines of credit. Bankers were prone to the chilling repetition of the phrase "prompt repayment of the loan," just when it was most inconvenient to hear it. Bankers wanted to lend you money when you didn't need it, charged horrible interest rates when you did, and all too clearly preferred that two hundred meals with a profit margin of 75% be pumped out by a raft of *sous* chefs and dumped in front of gluttonous hordes instead of carefully chosen, beautifully cooked meals presented to a discriminating few.

To Quill, fully booked Saturday nights were an etching by Thomas Hobbes, a perception reinforced this evening because of the costumed Chamber members. But given the Rabelaisian noise level and rate of consumption in the dining room, the Hemlock Falls Savings and Loan guys were undoubtedly pleased as Punch.

There was no accounting for taste.

A place had been set for her at the Chamber table and she sat down between Elmer Henry and Howie Murchison. Mavis was four chairs away. Keith Baumer had invited himself to the dinner and had squeezed himself next to her. His right hand was under the table, his left busy shoveling bites of potatoes *duchesse* into Mavis' open mouth. Mavis squealed at periodic intervals; Dookie Shuttleworth, eyes fixed on his plate, frowned disapprovingly on her opposite side. Directly across from Dookie, Marge and Betty slurped Zinfandel with abandon.

"Meg's surpassed herself with this lamb," said Howie to Quill, his tricorne tilted rakishly over one eye. "What's in it?"

Peter Williams set a plate of lamb in front of her. Quill unwrapped the tinfoil encasing the chops.

"It's coat dew agnes ox herbs!" said Keith Baumer loudly. Mavis and Marge shrieked with laughter. He waved the handwritten menu card at Quill and grinned sweatily. "Says so right here, Howie. But—oh!" He pulled a face of mock horror. "See Quill's face? Is it my French, Quill? Tell her how good my French is, Mavis."

"You *bad* boy!" Mavis shrieked, whacking him energetically with the menu.

Quill ate her lamb absentmindedly, trying to figure out a way to get Mavis alone. An after-dinner brandy in the Lounge was clearly a bad idea—she was three sheets to the wind, if not four. Maybe Mrs. Hallenbeck could help. Quill glanced across the table. The widow was listening with glazed attention to Norm Pasquale, who was able, without any encouragement at all, to recite the entire high-school band program listings for the past twenty years. ". . . clarinets in 'Mellow Yellow'," Quill heard him say. He was up to 1976.

"Lemon?" said Howie in her ear.

"I'm sorry, what?"

"I said you don't want to eat your lemon, and you were about to." He took her fork, dumped the lemon slice on his plate, and placed the fork back in her hand.

"No. You're right, I don't. Howie, could you do something for me?"

He peered at her over his wire-rimmed glasses. "You *do* want that stuff from the drugstore . . ."

"I want him"—she pointed to Baumer—"out of the way so I can talk to Mavis."

"I suppose I could take him into the Lounge for an after-dinner brandy."

"What a good idea," she said cordially. "It'll be on the house. As a matter of fact, why don't you give him several?"

Howie looked at Baumer doubtfully. "He's had quite a bit already."

"He's not going to drive anywhere, so I don't care if Nate has to carry him upstairs feet first. Drink," she said recklessly, "as much as you want, as long as you keep him occupied."

Quill stood up, tapped her water glass, and thanked the Chamber for its continued support of the Inn over the years. This was met with warm applause. She expressed her conviction that Sunday's presentation of *The Trial of Goody Martin* would be the best yet. This was met with enthusiastic shouts. She invited the members to have brandy and *crème caramel* on the house in the Lounge, which was met with more cheers, except for Marge, who rolled her eyes and yelled, "milk puddin'!" to no discernible purpose. Esther leaned across Elmer Henry and interpreted helpfully. "She wants to hold the meetings at the diner next year. She says these foreign puddings make Americans sick. She says . . ."

"Thanks, Esther. I get the picture."

In the general scraping of chairs, Quill edged around the table and grabbed Mavis by the arm. "I'm going to the ladies room before I go to the Lounge. Want to come with me?"

"Why, sure, sugar."

Mavis moved like a rudderless boat, amiably correcting course as Quill guided her to the main-floor bathrooms. Inside, she peered blearily at herself in the mirror. "Shee-it. Would you look at this *hair*?" She patted the stiffly lacquered waves delicately. Quill, confronted with a real live opportunity for detection, wondered wildly where to start. What would Myles do? Ask to see some identification, probably, which was no help at all, since she doubted that much would be gained by asking to see Mavis' driver's license. Besides, she already knew Mavis.

Or did she?

"Mrs. Hallenbeck seems a little . . . difficult . . . at times. I really admire the way you handle her. Have you known her long?"

Mavis stretched her lower lip with her little finger and applied a layer of lipstick. "Long enough."

Well, that answer was loaded with information. Quill took a moment to regroup. "I was absolutely fascinated to learn that you and Marge are old friends," Quill tried again. "Have you visited her in Hemlock Falls before this trip?"

"That ol' girl don' like you too much," said Mavis. "Why you want to know that?"

"John Raintree mentioned that he'd seen you before . . . I *think*," Quill said hastily. "I may have misunderstood."

"That Indian fella? You know what we say down South?"

From the sly look in Mavis' eye, Quill didn't think she wanted to know what they said down South.

"Indians're worse liars than niggers."

Quill drew a deep breath. Doreen pushed the swinging door to the bathroom open, stuck her head in, and said brusquely, "You're needed, Miss Quill."

Mavis dropped her lipstick into her evening bag and closed it with a snap. "I better be gettin' back to that party." She grabbed Quill with a giggle. "Think I'm gonna get lucky tonight. That ol' boy Keith may be baldin' on top, but there's fire in that oven, or I'm Mary Poppins." Her grip tightened and her eyes narrowed. "So I'll be in the Lounge for a while, if you want to have a little more innocent girl talk." Her long fingernails dug painfully into Quill's wrist.

"After that, I'll have a sign out—readin' 'Do Not Disturb.'" She released Quill's wrist. Bosom outthrust, she sailed out the door.

"Huh!" sniffed Doreen, skipping aside as the door swung closed. "That's one of them wimmen that needs her devils cast out for sure."

"What women?"

Doreen dug into her capacious apron pocket and thrust a fistful of pamphlets at Quill. THE LORD DESPISES THE SINNER WITH LUST IN HIS HEART! the first one thundered in scarlet ink. HE SHALL CAST OUT THE DEMON OF UNRIGHTEOUSNESS screamed the next. And third, YE SHALL EXERCISE THE DEVILS OF HOT DESIRE. The line art featured large men with beards shaking impressively large forefingers at big-breasted women. Lightning featured prominently in the background. "Oh, my," said Quill.

"We exercised a right number of devils at the meetings in Boca Raton," Doreen said in satisfaction. "Bit noisy, but those devils skedaddled out of the sinners like you wouldn't believe."

"It's *exorcise*, Doreen, not exercise."

"We got right sweaty doin' it," said Doreen indignantly. "I mean to show these to the Reverend Shuttleworth. He ain't got enough fizz in his preaching. I'll bet the Reverend would fill the pews right up if he had a bit of exercising in his sermons. Stop puttin' people to sleep. There's this 1-800 number he can call any time of the day or night to get the lowdown on this stuff." Quill opened her mouth to lodge a protest, and Doreen swerved into an abrupt change of topic. "You're wanted at the reception. What're you standing around here for?"

Quill gave up. "What's the problem?"

"Somebody's here to check in."

"I think we're full."

"Hey, do I run this joint or do you?"

A strong impression of smug hilarity hung around Doreen. Quill's misgivings strengthened to dismay when she arrived at the reception desk, Doreen at her heels. The woman who stood at the front desk was both sophisticated and annoyed, a combination that guaranteed trouble. Dressed in a short tight skirt, platform shoes, and a well-cut jacket, she had the smooth, expensive hair and skin that meant money with access to Manhattan.

"Are you the manager here?" she said crossly.

Quill cocked an eyebrow at Doreen; there'd been a lot of women like this at the gallery when she was painting, and if Doreen thought she'd see her boss discomposed, she had another think coming. "I'm Sarah Quilliam," she said, extending her hand. "And excuse me for saying so, but that's the most marvelous jacket I've ever seen. It simply *screams* Donna Karan. Not everyone can wear her as well as you do."

The fashion plate relaxed a little. "Darling, the cut hides the most awful flaws. She's easier than you think. Can you help me out here? I'm trying to check in, and this little person behind the desk keeps saying she has to ask the manager. Nobody seems to be able to find the manager, for God's sake."

Quill winked comfortingly at the young Cornell student behind the counter. "He's on an errand for me," said Quill. "I'm the owner. What can I do for you? I'm afraid we're booked solid at the moment."

"But I've got a room."

Quill moved behind the front desk to check the bookings. The missing ledger had reappeared as mysteriously as it had gone. "And your name?"

"Celeste Baumer. Mrs. Keith Baumer."

If that was a snigger from Doreen, Quill thought furiously, she was going to do some "exercising" of her Inn's own devils: the housekeeping kind.

"She's got ID," said the Cornell student apologetically. "But I called Mr. Baumer's room, and he doesn't answer. Mr. Baumer's booked a single for the week, not a double, and John always told us to check with the customer when something like this happens."

"And he was right," said Quill. "Was your husband expecting you, Mrs. Baumer?"

"Oh, no." She exposed a bright row of teeth in what Quill took to be a smile. "I wanted it to be a surprise."

"Why don't you sit and have a glass of wine in the bar, Mrs. Baumer? On the house, of course. We'll see if we can find Mr. Baumer."

"Are you going up to his room?"

"Um," said Quill, "actually I think he's out on . . . on . . . a sales call or something."

"I've been on that damn train for hours. I want a bath and then I'll take you up on that free drink. But first I want to check in."

Maybe, Quill thought as she, Celeste Baumer, Doreen, and the Cornell student (who was carrying the suitcases) trooped up the stairs to the second floor, Keith Baumer left Mavis at the bar and was freshening up. Maybe he was making phone calls to his neglected customers. Maybe he'd fallen asleep dead-drunk. And alone.

Quill knocked on the door to 221.

"I don't think he's here," she said after a few moments.

"Open it up, darling," Celeste Baumer demanded. "You wouldn't believe how I have to pee."

Quill unlocked the door. Mrs. Baumer pushed past her and switched on the lights. Two twenty-one was decorated in Waverly chintz with scarlet poppies against a cream background.

The poppies on the tailored bedspread moved up and down with the briskness of waves on a breezy sea.

"Oops," said the Cornell student.

"Dang!" said Quill.

"You bastard!" shrieked Celeste Baumer with enormous satisfaction.

"Heh-heh-heh," chortled Doreen.

"God-*damn*!" shouted a nude and sweaty Keith Baumer.

Mavis screamed in a very ladylike way.

CHAPTER 8

July in Central New York is not the usual mating season for songbirds, but the repeated attacks of the cardinal flying into its own image on the sunrise side of Quill's bedroom window woke her at six. She squinted against the sunshine pouring in and addressed the bird. "That's not a hostile rival, that's you," she said.

Ta-ching! The bird flattened its beak against its reflection, intent on assassination.

"Has the word gotten to the bird world, too? You think your sweetie's in here with some other guy?"

Ta-ching!

"You're related to Baumer, maybe, and have faith in the triumph of hope over experience."

Ta-CHANG! The bird, with one last mighty effort, hit the window and dropped out of sight. Quill got out of bed and peered out the window to the lawn. The cardinal lay on its back, feet up. It chirped, righted itself, and flew at the window, beady eyes glittering.

Ta-ching!

Quill went back to bed and pulled her pillow over her head.

Myles, dressed in his grays, came out of the kitchenette carrying two cups of coffee. Quill groaned, sat up, and peered at him. "Are you going to let Mrs. Baumer out of the pokey?"

"Probably." He handed Quill a cup, then sat at the foot of the bed.

"You think it'll hit the papers?"

"Probably. The local's stringer's in town to cover the opening ceremonies of History Days."

"Oh, God."

"It'll blow over, honey." He rose, stretched, and drained his coffee. "Of course, you could always give up innkeeping as a profession and marry me."

"No, Myles."

"Or you could continue being an innkeeper and marry me."

"I tried marriage. It stinks. You didn't find marriage all that terrific, either."

"Youthful folly. On both our parts."

The cardinal hit the window again.

Quill got out of bed. Further sleep was impossible. "Would you like some breakfast? Meg's got an assistant in the kitchen that makes a mean Eggs Benedict."

"I'm going down to the jail to let Mrs. Baumer go. Unless you want to press charges for the damage to two twenty-one."

"I don't think so. I didn't like that lamp anyway, and I can fix the dent in the wall. Just a matter of replacing the sheetrock and repainting. I feel so sorry for her, Myles. I can't believe that jerk Baumer."

He kissed her, a process that always softened Quill's resolve to never marry again. "I don't know when I'll see you today, kiddo. Just relax and enjoy yourself."

"Easy for you to say—all you have to do is make sure that four thousand tourists in Dodge Caravans don't all crash into each other on Main Street."

"All you have to do is keep the doors barred against irate spouses, supervise the extra help, keep Doreen from rending Keith Baumer limb from limb in fine Old Testament outrage, hold your sister's hand if her soufflé flops, and generally wear yourself ragged."

"It's not that tough, Myles. Not when you've got good staff. And I've got good staff."

They both carefully avoided any mention of John Raintree.

She closed the door after him and took a long leisurely shower, getting down to the dining room at seven o'clock. Meg was seated at their table for two by the kitchen door, and Quill went to join her. Meg had abandoned her leggings, ratty tennis shoes, and sweatbands for well-pressed jeans and a lacy top. She'd taken a curling iron to her dark hair, and wore a pair of gold hoop earrings.

"Well *you* look totally cool," said Quill.

Meg batted her eyelashes. "Guess who's going on a picnic with the best-looking gourmet critic in Hemlock Falls?"

"Really? Did you pack the basket?"

"Cold gravlax with my Scotch Bonnet salsa. Homemade flatbread, dilled potato salad. Nice chilly bottle of a sparkling Vouvray. Strawberries with that *crème brûlée* from last night. If we get a good seat for the opening ceremonies, I guarantee you that fourth star."

"Everything okay in the kitchen?"

"Frank's supervising. All we're going to get today is a zillion orders for roast beef sandwiches to go." She hesitated. "Any word from John?"

Quill shook her head.

"Jeez." Meg sighed. "Poor old you. At least you've got that creep Baumer out of your hair."

"Nope."

"Nope? Are you serious? After all that ranting and raving last night? I would have thought the son of a gun would be embarrassed to show his sniveling face in town."

"He's booked for the week. He's paid for the week. He'll stay for the week. That's what he said."

"In-credible."

"I assume it has to do with the sales convention at the Marriott." Quill sighed. "I can't think how that guy keeps a job."

"And the marvelous round-heeled Mavis?"

"Mrs. Hallenbeck said, 'Booked for the week, paid for the week.'"

"They'll stay for the week?"

"Besides, I think both of them are looking forward to the play this afternoon. Ow!"

Meg kicked Quill's ankle as Keith Baumer, Mavis, and Mrs. Hallenbeck arrived simultaneously at the entrance to the dining room. Conversation in the dining room came to a halt. Mrs. Hallenbeck, Quill thought, was superb. She ignored Baumer with aplomb bordering on the magnificent. Mavis meekly trailing in her wake, she swept past Baumer—whose face was tinged a dusky pink—to their regular table. Head down, Baumer slunk to table eight.

"Oh. There's Edward," said Meg eagerly. Lancashire, in cotton Dockers, boat shoes, and a dark green denim shirt, walked in, and with a casual wave at Meg and Quill, began to come toward them. He stopped at the Hallenbeck table and spoke briefly to the widows. Mavis, in an off-the-shoulder tank top that showed more décolletage than her Empire-styled gown of the evening before, smiled invitingly up at him.

"Would you look at that!" hissed Meg. With a brief, apologetic glance at Meg, Edward pulled out a chair and sat next to Mavis. One of the Inn's impeccably trained waiters was instantly at his elbow with a cup and freshly brewed coffee. "How does she *do* it?" said Meg, awestruck.

Mavis flirted, giggled, and ignoring Mrs. Hallenbeck's imperious frown, beckoned to Baumer. Baumer shuffled over from his table and sat on Mavis' left. Sprightly conversation wafted through the air. Meg pulled at her lower lip. Quill looked at this familial symptom of deep thought in alarm. "Meg, I know that look. What are you going to do?"

"Me?" said Meg innocently. "Not a thing, sister dear, not a thing. Excuse me a moment." She sprang up and went into the kitchen. Quill swallowed her French toast, took a gulp of tea, and followed her hastily.

"A *lot* of tarragon, I think," Meg was saying to her *sous* chefs, "and what else? Ideas, guys, I need ideas."

"Baking soda instead of baking powder?" said the shorter one. His name was Frank Torelli; his father ran a good restaurant in Toronto, and Frank was slated to take over the family kitchen when his apprenticeship with Meg was up. The taller one was a Swede from Finland, studying at the Cornell Hotel School on a green card. Bjorn's blond hair and blue eyes had the pale, icy look of plain water in a glass.

"Salt," said Bjorn. "A lot of it."

"Too obvious," said Meg. "I want subtle stuff. So he's not really sure what it is."

"I got it. I got it!" said Frank. He ran excitedly to the cupboard, pulled out a small bottle, and waved it in the air. "Eh? S'all right?"

"All right!" said Meg.

They burst into laughter.

"What's all this, then?" said Quill, feeling a little like a policeman in a medium-grade British mystery.

"Never you mind," said Meg. "Don't you have a lot of stuff to do today? Beat it."

"Peter's going to manage the front desk today. Doreen's taking care of the housekeeping staff. And I thought that Bjorn and Frank were in charge of the kitchen shifts." Quill folded her arms and leaned against the butcher's block. "One of the advantages of taking management courses at Cornell at nights is that you learn to empower your employees. So, I've got lots of time to spend with you guys, since you seem to be making all the decisions, anyway."

"Hey. Wouldn't your life be a lot easier if that miserable Mavis and sleazy Baumer beat feet?" demanded Meg.

"Well, yeah. Baumer at least." Frank had the mysterious bottle in his large hand and she couldn't see the label. Quill didn't know if she wanted to see the label. "But if Mavis doesn't stay the week,

I have to play Clarissa. And you could rate my enthusiasm to be dunked and squashed right up there with getting nasty letters from the Board of Health. Not only that, but Mavis is going to be subpoenaed as a witness in Gil's drowning accident. So she can't leave."

"Just Baumer, then," said Meg. "We're just going to encourage Baumer to leave a leetle bit earlier than he had planned to. He's going to find the food not to his taste." Gales of giggles came from the *sous* chefs. Meg flung out both her hands at Quill's outraged expression. "Nothing illegal, immoral, or actionable. I swear."

"Please, Meg," said Quill. "Think of the bad publicity."

"From a guy whose wife shows up while he's in the sack with Mavis the Bimbo? From a guy whose wife whacks him up the side of the head with a lamp? He's lucky we don't turn him in to his company. *One* call to his boss at the Marriott, one call, that's all it'd take! He's lucky we don't sue him for damages. He's lucky he's alive!" Meg raked her hair back with both hands. Her cheeks were flushed. Her eyes glittered. Frank and Bjorn exchanged meaningful glances and melted into the background. "I will SHUT DOWN MY KITCHEN before I serve my good food to pigs like that!" Meg shouted. "I will THROW MY SPATULAS INTO THE FIRE!"

"Mornin'," said Doreen, stumping into the kitchen. She was wearing her best polyester pantsuit and a small straw hat. She put her hands on her hips and stared at Meg. "Well, missy. Looks like the Devil's got ahold of you."

Meg drummed her fingers on the countertop.

"You look nice, Doreen," Quill ventured into the charged silence.

"Been to see the Reverend," she said. "Givin' him tips on how to wake up the sinners. Gave him a couple of ideas for his sermon, he said." She went to the locker room to change into her work clothes. Her voice floated back to them. "Told him about last night. Said he'd never heard of such a scandalous thing." She reappeared, tying her capacious apron neatly around her waist. "Thinks that there Baumer's goin' straight to Hell. Along with Mavis. Called her a right fine name, too." She rummaged in her purse, withdrew a piece of paper, and squinted at it. "Wrote it down. Suckabus."

Meg started to laugh.

"Succubus," said Quill. "Oh, dear."

"Sounds nasty," said Doreen hopefully. "Innit? What is it, exactly?"

"Succubi are female demons," said Quill. "They visit afflicted men in the dead of night and . . . ah . . . ."

"Sap their life force," said Meg with a wicked grin.

"You mean there's more than one?" said Doreen. "It's not just this Mavis Collinwood?"

"Quite a few in Times Square, when I visited," said Frank. He and Bjorn, noting the ebb of Meg's temper, had rejoined the women.

"They aren't real, Doreen," said Quill. "A succubus is a metaphor for the way the people of Old Testament times viewed a certain type of woman, and as far as I'm concerned, it's a bunch of male chauvinist hooey. I don't want any more discussion about sex vampires of Hemlock Falls, or for that matter, foul substances in Keith Baumer's food. I want everyone to go back to work."

"Yes, *ma'am*." Meg saluted. "Whatever you say, *ma'am*!"

Quill marched back to the dining room, ignoring the snickers from the kitchen with the dignity befitting a manager who had successfully quelled an employee revolt. A hoot of laughter with distinctly Swedish overtones modified her conclusion to a half-muttered, "Well, I told them, anyway."

She sat down at the table to finish her breakfast.

In a few minutes, Edward Lancashire joined her. "Ready for the big day?"

"It's not really a big day for me," Quill explained, "or Meg either. Everyone's checked in; the dining room, Lounge, and bar are all booked, and the staff knows what to do."

"It's the front-end preparation that's the toughest," said Edward.

"You'd know about that," Meg said cheerfully, as she rejoined her sister at the table. "You're not planning on dinner here tonight, are you, Edward?"

"No. I've booked a table at Reneès in Ithaca. Opening day of History Week is a little too raucous for me."

"You're going to the play this afternoon, though," said Meg. "We're having a picnic. Nobody should miss the play. And you shouldn't miss my gravlax. The Scotch Bonnet salsa is *fabulous*."

"Oh, I think everyone will be there," said Edward Lancashire. "Mrs. Collinwood. Mr. Baumer. The delightful Ms. Schmidt. I've eaten at her restaurant, by the way. It's quite good for American diner food. Perhaps even Mr. Raintree will join us? I haven't seen him around lately."

"He had some personal errands to run," said Quill hastily. "But I'm sure he'll be there, too. Nobody within fifty miles of Hemlock Falls misses *The Trial of Goody Martin.*"

Seeing the crowds that afternoon, Quill revised her estimate upward; tour buses brought day trippers from Rochester, Buffalo, and Syracuse. Myles and his men cordoned off Main Street, and allowed cars to park on the shoulder of Route 96 outside the central business district.

The Kiwanis beer tent did a thriving business, the Lions hot dog stand ran out of buns at two o'clock, and the Fireman's Auxiliary kiosk posted a triumphant SOLD OUT sign on the counter that had displayed wooden lawn ornaments of geese, pigs, cats, ducks, cows, and the rear ends of women in long print dresses. Gil's Buick dealership always took a booth for History Days. Quill, intent on finding out more from Tom Peterson about John and Gil, caught a glimpse of the awning over the late-model car that the dealership always planted in front of the booth. She wound her way through the tourists to it. Tom Peterson greeted her with a wave and a smile. Nadine sat under the awning, hands folded in her lap. Freddie, unexpectedly garrulous, was there, too.

"Missed you in church this morning," said Tom, who was a deacon at Dookie's church.

"John's out of town for a bit, and I got caught up," Quill apologized. "You know how it is in the summer. John's due back today, though. So I'll be sure to try next week."

"I wouldn't miss it, if I were you," said Freddie. "Something sure lit a fire under the Reverend this morning. Whoo-weee!"

Quill, intent on forming questions that would give her some clues as to Gil's relationship with the girl in John's picture, gave him an encouraging, if absentminded, look.

"Hellfire and brimstone. Quite a little sermon." Freddie leaned forward and said in a low voice, "Just between you and me? Collections were up pretty near seventy-five percent. The Reverend was as pleased as Punch, said the Lord was showing him the way to a resurgence of faith. And where there's a resurgence of faith, there's a resurgence of cash. Now, Miss Quill, wish we could come up with something for you that would give us a resurgence of cash. You think about tradin' in that old heap you've got for a good late-model car?"

"You're taking over from Gil?"

Freddie shot an anxious look at his boss. "Just temporarily, like. Now, about that old heap . . ."

"Gil sold me that 'old heap' two years ago," said Quill indignantly. "It wasn't an 'old heap' then."

"Got to have the look of success in your business," said Freddie wisely. "Now, I could show you . . ."

Quill laid a hand on Freddie's arm and promised to look at new cars. Then she walked up to Tom and said flatly, "Was Gil worried about the business?"

"Hell, we both were. I floated him a couple of private loans to tide him over first and second quarter. He expected business to pick up."

"Was that John's recommendation? The private loans?"

"John? He didn't have much to say about it."

"Does he audit all your books, Tom? You know, for the transport company and your private affairs?"

Tom's face closed up. "I don't know that that's really any business of yours, Quill. No offense."

Quill flushed. Great detectives of fiction were never accused of rudeness; she'd have to brush up on her technique. "I was just thinking of having John do my personal taxes, that's all. Wondered if you found him as good at that as he is at the commercial end."

Tom frowned. "Quill, you hired him. You know him better than I do."

"Just wanted your opinion," she murmured. She cleared her throat. "Will you have a new partner now? Did Gil leave key-man insurance, or do you get the whole dealership?"

"Quill, I don't know what game you're playing at. But you don't play it with me. I'm warning you." He held her eyes for a long minute. Quill gazed coolly back. He turned away from her. "Time for you to be going down to the Pavilion, isn't it? Wouldn't want to miss the play. Unless you'd rather continue to stick your oar into my personal business."

The sun was hot, but not hot enough to account for the heat in her face. Quill decided her chief irritation was with Myles, who had failed to clarify the embarrassing pitfalls awaiting inexperienced interrogators. She shoved the recollection of Myles's prohibitions against any kind of detecting firmly out of her mind, waved cheerfully at Nadine, who raised a hand listlessly back, and walked the two blocks to the Pavilion, absorbed in thought.

The open-air Pavilion was ideally situated for the presentation of *The Trial of Goody Martin*. Thirty wooden benches, seating three to four people each, formed a series of half-circles in front of a bandstand the size of a small theater stage. A forty-foot, three-sided shed had been built in back of the bandstand in 1943 to provide space for changing rooms, sets, small floats for parades, and band instruments. Between the shed and the municipal buildings that housed the town's snowplows, fire engines, and ambulances was an eight-foot-wide gravel path. The path debouched onto the macadam parkway that circled the entire acreage of the park. The action in *The Trial of Goody Martin* required that the audience sweep along with the actors and props in a path from the duck pond to the bandstand to the bronze statue of General Frederick C. C. Hemlock.

The statue of the man and his horse had been erected in 1868, two hundred years after the founding of the village. Something had gone awry in the casting process, and the General's face had a wrinkled brow and half-open mouth, leaving him with a permanently pained expression as he sat in the saddle. On occasion, roving bands of Cornell students on spring break heaped boxes hemorrhoid remedies at the statue's base, which sent the mayor into fits. Most years the statue sat detritus-free, except for the six-foot heap of cobblestones piled at the foot and used to crush the witch each year.

The crowd was enormous, the benches jammed. Quill stood at the periphery and scanned the mass of people for Meg and Edward Lancashire.

Esther West jumped up on the lip of the bandstand, and shaded her eyes with her hands. She caught sight of Quill, pointed at her, and waved frantically.

Elmer Henry appeared out of the crush of people and grasped her arm. His face was grim. "You memorize that Clarissa part?"

Quill's heart sank. "Why?"

"That Mavis is drunker than a skunk. Esther don't want her to go on."

"Elmer . . . I . . ."

"You're the understudy, aren't you? You got to do this, Quill. For the town."

"Maybe we can do something," said Quill weakly. "A lot of black coffee?" The mayor looked doubtful. "Come on. She may not be drunk, Elmer, she may just have stage fright. I mean, look at all these people."

"That's what I'm looking at. All these people. We can't have the Chamber look like a durn fool in front of these folks. Do you know that some have come all the way from Buffalo?"

Quill plowed her way determinedly through the sightseers to the shed at the back of the bandstand, the mayor trailing behind. The shed was seething with a confused mass of costumed players and uniformed high-school band members. Harland Peterson's two huge draft horses, Betsy and Ross, stamped balefully in the corner. The sledge, the barn door, and the band instruments squeezed the space still further.

"Quill! Thank God! Do you see her, that *slut*?" Esther gestured frantically at Mavis, then clutched both Quill and a copy of the script in frantic hands. Sweat trickled down her neck. Mavis, blotto, swayed ominously in the arms of Keith Baumer. Her face was red, her smile beatific. Esther shrieked, "Can you believe it? Here's the script. You've got ten minutes until we're on."

Surrounded by Mrs. Hallenbeck, Betty Hall, Marge Schmidt, and Harvey Bozzel, Mavis caught sight of Quill and caroled, "Coo-ee!"

"Coo-ee to you, too," said Quill. "Esther, I can fix this. I need a bucket of ice, a couple of towels, and Meg and her picnic basket."

The ice arrived before Meg. Quill ruthlessly dropped it down Mavis' dress, front and back. Someone handed her a towel. She made an ice pack and held it to the back of the wriggling Mavis' neck.

Meg and Edward Lancashire joined them a few moments later. "Oh, God," said Meg. "Will you look at her?"

"You've got your picnic basket?" Quill asked through clenched teeth.

"Sure."

"You have those Scotch Bonnet peppers for that salsa?"

A huge grin spread over Meg's face. "Yep."

"You have your special killer-coffee?"

"Uh-huh"

"Then let's get to work."

The Scotch Bonnet had the most dramatic effect. Mavis gulped the coffee, squealed girlishly at the reapplied ice pack, but howled like a banshee after Meg slipped a pepper slice into her mouth.

"Language, language," said Meg primly.

The two sisters stepped back and surveyed their handiwork. Mavis glared at them, eyes glittering dangerously.

"And Myles claims you can't sober up a drunk," said Quill.

"Actually, he's right," said Edward Lancashire. "All black coffee does is give you a wide-awake drunk. I don't know that Scotch Bonnet has ever been used as a remedy for drunks before. I'd say what you've got there is a wide-awake, very annoyed drunk."

"You can write about it in your column," Meg said pertly. "Well, Esther? What d'ya think?"

"I think we've got ourselves a Clarissa," said Esther grimly. "Just in case, Quill, I want you to study that script. She'll make the ducking stool, but I don't know about the trial. C'mon, you."

In subsequent years, Chamber meetings would be dominated periodically by attempts to resurrect *The Trial of Goody Martin*, and it was Esther West, newly converted to feminism, who firmly refused to countenance it. "Anti-woman from the beginning," she'd say. "It was a dumb idea in the first place, and a terrible period in American history, and we never should have celebrated it the way we did. Now, *Hamlet*—that play by William Shakespeare? I've always wanted a hand in that."

Mavis handled the ducking stool and the swim with a subdued hostility that augured well for the artistic quality of her impassioned speech at the trial to come. Marge Schmidt, Betty Hall, Nadine Gilmeister, Mrs. Hallenbeck, and others in The Crowd, may have yelled "Sink or swim" with undue emphasis on the "sink" part, but the audience failed to notice a diminution in the thrust of the whole performance, and joined in with a will.

Elmer Henry, Tom Peterson, and Howie Murchison dragged

Mavis the forty feet from the pond to the bandstand, and the trial itself began. Dookie Shuttleworth, surprisingly awe-inspiring in judge's robe and wig, pronounced the age-old sentence:

"Thou shall not suffer a witch to live."

Mavis soggily surveyed the audience, smoothed her dripping gown over her hips, and addressed the judges. "My lords of the Court, I stand before you, accused of the crime of witchcraft . . ."

So far so good, thought Quill, perched on a bench in the front row. The *S*'s are mushy, but what the heck. Half the crowd's mushy from the heat and the beer.

"A crime of which I'm innoshent!" She burped, swayed, and said mildly, "I'm not a crimin'l. Jush tryin' to get along. Good ol' Southern girl in the midst of all of you"—She paused and searched for the proper phrase. "Big swinging dicks?" she hazarded.

"She's off script!" screamed Esther.

Apparently finding the response from the audience satisfactory, Mavis raised her middle finger, wagged it at a blond family of three in the front row, and took a triumphant bow.

Quill pinched her knee hard, a defense against giggling she hadn't needed since high school.

Dookie thundered his scripted response, "Scarlet whore of the infernal city! Thou shalt die!" then called for the sledge. Harland Peterson drove Betsy and Ross to the side of the stage, the straw-filled sledge dragging behind them.

Mavis spread her arms wide, in her second departure from the script, and leaped into Harland's arms. He staggered, cussed, and dropped her into the straw. Responding to a harmless crack of his whip, Betsy and Ross phlegmatically drew the sledge down the path behind the shed.

As the business of trading Mavis for the hooded dummy went on in the back, Howie, substituting for Gil, read the grisly details of the sentence aloud, straight from the pages of the sentencing at Salem three hundred years before. ". . . planks of sufficient weight and height to be placed upon the body of the witch . . ."

Harland Peterson appeared at the edge of the stage, scowling hideously. He waved at Howie, who ignored him.

". . . and the good citizens of this town to carry out the justice of the Almighty . . ."

Harland gestured again, furiously.

". . . and the law of the Lord is as stones, and as mighty as stones . . . *What*, Harland?"

"Barfed on my boots! I ain't drivin' that sledge! You git somebody else to drive that sledge." He stomped off. Howie looked around helplessly. The crowd sniggered.

Harvey Bozzel, teeth displayed in a wide shiny grin, jumped off the stage and reappeared some minutes later on the front seat of the sledge, reins in hand. There was a scattering of applause. "Gee!" he hollered firmly. Betsy and Ross turned obediently to the right. Meeting the wall of the municipal building, they stopped in their tracks.

Ripples of laughter washed through the audience. Quill stole a look at Elmer and Esther out of the corner of her eye and pinched her knee. She was going to have an almighty bruise.

"Haw! You durned fool. Tell 'em to haw!" Harland yelled.

"Haw!" said Harvey, in a more subdued manner.

Betsy, or perhaps it was Ross—Quill couldn't tell for certain—flicked an ear, gazed inquiringly at her partner in harness, then pulled to the left. This brought the forward edge of the sledge frame into view. Failing further direction, Betsy and Ross continued to pull left, and the sledge frame hit the shed side with a thud.

"Giddyap!" roared Harland at his horses. "Ignore the durn fool up there."

Ross, or perhaps it was Betsy, snorted, shook his head in genuine disgust, and pulled straight in response to the man who fed him oats twice a day—not to mention the occasional sugar cube. The sledge with the dummy finally emerged intact from behind the shed.

"You got that, Harvey, you idjit?" Harland shouted as he spelled out the commands to make them clear. "H-A-W means *left*. G-E-E-U-P means *right*. 'Giddyap' means *straight*."

Betsy and Ross broke into a rumbling jog. "Giddyap" was something they understood. The dummy bounced on the sledge, black hood flapping in the breeze.

" 'Giddyap' twice means faster," Harland said in a normal tone of voice. "Never knowed you was such a durn fool, Harvey."

The band broke into the strains of Gounod's Funeral March and the procession moved down the path to General Hemlock without further incident.

Quill wondered if she should check on Mavis. If she'd gotten sick to her stomach, she was going to feel a lot better, and she might want to see the conclusion of the play. On the other hand, Mavis sober was probably meaner than Mavis drunk, and she had taken grave exception to the dose of fiery pepper. Quill decided guiltily to spare herself the experience.

She strolled on down to the statue, behind the crowd.

Howie demanded the laying on of the barn door, while Dookie and Elmer beat a slow and solemn rhythm on a large drum. The dummy, indefinably lifelike, sprawled in the straw. The sacklike hood had been drawn tightly around the high neck of the dress.

She heard the thunk of stone on wood, and the final prayers of the "judges" condemning the witch's soul to hell.

The crowd usually entered into the spirit of the thing, and so it was with no surprise that Quill saw Keith Baumer heave a stone weighing a good hundred pounds onto the stones already piled high, to shouts of Go!Go!Go! from the crowd.

She saw the stage blood seeping from under the wooden planks.

It was the smell that alerted Quill: the coppery, unmistakable scent of blood—mixed with worse odors. The crowd quieted, then stirred uneasily, like water snakes in a still pond.

The dummy's hand stiffened, convulsed. The nails turned blue.

For a few terrible moments, Quill saw nothing else at all.

CHAPTER 9

"Squashed flatter than a bug on a windshield," said Marge, awed.

Myles had taken immediate control, separating those townspeople and Inn guests nearest the stage from the audience at large and sending them to the Village Library. Davey Kiddermeister escorted them to the ground floor, then set up a methodical interview system. One by one, each of the group was called and disappeared into the librarian's office behind the checkout desk.

Pale and sweaty, Keith Baumer paced to the front window and looked out at the Pavilion, where Myles was getting names and addresses from the out-of-towners. "Are we gonna put up with this? Who does that damn fool think he is?" He borrowed a cigarette from Harland Peterson and lit it with shaking hands. "He's going to hear from me on this one. I know people."

Mrs. Hallenbeck coughed and waved her hand elaborately in front of her face.

"You can't smoke in here," Esther West said.

Baumer stubbed out the cigarette with an angry glare. "Murchison, you know about these things. What are our rights here?"

"I practice family law, Baumer," said Howie dryly. "Probate, real estate. I'm not much on problems like these."

"It wasn't anybody's fault."

"That rock you heisted onto the shed door was a hundred pounds if it was twenty," said Harland Peterson brutally. "I'd say it was your fault."

"But you have to have knowledge beforehand," said Baumer. "I had no idea she was there. You people all piled the rocks along with me. If there's criminal negligence here, we're all in it together. I'd like to retain you as counsel, Murchison, until my own lawyer gets here from New York."

"'Fraid I can't help you," said Howie.

Quill wondered at the sudden drop in Baumer's buffoonish façade; he was pretty quick to stand on his rights. Had he been in trouble before?

Tom Peterson came out from the librarian's office. "He wants to see you next, Quill." He looked at the assembly. "Don't worry, everybody, Deputy Davey's keeping it short."

Elmer stopped Quill as she headed to the office. "Emergency meeting at the Lounge tonight, Quill? Chamber's got to discuss this."

Quill nodded her agreement and went into the librarian's office.

Davey sat at Miriam Doncaster's desk, his black notebook an incongruous official object among the china ducks, geese, and dogs that the librarian collected. "Will you sit down, please, Ms. Quilliam?"

Quill sat in the straight chair in front of the desk and folded her hands in her lap.

"Your name and home address, please, and don't tell me I already know it like Tom Peterson just did, because I have to go through this exactly the same way with everybody, or Myles'll have my head on a platter, like that poor fella that messed with the stripper."

Quill took a moment to sort this out. Davey was a faithful member of Dookie's church. He must mean John the Baptist.

"Sarah Quilliam, the Hemlock Falls Inn, Four Hemlock Road, Hemlock Falls," she said. "My zip code . . ."

"Don't need no zip code." Breathing through his mouth, Davey peered at the notebook. "May I see your driver's license, please?" Quill fished in her purse and handed it over. Davey made a check mark in his notebook without looking at it, and handed it back. "Did you know the name of the deceased?" he read aloud.

"Mavis Collinwood."

"Do you remember what she was wearing when she left the stage on the sledge? Before Harland pulled her around to the back?"

"A long, black cotton gown. A white ruff around her neck. A black cloth cap tied with strings under her chin."

"Anything else?"

"Well—" Quill blinked at him. "Shoes . . . stockings . . . and, um, underwear?"

"Thank you. Please leave the library without speaking to anyone out there. Except to tell your sister that she's next."

"That's all?" Quill rose to her feet.

"Yes, ma'am."

"Do you think you could interview Mrs. Hallenbeck next, Davey? It's been a long day for her, and she's had quite a shock."

Davey's eyebrows drew together; an obdurate state official following an inflexible routine. "Myles told me to do these interviews of the people who actually knew Ms. Collinwood in this exact order. Mrs. Hallenbeck's at the bottom, right before the people who were next to the stage."

"Why isn't he interviewing the people who piled rocks on the barn door?" asked Quill, exasperated.

"I don't know, ma'am. Just doing my job."

"You'll be doing your job a lot better if you let me get that little old lady back up to the Inn so she can recover from the shock," said Quill with asperity. "I'm sure Myles would want you to see to the needs of the elderly."

"He did tell me to make sure she was comfortable. I got her a glass of water. And a cookie." Davey slowly erased a line from the bottom half of his notebook and laboriously wrote at the top. "I'll see her right after your sister and Mr. Lancashire."

"Would you tell Meg and Mrs. Hallenbeck that I'll wait for them outside?"

"Yes, ma'am. And you're not supposed—"

"To tell anyone you belted me with a rubber hose to extract important information."

Quill walked outside and sat on the steps of the library. Across the green lawn of the park four lines of tourists stood restlessly in the July heat. Myles had assigned uniformed officers to take the names and addresses of members of the audience. Others patrolled the lines, seeing that the elderly had a place to sit in the shade, and taking little kids to the Porta-Johns. Quill figured the interview took about three minutes, minus the demands she'd made of Davey, and did some calculations on her fingers. At eighty people an hour, it'd be several hours before she could ask Myles what the heck was going on.

Meg bounced out the library door. "Edward will be out in a minute," she said. "I told him we'd wait for him. What do you suppose that clothes stuff was all about?" she continued, coming down the steps to sit at Quill's side. "I mean, who cares what she was wearing? Does Myles ask people in a car crash if the driver was wearing designer jeans, or what?"

Quill, who had been wondering the same thing herself, let out a gasp.

"Well?" Meg demanded.

"The hood."

"The hood?"

"The hood. Meg, *somebody put the hood on Mavis*. She was never supposed to wear the hood. She was supposed to ride on the sledge to the back of the stage, jump off, put the dummy in her place, and stroll on out to watch the rest of the fun and games. But

Harland came stomping out complaining that she'd thrown up all over his shoes, and then Harvey said he'd drive the sledge. Mavis could have passed out on the sledge, which would account for the fact that she was there instead of the dummy, but she had no reason to put on the hood."

"Wow," said Meg. "Oh, wow. Murder. Oh, my God. Who did it?"

"How should I know?" demanded Quill. She watched the sheriff's patrol across the green. "All kinds of people had motives to murder Mavis."

"Who?"

"Who? I'll tell you who." Quill, upset, couldn't think of anyone but John and Tom Peterson. But they had wanted Gil dead, hadn't they? Or had they? "Celeste Baumer for one."

"I thought she went back to Manhattan after Myles let her out of jail."

"Maybe she didn't. Maybe she stayed here, lurking until an opportunity presented itself."

"Dressed like she was, she'd stick out a mile. Who else?" Meg's eyebrows shot up. "I know! Mrs. Hallenbeck!"

"Why? She's out a companion, and I really doubt she'd find it easy to get another one. She's terrified of being alone. Not to mention the fact," Quill added sarcastically, "that she's eighty-three years old and more than likely a grandmother six times over."

"The Grandmother Murders," said Meg. "I like it."

"Now Keith Baumer—*there's* a murderer for you."

"Too obvious," said Meg. "I mean, he was the one who lifted the heavy stone onto her."

"Not if he wanted to divert suspicion from himself." Quill locked her hands around her knees. She could see Myles's broad shoulders in the distance. "Maybe Mavis was pressuring him to marry her, or something."

"I wish John would get back," said Meg, who obviously wanted to avoid a serious discussion as Quill did. "This is a mess. Do you suppose they'll cancel the rest of History Days?"

"I don't know." Quill rubbed her hands over her face. "Maybe I'm crazy. Maybe it *was* an accident. Mavis was so drunk, she could have put the hood on as a joke or something, and then passed out on the sledge."

"Myles will take care of it." Meg sat up and brushed the seat of her jeans briskly. "Let's walk over and ask him what's going on."

"He'll just tell us to butt out, Meg. He always does." Quill was seized with a desire to get back to the Inn, and jumped to her feet. "Where's Edward? He's been in there quite a while. Did he go in right after you?"

"Yep. I'll go check."

"Meg, we're not supposed to go in there. Davey said . . ."

"Bosh!" Meg jumped up, disappeared into the buildings, then reappeared a few moments later with Edward Lancashire.

"Mrs. Hallenbeck just went in to see Officer Kiddermeister," he said in response to Quill's inquiry.

"You were in there a long time," said Meg. "Did he ask you the same questions he asked us?"

"I'm sure he did," Edward said easily.

The door to the library swung open, and Mrs. Hallenbeck felt her way carefully down the steps. Quill went up and took her arm. "Are you feeling all right? This must have been such a shock!"

"This has been quite an experience," the old lady said. "Most interesting. I warned her that liquor would be the death of her someday—that, and those pills." She gazed around with satisfaction. "It's a lovely day."

"Did Mavis drink much, Mrs. Hallenbeck?" Edward asked.

"A cocktail every evening, without fail. I myself neither smoke nor drink, nor put any drugs in my body," she said firmly. "I am often complimented on my youthful appearance. It is the result of taking care of myself. Shall we walk to the Inn? I could use a cup of tea."

"Would you like me to call the van from the Inn, Mrs. Hallenbeck? It's all uphill." Quill was worried about her in the heat.

"What a thoughtful child you are, Sarah. You take such good care of me. No. I shall walk. I walk four or five miles a day most of the time. I am frequently complimented on my stamina."

The four of them set off at a rapid pace, Mrs. Hallenbeck leading the way.

"Had you known Mavis long?" asked Edward of her.

"Oh, yes. She worked for my late husband, you know. Had a title—Human Resources Director or somesuch. Quite a stupid woman, really, when you think about it."

"Such a terrible way to die," murmured Quill, half to herself.

"Perhaps the sheriff will find some evidence on the barn door," suggested Edward.

"I did not so much as pick up a stone, so I clearly am not responsible," said Mrs. Hallenbeck with immense satisfaction. "But that terrible Baumer person. Someone should put people like that in jail. Imagine being responsible for an accident like that."

They reached the bottom of the incline to the Inn. Mrs. Hallenbeck looked girlishly up at Edward. "I believe I'll take this handsome young man's arm up these little stairs."

Edward presented his arm with a gallant gesture, and the two sisters fell behind. The words "frequently complimented" floated back to them more than once, and Meg muttered crossly, "I don't think that woman's elevator goes all the way to the top, Quill."

"Meg, she's eighty-three years old. We can't imagine what that's like. All the people that she grew up with, her husband, her friends, are either gone or going. The line between life and death must seem very thin to her, each day more of a struggle to stay on this side and not slip to the next."

Meg started to hum the portentous strains of "Pomp and Circumstance," and Quill told her to shut up. "That doesn't make you think of fat guys with double chins making speeches full of hot air?" said Meg innocently. "It does me."

"I'd rather think about what to serve the Chamber tonight."

"Something comforting, but not depressing," said Meg. "Pasta in sauce ought to set Marge right up. As long as I don't have to make it, smell it, or eat it. Frank'll make it."

"Pasta in sauce," said Marge with satisfaction some three hours later. "Finally something I rekonize."

"Very diplomatic," said Howie dryly. "Traditional village fare for weddings, anniversaries, and funerals." He rolled a forkful around in his mouth. "Do I detect fresh basil? The last of the Vidalias?"

"Do I detect bullshit?" asked Marge, raising her eyes to the ceiling. "Or is it Heinz spaghetti sauce, like any sensible person uses?"

"We need to get to the purpose of this meeting," said Elmer Henry. He rapped the gavel and stood up. Seventeen faces stared back at him. "This emergency meeting of the Hemlock Falls

Chamber of Commerce is now in session. Will you lead us in a prayer, Reverend?"

"He's not here," said Betty Hall. "He called his own emergency session of the deacons at his church. Said he'll be right along as soon as it's over."

"So Tom Peterson isn't here either," said Elmer. "And Myles is off on his investigation. We have enough to vote, Quill?"

"You need a certain portion of the membership," said Quill hesitantly. "I'm not sure just how many."

"Two-thirds," said Howie impatiently. "There's twenty-four active members."

There was a pause while everyone figured this out.

"We're two short," said Esther, which, unknown to Quill, helped enlighten Mark Anthony Jefferson, the vice-president of the Hemlock Falls Savings and Loan, as to Esther's cash-flow troubles.

"No, we're one over," said Marge promptly, which would have surprised Mark Anthony not at all. "So, do we cancel the rest of the History Days or what?"

"If I might say something," said Harvey Bozzel. He stood up, tucked his hands boyishly in the back pockets of his cotton Dockers, and composed his features into a grave, but not solemn, expression. "We've experienced a terrible tragedy here. Just terrible. And we sincerely mourn the passing of this celebrity in our town."

"Celebrity?" said Betty Hall. "She was a paid companion to that old lady. What's with the celebrity stuff?"

"She was a professional actress," Harvey said gently.

"She was a dancing hot dog!" said Betty. "1 don't call that being a celebrity."

"A story . . . now, Ralph, you can help me on this . . . that will probably be picked up by the national media."

"A TV station was here," admitted Ralph Lorenzo, editor and publisher of the *Hemlock Daily News*. "But it was just the affiliate from Syracuse."

"With the proper handling," said Harvey, "this can be a story of national scope." He ran one hand through his styled blond hair and asked rhetorically, " 'Does an ancient curse haunt the peaceful village of Hemlock Falls? Story tonight at eleven.' With absolutely no disrespect to the dead, think of the publicity." He lowered his voice and looked at them earnestly. "Think of the good it can do the businesses of Hemlock Falls. Quill, has anyone decided to shorten their stay with you because of this?"

"I thought it might," said Quill, "but no. Everyone seems to be ghoulishly interested in what's happened."

"No, no, no, no, no. Not ghoulish, Quill. It's the universal need to validate your own existence. In the midst of death, there is life. This is a well-known phenomenon in advertising."

"It is, huh?" Harland Peterson banged his fist on the table. "If you're talking about keeping this play going all week, I say it ain't right and it ain't fit, and I'm going to vote against it."

"I have to agree with Harland," said Quill. "This is capitalizing on—"

"On an accident that could have happened to any one of us," said Harvey. "Quill, if you had decided to go on, it could have been you! Don't you see? You get on the expressway after a tractor-trailer hits a bus—you drive more carefully. These occurrences, terrible as they are for the victims, can help prevent such things from happening again. Now, if the town were to approve a small advertising budget, I'd be happy to handle the necessary press releases, to interface with the media, perhaps conduct tours of the fatal spot."

The members responded with vehemence. Marge offered the practical opinion that it'd be good for the diner business, and probably the Croh Bar, too. Howie Murchison drew an analogy between Harvey's proposal and the behavior of ghouls; Miriam Doncaster offered a precise definition of ghoul and agreed with Howie. Freddie Bellini, the mortician, said death was a decent business and he wasn't going to sit still for nasty shots from lawyers and librarians. Quill abandoned any pretense at taking notes and wondered if John Raintree had been in a car wreck, and maybe that was why he'd gone missing.

Myles walked into the room and the squabble stopped abruptly. He was still in uniform. The lines around his gray eyes had deepened a little, and his mouth was grim. Quill thought he looked terrific, like Clint Eastwood riding into town to deal out frontier justice to the mob. He pulled a chair up to the table and sat down.

"We were just discussing the rest of History Days," said Elmer. "Talking about whether or not to continue with the play. What do you think?"

Myles shrugged. "We've found all we're going to find at the site. Go ahead."

Quill would have preferred a response more in the heroic mode. A man who looked like Myles should wither the Harvey Bozzels of this world with a phrase or two of devastating pith. A direct blaze of contempt from his steely eyes would do it, too.

"I'm hungry," said Myles. "Any more of the pasta around?"

Quill handed him her plate. "Take mine."

"So we have the sheriff's support," said Harvey. "I can work up a fee schedule for you right now, and then we can take a quick vote."

Myles wiped his mouth with Quill's napkin. "You don't have my support. I said the site's not off limits."

"What's your opinion, then?" asked Esther. "Harvey said you don't close the expressway after a car accident, so why should we lose the business from History Days?"

"I don't have an official opinion. My personal opinion is that we've had two deaths in the past forty-eight hours and that's no cause for celebrations of any kind."

"We can always tell when it's not an election year, Sheriff," said Harvey nastily. "These two accidents could have happened any-where, at any time . . ."

"They weren't accidents," said Myles. "Gil Gilmeister and Mavis Gollinwood were murdered." Myles swallowed the last of the pasta and stood up. The silence was profound. "Quill, you're to notify me if any of the guests here at the Inn check out. Any of you here have planned to take any time away from the Falls, let Davey know first." He stopped at the door, and looked directly at Quill. "I'm going to need to talk to John Raintree. There's an APB out on him. Any of you see him, call me."

"Murdered!" said Miriam Doncaster.

"Bullshit," said Marge. She wiped her forehead with her napkin.

"S'cuse me," said Ralph Lorenzo, "seems to be a story here." He jumped up and ran after Myles, almost colliding with Dookie Shuttleworth and Tom Peterson as they came into the conference room.

"Forgive us for being late," said the Reverend Shuttleworth.

"We had a most important meeting at the church."

"Sheriff says Gil was murdered, Tom," said Howie Murchison.

"Gil?" Tom stood uncertainly for a moment. The Reverend Shuttleworth took his arm and put him into a chair.

"Murder," said Harvey Bozzel. "Can't see that anybody would want to murder Gil, and if they did, whacking him over the head with that front loader was a piss-poor way to do it."

"That Mavis Collinwood, too," said Elmer. "Marge, you were there at the duck pond. What the hell happened?"

"You know what happened," said Marge sourly. "Sheriff's full of baloney. Coulda been me, coulda been Mavis sat in that ducking stool. You have some gripe with Gil, Harland? You set that tractor up somehow?"

"That tractor's been used for thirty years, and it's got another thirty in it. Ain't nothin' wrong with that tractor!" Harland roared.

"We must not assign blame," said Dookie Shuttleworth. "This is just further evidence that there is some devilish device at work here in town. Quill, the deacons and I have decided to hold a prayer breakfast. This distressing news makes it all the more urgent that we do so. Would the dining room at the Inn be available to us tomorrow morning? For perhaps forty people?"

"Of course, Mr. Shuttleworth," Quill said. "I'll speak with the kitchen about the menu."

"The church is not exactly in funds at the moment," he said apologetically. "Perhaps we could work something out?"

The wail of a siren jerked Quill upright.

"That's the ambulance!" said the mayor. "What the heck? What's happening to the town now?"

Quill ran into the hall and out to the front lobby. Two paramedics burst in through the door. The woman, a substantially sized brunette Quill had seen in town before, said, "Room two twenty-one, miss?"

"This way," said Quill, They followed her up the short flight of stairs. Two twenty-one was Baumer's room. Quill, her heart pounding, rapped on the door as she opened it with her master key. "Mr. Baumer!" she called. "It's Sarah Quilliam. Are you all right?"

"In here!" Baumer's voice was whispery, faint. Quill froze with anxiety bordering on outright fear. Some lunatic must be abroad in Hemlock Falls. Maybe Harvey Bozzel was right. The paramedics shoved her unceremoniously out of the way and charged into the bathroom.

Quill sat down on the bed and took several deep breaths.

"Was that the ambulance?" Meg stood at the open door. She snapped her fingers nervously, a habit which had irritated Quill since their childhood. "Is Baumer okay?"

"Yes, to the ambulance, and I don't know about Baumer," said Quill. "The paramedics are in there with him." Thumps and mumblings from the bathroom indicated the presence of too many people in too small a space "Have you seen him tonight?"

"Umyah."

"What do you mean, 'umyah'? Was he at dinner?"

The brunette opened the bathroom door. Her partner, a thick-set guy with a mustache, supported Keith Baumer. Baumer's face was furious. And green. Quill couldn't decide which condition was uppermost.

"This," Baumer rasped, "is the hotel from hell." The male paramedic dumped him unceremoniously on the bed. Baumer groaned theatrically and closed his eyes.

Quill, who had a growing, uneasy suspicion about the cause of Baumer's illness, asked the medics what happened.

"He has food poisoning," said the brunette. "We got a sample." She held up a clear tube. Quill averted her eyes from the loathsome contents. "I just think he ate sumthin' that didn't agree with him."

"He have anything with raw egg in it?" asked the male medic. The tag on his white coat read O. DOYLE. "This could be salmonella."

"Salmonella," agreed his partner. "Deadly stuff. Ought to take him to the hospital." She nodded her head in gloomy relish. "Might not last the night otherwise."

"There is no salmonella in my kitchen," snapped Meg. "And if he's sick, it's because he grossed out on my food. Pork roast, potatoes *duchesse*, asparagus with hollandaise—and the eggs were cooked, thank you. He started the meal with sausage-stuffed mushrooms, and ended it with a chocolate *bombe*, and nobody's gut can take all that, even a cow, which has four stomachs instead of that guy's one."

"He looks a little better, Mr. O'Doyle," said Quill, eyeing Baumer with hope.

"It's Doyle, ma'am. Oliver Doyle. And I think he does, don't you, Maureen?"

"I'll take his temperature." She opened a black bag, took out a thermometer, and rolled up her sleeves. "CAN YOU HEAR ME, MR. BAUMER!"

"I can hear you fine," he snapped. "It's my stomach, not my ears."

"CAN YOU ROLL OVER ON YOUR STOMACH FOR ME? WE'RE GOING TO TAKE YOUR TEMPERATURE." Maureen advanced on him, the thermometer held aloft.

"We'll wait in the hall," said Quill. She shoved Meg out of 221, across the hall, and flat against the opposite wall. "What the hell have you been up to, Meg!"

"Nothing," said Meg, meekly.

Quill knew her sister's literal mind. "Then what have Frank and Bjorn been up to?"

"A little creative cooking, that's all," said Meg. "Nothing remotely harmful."

Quill stood back and glared at her, hands on her hips. "That little bottle. What's in it?"

Meg opened her mouth, closed it. "Ipecac," she said. "A very weak solution."

Maureen and Oliver came out of 221, closing the door behind them. "Temperature's normal," said Maureen regretfully. "Pulse is normal. And he only threw up five or six times and he's not gonna heave again, he says. Told him to stay in bed for a few days, eat boiled eggs and tea, maybe a little toast."

"Aw, Maureen, the guy's going to be fine," said Doyle, "just ate something that didn't agree with him. I seen guys a lot sicker come out of the Croh Bar and work the late shift at the paint factory, no problem."

"Still got to report it to the Board of Health," said Maureen. She waved the test tube. "Send this in for samples." She brightened. "Might be salmonella. Just a teensy little bit."

"Nah." Doyle shook Quill's hand. "He heaves again, give Doc Bishop a call. You won't need us. Bit of a waste of time, this. Took me away from a great video and the girlfriend."

"You must let the Inn make a contribution to the ambulance fund," said Quill hastily. "I mean, on top of the one we give every year." Quill drew them to the stairs. "And we'll take good care of Mr. Baumer. We'll see that he stays in bed a couple of days. Meg will see to the menu herself."

"Told him you prob'bly wouldn't charge him," Maureen tossed over her shoulder as they carried their equipment out, "on account of you wouldn't want a lawsuit or nothing." She waved the test tube aloft in farewell.

"Thank you," Quill said to the closed door, "very, very much." She turned to her sister. "What were you thinking of?"

"That we'd get rid of him!" said Meg with spirit. "Have him move to the Marriott or something. Let them put up with him."

"Good plan," Quill said cordially. "Excellent plan. I like a plan that means we're going to have to wait on him hand and foot for the next three days. *For free!*"

"Tell you what," said Meg with a charitable air. "Since you're so upset about this, let me take care of it. You don't have to worry about a thing."

"That's big of you."

"It's the least I can do."

A shout came from behind the closed door of 221. Quill smiled sweetly. "That call's for you."

The Chamber members were eating lemon tarts when Quill returned to the Lounge. She sat down, looked at the yellow custard filling, and pushed it away.

"Everything all right?" asked Howie after a moment. "Elmer wanted to come stampeding to the rescue, but I convinced him that another eighteen bodies stuffed into your front lobby would only confuse matters."

"Seventeen," said Marge. "I hollered at Ollie Doyle out the window. Said your sister finally poisoned somebody."

"Don't be absurd, Marge," said Esther. "What we have to worry about is whether a murderer's running around loose in Hemlock Falls. He might be staying right here at the Inn!"

"The only person who'd want to murder Keith Baumer is his wife," said Quill. "And she went back to Manhattan this morning after Myles let her out of jail." Well aware of the town's propensity for gossip, she came to a decision. She ground her teeth, looked Marge in the eye, and said, "You were right. My sister thought Keith Baumer was the ultimate pest. So she put ipecac in his food." She shut her eyes, waiting for the barrage of indignation sure to follow.

"Really?" said Betty Hall with interest. "Marge tried that once with this smartass yuppie from New Jersey that kept sending his food back. Worked a treat. Never saw him again."

"Made him pay the bill, too," said Marge with satisfaction. "Tell Meg baking soda in the scrambled eggs works just as good. And there's no mess to clean up."

"Well, we all hope that Meg's efforts are rewarded," said the Reverend Shuttleworth. "There are certain signs about the man that are very disturbing, very disturbing. There is strong evidence that he was an instrument in the downfall of that poor creature who went to her reward this afternoon. And I have your Doreen Muxworthy to thank for first bringing them to my attention."

"The staff at the Inn aims to please," said Quill. "Mayor, if the meeting is going to go on much longer, I'll need to leave you to your coffee. I've got to see to some things."

"Yes. With John being accused of these murders, you will have many extra duties," said the Reverend Shuttleworth. "The members were telling me about this APR."

"APB," said Quill, "and John has *not* been accused of these murders, Mr. Shuttleworth. And I'd appreciate it *very* much if you all understand that. Myles just wants to talk to him. That's all. He has . . . evidence germane to these incidents."

Nobody would meet Quill's eye. She wondered just exactly what had been discussed while she was occupied with Baumer. "You've known him for years," she said. "He grew up in this town. He does the books for half the businesses in town. You've trusted him in the past. Has he ever betrayed that trust?"

Mark Anthony Jefferson cleared his throat. "Well, that's just it, Quill. We've been talking the matter over and—" Quill drew breath to protest, and Jefferson held his hand up.

"Please. He knew, for example, quite a bit more about Gil's car business than Tom here—his own partner—did. I'm going to go over the books tomorrow with Tom, at the bank, to see if there may have been any irregularities that Gil could have discovered."

"You have no basis for that belief," said Quill hotly. "None!"

"It's wise to take precautions," said Mark Anthony. "As for Ms. Collinwood . . ."

"He'd never even met Mavis Collinwood before she came here!" said Quill. "This is all—There's a word for it. Howie?"

"Supposition?" said the lawyer.

"No!" Quill knew her face was red with anger. "Slander!"

Howie looked at Marge and raised his eyebrows.

"I'll tell her," said Marge gruffly. She rocked back in her chair. "Mavis told me something about John that you have to know, Quill. I'm sorry to be the one to do it, too, because although I ain't sure about this fancy schmancy kwee-zeen you all serve, you've been a good enough friend and neighbor over the years. And you know I'm mostly joking when I give you a little bit of hassle over stuff. The way I figure, we've got a friendly rivalry, that right, Howie?"

"You ought to get to the point, Marge," said Howie.

"John was the head of the accounting department for Doggone Good Dogs some years back. After my time. Mavis figured he was the one who embezzled near three hundred thousand dollars from their company. Then he disappeared and nobody saw hide nor hair of him for a couple of years. Mavis was that shocked when she met him here at your Inn." Marge looked around the table. "So what we figure is, John had himself a real good motive to get rid of both of them, Mavis and Gil."

Quill left them sitting there without a word.

CHAPTER 10

Quill wanted a place with no phones, no people, and no problems. When being nibbled to death by ducks, she thought, the best thing to do is leave the pond. Meg was the sort of person who'd mince the ducks into pâté, and not for the first time, Quill envied her sister's direct, assertive approach. For Meg, all odds were surmountable.

Even murder.

She left the Inn and walked to the gazebo in the perennial garden. Evening was coming on like high tide on a still night, the purple-blue darkness flowing over the Falls' ridge to touch the crescent moon. The dark hid the colors of the roses, but their scent recalled their names, and their names their sturdy beauty—Maidens' Blush at its peak; the damasks Celsiana and La Ville de Bruxelles in full bloom; the hybrid teas Tiffany and Crimson Glory a constant undernote, as they had been all summer. Quill's hand flexed as though it held a paint brush. She sat in the gazebo and let pictures of new paintings drift through her mind's eye. The heart of a Chrysler Imperial rose would make a wonderful painting—a man-made rose with a man-made shape at odds with the essential nature of flowers. It would give the painting an energetic irony. And the color—an aggressive, insulting, dangerous red.

Like blood seeping from under a barn door.

"Ugh!" said Quill into the dark. She asked herself the logical question: Who wanted Mavis dead? She shut her eyes and thought about the scene of the crime as a painting. The bandstand with the three witnesses—Howie, Elmer, and Tom Peterson; Dookie, in the judge's seat; the crowd immediately in front of the bandstand.

Who in this picture had the opportunity to kill?

Baumer had been standing extreme stage left. If he'd looked over his right shoulder, he would have seen the sledge stop and Harland dismount. He could have waited until Harland stomped around stage right to accost Howie and tell him he wasn't going to drive anymore.

Did Baumer take the chance to pull the hood over Mavis' slack mouth and dulled eyes?

Tom Peterson had been standing at Baumer's elbow after he moved offstage. The two men hadn't known each other, and hadn't spoken together, at least not in the replay Quill saw before her. Tom, too, could have ducked around the stage and gone into the semidarkness of the shed. Except that Quill could find no link between Tom and Mavis. And Mavis had been the target of the murderer, who had succeeded the second time, after failing the first.

Harvey Bozzel had jumped from the stage to the rescue like some half-baked Dudley Do-Right. The crowd had surged forward when Harvey made his dramatic gesture, and Baumer and Tom Peterson had disappeared in the melee.

Quill concentrated hard: Mrs. Hallenbeck, Nadine Gilmeister, Marge Schmidt, Meg, and Edward Lancashire had all been shoved back as the crowd moved forward.

There was herself, of course, sitting on a bench with two teenaged girls who'd been restless during the trial scene, and able, in the confusion, to walk away unnoticed. "And I sure as heck didn't do it," said Quill aloud.

So all of them had been close enough to slip around the bandstand and assist Mavis Collinwood down the gravel path to death at the foot of General Hemlock.

Who had been at the scene of *both* crimes? Tom Peterson, Nadine, Mrs. Hallenbeck, and Edward Lancashire had all been in the vicinity, but Marge and Baumer were the only two who'd been there at the time of both killings. Unless one of the others had *returned* to the scene.

Mrs. Hallenbeck certainly wanted Mavis alive; "Old age is lonely," she'd said. "You have no idea how lonely. And Mavis is a warm body in the house. She's nowhere to go, but to me. Do you know how hard it is to find a healthy, reasonably responsible person to take care of me?"

It was conceivable that Mrs. Hallenbeck had accomplished the murder, but there was no motive. Quite the reverse.

Did Tom Peterson want Mavis and Gil dead? Had he tried three times to kill her? She knew the car business was in trouble. Had Mavis and Marge offered to buy Tom out, using Mrs. Hallenbeck's money? Was there a reason that Tom couldn't/wouldn't sell? He said he'd been home watching a videotape the night Gil died, and his wife was gone for the evening. His house was the only residence even close to the park; he could have watched the three of them mooching around in the park; he could have slipped out, loosened the bolt, watched Gil's death, and taken the bolt with him. He'd have been back home in less than ten minutes.

What was the motive? Tom would have wanted Mavis alive, and able to buy Gil out.

What about Nadine? Quill thought long and seriously about Nadine. It didn't fit. In almost any other marriage, jealousy would have been a dandy motive. But it would have been Marge, not Mavis, who Nadine would have wanted out of the way. Besides, Nadine had been shopping in Syracuse with her sister the night of the ducking-stool incident. Her parking validation from the Mall had the time on it; she couldn't have physically been there in time to do the first murder.

And finally, Edward Lancashire. Quill could see no reason why the food critic for *L'Aperitif* would want to kill Mavis Collinwood. But he had the opportunity. And he'd been asking a lot of questions.

Marge was a most attractive candidate for born murders. Quill scrupulously cleared her mind of prejudice. You didn't pursue a potential murderer because the potential murderer called your sister Megia Borgia, and threatened you and yours with polyester-suited employees from the Board of Health. You investigated reasons why persons of such lousy taste would hate the victim.

"One," said Quill to the Sutter's Gold rosebush at her elbow. "Marge and Mavis worked together at Doggone Good Dogs. Marge claims Mavis told her three hundred thousand dollars was missing. And that John took it What if Marge had taken it? And what if Mavis found out?" Everyone in town wondered why Marge did so well out of that little diner. She'd lent money to Gil more than once. Even Esther West had once confided to Quill that in times when the banks clamped down on lending, Marge was a good, if usuriously inclined, source of cash. Marge's behavior was definitely suspicious. She loved Gil—or did she? Gil owed her money. Her activities and motives *both* would have to be investigated. Maybe Marge had been after Mavis all along. Gil could have hopped on that ducking stool *before* Marge could stop him. Quill shuddered at the thought of Marge screaming No! as Gil went drunkenly to his death.

Quill began to feel better. She was getting that I'm-really-good-at-managing-people feeling so often rebutted by the skepticism of her nearest and dearest. She jumped up and moved briskly along the gravel path, hands clasped behind her in the best Sherlock Holmes tradition.

Baumer. Another prime candidate. Quill pulled at her lower lip. She'd read with great interest various books on the personalities of murderers. Motive was frequently rooted in the character of the killers; given a variety of motives in a given number of people, only one would kill. Just considering his character, Baumer fit better than anybody. At least, he'd been positioned right; of all the members of the audience at the *Trial*, he was in the best position to pop backstage and hood the bird, so to speak. And he'd been with Mavis, Marge, and Gil the night of the duck pond killing. But why? No reason to kill Gil, but, like Marge, perhaps Mavis had been his target. Would he kill to keep his marriage together? Was he afraid that word of his shenanigans would get back to his boss?

"Probably not," said Quill, this time to the concrete fish pond by the French lavender. "But it wouldn't hurt to explore possibilities." She could start tomorrow, ask some tactful, discreet questions of Baumer's employers at the sales conference at the Marriott; go to the diner and confront Marge; investigate Peterson.

Quill heard the sounds of people leaving the Inn. Car doors slammed in the distance. Voices shouted goodbye. Motors revved, taillights blinked red; the Chamber members had gone home.

Feeling it was safe to go back in the water, Quill went to the kitchen and laid her conclusions out for Meg.

Meg sipped coffee—she was immune to the effects of caffeine, and had been known to drink her special blend to put herself to sleep—and drew circles on the pastry marble with her forefinger as Quill narrowed the number of suspects to two.

"So I'm going to go to the Marriott tomorrow and start with

some questions about Baumer's past. The other thing I can do is have Doreen search his room for that bolt. And I thought I'd drop by the diner. If Marge is lying about John's connection to Mavis and Doggone Good Dogs, she did it under the guise of presenting an olive branch. I'll just walk into the diner for lunch, waving my own olive branch, and asking innocent questions."

"Have you talked this over with Myles?"

"Of course I haven't talked it over with Myles. You know that Myles is practically prehistoric in his attitude toward women's ability to do certain things."

"I haven't noticed that at all," said Meg. "He's got two patrolwomen in the Sheriff's Department, he voted for our woman senator in the last campaign, and he does his own housework. Doreen's after him all the time to hire her cousin Shirlee to clean for him. He cooks for you all the time, and I remember distinctly, Quill, that he took his two little nieces to Disney World all by himself last year. Myles isn't a male chauvinist. He doesn't want you messing in his police work, because you're an emotional, biased *person*. His bias is *not* gender-specific."

"I am *not* an emotional, biased person!"

"Yes, you are, Quill! You're a crusader. You've always been a crusader. Remember the protest?"

"Meg, don't bring up the protest."

"I remember the protest . . ."

"Meg, you always bring up the protest. That was thirty years ago, for Pete's sake, and you bring it up when the least little thing happens."

". . . I was four years old. *Four years old!* You had me protesting the Vietnam war in front of my *kindergarten*. Here I was, this totally innocent little kid whose big sister had this sign STOP THE WAR with the R backward, and we made the six o'clock news. Mom was so embarrassed she didn't go out of the house for weeks afterward. The neighbors thought she put us up to it."

"Dad thought it was great," said Quill stiffly. "He sneaked me a Mars bar when he came to get us at the police station."

"You never told me that," said Meg. "I never got any of it, either." She regarded her sister with exasperation. "Your analysis of the situation is clean, cool, and precise."

"Thank you," said Quill.

"It's also bogus. You're ignoring one screamingly obvious set of facts which bring the whole house of cards to the floor, Hawkshaw."

"And what's that?"

"John," said Meg. "John appears to have the best motive of all. What about that picture!"

"Why should the fact that Nadine and Tom's sister-in-law was John's sister have anything to do with anything?" said Quill crossly.

"Because you were the one that 'deduced' the picture really belonged to John, and Gil had it! Honestly, Quill. It makes perfect sense to me that if Gil saw it lying on the ground, he'd pick it up and put it away so he could return it to John later. It also makes perfect sense that the Gilmeisters knew about John's prison sentence and never told anybody. You know what Hemlock Falls is like. Nadine would be embarrassed to the tops of her ears to have everyone know they'd had an ex-con in the family. I love you, Quill, but there's caramel where your brains should be. You're letting your friendship with John get in the way of the facts." She shook her head. "I'm beat. I'm going to bed. I'll see you in the morning."

There was a mass of telephone messages under her door. Quill flipped on the overhead lights and sank into the Eames chair in front of the fireplace and riffled through them. The insurance adjuster would be by in the morning to examine the balcony. She could hand off the task of showing him around to Peter Williams. Myles had called; he was in Ithaca until Tuesday. The forensic lab tests on Saturday had been positive for sulfuric acid, which meant, thought Quill, that it was highly possible there'd been a first attempt on Mavis' life. She paper-clipped that message to the three from Mrs. Hallenbeck, inviting her to dinner, to a cup of late-night tea, and then to breakfast tomorrow morning. "We must talk," each message read.

"That we must," Quill said to herself. "About our bill, about Mavis. About what you discussed at dinner with Mavis, Marge, and Gil."

She scrawled a short list. "Things To Do—Monday: Hal; Pet; Mar; Baum," and muttering the names HalPetMarBaum like a charm against disaster, fell into a deep, dreamless sleep.

The phone rang. Quill jerked awake. The digital clock radio blinked two-thirty. Quill regarded it with baleful eyes and picked the phone up. "This is Quill."

"Is Myles with you?"

"John!"

"He's not there?"

"No. He's in Ithaca and won't be back until Tuesday. John, I've been so worried about you. Where are you?"

The line went dead. Quill jiggled the cutoff button. Two quiet taps sounded at the door. Quill jumped up and flung it open. John stood there, white shirt rumpled, tieless, his sports coat filthy. The gray shadows under his eyes made his cheeks gaunt and his expression haunted.

"Come in and sit down," said Quill. She ushered him into the room and shut the door. John slumped on the couch and rubbed his hands over his face.

"You look exhausted, John. Have you had anything to eat?"

"A Big Mac, this afternoon."

"Meg will have a fit."

He chuckled. "Actually, it tasted pretty good. Sometimes you just get a craving for junk food, you know?"

Quill paced restlessly around the room.

John watched her for a moment, forearms on his knees. "I want to tell you about my prison sentence."

Quill sat in the Eames chair, relieved.

"I went to my rooms first, before I came to see you. I wanted to show you a picture I have there, but the police . . ."

"Yes, I know."

"Then you know about my sister?"

"I didn't know who she was, John, until I showed it to Nadine. Myles found the one of her in the waitress uniform at the scene of . . . where Gil drowned."

"By the pond?"

"Yes. I matched it with the one you had in your room."

"Gil was going to put it in the family album. He never had much sense. So, that explains the APB. Myles thought it connected me to the scene of the crime."

"Yes, John. Where have you been all this time?"

"I made some—acquaintances in prison. There's a network, if you know who to talk to, where to look. That's one of the things I did while I was gone. I spent a lot of time trying to find out why Mavis came here, what she was after, what she'd been doing since I saw her last at the company."

"So you did work together, then?"

"For about six years. It was just after I got my MBA from RIT." He shook his head. "I really thought I was going places, then." His face shuttered closed. Quill waited patiently.

"We were a close family, growing up," he said. "My dad worked the high steel and was gone a lot. My mom stayed home. My sister Elaina was quiet, shy, never dated much in high school." John stopped, sighed, then went on. "I was a rowdy kid in high school, ran around with a bunch of guys who got into stupid small-time things. Lifting cigarettes from drugstores, joy-riding in other people's cars. I straightened up my senior year, and left all of it behind me when I got the scholarship. All but friends, one in particular, who married my sister. Tom Peterson's brother, Jack." He looked at Quill, the skin drawn tight over his cheekbones.

"My dad died in a fall from a high beam. My mom passed on soon after that. Cancer. Elaina had no one but me. And Jackie, of course. Jackie who got into the booze every Saturday night, then every Friday and Saturday night, then every day of the week and came home from the bars and beat her.

"She never said a word. Not for all the time I was in school, not for the years I started working my way up, to D.G.D.'s headquarters. I'd drive in from headquarters in Syracuse. We'd get together now and then, and I noticed things, as you will, in passing. A black eye. A fractured elbow. A cracked rib. Falls, she said, or clumsiness. Any one of the million transparent excuses you hear from battered women."

John stared at his clasped hands. "I was into the booze pretty good myself. Earning good money. On my way up. Ignoring all the signs that told me I was in trouble, refused to believe I was another alcoholic Indian. I'd beat the stereotype, right?

"I dropped by Elaina's one Saturday afternoon. Hadn't seen her for a couple of months. I'd been to a sports bar with some of the guys from the company and we'd gotten into the Scotch. Somebody had called me at the bar. Said there was trouble. I knocked on the front door and waited. Nobody answered for a long, long time. I went around to the back. I looked in the kitchen window. The place was a mess; pots and pans all over the floor. There was a huge smear of chili on the ceiling, from where a pot'd been thrown off the stove, I guess.

"Elaina lay facedown in the middle of the kitchen floor. I kicked in the lock. Went to her. Called her name. I turned her over." A shiver went through him. It didn't reach his face. Quill swallowed, and dug her nails into her hands.

"Tomatoes get hot. He'd thrown the chili into her face, after hitting her with the pot, I guess. She was burned, from her temple, here"—he touched his own—"to her chin. Later, we found out that she'd lost the sight of one eye. That pretty face. Gone.

"I shouted. I shouted again. I could hear the TV yowling from the living room. I ran in. Jackie was passed out on the couch. His mouth was open. He was snoring. There was tomato sauce down his shirt, on his hands. I beat him to death. And they sent me to prison."

Quill was cold. She couldn't speak. "Why don't I make you something to eat?" She went to her small kitchenette and busied herself. When she returned, she brought a small bowl of soup.

John sipped it, then said, "It didn't make a big splash in the papers. But everyone in the company knew, of course. And that included Mavis. "Mavis had a nice little sideline going."

"She was Human Resources Director, wasn't she?" Quill's voice was rusty. She cleared her throat.

"The employees had a joke. That she directed the resources into her own pocket. Nobody knew how much money she made, but she was in a position to find out things. And she did. Have a little problem with your former employer? Mavis would approve your hiring on the condition that ten percent of your paycheck be turned over to her, every Friday. Swipe a few cartons of frozen meat from the storeroom? Same deal. You couldn't turn her in without turning yourself in. And nobody complained, of course. Nobody in management knew, or at least I like to think they didn't. I sure didn't find out until I came to work here. She tracked me down and gave me a call."

"She was blackmailing you?"

"Mavis was blackmailing everybody. By that time, she'd weaseled herself into the old lady's back pocket, and when the old man was alive, you couldn't touch her. Mavis had something on the guy who took over the accounting after I left—I don't know what it was, but it gave her access to the books. And she cooked them. Three hundred thousand dollars were missing soon after I went to jail. After I got out, she called me, and sent me documents that "proved" I'd been systematically bleeding the company during my time as head of accounting. A small monthly stipend, she said, would keep this news from my current employer."

"I wouldn't have believed it for a second," said Quill indignantly.

"No? How well do you know me? I've been here less than a year, Quill. And if you'd been approached by a woman with proof of my prison trial, my alcoholism, and 'proof' I'd diverted three hundred thousand dollars for my private use, what would you have done? What would anybody have done? I would have stopped you from hiring someone like that myself."

"I would have asked where the three hundred thousand went," said Quill. "The way you live it's obvious you haven't got it."

"Mavis had that covered, too. Elaina is . . . not right. She's been in a hospital down in Westchester for a long time. The state pays a part of it, but it's not enough." He reddened. "Gil and Marge and most of my clients pay me in cash. My income from my business is unrecorded, and I pay it directly to the institution. It'd be a bit of a job to prove where that money came from—and get a lot of other people into tax trouble."

"So between Mavis and your sister, it must be quite a stretch to make enough money to live."

"I live pretty well, Quill. Except for the lack of junk food. I think we should try to convince Meg to add potato skins to the appetizer menu."

"The kind loaded with Baco-s," said Quill. "No problem."

"You want to tell her, or shall I?"

"Flip you for it."

The lighthearted game wasn't working. Quill set her coffee cup on the end table. "So you must have been pretty upset when she showed up here."

"Quite a motive for murder," John agreed. "Quill, on my sister's life, I didn't kill Mavis. And I didn't kill Gil."

"Then we'll have to figure out who did."

"The woman of action," mused John. "I haven't seen you like this before, Quill."

"Well, there aren't that many crimes to solve in Hemlock Falls."

"Just put one in front of you, and you drop your normally diffident manner and charge?" John asked. "I mean, I *have* heard the story about the kindergartener's protest march, but I thought it was apocryphal, at least until now."

"Hah," said Quill. "Let me bring you up to date."

She summarized the discovery of the photograph among Gil's effects, the conversations with Tom, Nadine, and Myles, and Marge's disclosure at the Chamber meeting. Her review of the deadly conclusion to *The Trial of Goody Martin* was succinct but accurate.

"So you believe that Baumer and Marge are the likeliest suspects, with Tom Peterson running a poor third just because he had the opportunity."

"Don't you? I mean, that matchbook's pretty significant."

"There's an old saying in the audit business, Quill: 'Follow the money.' When I left here Friday, I was in a panic." He smiled slightly. "Not usual for me, I know. But I thought if I could find out what happened to that three hundred thousand three years ago, I might be able to discover who was being squeezed by Mavis badly enough to kill her."

"It did occur to you, didn't it, that Mavis took it herself?"

He hesitated. "It's possible. But I don't think so. I have a friend who's pretty good on the computer. We got into Mavis' financial records this morning. If she did have it, she doesn't have it now. Mavis is just about broke. She needed that job with Mrs. Hallenbeck."

"But what about the money you sent her?"

He shrugged. "A couple of hundred dollars a month. I found that, all right, along with a few other contributors to Mavis' nest egg, who are more than likely in the same position I am myself. She appeared to be taking in about eight hundred a month. That's enough to keep her in red lipstick and mid-range designer clothes, but that's it."

Quill hesitated to ask the next question. Somehow, theorizing in the perennial garden was a lot different than a cold discussion of facts with your accountant. "What about Marge? Was she being blackmailed, too?"

"I don't know. I was reviewing records of deposits, Quill, and they don't list the origin of the money in any bank I ever heard of. If I have a little more time, I can take a look around Marge's accounts." He shook his head. "I have a hard time believing it, though. Two hundred a month is a pretty slim motive for murder. Then there's the fact that I *like* Marge. I've known likable murderers in the joint, but I can't believe she'd have to resort to killing Mavis to get rid of her."

Quill explained her theories. John, unlike certain sheriffs she could name, listened with interest.

"Baumer's a possibility. The guy dresses like he's on the edge. Tom Peterson? I don't know. The partnership . . ." He stopped.

Quill waited. "What? What about the partnership, John? Don't stop now. We may solve this, just sitting here!"

"You mustn't repeat any of this, Quill. When people hire me to handle their books, they trust me with a fundamental part of themselves."

"You're worried about my finding out about Gil Gilmeister's financial affairs, when you're being hunted for murder?" Quill said. "Oh, for goodness sakes, John. That's absurd."

"Not to me."

Quill bit back her laughter, figured she never in this world would figure out why men behaved the way they did, and promised never to reveal to anyone the state of Gil Gilmeister's general ledger. "Plus," she said dramatically, "I hereby absolve you of the least little suspicion that You Did It. No one with that kind of honor system could possibly have swiped that bolt. And since you weren't even here when Mavis was . . . you know . . . you're totally in the clear."

John looked at her gravely for a moment. "Let's get back to the partnership. Gil and Tom have a fifty-fifty partnership in the business, not ideal for a number of reasons, because they had to agree jointly on every decision they made, and sometimes the interest of one partner conflicts dramatically with the needs of another. This was very true in Gil's case. Nadine was quite a consumer, and Gil's drinking problem didn't help matters either. Toward the end, Gil was drawing heavily against the equity in his part of the business; and business isn't all that good to begin with."

"The cash loans came from Marge?"

"Yes. And I'll say this for her, Marge Schmidt is a hell of a good businesswoman. She didn't let her affection for Gil stand in the way of liens against the units."

"You mean Gil borrowed money from Marge against the cars he hadn't sold?"

"Against the cars he sold. You know most of the profit from that business comes from the car loans."

It seemed to Quill that John's admiration of Marge's business acumen was misplaced, and that the nature of business itself was perverse. Marge's stranglehold on Gil's business was a *good* thing? She forebore comment and said, "But none of this has to do with Tom Peterson's half."

"No. Although Tom was getting fed up, and looking actively for a new partner. Funny thing was, he wasn't helping Gil get the loan he needed from the bank. They require an audit, and Tom kept ducking me, putting me off. Gil knew this. Gil also knew that Tom could force Marge to call those loans in by threatening to take his profitable side of the business elsewhere. He was even talking about setting up in competition with Gil. Marge had lent Gil a lot of money, and it'd be a case of her business or his. As I said, Marge is good. She wouldn't let her and Betty's ship go down to save Gil."

"So my theory about Marge and Mavis bringing Mrs. Hallenbeck's millions into Gil's business wasn't all that farfetched."

"No. Although from the little I knew of Mrs. Hallenbeck when I worked for the company, she'd be a hard sell. She was a tough cookie right from the start. Nobody was real surprised when old man Hallenbeck locked himself into the garage and turned the car motor on."

"Oh," said Quill softly. "How terrible!"

"Yes. She's got the life, though, doesn't she? Or she did. Doggone

Good Dogs was sold to Armour's. She retired with a tidy sum, to say the least. And she had Mavis to run her errands for her."

"Not anymore," said Quill.

"Will she find someone else?"

"I don't know—it's very difficult. There's very little help for the elderly these days—unless they're willing to accept a nursing home, and I can't see Mrs. Hallenbeck doing that."

"It'd be a heck of a *nice* nursing home, with her money."

"But none of that explains why Tom Peterson would have a motive to kill Mavis."

"There's something funny going on." John's habitual self-containment kept him on the couch; any other man would have been pacing the room. He allowed himself a slight frown. "I knew Mavis was coming. She called from the gas station in Covert to tell me that we had to discuss what she called a 'rearrangement' of the payments."

"You paid her once a month?"

"Yes. To a post office box in Atlanta. The envelope was addressed to Scarlett O'Hara."

"Good grief," said Quill. "It figures."

"She was . . ."—John hesitated, searching for the right word—"ebullient. Chattering." He moved his thumb and forefinger together rapidly to indicate mindless babble. "Said the money was rolling in from every side."

"She's got the wrong heroine in Scarlett O'Hara," said Quill. "Behaving much more like the rapacious Evita, don't you think?"

John dismissed this excursion into light-mindedness with a tolerant twitch of his mouth. "I guess. The point is, Quill, she chose Hemlock Falls for a purpose. Not just because I was here. I got the impression that she'd come to some crossroads."

What, thought Quill, would be considered a career milestone for a professional blackmailer? "She must have come across something that would really feather her nest. Big money," she said aloud. "More than you could afford. And since she obviously came to Hemlock Falls for a reason, it must have to do with people she knows here. Something that Marge is involved with?" Quill guessed. "Something Tom Peterson is involved with?" She jumped to her feet. "*John!* The matchbook! The memo from the D.O.H.!"

"The mysterious folded-into-threes matchbook?"

Quill waved her arms excitedly. "You said that Tom was ducking an audit. That you couldn't get his personal finance statement out of him. That Gil was getting desperate, because without it the bank wouldn't give him a loan. That's fact one."

John nodded. Quill began to pace around the room. "Fact two is that the matchbook showed up on the balcony. He must have been there. He must have tried to push her over the edge."

"Wouldn't Mrs. Hallenbeck have seen him?"

"She said she was in the bathroom. He's been in our back room any number of times, delivering meat; he'd seen the drum of sulfuric acid. If Mavis called him, like she called you, he'd have a lot of time to set it up. The register's out all the time at the desk; he could have found out what room they were staying in, no problem. And he was here in the Inn while Mrs. Hallenbeck and Mavis were at dinner. And he lives right across from the pond. He said himself he was home alone. And of course, he was right there at the play."

"But what's his motive? And how would he know Mavis before she came to the Falls?"

"Did his brother work for the company?"

"For a while. He was a salesman. Most kids from Hemlock Falls end up either at the paint factory, or working for Doggone Good Dogs."

"And Mavis knew all the dirty secrets." Quill stood still, closed her eyes, and concentrated hard. "Meat . . ." she said slowly. "Tainted meat. That D.O.H. memo Marge was waving at me said something about tainted meat. E. coli bacteria. I went to Tom's to check on the shipment of beef that Meg said was spoiled. Tom got very weird about it. Doggone Good Dogs is a large customer for meat shipments. Help me out here, John."

Quill opened her eyes and discovered that Indians could turn pale.

"Jesus Christ," said John. "That's it. The beef is delivered directly to the franchise from the slaughterhouse. The franchise is the point of inspection. We had a real run on rejections from the restaurants just before I . . ." His lips thinned. "I was just about to take our inspector out to an Ohio supplier when . . ."

"Elaina happened."

"Yes."

"But what would Tom Peterson want with tainted meat?"

"Resale," John said. "Selling meat to third-world countries would give you the biggest money. Reselling to small restaurants and diners wouldn't be worth it. But if you shipped the containers offshore . . . I don't know, Quill, this is all guesswork."

"We'd need proof," said Quill. "What if we checked out Peterson's warehouse?"

"There'd be no need for him to have the trucks move through here."

"Somehow we got some of it," said Quill. "Isn't there some indication where the stuff came from? If we could find the truck that had the stuff we got, wouldn't there be some bill of lading, or whatever, that would tell its point of origin?"

"The carcasses are tagged," John said. "But there's all kinds of ways to fake the documentation. Except for the tattoos."

"The tattoos?"

"On the carcasses. They're stamped by the USDA. If they've been rejected, there's a code for that. It's inked onto the carcass. Of course, it can be cut off, but if we could find a whole carcass we'd have proof."

"I'm going over there," said Quill. "Right now. Coming with me?"

John grinned. "Sure. What the hell?"

"What the hell," Quill agreed. "Just give me a few seconds to change into my burglar outfit."

"We'll need a rope, a camera, and a flashlight."

Quill pointed to the credenza. "Camera and flashlight in there. Rope's in the car trunk."

Quill re-emerged from her bedroom minutes later dressed in a black turtleneck, jeans, and running shoes. "Do you think I should black my face?"

"No. But it's a good thing you're not blond."

The July air was soft and still. John and Quill crept to her car. After a fierce whispered discussion about who should drive, Quill started the motor, and kept the lights off until they reached the end of the drive and turned onto Route 96. Quill's heart was beating faster than usual. Her palms were damp. Her sense of time was warped; the ride to the Peterson warehouse seemed endless, but when she pulled into the gravel road to the buildings, it seemed as though no time had passed at all.

"Park behind that shed," said John in a low voice. "We'll walk up on the grass. It'll be quieter."

In the open air, Quill felt exposed, sure that a floodlight would go on and a siren sound any minute. "Over the top, Ma," she hissed at John's back. She bit her lip to keep the nervous giggles down.

"Only you," John whispered, "would do Jimmy Cagney imitations at a time like this."

The chain-link fence loomed up at them. John put both hands in the wire and leaped lightly upward. The wire *chinged* in the darkness. John clung for a moment, then moved rapidly toward the top, his feet finding purchase where Quill could see none at all. She grabbed the fence, and the wire bit into her palms. John dropped lightly to the other side. Quill pressed her face close to his. "I don't think I can climb this," she mouthed. "There's a dug-out spot a little farther down. I'm going to go under."

She followed the line of the fence to the hole where the German shepherd had made his escape, and wriggled under. Her long hair caught in the torn wires at the bottom, and she bit her lip to keep from yelling. She rolled free and got to her feet. John was already at the warehouse door.

"Can you pick the lock?" she said into his ear.

He shook his head. "It's bolted from the inside." He pointed up, then motioned her to wait. He unwound the rope at his waist and made a quick lasso, spun it rapidly a few times, and tossed it into the air. It caught on the roof joist. He pulled the rope taut, then rappelled quickly up the side of the building. The thud of his tennis shoes on the metal wall sounded like thunder. He disappeared through a ventilation duct. Quill pressed herself against the building and quivered. The moments before John opened the door seemed endless. She let out her breath, only half-aware that she'd been holding it, when she heard the quiet click of the bar being drawn from the inside door.

Moonlight leaked through the open ventilation shafts in the roof, picking out the cab of a semi truck and four Thermo King refrigeration units. John took her hand, and they made their way carefully across the floor.

"If anyone comes in," John said very quietly, "roll under the cab and stay there."

Quill nodded. "These things are locked, aren't they? How are you going to get in?"

"There's a maintenance door under the roof. Give me a leg up."

Quill crouched down and cupped her hands together. John put his hands on her shoulders, stepped into her cupped hands, and sprang up. Quill staggered back; he was unexpectedly heavy.

She waited, searching the darkness. It was quiet. Too quiet. Quill bit back hysterical giggles. Time stretched on. Suddenly, a dark shape appeared at the back of the unit. Adrenalin surged through Quill like a lightning strike.

"Safety door," said John. "You can open the units from the inside once you get in."

"God," said Quill, "did you find anything?"

A low growl cut the air. Quill's breath stopped. John grabbed her hand. The growl rose, fell, and turned into a snarl.

"The dog's back," said Quill. "Oh hell!"

John thrust her behind him. Quill could smell the rank, matted odor of an animal neglected. The snarl spun on, a sinister, mesmerizing purl of sound. John flattened himself against the metal unit and pulled her carefully with him. The snarl died. Quill could hear the dog panting. It wriggled out of the dark, ears pinned against its head, lips pulled back, eyes slits of red in the moonlight. The dog sprang. John hurled himself in front of her. Quill, her lip bloody from the effort not to scream, swung the flashlight hard and connected with the dog's thick furry skull. The animal shrieked and dropped back. The door to the unit was slightly ajar. Quill swung it open, scrabbling frantically in the frigid air. She pulled a box from the unit. It fell to the ground. Packages of hot dogs spilled into the dirt. The dog shook its head and got to its feet.

"Good doggie," said Quill, "nice boy." Moving carefully, eyes on the dog, she bent and picked up the frozen hot dogs, rolling them to the dog like bowling balls. The dog sprang on the meat, both paws protectively over the package. It glared at them. The growl heightened to a snarl, the snarl to a bark which split the air like a hammer.

"Okay," gasped John. "It's not going to charge if it's barking. Back off, slowly. Don't run until we get outside."

He forced Quill behind him. She held on to his arm; he grunted in pain, and she let him go. Her palms were wet and she smelled blood. The dog's barking grew intermittent, interspersed with snarling gulps of the frozen meat.

They reached the warehouse door. Backed out slowly. Quill slammed it shut. Lights in the trailer snapped on.

They ran. John forced Quill under the fence and followed her. Freddie Allbright shouted into the dark. Quill fumbled for the keys to the car, threw herself into the driver's seat, and was out on Route 96 before John had the passenger door closed.

"Good Lord," said Quill, when they were back in her room. She peeled John's shirt back from his forearm. "He got one good chomp in, didn't he?"

"It was worth it," said John. "There's a carcass there with the reject stamp." He waved the camera. "And I got the pictures. Now, Quill, I have a favor to ask. I'll need until Tuesday at least to go through Tom's financial records. Myles is gone until then, right?"

"Yes."

"I'm going to turn myself in. But not for another forty-eight hours. I'd appreciate it if you gave me some time."

"Gave you some time? You mean, you think I'd turn you in? John, how could you?"

"How could you not?" he said wryly. "You can't harbor a fugitive. I wouldn't let you, anyway."

"Just tell me where you're going to be, so I can report on my progress to you. I'm going down to the Marriott tomorrow, and I'm going to pump Mrs. Hallenbeck for everything that she knew about Mavis' affairs. Peterson's got to be connected with her somehow. And . . . now, this is the worst sacrifice of all, John." She paused impressively. "I'm going to eat lunch at the Hemlock Hometown Diner—Fine Food and Fast. Are you grateful, or what?"

For the first time that evening, a real smile crossed John's face. "Pretty noble, boss."

" 'Pretty noble'? I'd say that's incredibly noble."

There was a hard, imperative knock at the door.

"I didn't lock it," Quill hissed, then loudly, "Just a moment, please."

The door swung open and Mrs. Hallenbeck walked into the room. "So!" she said. "You finally caught him!"

CHAPTER 11

Mrs. Hallenbeck marched into Quill's quarters frail, rude, and triumphant. Quill, astonished, looked at her watch: six-thirty in the morning.

"You didn't answer my phone messages," said Mrs. Hallenbeck. "I thought perhaps you didn't get them. I woke up and Mavis wasn't there to get my coffee. I always have just one cup, cut with hot water before I take my walk. Would you get it for me, please?" She sat down in the straight-back chair near the easel, and frowned at John. "What are you doing in Sarah's room? Have you spent the night here?" She lifted her chin. "If you have, I shall think twice about offering Sarah the opportunity to be in my employ." She smoothed her linen trousers with a precise hand. "Now. Tell me why I shouldn't call the police immediately. Everyone has been looking for this man."

Quill, unable to think of an adequate response, heated a cup of weak coffee in the microwave and handed it to Mrs. Hallenbeck. She sipped it and gave it back to Quill with a demand for more hot water. "You are extremely dirty," she said to John. "I suppose you have been hiding out."

"Do you remember me, Mrs. Hallenbeck? I thought you might have when you checked in three days ago, but you didn't say anything. Did Mavis tell you about me?"

"I thought I'd seen you before. I mentioned it to Mavis. She said I was mistaken. I am rarely mistaken."

"I worked for your husband a long time ago, in the accounting department."

"My husband?" Mrs. Hallenbeck didn't seem to hear John. She mumbled slightly. Her eyes clouded. She held her coffee cup out to Quill with a wordless demand that it be taken away. Quill put it in the small sink in her kitchen, and wondered what to do. Finally Mrs. Hallenbeck said in a querulous voice, quite unlike her usual crisp tones, "You remember my dear Leslie? Of course, he would have been Mr. Hallenbeck to you. Well, I don't recall you specifically. There were so many employees. They all simply adored Leslie. As I did."

Quill and John exchanged a cautious look.

"I only met Mr. Hallenbeck once a year, at the company Christmas party," John said. "I saw you there, too, of course, but we never spoke before you came here."

"I should have remembered you if I had. I am frequently complimented on the accuracy of my memory."

The spell, or whatever it was, seemed to have passed. Quill wondered at the harshness of memory; a husband's suicide would be an intolerable burden to bear, the guilt horrific. Had John's quiet reference to her dead husband touched off memories too painful to bear?

The morning sun poked an exploratory finger through the southeast window. Its light made Quill aware of just how old eighty-three was. Blood, muscle, and bone all shrink, she thought, as though a tide has ebbed. Does the spirit shrink, too, and the healthy young become the senile old? Or does it wear away, as the physical does, to leave bedrock character behind? She thought of her own mother, and her mother's loving, changeless heart trapped in a body diminished, but not conquered, by age. She couldn't begin to make sense of it, and wouldn't bother.

"You have not yet given me a reason as to why the police haven't been called. What are you going to do about him?" Mrs. Hallenbeck jerked her chin at John. Her eyes were suddenly clear and shrewd. "He's wanted for murder, I understand."

"It's a mistake," said Quill. "And John's going to clear that up. He'll be back managing the Inn again. In the meantime I'd appreciate it if you wouldn't say anything about seeing him here. We're keeping it a bit quiet until John gets a chance to talk to the sheriff himself."

"So you're going to solve the murders. Huh! It's obvious to me that he did it. Killed that Mr. Gilmeister and Mavis, too." Her eyes widened in alarm. "You're not going to kill me, are you?"

"But he didn't, Mrs. Hallenbeck. He's innocent. And why in the world would anyone want to kill you?" The doubt was back; perhaps she was senile.

"I know things, of course. I know all about Mavis, and what she was like." Her hands shook. Her lips tightened in disgust. "Dreadful girl. I should have fired her years ago. I am far too tender-hearted. It's very easy to take advantage of me." She looked at Quill out of the corner of her eye. "As an example, I believe it was Mavis who staged that little—ah—incident with the balcony for the insurance money. I'm afraid she's done it before. If that is so, I have a great deal to make up for. You will, of course, present the bill for repairs to me. Sometimes I believe that all the trouble that has come since then is a result of Mavis' foolishness. If I had kept better control of her, if I had refused to allow her to go out with those appalling people, the rest of this would never have happened." She pursed her lips, and said anxiously, "You don't think people will blame me, do you? I confess to feeling a small portion of responsibility for what happened to her, and to Mr. Gilmeister. I believe the trap on the ducking stool was set for her. I should have managed her better. But I've never had a head for people like Leslie had."

Quill, reeling from the news that Mavis had made a career of conning hotels, couldn't respond for a moment.

"I don't think that's true, Mrs. Hallenbeck," said John. "I didn't know you well, and you know what employee gossip is like, but everyone agreed that you were probably better at managing the business than your husband. And successful business is all about how well you manage people. Mr. Hallenbeck always used to say that at the Christmas parties. My boss, Carl Atkinson? You may remember him. He had the greatest respect for your abilities. Someone with your kind of intelligence doesn't suddenly lose it. You can't blame yourself for Mavis' behavior."

Mrs. Hallenbeck smiled primly.

Moving quietly, as though not to startle a small animal, John got up from the couch. "Can I get you another cup of coffee?"

"Just a little, perhaps. Quite weak. I am very sensitive to caffeine."

Quill heard John making a fresh pot. She waited. She wasn't entirely sure what he was up to, with these flagrant compliments, but at least Mrs. Hallenbeck hadn't reached for the phone to call the cops yet.

"I think," said John, coming back into the room, "that Mrs. Hallenbeck could be very helpful in the investigation to clear my name."

"Oh," said Quill, enlightened. "Yes. Absolutely."

"I?" said Mrs. Hallenbeck with a gratified inflection.

"The reasons for Mavis' murder must rest in her past. I left the company a long while ago, Mrs. Hallenbeck, and I have very little idea of what went on in the past five years or so. You were there. You knew Mavis. You've even had her living with you for . . . how long?"

"Just a year. My son insisted that I have a companion to live with me."

"So, you know her better than any of us. Now, Quill and I have a suspicion that Mavis was a blackmailer."

"Wouldn't surprise me in the least," said Mrs. Hallenbeck. "I had a suspicion of that right along."

"You did?" said Quill, fascinated. "And you didn't get rid of her, or anything?"

"Well, she wasn't blackmailing me. And Mavis could be a great deal of fun, you know. Huh. Blackmail. *Who*, do you suppose?"

"That's what we were hoping you could tell us," said Quill. "Had you heard her mention Marge before, for example? In any way that would lead you to believe that she had something on her?"

"Marge Schmidt? No. I mean, of course, they worked together way back when. Margie was good, I'll give her that. Never had a proper respect for me or for Mr. Hallenbeck, but then, with that background, what can you expect? Blue-collar all the way, high-school education, no proper home life at all. But she was quite efficient at running the East Coast operations. I told Mr. Hallenbeck he should offer Marge more money when she quit. The profit margin in that was never the same after she left. I would guess," said Mrs. Hallenbeck with a twinkle, "that Mavis met her match in Marge Schmidt."

"You must have a good reason to suspect Mavis of blackmail," said John. "Think back. Any phone conversations, or letters, or people she mentioned? Especially if you've seen them here."

"Gil Gilmeister never worked for Doggone Good Dogs, for example?" said Quill. "Or Tom Peterson?"

"Oh, no. The first time Mavis met Tom was at the play rehearsal when Marge introduced him to both of us."

"And then you went to dinner with Gil at the diner."

"Yes. Marge had a loan outstanding against Mr. Gilmeister's half of the auto business. She suggested that I buy him out. Mavis knew that my investments hadn't been doing too well lately. The market these past few years has been simply appalling. I used to get quite a decent return on my portfolio, and it's been halved. *Halved.* I'm seriously considering suing my broker."

"How did you leave it with Gil?" asked John.

"I wasn't averse to a good return. I told Mavis to speak to his partner, Tom Peterson, to get an idea of what the business could do under decent management."

"Did she speak to him?"

"Yes. She was never one to let grass grow under her feet, I'll tell you that. Mr. Gilmeister, Marge, and Mr. Baumer brought me back to the Inn, while Mavis went across the green—to whatever it is that you call it. . . ."

"The Pavilion," supplied Quill.

"Yes, where the—incident occurred—to speak to Tom. Gil was most anxious for a quick decision. He didn't seem a bad sort, apart from his drinking problem. Whereas Keith . . . Tcha! A dreadful employee and a dreadful man."

"Keith," said Quill stupidly. "You mean Keith Baumer?"

"Yes, do you know him? Of course, he's staying here, isn't he? He was there when Mavis . . ." She shuddered. "I know there is a great deal of violence in the world today. I know at my age I should be more immune to it. But I cannot get the incident out of my mind. I dreamed about it, last night."

"Mrs. Hallenbeck!" Quill uncurled her clenched fists and forced herself to speak in a normal tone of voice. "Did you know Keith Baumer before you met him here at the Inn?"

"Of course. He was Meat Manager for the Central portion of the United States."

"For Doggone Good Dogs?"

"Yes." Mrs. Hallenbeck's tone was impatient. "As I was saying, I wonder if I should see that nice Dr. Bishop about my disrupted sleep. I've never needed much sleep, even as a young woman, but—"

"Mrs. Hallenbeck," said John. "You may have solved the case!"

"I?" A look of utter confusion crossed her face. "What do you mean? What did I say?"

"When did Keith Baumer work at Doggone Good Dogs?" John was marvelous, thought Quill, quiet, unexcited, yet properly deferential.

"Is it important?" said Mrs. Hallenbeck, her cheeks flushed. "You mean he and Mavis may have known each other before? That they had arranged to meet here? Of course! *Mavis* suggested we come to this place. There could be some reason for him to . . . to have made the accident happen? Well!" She was obviously pleased with herself. "I have an excellent memory. Let me think a moment. He was Meat Manager for about four years, approximately ten years ago, before your time, Mr. Raintree."

"And Mavis was Director of Human Resources at that time?"

"Not then. She was part of the department. She moved on to become Mr. Hallenbeck's assistant. Human Resources was headed at that time by a fiery young woman, most impractical. A Democrat, I believe. At any rate, Keith was fired under a cloud, as they say."

"Not embezzlement?" said John.

"No. Something to do with the way things are run nowadays. Stupid laws, when it's usually all the woman's fault. The way these young girls dress!"

"Sexual harassment," said Quill, "it figures."

"That was it. How clever of you, Sarah."

"How clever of *you*!" Impulsively, Quill walked over and gave her a hug. "This could be it, John!" She sank to her knees beside Mrs. Hallenbeck's chair. "Listen. We're going to need some time to track down Baumer's movements. My guess is that we can discover enough evidence to put him away for a long, long time."

"You mean you think he killed Mavis?" She looked old and bewildered. Her lips moved soundlessly for a moment and then she looked at John. "I thought *he* killed Mavis!"

"No, Mrs. Hallenbeck, that's one of the things you are going to help us to accomplish. Remember? We're all working together to clear John's name."

"We're investigating," said Mrs. Hallenbeck with satisfaction. "You and I."

"And John. It's almost seven-thirty now, Mrs. Hallenbeck. Why don't you go down to the dining room? Meg and I usually eat about now, and you can join us. Just ask Peter to seat you at our table. Tell him I told you to sit there. I'm going to bathe and change, and then I'll join you." She helped the old woman out of her chair and escorted her to the door. "Remember. John isn't going to go to the police until the sheriff gets back. We have twenty-four hours to solve these murders. So part of your job as a member of the investigation team is not to let anyone know that John's come back."

Mrs. Hallenbeck nodded wisely. "I'll be downstairs, waiting for you, and"—she leaned forward and whispered in Quill's ear—"I shall be on the alert for clues."

Giddy from both lack of sleep and relief, Quill collapsed on her sofa with a sigh when the door closed on Amelia Hallenbeck.

John, more reserved, said, "It's not over yet. I'm going to spend the rest of the day with my hacker friend. I'll pull Baumer's address from the register and see what we can find in his financial records. But, I don't know, Quill. This all seems pretty tenuous."

"I'll talk to Marge, Tom Peterson, and Baumer himself, after I get back from the Marriott," said Quill confidently. "John, we'll solve this by the time Myles gets back. Let me know where I can call you. Is your friend in Ithaca or something?"

"No. Here in town. I'll give you the phone number." He wrote it down and handed it to her.

"You mean all this time you've been in Hemlock Falls?"

"Yes. And yes, Quill, I was within a block of the Pavilion when someone pulled that hood over Mavis' head. To someone like Myles, I'm still the ideal suspect. I had means, motive, and opportunity, for both murders."

He left as quietly as he had come. The coffee John made was untouched. She gulped two quick cups. Then she stripped out of her robe and nightgown and gritting her teeth, took a shower as cold as she could stand it. She dressed and went downstairs to breakfast. Meg would be fascinated with recent developments.

Meg, smoking one of her infrequent cigarettes, was propped back in her chair at their table, staring at the wall over Mrs. Hallenbeck's head. Mrs. Hallenbeck herself was tucking into a soufflé. Quill dropped into the chair next to her; she noticed through her haze of fatigue that Meg's hair was flat.

"Morning, Meg."

Her sister's gaze dropped from the wall to Quill's face with the suddenness of a bird after a worm. "Have you entirely lost your mind?" Meg demanded.

Quill put down her orange juice. Mrs. Hallenbeck couldn't have told Meg about John already. "I don't think so. Why?"

"Why? WHY?! We've got *forty people* showing up for breakfast in twenty-two minutes. Expecting food, I'll bet. Does anyone need to tell the chef about forty people arriving for brunch on a Monday when we average twenty servings in the dining room total, if we're lucky? Well!?"

"Forty?" said Quill bewildered.

"If that sanctimonious prat Tom Peterson hadn't called to confirm he had reservations, they would have all shown up to eat what? What, Quill?! Do I send out to the Burger King down the road for what they laughingly refer to as breakfast croissants?"

"Dookie's prayer meeting! Meg, I'm so sorry, it completely went out of my . . ."

"Do you know what I've got in stock? Do you? Doughnuts! Four dozen Little Debbie doughnuts that the bread guy left here by mistake. Those doughnuts are so filled with artificial crap that people's arteries seize up just looking at them!"

"Meg, I'm *really* sorry. Honestly, there's been so much going on, it just . . ."

"Fell out of what passes for your mind." Meg stubbed out her cigarette, raked her hair back with both hands, and shoved herself away from the table. "This is just *it* for my reputation. Just *it*. You want me, I'll be in the storeroom. Hanging from the rafters."

The swinging door to the kitchen banged shut. Silence descended on the dining room.

"That is a very rude young woman," said Mrs. Hallenbeck.

"It's just Meg," said Quill. "You watch. She's probably whipped up a bunch of omelettes, or quiche, or Eggs à la Reine, and the deacons will think they've died and gone to heaven."

"You don't seem perturbed by the temper tantrum."

"Meg's cooking is her life. She takes it seriously. It's part of what makes her great. Running this kitchen is the best thing that ever happened to her."

"She should be married." said Mrs. Hallenbeck. "It would settle her down. You wouldn't have to spend so much time taking her abuse."

"She was married. To the sweetest man I've ever met. He was a stockbroker, and I swear, when he died I thought Meg was going to die. But we invested in the Inn together, and you wouldn't believe the change in her. It look a year or more for Meg to get over his death. The cooking was what did it."

"How did the young man die?"

"Automobile accident. He was thirty."

"She should manage on her own," said Mrs. Hallenbeck. "If you'll pardon an old woman's interference, my dear, she needs to lead her own life. You've cocooned her here."

"Do you think so?" Quill's eyelids drooped and she jerked herself awake. "Sorry, I used to be able to stay up all night in college. I seem to have lost the knack."

Mrs. Hallenbeck patted her hand. "Why don't you go up and take a nap? I will sit here and be alert for any unusual circumstances. I have a notepad, right here"—she tapped her black purse—"and I will write down anything untoward."

"You know, I think I will. I'm sorry we missed our breakfast"— Quill yawned—"but you're right. I'm hot going to be much good at investigation if I'm falling asleep on my feet. I'll just check and make sure that everything's set up in the Banquet Room for the prayer meeting, and then take maybe an hour's nap."

"I will meet you for tea," said Mrs. Hallenbeck, "at five o'clock." Quill got up, and she added, "You know, my dear, you might think seriously about retiring from the Inn. It's a great responsibility, far too much to carry alone. Perhaps we could talk, at teatime, about other things you could do. Painting for instance. When do you ever have time to paint?"

"Not much recently, that's true. But I love the life, Mrs. Hallenbeck. It has a lot of rewards that might not be obvious to the outside eye. The Inn is a very peaceful place, you know. The past few days are definitely an exception. Our guests are almost always nice, like you, and come here to relax. Like this prayer meeting this morning," said Quill earnestly, aware somewhere in her sleep-deprived brain that she was rattling on, "nice people, church people, peacefully praying in the Banquet . . ."

"Ah, Quill?" Peter Williams tugged at her elbow. Quill blinked at him. "We've got major trouble with the prayer meeting."

CHAPTER 12

"They came in a van about half an hour ago," said Peter as they walked through the lobby to the Banquet Room.

"They?" said Quill. The coffee she'd drunk to stay awake must have been decaf; either she was asleep on her feet or Peter didn't make sense. "They who?"

"Right out there." He pointed to the front door.

Quill opened the door and went outside. A white Chevy Lumina van was parked on the drive. The side panels were lettered in a screaming orange. "We Save Sinners!" Quill read aloud. "Call 1-800-222-PRAY!" She walked slowly around the van. "THE ROLLING MOSES—The Rev. William Maximilian" was printed on the hood in black Gothic letters intertwined with lightning strikes. Quill shut her eyes and opened them again. The design was still there. And the phone number. They were both very familiar.

Those pamphlets Doreen was carrying around in her apron pocket.

The license plates on the van read "Florida, the Sunshine State." The inspection sticker was a year out of date.

"Quill?" Peter called to her from the lobby. He sounded worried. "They're starting the prayer breakfast now."

Quill drifted slowly back in. "I don't think I want to know

what's going on," she said dreamily. "I'm on overload. As a matter of fact, I'm going upstairs to take a quick nap." She thought of her nice comfortable queen-sized bed with the muslin comforter and the cool white sheets.

Peter hesitated. "I'm the last one to judge by appearances . . ."

"Yes," said Quill.

"But these guys showed up at the prayer meeting this morning. They look pretty . . . unsavory, I guess you'd say. They said Doreen had called that 1-800 number and they were here to . . . to . . ."

"To what?"

"Perform an exorcism," said Peter.

"A *what*?"

"To rid the Inn of succubi and other stuff. I thought we'd better sit in."

Quill walked the short length of the hall to the Banquet Room. Most of the deacons were already there; Quill saw Harland Peterson, Elmer Henry, and Tom Peterson and smiled "Hello."

Dookie Shuttleworth stood by the open door, looking confused. He started forward when he saw Quill, took her hand, and patted it warmly. "We haven't seen you in quite a while, Quill. Please come in and join us." He drew her into the Banquet Room.

Despite the short notice, Meg and the kitchen crew had done themselves proud. The staff had set up a long buffet table; Kathleen Kiddermeister was making crêpes to order at one end. Chafing dishes filled with The Sausage, bacon, caramelized apple, puffed potatoes, and a large Heavenly Hoggs Ham were displayed along the rest of the table length. Bowls of fresh strawberries and blueberries sat in the center of round cloth-covered dining tables set with Spode china. The room was filled with most of the regulars of the Hemlock Falls Word of God Reform Church—and a few who weren't. Doreen sat at a table with Esther West. The ubiquitous Keith Baumer had apparently invited himself and was swallowing food at an enormous rate. Quill decided testily to put the cost for Baumer's breakfast on his bill instead of the one that went to the church.

She paused to reconsider. She wouldn't throw Baumer out. She'd perform a charitable act. Let Baumer horn in if he wanted to. She was becoming more and more convinced that he was the best suspect of all. She was not averse to supporting the admonition to let the condemned eat a hearty meal; the food in prison would be a punishment all the greater in contrast.

The happy, contented buzz of satisfied breakfast-eaters bathed Quill in a warm glow. "Isn't Meg terrific?" she said aloud.

"She is wonderful!" said Dookie. "After this delicious breakfast, Quill—such a generous contribution to the church, my dear—I had no idea when I mentioned our money troubles that you would give us so much!"

Quill had forgotten her promise to fund the breakfast. She waved away the uneasy feeling that she'd been giving away a lot of free food since John had been gone. "Reverend Shuttleworth, there's a van outside . . ." Quill stopped, not sure how to continue.

"Yes. The Rolling Moses." The confused expression returned to Dookie's face and seemed to settle there. "They said Doreen Muxworthy called them early yesterday to tell them a succubus was inhabiting the Inn and their help was needed to get rid of it."

"Doreen?" said Quill, keeping her voice low with an effort.

Dookie brightened. "The Reverend William Maximilian said these—er—performances have a very positive effect on the urge of the congregation to donate to worthy causes. We agreed to split the collection plate today—and since we're in desperate need of funds, Quill, I thought perhaps . . . Ah! Here is the Reverend Mr. Maximilian now. Mr. Maximilian, I would like to introduce Miss Sarah Quilliam, who has so generously donated today's breakfast."

"Good eats. God bless you, sister."

The Reverend Mr. Maximilian breathed heavily through his open mouth. He was fat, hairy, and his five o'clock shadow rivaled the late Richard Nixon's. Quill hadn't seen sideburns like that since Elvis Presley gave his farewell performance.

The Reverend Mr. Maximilian engulfed her hand with his own sweaty palm and held on to it "Revrund Shuttleworth is mighty lucky in his flock, little lady. Red hair like that means a passionate nature. A passionate nature. I hope you are going to join us for the service?"

Quill's response was a noncommittal "Um."

"And these are my helpers in the Lord. Byron? Joe-Frank? This little lady owns the Inn."

Guys a lot like Byron and Joe-Frank parked their Harley Davidsons outside the Croh Bar on Saturday nights. Joe-Frank had tattoos on his heavily muscled upper arms that said PRAISE GOD on the left and PUNISH SINNERS on the right. Byron's black leather jacket covered any tattoos he may have had, and just barely concealed a blackjack on his hip. His lack of visible skin ornamentation was made up for by the ring in his nose.

Quill nodded politely. She sat down next to Mark Anthony Jefferson, prey to misgivings.

"Fellows in Christ!" Dookie tapped a water glass with a spoon for attention. "We are privileged to bring a unique guest to our meeting today. I would like to introduce to you my brother in Christ, the Right Reverend Mr. William Maximilian. Willy Max has come to us all the way from Newark, New Jersey, where he was administering to another church such as ours—a church in trouble."

Dookie's eyes brightened as he warmed to his favorite topic. "Declining attendance, scanty donations, all these things are troubling the church here at Hemlock Falls, my friends. We have brought Reverend Mr. Willy Max here to support our spiritual renewal—to help us cast out the demons of avarice and miserliness, and invite in the angels of charity and openhandedness."

Elmer Henry cleared his throat in a marked manner. Dookie concluded rapidly, "Ladies and gentlemen, Willy Max and the Church of Rolling Moses!" Dookie led the applause and sat down.

Willy Max rose to his feet, tucked his thumbs into the substantial flesh hanging over his cowboy belt, and surveyed the room in silence. His brow beetled. His lower lip thrust out. He scanned the crowd, one by one, until the silence was utter. Absolute. The Banquet Room became as silent as a Carmelite nunnery at lunch. "I don't know about angels of charity," he said slowly, "I know about scarlet wimmin, and the Devil who sends them to torment our poor male flesh. Brothers and sisters," intoned the minister, "let us bow our heads and pray."

Obediently, the congregation bowed its head as one.

"Lord? It's me here, Willy Max. Your servant. Once again, Lord, I offer praises for the light of knowledge and redemption. Like Paul on the road to Damascus, Lord, I was struck down in stone by a vision of Hell. ('Cept it was in that CPR class in Sarasota, Lord, and not on a road a'tall.) Lord, we are poor cree-turs and wicked. We have fallen into temptation and into snares . . ."

"Snares . . ." said Byron and Joe-Frank together.

"The snares of lust." His voice rose, beefy hands clasped. "The traps of temptation, the *pits* of *promiscuity*!" he thundered. "There are those among us who have been plagued by visions of the Scarlet Woman of Babylon at night . . . is it not so, brothers and sisters?!"

"Amen," said a few of Dookie's flock tentatively.

"There are those among us who have been *inflamed* by the thought of wimmin. Scarlet-lipped, rouged, and scented wimmin."

"Amen." The chorus was swelled by several more parishioners as the plates were cleared.

Willy Max raised his hands to the ceiling. His voice slid upward like the tenor sax at the start of *Rhapsody in Blue*. "YOU HAVE BEEN DRAWN TO SALACIOUS AND HURTFUL LUSTS!"

"LUSTS!" shouted those citizens of Hemlock Falls who had finished their breakfast.

"WHO AMONG YOU IS DRAWN TO DAMNATION?"

A surprising number of voices said they were.

"ARE WE NOT ALL SINNERS IN THE EYES OF THE LORD?"

General agreement was expressed by the majority.

Willy Max began to move about the room, face red, arms waving. "BRING ME A SINNER, LORD, THAT I MAY SHAKE THE DEMONS FROM HIS SOUL! GUIDE ME, LORD! SHOW ME THE BLACK-HEARTED BUCKET OF SLIME."

"Right here!" said Doreen, pointing at Keith Baumer.

Baumer put his fork down, gazed around with a bemused expression, and said feebly, "Look here . . ."

Max raised his eyes beseechingly to the ceiling. "Who, Lord, who?"

"*Him, Lord, him!*" Doreen screamed.

"Uh, just a minute here," said Baumer. "I'm an agnostic."

"THIS IS THE ONE, REVRUND. THIS-HERE'S THE SINNER." Doreen grabbed Baumer by the tie. His eyes bulged. Doreen pulled. Baumer rose from his seat. Some hours afterward, opinion was divided as to whether this was strictly voluntary, since strangulation wasn't held to offer a genuine alternative to repentance.

"Have you lusted in your heart?" Willy Max demanded.

"Urgh," said Baumer.

"HAVE YOU LUSTED IN YOUR LOINS!" then, in an aside to Doreen, "Leave him go, sister."

Doreen released Baumer's tie. Byron and Joe-Frank grasped him by both arms, perhaps in a humanitarian attempt to prevent him from falling.

"Fall to your knees and PRAY!" hollered Willy Max. Byron and Joe-Frank assisted Baumer to his knees with good-humored alacrity.

"ooOOOOHHHLORD!" Willy Max shouted. "Shake these dee-mons from his breast!"

Joe-Frank tapped Baumer's knees with the blackjack. Baumer fell flat, face-up.

"GET THEE BEHIND ME, SATAN!" Willy Max implored the ceiling tiles. "BOYS! PUSH THE DEVIL OUT!"

Byron held Baumer's head. Joe-Frank thumped Baumer's chest and stomach with both fists, an ecclesiastical tribute, perhaps, to the CPR class where Willy Max had first received divine inspiration.

"Help-me, help-me, help-me," Baumer wheezed, in time with the thumps.

Tom Peterson scowled. Mayor Henry jiggled one large knee up and down. Harland Peterson's lower lip stuck out like a granite ledge. Dookie Shuttleworth's expression was an interesting mixture of agony and apprehension.

"Shake the demons outa him!" yelled Byron.

"Yay, bo!" Joe-Frank responded enthusiastically.

"Mr. Maximilian?" Dookie Shuttleworth got to his feet. "Mr. Maximilian!"

The bikers stopped pummeling Keith Baumer. Willy Max gazed benignly at Dookie. "Yes, Revrund?"

"The ah—devils—seem to have flown. I think perhaps if you could sit down . . ."

"There's a whole lot more shakin' to go on," said Willie Max sternly. "And a lotta prayers to holler."

Dookie picked his way apologetically to the front of the room. He gave Keith Baumer a hand and drew him up, then patted him on the shoulder. "Sit down, son."

Baumer sat down, mouth moving soundlessly.

"And you, Mr. Maximilian, we'd like to thank you for your support, but I think . . ."

"Hell!" Baumer gasped, to mildly disapproving looks from his near neighbors.

". . . it's time for you and your followers to go now."

Quill held her breath. There was a moment's tense silence. Elmer Henry, Harland Peterson, and Davey joined Dookie, shoulder to shoulder. Byron and Joe-Frank cracked their knuckles ominously. Harland Peterson reached out one large hand and removed the blackjack from Byron's grasp like a mother taking a bottle from a beloved baby.

Quill wondered if she ought to pull the fire alarm.

"Thank you, brothers and sisters," said William Maximilian finally. "We'll leave you now, to continue on our mission. Revrund Shuttleworth, with your permission, sir, we'll pass the plate before we go."

"I think not," said Dookie sternly.

There was a murmur from the assembly. Quill was impressed. She had never seen Dookie so decisive.

"You're all crazy," said Baumer, who had recovered his breath. Then, perhaps unjust in this sweeping oversimplification, "You're a bunch of fuckin' maniacs!" He stood up, swaying a little, and marched to the door; he turned and glared at William Maximilian. "You'll be hearing from my lawyers, you son of a bitch."

Quill stepped aside to let him pass. One eye rolled wildly at her. He shook his head, as if to get rid of flies. He wobbled down the hall, headed straight, Quill surmised, for the checkout desk and the Marriott on Route 15.

"Brothers and sisters," said William Maximilian, "we'll bid you all farewell."

Quill followed them down the hall, through the lobby, and out the front door. Joe-Frank, Byron, and Willy Max got into Rolling Moses. Joe-Frank turned on the ignition and gunned the motor. Rolling Moses took off like a cat with a stomped-on tail. She turned to Peter Williams, who had accompanied her, propelled, had she known it, more by concern for the look in her eye than a desire to make sure of Rolling Moses' departure.

"Bring me," she said, "Doreen."

"Yes, ma'am."

Quill took a few deep breaths. "And Peter? Mr. Baumer will undoubtedly be checking out. Will you make sure you know where he's headed? He's a material witness to the murder at the Pavilion, and Myles will want to know where he is."

"Yes, ma'am."

Quill went to her office and sat down behind her desk. Doreen tapped at the door, was given leave to enter, and came in.

"Now, I know what you're thinkin'," said Doreen engagingly.

"You can't possibly know what I'm thinking," said Quill coldly. "What I'm thinking is illegal in this state."

"First of all, the Reverend din't have those two with him in Boca Raton," said Doreen. "Honest. He had two helpers from the Sunset Trailer Park. Nice ladies." She paused reflectively. "Not as good at thumping as that there Joe-Frank." She heaved a deep sigh. "*Second* off, I din't call them."

"If you didn't, who did?" said. Quill evenly.

"I dunno."

There was a short silence.

"So, am I fired?"

Quill remained expressionless.

"If I ain't fired, you gonna fine me?"

Quill picked up the stapler and depressed the arm. Three staples littered her desktop before it jammed. She set it back into place.

"You want me to think twice about this here Rolling Moses religion," guessed Doreen.

"I don't want you to think twice. I want you to forget it. I want it totally, absolutely, entirely erased from your memory. I want no more harassing of the guests. No more Bible verses in soap on bathroom mirrors. No more bugs in the beds. I don't give a damn about the seven plagues of Egypt. This is Hemlock Falls, and there are no grasshoppers, no locusts, no SLUGS allowed. Got that?"

"Got that," said Doreen. "I was kinda going off this, anyways. Thinking maybe of taking up Amway."

"Why do you have to take up *anything*!" shouted Quill. "Especially now, when I need you and Meg to be relatively sane and even-tempered."

"Somethin' happen?" said Doreen alertly.

"Yes." Quill took several deliberate breaths. She knew Doreen to be absolutely trustworthy in every area but her brief and violent enthusiasms. Well—pretty trustworthy. On the other hand, she didn't have a lot of choice. Someone had to search for clues, and she didn't have the time. "John's back."

"Ayuh," said Doreen.

"I haven't had a chance to tell Meg. But Mrs. Hallenbeck knows."

"That one!"

"It was an accident." Quill briefly recapped her conversation with John, leaving out the personal details, but including the sudden invasion of Mrs. Hallenbeck's and her intention to investigate.

"Sheriff is after 'em," said Doreen. "We don't have much time for this here investigating."

"No, that's one of the reasons why I was furious about the evangelist. All those management courses I take, Doreen, I'm supposed to put you on probation for stuff like this. And here I am trusting you with something that's vitally important. It's John's life we're talking about here. I mean, they don't execute people anymore in this state—but another prison sentence? We have to do something."

"Even if he *had* killed that Mavis . . ." Doreen began darkly.

"Well, he didn't," said Quill, "and what we have to do is look for that bolt. The one from Harland Peterson's tractor. There's no way it could have fallen into the river, Doreen—and I know Myles and his men didn't pick it up at the scene. So the killer's got it. Motives for Baumer are piling up. I want you to pay particular attention to his room when you look."

"You got it. I'll search the whole dang Inn."

"If you find it, be sure not to pick it up with your bare hands," warned Quill. "There may be fingerprints. Use your work gloves and put it into a Baggie or something. And, Doreen?"

"Yes'm."

"There's really no need to mention this to the sheriff, or Deputy Davey, or any of the patrol guys."

"You don't want them to find out? I thought we were helpin' them."

"Well, we *are*; it's just that some people might think it was interfering with an official investigation or something." Aware that her management training courses were stern in the admonition to at all times maintain an executive demeanor and that she was, perhaps, being a bit tentative where direct and aggressive behaviors were what led to Maintaining Control of Employees, Quill folded her hands on her desk and said briskly, "Then you'll report back to me the instant you discover something *essential*. It isn't worth it to waste time coming to me with *nonessential* information, like Keith Baumer's swiped towels, or something. Come to me when you discover facts that will help us get this investigation over."

"Like the instant I do?" asked Doreen, her eyes on the window behind Quill's desk.

Quill, nettled by the inattention to her best executive style, snapped, "Immediately."

"Like, 'essential' is when the sheriff gets back?"

"Myles?" Quill shook her head. "Now, that's what I mean by essential versus nonessential, Doreen. Myles is a person who's nonessential to our investigation. The discovery of the bolt that clears John, that's essential to the investigation."

"Got it," said Doreen.

Quill began to recover her increasingly elusive sense of being in charge. She'd tackle Tom Peterson first; the prayer breakfast would be breaking up in a few minutes, and she could ask him to stay behind for an extra cup of coffee. Then the Hemlock Diner and Marge and Betty Hall. Then on to the Marriott, where Baumer had presumably settled after his expressed displeasure with the comforts offered by the Inn, and finally, Baumer himself.

She, John, and Doreen would have the case wrapped up and solved in no time.

On the way back to the prayer breakfast, Quill ventured a whistle. It stopped in mid-trill at the sight of a familiar broad back in trooper gray at the front desk. So *that's* who Doreen had seen out the window.

"Myles?"

He turned, frowning.

"Sarah."

"Sarah" was not good. The last time Myles had called her Sarah was early on in their relationship when he'd been contacted by the SoHo precinct station about a misunderstanding over a large number of parking tickets she'd forgotten to pay when she left Manhattan to move to Hemlock Falls. She had lent her car for a few weeks to a fellow artist who was down on his uppers, and between explaining that no, they weren't involved any longer and yes, it was pretty typical of Simon to pull stuff like that, it took a few days before she went back to being Quill.

"Your note said you wouldn't be back until tomorrow."

"I got lucky. Forensics owed me a favor or two, and the autopsy on Mavis was done early this morning. I was on my way back to the station when Davey radioed the complaint to me. What's going on, Quill?"

"Complaint?" Quill craned her neck around Myles's height and pulled a face at Dina, who rolled her eyes expressively.

Myles flipped his notepad open—just for effect, since she'd never known him to forget a thing. "Christian terrorism?"

"That Baumer! Dina! I thought he checked out."

"Nope. Sorry, Quill. He made a lot of phone calls, though."

Quill groaned.

"What's been going on?"

Quill explained, downplaying the chest-pounding to a few brotherly taps.

"I'm going to see him. I've got a couple of questions for him myself. I'll be a half hour or so. Will you be here? I want to talk to you."

"I want to talk to you, too," Quill said glibly, "but I have a few things to do today in the village. Can we meet for an early dinner?"

"Let me rephrase my request," said Myles cordially. "I will see you here in half an hour. Consider it a date, Sarah. The official kind."

"Oh." Quill pulled her lower lip. "Does this mean you won't tell me the results of the autopsy on Mavis?"

"Sure, I'll tell you the results of the autopsy on Mavis. The media already has the results of the autopsy on Mavis because some damn fool at the morgue leaked the results. So you can hear it from me, or you can wait for the six o'clock news. Take your pick."

"I'd rather hear even the weather report from you than some boring old reporter," said Quill earnestly, "or even the price of hogs, or arrivals and departures at La Guardia. The sound of your voice alone sends . . ."

"You do want to drive me to an early grave," said Myles. Quill wondered if the noise he was making really came from grinding his teeth, as she thought it might. "Mavis had ingested a large amount of alcohol an hour or two before her death. But the amount of alcohol wasn't sufficient to cause a blackout; she also took ten milligrams of Valium about eight o'clock that morning. The Valium and the alcohol weren't sufficient to cause unconsciousness, either."

Quill wondered for a wild moment if the Scotch Bonnet pepper had made her pass out.

"She had either taken—or someone had given her—five grains of Seconal, probably in a drink twenty minutes or so before she went on as Clarissa Martin. There was so much junk in her system, it's hard for me to believe that she didn't drown in the ducking pool.

"Seconal," said Myles, "means we can prove premeditation." He looked at her grimly. "You stay here. I'll be back after I talk to Baumer."

Baumer had been drinking with Mavis just before she went on. Quill caught her breath. "Why don't I come up with you?" said Quill. "We can give him the old one-two."

"No."

"Won't you need a witness?" asked Quill. "You know, in case Baumer tells you one thing in private and then lies to you later?"

"No."

"But, Myles, Baumer was with Mavis the whole morning before the play. He ate breakfast with her. He showed up at the play with her."

"And Baumer came down to the station at noon to put up bail for his wife," said Myles. "He was at the station until well after two-thirty. He left to walk down to the Pavilion—a twenty-minute walk from the station, Quill—and I saw him leave."

"But he could have gotten a lift and gotten there early."

"Mavis hadn't had any beer; four or five mint juleps, judging from the stomach contents, and only beer is served at History Days. You know the ordinance. She must have gotten them from a private source, or a bar. Baumer wasn't carrying a Thermos when he left the station."

So Nate would know who she'd been drinking with.

"So Nate will know who she'd been drinking with, since the Croh Bar sure as hell doesn't make mint juleps. Quill, you are *not* to question Nate. Do you understand me? I love you. I will also put you in jail for obstruction of a criminal investigation."

" 'Oh God of love, and God of reason sa-a-a-y,' " sang Quill, " 'which of you twain shall my poor heart obey?' "

Myles grinned. A reluctant, very small grin, but a grin nonetheless. "Stick to the contralto roles. Your voice cracks on the B flat. Gilbert, not to say Sullivan, would spin in his grave."

Quill bobbed a mock curtsy. She watched Myles jog upstairs to beard Baumer in his den, then went into her office to place a call to Nate.

"Nope, sorry, boss," he said. "Bar was busy at one, but I remember the damn mint juleps. I didn't make any on Sunday."

"Was Kathleen waiting tables? She sometimes makes up orders when we're busy."

"Nope. Two of the kids from Cornell were on the early shift. And I don't let them behind my bar."

Quill hung up the phone and pulled out a pad of paper.

She wrote: "Bolt. Must find."

Then she wrote: "Seconal: Who has?"

Followed by: "Follow the money!"

Then: "More matchbooks?"

And last: "Mint juleps: Who can make?" Then she drew a chart.

DUCK POND

	OPPORTUNITY	MOTIVE
Marge	Yes, if she and Mavis were together	Set up beforehand to get Mavis?
Tom Peterson	Yes	Business/tainted meat?
Baumer	Yes	Mavis blackmailing him?

She scrawled John's name in pencil, so she could erase it, and listed Yes, for opportunity and motive.

She scribbled and drew little arrows under "Motive." She was certain that the duck pond murder had been aimed at Mavis, not Gil. She considered the possibility that Mavis had murdered Gil, and that Marge had murdered Mavis in revenge. The chart exercise began to resemble her note-taking as Chamber secretary. She got irritated, balled it up, and threw it in the wastebasket. Mavis couldn't possibly have wanted to murder Gil, at least not until she'd gotten her hands on his car business.

A new chart would serve a more useful function.

THE PAVILION
MOTIVE (ALL HAD OPPORTUNITY)

Marge	Yes, if she stole $300,000; if Mavis was blackmailing her?
Baumer	Yes, if Mavis was blackmailing him?
Tom	Yes, if Mavis had leaned on him to give bigger cut of proceeds from car deal? Query: tainted meat?

Then again in pencil, for John, "Yes." She promptly erased it.

Quill perused her chart with a sense of accomplishment. She had a very satisfying list of suspects. It was becoming more and more clear to Quill that Mavis had drawn the unfortunate—although still revolting—Keith Baumer to the Inn the same week as she and Mrs. Hallenbeck had planned to stay. She was probably going to hit him up for an increase in the blackmail money. Stranger things had happened before, Quill mused. Far, far stranger things. If she could get Marge and Baumer to answer the right questions, she could solve this case.

The door to her office opened. Harvey Bozzel poked his head inside. "Hel-lo!" he said.

"Harvey? What are you doing here?"

The look (resignation mixed with hurt) on Harvey's face told Quill that this was probably his usual reception, and she hastily apologized.

"Yes. Our meeting was for ten o'clock, right?" Harvey edged into the office. He was carrying an oversize briefcase.

"Oh," said Quill, "the ad campaign for the Inn. I forgot . . . I mean, I'm delighted to see you."

"You'll be delighted to see *these*," said Harvey heartily. "Now, I never got a chance to properly pitch my first and, I believe, my best campaign for the Inn, Quill. If you could sit right here—" He grasped her by the shoulders and piloted her to the couch. Quill sat down. Harvey swept the top of her desk clear and set up an A-frame display. Next to it he placed a battery-operated tape recorder. "I have to show you the print ad first." Harvey flipped the A-frame open. A pen-and-ink sketch of the Inn, which, Quill admitted, wasn't half bad, covered the upper two-thirds of the display.

"What's that big wooden thing in front of the Inn?" Quill asked.

"I'll get to that," said Harvey. "What do you think of the copy?"

Quill leaned forward and read:

THE INN AT HEMLOCK FALLS!
- Four-Star Food (word of Edward Lancashire's intent must have gotten around.)
- And splendid views (true, thought Quill)
- Luxury rooms (absolutely)
- Splendid yews (?)

"There's no yew here, Harvey," said Quill.

"I couldn't think of anything to rhyme with Hemlock," said Harvey, "and it's a mnemonic aid. You know what a mnemonic aid is, Quill?"

"Yes."

"It's a rhyme that helps your customers remember your product. Very important, mnemonic aids. Essential principle of good advertising. Now," said Harvey expansively, "here's the best part." He reached over and turned on the tape recorder. There were a few bars of jazzy music, then a bark, then a "shit" from someone who sounded like Harvey. "The dog," said Harvey apologetically. "I recorded this at home." He fast-forwarded the tape. "Here we go.

I picked up one of those musical scores from a catalog. You know, where you can sing the lyrics along to the background music? Sounds pretty professional, if I do say so myself."

The tape played the intro to "Rock Around the Clock." A voice (Harvey's) sang the opening bars, with verve, if not with accurate pitch, and ending with *smash*! instead of the expected chord in A major.

"What's that smashing sound?" said Quill.

"The rocks! You know! On the barn door that squashes Clarissa. Wait-wait-wait. You gotta hear the verse after the intro."

Harvey's recorded voice finally reached twelve o'clock, assured his audience that there were "Rocks! Around! The! Park! Tonight!" and then attacked the verse:

> "*When you walk on through that old Inn door*
> *You'll find gourmet food and historic lore*
> *And yeah! There's more. That old barn door*
> *That turned into a coffin floor . . .*"

Quill reached over and turned the tape recorder off.

"See, what I figure is this—" said Harvey excitedly. "We get that barn door from the sheriff's office. You know that Tom Peterson would have burned that sucker if Myles hadn't gotten it away from him and held it for evidence? But the publicity, Quill! Think of it! It's the most fabulous PR campaign I've ever . . ."

"Stop," said Quill.

Harvey stopped.

Quill took a deliberate breath. "Now. Explain to me slowly. Myles has the barn door?"

"Evidence," said Harvey, knowledgeably.

"And Tom Peterson tried to burn it?"

"He was upset, he said. Want'd to get rid of the dang thing."

"Hmm," said Quill. "Now that is *very* interesting."

"Am I interrupting anything?" Myles eased in the door. "Hello, Harvey."

"Hi, Sheriff. Just presenting some new advertising ideas to Quill, here."

"And I'm thinking very hard about buying them, Harvey." Quill avoided Myles's penetrating eye. "Why don't I call you later this week, and we can discuss it further?"

Harvey shook hands with Quill and Myles, then gathered up his A-frame and his cassette recorder.

Myles waited until he was gone, then said bluntly, "What did you do last night?"

Taken aback, Quill found herself stuttering. "I went to bed."

"When did you last see John Raintree?"

Quill's face turned red. She could feel it.

Myles shuffled through the papers Harvey had shoved into an untidy pile. He picked up her charts. "Little sketchy," he said, "but not bad. The thing about a murder investigation, Quill, is just one thing. Facts. And more facts. You're right about the bolt and the Seconal." He read on. "I take it Nate didn't make any mint juleps yesterday. Who told you to 'follow the money'? John, I suppose. That's good advice, sometimes, but nothing's as direct and unambiguous as hard evidence." His eyes softened. "Sit down a minute, honey."

Quill sat.

"Doreen found two of the items on your list."

"The bolt? And the Seconal? So it *was* Baumer."

"She found them in John Raintree's room."

Quill sat upright, as though she'd been shot and didn't realize the extent of the damage. "That's impossible. I searched . . ." She stopped.

"I asked Davey to pick John up at a house on Maple about fifteen minutes ago."

Quill stared at Myles. He came and sat down beside her on the couch. "I'm going to place him under arrest on suspicion of murder, Quill. I wanted to be the one to tell you. I didn't want you to hear it over the grapevine. God knows there's enough gossip in this town." He put his arm around her and rested his chin on the top of her head. "I called Howie Murchison. He's going to represent John until we can get an expert in criminal law in from either Rochester or Syracuse. There's a guy named Sam Monfredo who's got an excellent reputation. We'll try and get him." His arm tightened. "Are you crying?"

"No!" said Quill. Myles handed her his handkerchief. She blew her nose. "This isn't right, Myles."

"I agree with you. It's too easy. It doesn't smell right. I swear to you, Quill, I'll do everything I can to keep the investigation open. But there's just too much evidence for me to ignore."

"I'd like to know when you had the time to get it," said Quill bitterly. "You've spent half the time in Ithaca. Have you got a spy here, or something?"

"I much prefer anger to tears," said Myles. "I'm glad it doesn't take you a long time to bounce back."

"You're evading the question. How did you know John was at that house on Maple? Don't try and tell me you put Davey on stakeout. He's on traffic patrol every single day of the week, and he has to count on his fingers to figure out if people are over or under the speed limit"

"No, it wasn't Davey."

"Who then?"

"We've been working with a private investigator from Long Island. Doggone Good Dogs hired him to tail Mavis. Apparently they were pretty convinced that she'd had the money—they just haven't been able to find it. And they're pretty sure she's involved with something else."

"The tainted meat," said Quill. "You know about that?"

"Edward's been tracking her and Tom Peterson for several months. He alerted the office a few days before . . ."

"Edward Lancashire!"

"Uh, yeah."

"Edward Lancashire's a private eye?" Quill slumped back and closed her eyes. "Oh, my God. We thought he was from *L'Aperitif.* Myles, Meg's been feeding that guy like a king!"

"He's a pretty good guy. It won't hurt him."

"You knew all along," Quill accused, "and you let us think he was the . . . the . . ."

"It was harmless, Quill. And if either Eddie or I had told you the truth, you would have kept it to yourself, and six of your closest friends."

"That's not fair," Quill raged. "It's a chauvinist remark of the most insulting kind."

"I didn't tell Davey, either. He's as upset with me as you are. And only three people knew that John was back, right? Doreen, you.

The widow. It's impossible for you to keep anything to yourself, Quill. Part of it's that you're too trusting, and the other part . . ."

Quill's voice was dangerous. "The other part?"

"That you're too trusting." He smiled again and kissed her. "We're going to do what we can for John. And I've got to go now." He eased himself off the couch. "Quill, do me a favor, please. Stop these amateur efforts at solving the crime, will you? Leave it to the experts."

"These are the experts that have John Raintree in jail for murder," said Quill, "based on what?—a bolt, some drugs, a prison term . . ." She trailed off.

As he left, Myles said, "That's the hell of it. Quill. There's always the chance that he did do it."

"Stubborn!" Quill shouted after him as he left "That's the second thing, isn't it? Stubborn!"

CHAPTER 13

Quill's first impulse was to march down to the jail carrying a sign: FREE JOHN RAINTREE. Maximum effect would have been created by a subheading: "Another Wounded Knee? Police harassment MUST be stopped to preserve our freedoms!" but she doubted Myles's wholehearted support.

She looked out the window of her office; the parking lot was less than half full, which meant Dookie and the deacons had left, along with her chance to nail Tom Peterson.

Her second impulse was to see if Meg was over her prayer breakfast hissy fit. The sooner she knew about Edward Lancashire, the better.

Meg was humming "I Come to The Garden Alone" while chopping herbs. White beans soaking in a crock on the butcher's block, and several pounds of The Sausage gave Quill two clues to her sister's mood: hymn and cassoulet meant a return to the traditional.

"How's by you, Hawkshaw?" Meg scattered the herbs into the sausage and vigorously worked the meat.

"Fine," said Quill cautiously. "How's by you?"

"I felt a definite impulse for Basque tonight," said Meg dreamily. "It's soothing. Satisfying. Besides, I'm getting tired thinking up new haute cuisine for Edward. It's time to give him the good straight stuff."

"The prayer breakfast buffet was terrific," said Quill. "You heard about the Rolling Moses?"

Meg grinned. "Anybody checked out yet?"

Quill hadn't thought of the effect of the Christian Terrorists on the rest of the guests. "I know Baumer hasn't. Do you think we'll lose people?"

Meg shrugged. "Probably. They've canceled History Days, right?"

"You seem pretty sanguine about this. I mean, between the practical joke about the cancellations and the murders, we're going to be hurtin' turkeys."

"Won't last," said Meg confidently. "I'm guaranteeing you a rave review in *L'Aperitif*. Edward thinks my cooking is fabulous."

This did not bode well for Myles's revelation. Quill weighed the relative merits of Meg's temper tantrum over Edward Lancashire's imposture—although to be fair, he'd never claimed to be anything at all, much less a food critic—against Meg's gradual realization that the *L'Aperitif* review wasn't going to appear. And of course, Quill thought optimistically, the magazine would have to review them sometime; they always checked on the progress of their starred restaurants. It was not at all cowardly, she decided, to neglect to mention Edward Lancashire's real occupation. Diplomacy was the province of successful innkeepers as well as long-lived kings.

"Myles is back early, Meg. The autopsy showed enough Seconal in Mavis' system to sink a tugboat. The stomach contents showed the Seconal was in the mint juleps she was drinking just before the play. He says this shows premeditation."

"Really?" said Meg. "That's interesting."

"There's something else." Quill told her of John's return and his suspicions about the embezzled three hundred thousand dollars.

"Jeez." Meg began stuffing the sausage meat into the casings. "Maybe you're right, after all."

"You think John's innocent, too?"

"I never thought he was guilty. All I said was that your reasoning was screwed up. The facts say John did it. But it doesn't seem to me that murder is a rational act—you know what I mean?" She waved a half-stuffed sausage aloft. "It's like recipes. People think they can learn to cook if they follow a recipe *exactly*. Remember the Armenian dentist?"

"Haaiganash? The one who thought she'd have a more profitable career as a pastry chef? Yeah. You threw her out of the kitchen."

"She didn't have any soul," said Meg. "She thought cooking was a science. She didn't understand the basic ambiguity of cooking. Something goes into the recipe you can't account for. Cooking isn't rational. Neither is murder."

Quill, who thought this was a somewhat dubious simile, ate some parsley.

Meg worked in silence for a moment "You know what I think?"

"What?"

"You're exactly right about the mint juleps. Find out who made those mint juleps for Mavis, and you've got the murderer."

"I've already decided mint juleps are the essential clue," Quill said testily.

"There's one other thing." Meg took the colander of beans to the sink and rinsed them. "A recipe's a pattern of ingredients. Everything that goes into it reacts so that you get something else. The whole is greater than its parts."

This foray into Jungian theory impressed Quill not at all. "So?"

"So look at everything that's happened since Mavis got here. All of it resulted in murder."

"All right," said Quill irritably. Meg hadn't been out of the kitchen once the entire four days, except for the play, and here she was giving Quill advice about the investigation. "Mavis shows up. She falls off the balcony. Mrs. Hallenbeck says this is a little con game she cooked up, which, for all we know, she's been running for ages. John disappears. Gil drowns in the duck pond, presumably because somebody set a trap for Mavis. Mavis gets squashed under a bam door. John comes back. We learn that Mavis is a blackmailer who's probably been getting money from Keith Baumer and Marge Schmidt for years. We learn that Mavis very probably approached

Tom Peterson with some scheme for buying the business, which Marge may have discovered . . . God! It's Marge. It has to be."

Meg looked at her. The water ran unheeded over the beans. There was a distant look in her eye. "Who called up our customers and told them the Inn was closed? Who called the Christian Terrorists to hold an exorcism at the Inn, which can only result in the worst possible publicity for us? Who poured the sulfuric acid around the balcony, which resulted in even worse publicity for us?"

"Marge?" said Quill doubtfully.

"She could have done stuff like that any time these years past," said Meg. "There's something odd going on, Quill. None of this fits. If it were a soufflé, it wouldn't rise more than an inch."

Quill glanced at the kitchen clock. "It's twelve-thirty. The lunch crowd will have left Marge's diner by the time I get there. It'll be a perfect time to talk."

"You're not going to eat there, are you?"

"Do you think she'll try to poison me?"

"Not on purpose," said Meg seriously. "Besides, it's too public."

Quill parked in the bank's lot, near the sign that said "FOR HEMLOCK FALLS SAVINGS AND LOAN BANK CUSTOMERS ONLY! VIOLATORS WILL BE TOWED," walked to the diner, and peered in the plate-glass window. Two of the Formica-covered tables were filled; the rest were littered with the small detritus of a busy restaurant after a herd of customers has left.

Marge slouched against the cash register, talking to Mark Anthony Jefferson. He smiled at Marge, teeth white in his dark face, and shook her hand with the enthusiasm of a banker happy with his deposits. Quill pushed the glass door open and went in.

"Hi, Mark, Marge."

"Hello, Quill." Mark offered her a prim smile and a genial nod. Quill wondered if bankers took affability courses. *The object of this course is smile wattage: the small depositor, or the cash-poor, should be greeted with the proper degree of reserve, say seventy-five watts.*

Mark shook hands with Marge a second time. "Drop by any time, Marge. Be happy to talk about that transfer. I'm sure I can get that extra point for you. Quill? I wonder if we could meet this week sometime to talk about who is going to take over from John. He's a great loss to the business, and we'll want to be sure that whoever replaces him has the same level of expertise."

Quill muttered, "It's a little soon, Mark," and both she and Marge watched him leave.

"Good fella," Marge said. "Knows his onions. What're you here for?"

"Lunch," said Quill.

"Yeah?" Marge eyed her with a certain degree of skepticism "Betty!" she hollered suddenly. "You wanna bring out a couple of Blue Plates? Have a seat, Quill."

Quill sat down at one of the small tables. Marge swung a chair around backward and straddled the seat, elbows on the back. She and Quill regarded each other in a silence that stretched on until Betty plunked a platter in front of each of them. The Monday Blue Plate was meatloaf and French fries smothered in gravy. A small dish of green peas accompanied the platter. Quill took a bite of the meatloaf. Her eyebrows went up.

"Marge, this is delicious."

Marge methodically cut both potatoes and meat into small squares, and just as methodically ate each fork-sized bite.

Quill tried a French fry. Both it and the gravy spooned over the contents of the plate were as delicious as the meat.

Marge swept her plate clean of gravy with a soft roll slathered in butter.

Quill started on the peas. "These aren't canned," she said in surprise. "They're fresh."

Marge burped. She held up a pat of butter; its significance was momentarily lost on Quill. "Good food is good business," she said, "but if you want to know somethin', leave this out of it."

"I'm not buttering you up, Marge. I mean it" Quill hesitated, then said, "I'll bring Meg up here, if you don't mind. She never lies about food. And you'll believe her, if you won't believe me. It's wonderful."

"Huh!" said Marge. Her cheeks turned pink. She grinned and shouted over her shoulder, "Hear that, Betty? Miss Fancy Food here likes the grub!"

"I more than like it," said Quill honestly. "I love it."

"Not everything has to be goormay," Marge drawled.

"It doesn't. Marge, can we talk a little bit about what's been happening over the last couple of days?"

"If you want. Been good for business, I'll say that for it. Everybody comes in here to talk. And when they talk, they eat. Good for Chris Croh, too. Gossip and drink are a good mix."

"How well did you know Mavis? Well enough to know her personal tastes? What she liked to eat, what she liked to drink?"

"What she liked to eat and drink?" Marge, for once, seemed at a loss for words. "I dunno. She didn't much like that French gunk you serve up there at the Inn."

Quill put this down to Marge's automatic rejection of Meg's cooking, and waited.

"And drink? Hell, I don't know that either." Her heavy brow creased in thought. "I know she asked for some damn fool thing at the Croh Bar Saturday night. Chris had to look it up in the bar book, which always pisses him off, and then he couldn't make it because he didn't have lemon or peppermint or something."

"So you've never made a drink for Mavis?"

"Served her beer," said Marge. "What the hell is this about, anyways?"

"Did Mavis take prescription drugs? Or ever ask you for prescription drugs?"

"I don't know what you're gettin' at, missy, but I can tell you one thing right now. I take aspirin. That's it. You ask Doc Bishop, you think I'm lying. I," said Marge proudly, "barf up most anything that ain't natural. Penicillin, and that. Barf it up right away." She patted her ample stomach. "I'm that delicate, Gil used to say to me."

"Did you—correspond with Mavis on a regular basis, say once a month?"

Enlightenment spread over Marge's face like the sun coming up over the gorge. "You mean you wanna know if she was blackmailing me as well as John?"

"You knew about that?"

"Not till she came here. But I had my suspicions. I was Northeast regional manager for Doggone Good Dogs for pretty near five years. Worked my way up from waitressin'. Heard a lot of gossip about Mavis, of course. Never could prove anything. And what the hell did it mean to me, anyways? She was a lot of fun when she came into the district to do the personnel stuff. We'd go out, have a few pops—Mave knew how to have a good time.

"I decided to come back here and open my own business. Didn't much like having to run things other people's way, wanted to do it on my own; I grew up here"—Quill caught the unspoken message: unlike you and your sister, who moved in and tried to take over— "and this is the natural place for me. 'Sides, Betty and I'd been best friends in high school, and you can't run a place like this all by yourself.

"Anyhow, Mavis came to see me just before I quit the company. Said the home office wanted to keep me, and she offered me a raise and all that. I said no thanks.

"Didn't hear much from her a-tall until she hove into town with that Mrs. Hallenbeck. You know what it's like seein' somebody from way back. You may not have been all that good buddies, but there's some stuff to talk about. That's about it."

"Did you know John well?"

"He was after my time at the company. Heard about it, of course. Not every day the company has an employee what turns out to be a murderer. He come in here on his way back from Attica, as a matter of fact." She eyed Quill sharply. "You know about that?"

"Yes," Quill said.

"Headin' on out to Syracuse to look for a job there. We got to talkin'. Don' matter to me a guy that's been in the joint, so we cleared that up right away. We swapped a couple stories about the company. Things changed quite a bit after Armour bought us out, and ol' John got a couple of laughs out of it. I needed someone to do the books once a month; not enough for a full-time job, and Gil, bless his soul, needed somebody, too, and he always liked John and felt he had to make up for his sister bein' a vegetable and all. The two of us offered him wages for a couple of hours a month work. Then you placed that ad in the paper for a business manager, and he just settled in."

"And you know about Mavis being a blackmailer?"

"Do you know that old girl wanted me to come in on it?" Marge's astonishment was genuine. "We got to swapping stories

Saturday about how we each was doin', and she said she was on to a good thing. Wanted me to cut a separate deal with Tom if the old lady coughed up the investment, as kind of, what'd she call it, a fee for brokering the deal. Then we'd split it." Marge shook her head. "Mavis couldn't spit straight, much less do a good honest deal. Just wasn't in her nature."

"John said she insisted the letters with his money be addressed to Scarlett O'Hara. Some Southern belle."

"You mean like that movie, *Gone With the Wind*?"

"Yes. Marge? What happened when you refused?"

Marge shrugged. "Guess she talked to Tom herself. I tolt her to pound salt. I wasn't so hot on Gil gettin' out after that. I mean"— Marge colored painfully—"I wanted the old biddy to cough up the cash for the dealership. We had this idea, Gil and me. He'd get enough cash together to pay off that Nadine and he'd come into the business with Betty and me." She cleared her throat with an attempt at carelessness. "Said he'd always wanted a wife who'd help him, you know. Rather than being a drag. Didn't matter I was no beauty queen, he said; I had something better than that. I had some sense." Marge crumpled a paper napkin in her fist and blew her nose. "Said our kids would have some sense, too."

Quill bent her head and concentrated on the meatloaf. She waited a few minutes, then said, "I thought maybe you killed them, Marge."

"Me!" As she'd hoped. Marge's outrage doused the tears as effectively as a candle snuffer. "You gotta be kidding!"

"Well, it seemed logical," Quill apologized. "I mean, all this weird stuff's been going on at the Inn, and Meg and I thought you might want us out of business, and then Mavis shows up and you two are connected in what appears to be a shady deal over tainted meat and . . ."

"Tainted meat?" Marge demanded.

Quill, alarmed, not trusting Marge, stammered, "And I thought maybe *you* thought John would be a good scapegoat, because of what you knew about him."

"Jee-sus Kee-rist and eight hands around," said Marge, appearing to drop the tainted meat issue. "What the hell do you think I'm made of?"

"I didn't know," Quill said frankly. "Any more than I knew what kind of cook Betty is. She's good, Marge. I should have been down to your diner before. It's my fault that I never made the effort. But I will from now on. And so will Meg."

"Good," said Marge flatly.

Quill extended her hand cautiously. "I apologize, Marge."

Marge shook it. Her hands were calloused. "Don' mention it."

Quill swallowed the last of the peas, then leaned forward and said, "I've been doing a bit of a . . . well . . . an investigation into this."

"Do tell," said Marge sarcastically. "Myles know anything about this?"

"Yes," said Quill, which was the literal truth. "Actually, he doesn't approve, but Marge, this stuff can't keep up. I mean it can't be good publicity for the town, no matter what Harvey Bozzel says."

"That boy's a bozo." Marge rubbed her second chin with one massive hand. "So now that I ain't a suspect, who is?"

"Keith Baumer."

"That one!" Marge appeared to consider this. "He's an asshole, that's for sure."

"Do you think Mavis could have been blackmailing him?"

"Hell, yes. Wouldn't put it past her. And that jerk's done enough in this life to be ripe for it."

"You remember him from Doggone Good Dogs?"

"What female there didn't!" Marge scowled. "Went after two of my girls in the region. I would have been next, excepting he finally got his ass canned. I'll tell you something, though, never met anyone with as good a taste buds. Good nose, too. Could sniff one twenty-pound pack of froze hamburg meat and tell you what kinda cow it come from."

"John told me three hundred thousand dollars had been embezzled from the company just before the acquisition. He also said you had one of the best heads for business of anyone he'd ever met. Do you know of any way we could find out if Baumer had that money?"

Marge, preening at the compliment to her business acumen, was by now as chatty as Kathleen Kiddermeister's mother, who'd been known to talk to telephone solicitors for hours at a time. "Lemme think on it. To tell you the truth, I don't know what the hell happened to Baumer after the company canned his ass. If John wasn't in the slammer, he and I could probably figure it out. Be best if we knew where Baumer came from, and who he's working for, though."

"He's with some sales convention at the Marriott," Quill said. "His booking got messed up and that's why he landed on us. I'm going over there and see if I can find out a few facts."

"He use a credit card to pay for the room?"

"Traveler's cheques," said Quill regretfully. "And Peter deposited them in the bank Friday afternoon, so we can't trace him through the registered numbers. But if I can find his boss at the Marriott, I'll bet I can get a little more information."

"Maybe I'll truck on down to the bank. See if Mark'll let me on to the computer," said Marge. "If the two of us put our heads together, we can figure out somethin'."

"Then you don't think John did it, either?" said Quill.

"Hell, no." Marge reconsidered this. "At least, if he did, he musta had a damn good reason."

"I can't think of any reason that would force John into premeditated murder," said Quill. "I understand—at least I think I understand—the reasons that drove him to the defense of his sister. But this is different."

"It's all different," said Marge obscurely. "And it's all the same."

Quill left the diner with hope burgeoning, if not exactly springing, in her breast. Marge maybe was innocent of involvement with Peterson's scam. Quill would bet a year's income from the Inn that Marge was innocent of murder.

The Marriott lay twelve miles south of town on Route 15, and served both Ithaca and the surrounding small towns. Traffic was light, and it took Quill less than twenty minutes to pull into the hotel parking lot. She knew the manager from meetings of the local Hotel and Motel Association meetings. A big, tall, open-faced man in his thirties—and single. Completely charmed by him after they met, Quill had bullied Meg into attending the next Association meeting with her, only to discover that Sean was quite happily gay. The three of them made a point of getting together for lunch at least once a month.

She asked for Sean at the reservations desk, and the ubiquitous Cornell student trotted cheerfully away to find him. The hotel business would certainly suffer if Cornell ever decided to move to, say, Seneca Falls or Waterloo.

"It's Sarah Quilliam!" Sean greeted her with a smile.

"So it is." She raised herself on tiptoe and kissed him. "How's the hotel biz?"

"Fine. Fine." He looked at her sidelong. "I understand you're making a killing."

"Yes. It's why I'm here."

"Serious discussion? Come into my office, said the spider to the fly." She followed him into the manager's quarters, impressed as usual by the array of computers, the NYNEX phone system, and the middle-class expensiveness of the furniture and carpeting.

"Can I get you some juice? Coffee?" he asked, as they settled into comfortable chairs.

"Not now, thanks. What you can do for me is give me some information about a guest. Or rather, a non-guest."

"Can't do it, Quill." He shook his head. "HQ would send small fierce people down with large weapons to kill me."

Quill pulled her lip. "You've got a sales convention here?"

"It's listed right outside on the welcome board. AmaTex Textiles, out of Buffalo . . ."

"Do you have a list of convention attendees?"

"As a matter of fact, I do. You can pick one up in any of the meeting rooms they're using, and I just stuck one in my file. Hang on a second." He reached one long arm out to a filing cabinet, and within a few seconds, pulled a manila folder out of the drawer. "Here it is."

The names were listed alphabetically. Quill scanned the B's. There was no Keith Baumer listed.

"Are all the convention-goers listed, Scan, including the ones that don't have rooms here?"

"I believe so. But we were able to accommodate everyone that came in from out of town."

"Are you at capacity?"

"About seventy-five percent. Good for us this time of year."

The address and phone number of AmaTex headquarters was

listed at the top of the page. "Can I use your phone to make a call to AmaTex?"

"Of course." He eased himself out of his chair. "Tell you what, I'll go get us some Coke."

Quill waited until his office door swung silently shut behind him. She dialed the 716 area code for Buffalo, hesitated briefly, then the rest of the number.

"AmaTex Textiles," said a young voice.

"Could I speak to Personnel, please?"

"Human Resources, Compensation and Benefits, Pension Funding, or Training Department?" the voice asked.

"Um. I'm checking out a résumé. I wanted to confirm a prospective employee's background."

"One moment, please." Canned music blared onto the line: Tom Jones singing "The Green Green Grass of Home." Quill held the phone away from her ear.

"Department of Human Resources. This is Miss Shirley, may I help you?"

"Miss Shirley, this is Sarah Quilliam. I have an application for employment from a gentleman who lists AmaTex Textiles as a reference." Quill felt a modicum of remorse. If word circulated among Baumer's employers that he was job hunting, he'd probably lose his current job for certain.

"And?" said the insistent voice of Miss Shirley.

"I'm sorry. His name is Keith Baumer. I asked him for a résumé." Quill said hastily, "I wouldn't want you to think he was actively job hunting or anything."

"How do you spell that last name?"

Quill spelled it, waited the requested one moment for Miss Shirley to come back on the line, and smiled at Sean as he came back into the room bearing a tray.

"We have no record of a Mr. Keith Baumer ever being employed by AmaTex Textiles," said Miss Shirley.

"Are you certain?" said Quill. "How far back do your records go?"

Miss Shirley chose to take Quill's question as an affront to the efficiency of AmaTex Textiles' record-keeping. "Our files go back fifteen years. They're computerized. And who is this calling again?"

Quill apologized for the inconvenience, thanked her, and hung up. She turned to Sean. "Have you had any other sales conventions here in the past couple of weeks?"

"Nope. Not a one. What's up?"

"I don't know, Sean. This just doesn't make any sense."

CHAPTER 14

Driving back into town, Quill tried to make sense of Baumer's lie, and couldn't. Had Mavis summoned him to Hemlock Falls to increase the blackmail payment? Was the sales convention a cover for involvement in the spoiled-meat scam? Were he and Mavis partners? Quill worked through this possibility. Baumer and Mavis could have made a practice of bilking inns and hotels of insurance monies. Quill got dizzy at the prospect of a litigious Baumer. She grasped the steering wheel firmly, and forged ahead. If so, there was likely to be a record through the cross-index maintained by insurance companies to track fraud. The person who would know about that would be Edward Lancashire.

If Baumer had made phone calls canceling the Inn business, it was out of malice. Assuming that Baumer and Mavis were partners, why would Baumer murder her? Could Baumer have found out about Mavis' separate deal with Tom and murdered her to keep Mavis from running off with the loot collected from the insurance scams?

This, Quill thought to herself, was pure supposition: Myles was right. What she needed were facts. Who placed the bolt and the Seconal in John's room? Who fed Mavis those mint juleps?

She parked at the Inn's back door, and went to find one of the people who could give her the answers.

Edward Lancashire was sitting at a table in the bar, feet propped up on a neighboring chair, contemplating a painting she'd finished shortly after the Inn had opened. It was an iris, a miniature Dutch variety spread across the canvas in a tidal wave of purple and sun-yellow.

"A lot of relief in that," he said as she sat down. "Retirement must have seemed good to you, then."

Quill blushed. "I didn't realize private eyes were art critics, too."

"I looked at the signature and date before I sat down," he said. "Not too hard to figure out."

Quill laughed. Nate brought her an iced tea and refilled Edward's coffee. "I quit because I peaked," she said frankly. "There weren't any more edges for me to push."

"There was a nice article in *Art Review* about the abrupt truncation of a promising career." He smiled at Quill's surprise. "Private eyes read *Art Review*, too. I don't know much about art . . ."

"But I know what I like," Quill finished for him. "I could feel it, the fact that the work wasn't growing. To stick with it and repeat myself"—she shuddered—"kind of a little death."

His eyes wandered back to the painting. "You may have been wrong."

"I had an idea for the heart of a hybrid tea rose yesterday," she admitted. "A Chrysler Imperial. It's a dumb name for an artificial organism. It was to have been a painting awash with irony and the angst of modern life."

He raised an eyebrow. "Do you miss it?"

Quill nodded. 'The thing that's important about the rose is that I'm starting to think in concepts again."

"So it's a hiatus. Not a total break."

"You're right," said Quill surprised. "Although I hadn't thought of it that way. Somehow, that's a very reassuring idea. Thanks."

"You're a nice woman, Quill."

Quill, momentarily tongue-tied, finally said, "Well, you are definitely not a nice guy. How could you trick my poor sister?"

"So Myles told you I'm not the food critic for *L'Aperitif*, incognito."

"Yes."

"I take it you haven't told her yet. My food is still ipecac-free. I'd appreciate it if you wouldn't, at least until this is all over."

"What is it, exactly, that's going to be all over?"

"You mean the investigation?" He sighed, straightened up in his chair, and put his feet on the floor. "I uncover corporate crime. Stolen product. Embezzlement. Industrial espionage. When Armour went through the discovery process to purchase the Hallenbeck Franchise, the auditors discovered a total of three hundred thousand dollars had been drained away from the corporate coffers over a period of time. That's not a lot of money, and normally, in a deal the size of this one, Armour wouldn't have brought someone like me in . . ."

So that's why he can afford the Armani suits, Quill thought.

". . . but the search for the funds led to something a little bigger than that." He stopped and looked into his coffee cup.

Quill didn't move, afraid that he wouldn't tell her.

"The origin of the three hundred thousand was interesting. Eventually, we discovered that two managers in the meat division had been diverting meat that didn't pass USDA or Hallenbeck's inspection to third-world countries."

"Contaminated meat?"

"Yeah."

"Any idea who's behind it?"

"Maybe."

Edward needed a nudge. "Baumer!" said Quill. "That weasel."

"Keith Baumer?" Edward grinned. "You really have it in for that guy, don't you? I haven't ruled out Baumer. But the scam occurred both before and after his short career at the company. Mavis, on the other hand, knew all about it. We also know that the three hundred thousand passed through her hands, but it disappeared about a year ago. I haven't been able to track it."

"Do you think you're close?"

"To finding the money? My client's not all that concerned about recovering the cash, although it'd help pay my fees."

The Armanis, thought Quill, must be his knock-around clothes. She'd love to see what he wore when he had to dress for the occasion. She examined him through narrowed eyes. Edward, she decided, was not to be forgiven his deception. His client was going to be *very* impressed when she and John turned up with the photographic evidence of Peterson's involvement.

"We haven't enough to convict the people responsible for sending the contaminated food overseas." He paused. "A number of children died after eating the meat. Believe it or not, my client's got a conscience. Not all that usual with big business. It's a bit of a pleasure, working for them. They aren't as concerned with the money as they are with nailing the people responsible for the shipments. And we were all pretty sure that Mavis knew who they were. That's why I came here. I was going to offer her a deal; the company wouldn't prosecute for the embezzlement if she'd give us some names."

"And did she?"

"Somebody took care of her before I could get to her. I tried to set up a meeting with her Sunday morning, but it was hard to find Mavis alone."

"Do you think these people are in Hemlock Falls?" said Quill cleverly.

"I'm pretty close to finding out. But Mavis got herself murdered for another set of reasons entirely. At least, that's what Myles and I think."

"So you've talked to Myles about this. You don't think John was responsible, do you?"

"I don't know," said Edward. 'There's a lot of physical evidence against him, Quill. And he had a pretty compelling reason."

"What! The two hundred dollars a month he sent to that miserable Mavis?"

"No. How much did he tell you about the death of his brother-in-law?"

"That guy Jackie?" Quill settled back in her chair, trying to remember. "He said that he found his sister in the kitchen . . ."

"How did he know she was in the kitchen?"

"He got a phone call."

"Did he ever find out who?"

"He didn't say that he did." Quill, utterly bewildered, pulled her lower lip.

Edward took her hand and held it. "John was the one who initially reported his suspicions of the tainted meat scandal to company headquarters."

It took Quill a minute. She felt her face pale, and withdrew her hand from his. "You mean he was set up?"

"There's a strong suggestion that these people waited for an opportune moment."

"Oh, God," said Quill. "Poor John."

"I have an idea that John suspected it, too. He had quite a bit of time to think about it, in prison."

"And Mavis was the logical informant."

"That's occurred to both Myles and to me."

Quill shook her head. "I refuse to believe it."

"Myles said you were stubborn."

"*Excuse* me!" an outraged voice demanded.

Quill jumped.

Mrs. Hallenbeck stood in front of them. The Glare was in full force, "We had an appointment, Sarah. At five o'clock, for tea. It is now five-fifteen. You have kept me waiting." The old lady's face was pink with outrage. "I went to the kitchen, and waited there, thinking perhaps you were wasting your time with that sister of yours. You weren't there. I searched the entire dining room and the lobby, and I find you here, with this man. Do you have an explanation?"

"I'm sorry, Mrs. Hallenbeck," said Quill. "It's been a long day, and it slipped my mind."

"It slipped your mind! I've mentioned before that I'm considering offering you Mavis' job. Do you really want to jeopardize that offer?" Her eyes filled with sudden tears. "I have something to report on the progress of our investigation."

Quill, whose temper had been rising in a way quite unbecoming to an innkeeper of principle, was disarmed by this last statement. She smiled a little ruefully at Edward, then got to her feet. "Why don't we go into the kitchen to have our tea?"

"The kitchen?"

"None of the guests are allowed there," said Quill comfortingly. "Just our special friends. We'll have Meg make us something delicious. And then we can pool our information."

Meg had been out jogging, and her face was flushed and sweaty. "I just stopped to make sure everybody was here and the breads were rising properly," she said as Quill steered Mrs. Hallenbeck into the kitchen. "I'm going up to take a shower."

"Would you have time to make us some tea?" said Quill. She sent a pleading glance to her sister over Mrs. Hallenbeck's head.

Mrs. Hallenbeck settled herself into the rocker by the fireplace. "We are going to discuss the progress of our investigation," she said complacently. "I will have hot water only. Out of the tap. With a little lemon."

"Oh, okay. I could use a cup of coffee." Meg filled the electric teakettle, then her own espresso machine with spring water, and cut three slices of seedcake. "So, how'd it go with Marge?"

"You wouldn't believe that food, Meg. It's great."

"It is?"

Quill nodded emphatically.

"You're not serious. Jeez!" She bit her forefinger. "How great?"

"Oh, it's quite good," Mrs. Hallenbeck assured her. "Perhaps you could get a job there after the Inn closes."

"The Inn is not going to close," said Meg, astonished. "What are you talking about?"

"Well, that's what I have to report." Mrs. Hallenbeck opened her purse and withdrew her little notebook. "I made notes every half hour. My memory," she admitted, in a rare moment of humility, "is not quite what it was." She cleared her throat. "I sat on the leather couch in the lobby. From there, you can see people going to all parts of the Inn. I thought it would be a good observation post."

"Yay, Miss Marple!" said Meg, by now fascinated.

"As I sat mere, precisely fifteen people checked out of the Inn early. They were alarmed by the presence of what one party referred to as 'Devil worshippers.' "

"Oh, no!" said Quill, dismayed.

"You see my concern for the Inn," said Mrs. Hallenbeck. "I did not record the times of those departures. There were," she said frankly, "too many.

"You, Sarah, left the breakfast table at eight twenty-two. You stated you were headed for the prayer breakfast, and I had no reason to assume you were lying."

"Thank you, ma'am," said Quill. The sisters exchanged grins.

"I finished my breakfast and went to the, er, ladies room." Mrs. Hallenbeck flushed slightly. "When you drink as much hot water as I do, it is convenient to be near a WC. It is very good for the kidneys, however. I took up my post at nine-ten. At nine-eleven, three thugs came out of the Lounge, followed by you, Quill, and Peter Williams. You didn't notice me, which led me to conclude that my choice of observation post was correct."

"Willy Max and the Jerks for Jesus," said Quill.

"The guests will be back," said Meg. "Just wait for the review from *L'Aperitif*."

"You came back three and a half minutes later. You went into your office. Forty-five seconds after that, Keith Baumer crossed the landing upstairs and went down the hall. I got up to look to see who it was. He returned two and one-half minutes later. Seven minutes later, Doreen Muxworthy went into your office. Eleven minutes later, she left and went upstairs. Then, a young man named Harvey Bozzel knocked on your door and went in."

Meg rolled her eyes at Quill and poured herself a cup of coffee.

Mrs. Hallenbeck primly took a sip of hot water, replaced the cup in the saucer, and took a delicate bite of seedcake. "How am I doing so far?" She twinkled at Quill.

"Go on," said Quill. "I think you may have something here."

"Four minutes later Doreen came downstairs, carrying something in a plastic bag. She went out the front door. About five and one-half minutes after that, the sheriff came in the front door and went upstairs. He was upstairs for about ten minutes. Then he came down and went into your office."

"The bolt!" Meg cried, and took a triumphant gulp of coffee.

Quill yelled, "The pills. Baumer planted the pills in John's room! We have proof!"

Meg howled, "Jeez!" and spat the coffee into the sink.

"Good heavens!" said Mrs. Hallenbeck disapprovingly.

"What?" said Quill.

"Something miserable's in that damn coffee. Darn! I swallowed a slug of it, too. Yuck!"

"Sit down, Meg." Quill pushed her sister anxiously onto a stool. "I'm calling Andy Bishop."

"Why?" Meg demanded.

"Why? There's that damn Baumer wandering around the Inn putting God knows what into things, that's why. He knows we're on to him, Meg. Do you feel all right?" Quill, dialing Andy's number on the kitchen phone, looked worriedly over her shoulder.

"I feel fine," said Meg. She went to the espresso maker and looked critically at the coffee grounds. She held them to her nose and sniffed them, then poked them experimentally with one finger.

"Don't do that!" said Quill. "You're messing with evidence."

"Quill, if it'd been poison or something, I would have been dead by now, and I feel perfectly fine. Don't fuss!" She picked up the jug of spring water she used to make the coffee, unscrewed it, and sniffed the contents. "I can't smell anything. Whatever it was, I didn't get enough of it to matter."

A nurse-like Voice put Quill on hold for several long minutes. Suddenly, Meg yawned.

"Andy?" said Quill into the phone. "Could you get the ambulance over here? I think Meg's swallowed something. What? I don't know. Just a minute."

Meg sat down on the stool. Her eyelids drooped. She yawned again, prodigiously.

Quill set the phone receiver on the counter and put her finger into the coffee grounds, then tasted them. She picked up the phone. "Very alkaline. Very bitter. What?"

She heard the sound of a body falling. She whirled and shouted into the phone. "Andy! Get here right away! She's passed out!"

CHAPTER 15

Hair flatter than Quill had ever seen it, Meg lay prone in the hospital bed.

"I'm fine!" she insisted. "I am just bloody *fine* and I want to get out of here!" Her voice was hoarse from the esophageal tube that had been stuck down her throat. An IV drip ran into her left forearm. Quill was convinced that as soon as Myles, Andy, and the nurse were out of the room, Meg would detach the IV and escape out the hospital window. The Hemlock Falls Community Hospital was small, a single-story building tucked modestly behind the high school. The sounds of an evening baseball game came through the open window; to get back to the Inn, Meg would have to cross the field. Quill had taken Meg's jogging clothes and put them in the car, doubting even her sister would have the nerve to stalk across the diamond in an open-backed hospital gown. But she wasn't absolutely sure.

"Just for observation. One night. That's all. Then you can bounce out of here in the morning," said Andy Bishop.

"I didn't swallow enough of that stuff to kill a cat, much less an adult human being," said Meg angrily.

"The mineral water had a four-grain solution of Seconal dissolved in it," said Andy patiently. "You don't weigh much more than one hundred pounds, Meg, and you were dehydrated from running. That's why you passed out, and a patient who's been unconscious has to stay twenty-four hours for observation. Them's the rules." He hung her chart at the foot of her bed. "Why don't you settle down and go to sleep? We'll be right outside, in the hall."

"So you can discuss who dunnit without me? Not on your life." She sat up in bed. Quill folded one of the pillows in half and stuck it behind her back.

"You did not," Meg informed her, "save my life."

"No," Quill said. "But I thought I did at the time."

Meg squeezed her hand. "Were you scared?"

"I was scared." Quill squeezed back. "Not on your account. The paramedics were, guess who?"

"Not Maureen and Doyle?"

"Who else? Maureen's tickled pink. Guaranteed this woman will never ever eat in our dining room, but this is the most attention the Department of Health has paid her in years. She loves us. Oliver kept making noises about how this call interrupted him and his girlfriend and giving me hopeful looks as we passed the Croh Bar."

"It was the volunteer firemen you sent to the Croh Bar," said Meg. "You gave the volunteer ambulance a straight donation." She yawned. Quill glanced at Andy, who smiled reassuringly. "Quill, Myles. You know the thing that strikes me about these murders?"

"What?" Myles sat calmly in a green plastic chair near the open window, his arms folded across his chest.

"That they were so inept."

"Yes. There'd be no guarantee that the front loader would actually kill Mavis. The Pavilion was jammed with four hundred people, any one of whom could have noticed a live body on the sledge before the barn door was lowered onto her."

"And the balcony."

"Yes. If Mavis had gone over, she would have landed in five feet of water. Enough to break her fall, not enough to drown her."

"So you agree with me." Meg yawned again, hugely. "And as for me, that Seconal wasn't enough to stun a pig, much less Mad Margaret." Her eyelids drooped.

Myles smiled a little at Quill. "Mad Margaret?"

"We were Gilbert and Sullivan fans as kids. You know Mad Margaret."

He nodded. "From *Ruddigore*."

"Myles?" Meg forced her eyes open. "I'm not going to sleep until you tell me I was right. About who dunnit."

"You were right, Meg." Myles got up and drew the pillow from behind her back.

"Meg was right!" demanded Quill. "What do you mean? Who is it? I thought that I was doing the investigation!"

Meg slid down flat on the bed. She smiled seraphically at Quill. "Mrs. Hallenbeck, stupid." She closed her eyes and was almost instantly asleep.

"Mrs. Hallenbeck?" said Quill stupidly. "You said that just so she'd shut up and get some rest, didn't you?"

"Let's go out in the hall," said Andy.

They left the hospital room and went into the corridor. Quill could see the front lobby from where they stood. Mrs. Hallenbeck, who'd insisted on calling a taxi and accompanying Quill to the hospital, sat upright in one of the green plastic chairs. She was reading a magazine. From this distance, Quill couldn't tell what it was.

Myles leaned against the wall and regarded the elegant figure. "Meg's right."

"You're telling me that an eighty-three-year-old widow who's richer than all of us put together killed Gil and Mavis Collinwood?"

"She's got it right on the third try," said Myles. "And she's not richer than all of us put together. She's living on the three hundred thousand dollars she took from Mavis, who basically stole it from her in the first place."

"You mean because she was part owner of Doggone Good Dogs?"

"No. Because Mrs. Hallenbeck was ripping the company off by selling inferior quality meat to third-world countries. Mavis started her blackmail routine with the couriers, first Jack Peterson, and then, when he was killed, Tom Peterson; she had no idea what she was up against. When the couriers reported Mavis' attempts at blackmail to our lethal widow, Mavis didn't have a chance. Mrs. Hallenbeck swooped in, took the money, and convinced her she'd be jailed for blackmail. The two of them had a brief career bilking various hostelries across the country of insurance monies. That was confirmed this afternoon, too."

"I don't get it," said Quill. "What about the money from the black market sales?"

"Leslie Hallenbeck made restitution before he killed himself. Eddie thinks he knew his wife was involved, and so do I. We talked to John this afternoon, and he helped us confirm it. Hallenbeck didn't have much of an alternative. He couldn't turn his wife of sixty years in to the police. But he could give their personal fortune to the parents and relatives of the people who died after eating that meat. And he could take his own life. Which he did."

"But none of this is a reason for her to kill Mavis. They're all reasons for her to keep Mavis alive," said Quill.

"Oh, she needed Mavis to take care of her. But she found a replacement. And when Mrs. Hallenbeck wanted something, she didn't let much stand in her way."

"Oh, no. No, Myles. No."

"Let's go into this examining room," said Andy. He craned his neck; the elderly figure was still there. "She'll wait for you."

Quill walked blindly into the examining room, Andy and Myles behind her.

Myles leaned against the wall with a sigh.

"There were three things that stood in Mrs. Hallenbeck's way to having you substitute for Mavis. Mavis herself, the Inn, and the two people you most cared for, John and Meg. That first night, she summoned Tom Peterson to her room. We don't know what they discussed, but we can guess that it had something to do with the shipments. Peterson left the matchbook there. It's funny about nervous habits. At any rate, after he left, Mrs. Hallenbeck made her first attempt at murder. I had my suspicions then."

"You didn't say anything to me," Quill said indignantly.

"You noticed the scratches on Mrs. Hallenbeck's cheek? She sent Mavis down to find sulfuric acid in the storeroom. John saw her near the kitchen, remember? Mavis poured it around the wrought-iron balustrade. But when the time came to stage the accident, Mrs. Hallenbeck pushed her. Eighty-three's pretty frail, and that ended the first unsuccessful attempt."

"But why didn't Mavis *say* something?" Quill demanded.

"Because Mrs. Hallenbeck could send her to jail. She knew all about Mavis' blackmail schemes. And Mrs. Hallenbeck was right, you know. Mavis was a stupid woman.

"The second attempt you know about. Motive's the most important thing in a murder investigation, Quill—even more than the facts. You were right again—Baumer, Tom Peterson, and Marge all had the opportunity to remove that bolt from the front loader, but their motives were nowhere near strong enough. Mavis was a petty thief, and a small-time blackmailer. Mrs. Hallenbeck herself would have been a more likely candidate for murder. Baumer denies Mavis was blackmailing him—but I have a strong hunch she summoned him here, just like she contacted John. Baumer makes enough money so that the two or three hundred dollars a month Mavis demanded wouldn't have proven a strong enough motive to kill. And Marge is just plain too smart to have made an attempt that wasn't one hundred percent sure. Now, if Marge decided to commit murder, I wouldn't bet on my being able to prove it, but I'd bet a lot on the surety of the victim's demise.

"Mrs. Hallenbeck did get Mavis, of course. The day of the play, Mavis walked from the Inn to the Pavilion with Mrs. Hallenbeck. They'd been in their room drinking mint juleps. Mavis', of course, were laced with the Seconal Mrs. Hallenbeck takes to sleep."

"She said she never takes drugs," said Quill.

"She's a pretty good liar. Consistent, and with an excellent memory," said Myles.

"I checked the prescription register," said Andy. "She's had a refillable prescription for years."

"The barn door. Why did Tom Peterson try to burn the barn door? When Harvey told me that, I was *sure* . . ."

"Edward planted that idea, when the four of you were walking back to the Inn the day of the murder. Guilt's an odd thing, Quill. There could be all sorts of logical explanations about why a shred of clothing was caught on a splinter. But Mrs. Hallenbeck wanted no clues. So she ordered Peterson to burn it.

"So Mavis' death took care of obstacle number one," Myles continued. "Obstacle two was the Inn itself. You leave your guest register out for everyone to see far too often, Quill. She noticed it the morning they checked in. She always gets up early to walk every day. Saturday morning, she got up, took the register, and had time to make enough phone calls to clear the Inn's business for the rest of the summer."

"But a man claiming he was John Raintree made those calls," said Quill.

"You didn't listen carefully to what Dina said, or question your agents closely. Each of the guests who received the call got a message from someone calling on *behalf* of John Raintree. I checked with several of them, and each confirmed it'd been an elderly woman."

"I thought it was Baumer. I was *sure*."

"Nope. Although you'd given him enough reasons to do it by that time. Then Doreen's latest craze provided another opportunity to wreck the business; Mrs. Hallenbeck got a note shoved under her door, too, of course. All the guests did. And each of the notes listed the 1-800-PRAY toll-free line. Mrs. Hallenbeck called that one right from the Inn. You'll find it in the telephone records."

"And John?"

"She planted the bolt and the Seconal in his room, once you explained to her that this was the evidence the police needed."

"Ouch," said Quill.

"And of course, she knew about Meg's private stock of coffee. While she was waiting in the kitchen for you to show up for tea, she dosed the spring water."

"And Meg figured it out?"

"It was Meg who pointed out that Mrs. Hallenbeck had fixated on you," said Andy Bishop. "And she, of course, found the attempts at destruction both clumsy and ineffectual. The work not only of a rank amateur, but of the kind of pathology that may come with great age."

"You can't tell me that she's senile. Or has Alzheimer's," said Quill.

"No," said Andy. "We don't really understand what age does to the individual, Quill. But there's sufficient research to establish that in some kinds of personalities, age strips away the normal inhibitors to sociopathic behaviors. Mrs. Hallenbeck was undoubtedly as autocratic and self-focused in her youth as she is now; she just doesn't have the barriers to acting out that she had while young."

Quill took a moment to absorb this. "What's going to happen?"

"Eighty-three's pretty old for a trial," said Myles. "And our hard evidence is slim to nonexistent. We have the bolt, which has been wiped clean of fingerprints, but the chain of evidence has been broken. We can't establish for certain that it was in her possession, or even that she was at the park. We have a better chance with the Seconal; she's refilled the prescription a sufficient number of times to have the quantities on hand needed to drug Mavis and Meg's jug of spring water. Again, a good defense attorney would make mincemeat out of the evidence chain. It's all circumstantial."

"The phone calls to the Inn's guests? The call to Willy Max? Those aren't crimes?"

"Malicious mischief," said Myles. "A misdemeanor."

"So what now?" Quill looked at the two men.

"Eddie's client is Mrs. Hallenbeck's son." Andy Bishop cleared his throat. "He's agreed to commit her to a very comfortable institution. She'll be taken care of, confined, of course, and I will see to it that a complete record of what's happened here is in the psychiatrist's file."

"Have you met him, the son?"

"Just talked to him on the phone." Myles's expression didn't change much, but Quill knew he'd found either the man or the conversation distasteful. "He's made the arrangements to have her picked up. Refused to come himself. There's a secure room here at the hospital. Andy's arranged to have her checked in. I'll have Davey at the door until the morning. Just as a precaution."

"Does she know?" asked Quill.

"We were hoping," said Myles, "that you would tell her." He put his arm around her. She leaned into him and closed heir eyes.

Quill walked down the hall and sat in the chair opposite Mrs. Hallenbeck.

She set aside the magazine. *Vogue*, Quill saw.

"And how is your sister?"

"She'll be fine. She wants to go home now, but hospital rules say she has to stay. She's asleep."

"We'll go back to the Inn, then? I would like some dinner. It's late. But I suppose someone on the kitchen staff can be gotten up to make something."

"Dr. Bishop is a little concerned about you," said Quill carefully. "He's arranged for you to stay here tonight, too."

Mrs. Hallenbeck smiled. "Such a nice young man. I always find it easier to get along with men than with women, don't you?"

"No," said Quill truthfully. "I think it's about the same."

"I appreciate Dr. Bishop's concern for my welfare. I don't know how it is, but young physicians always seem to take the greatest care of me." She laughed girlishly. "I've been frequently complimented on my state of preservation, I suppose you'd call it. But I would prefer to go back to the Inn. You take such good care of me, my dear."

Quill took a long moment to reply. "The sheriff would like you to stay, as well. He called your son earlier this evening, and your son has made some very comfortable arrangements for you. The . . ." Quill stumbled, "hotel where you will be staying will send a limousine for you in the morning. He's concerned for your comfort now that Mavis isn't here to see to you."

Mrs. Hallenbeck's eyes clouded. Her lips trembled. The light from the lamp at her elbow strengthened the lines in her cheeks and forehead. She leaned forward and hissed, "You have no idea what it's like, being eighty-three. But it will happen to you, dear. Just like it's happened to me."

Once again Quill thought of her own mother, her loving spirit still strong in a body fine-honed by the years.

"No, it won't," she said.

CHAPTER 16

A July thunderstorm was brewing in the west when Quill brought Meg home from the hospital. It just goes to show you, Quill thought, the perversity of nature. After four days of hell, things were looking up. Doreen had seen to the discreet and tactful (she claimed) removal of Mrs. Hallenbeck's luggage and Mavis' effects. The American Association of Swamp Reclamation Engineers had called and fully booked the Inn for a week in August, which would help offset the fiscal consequences of yesterday's guest exodus. Best of all, Keith Baumer was checking out. Quill, heretofore neutral on the topic of religion, sent a prayer of thanks skyward, toward the thunderheads boiling over the top of the Falls, followed by a promise of a healthy donation to the American Association of Retired Persons, whose members had proved the exception to Mrs. Hallenbeck's homicidal tendencies, and who would undoubtedly be back, like the perennials, next spring.

"A trial would have been tough," she said to Meg as they sat in the kitchen watching the rain lash the windows.

"They came to get her while I was waiting for you in the hospital lobby." Meg poured white vinegar for the third time into her expresso machine in an effort to remove all traces of the Seconal. She was not, she'd informed Quill tartly, over her sister's protests, going to dispose of a perfectly good piece of equipment just because an inept murderer had used it in an attempt to kill her.

"Not so inept, with two deaths on her conscience. Did she seem . . ." Quill trailed off.

"Seem what? Remorseful? No. Upset? No. Tell me goodbye and thanks for the best meals she's ever had for free? No." The expresso machine hissed, and Meg fussed with it, not meeting Quill's gaze. "I'll tell you what you ought to do, though. Give Myles credit for calling in as many favors as he could to avoid prosecution and a trial. He knows how bad you feel, Quill. A trial would really do you in."

Quill rubbed the back of her neck. She'd dreamed, the night before, of Mrs. Hallenbeck soundlessly screaming her name, over and over again, and of long-nailed fingers shredding the canvas of the Chrysler Rose.

The back door slammed. Doreen stumped in wearing a yellow slicker. Water streamed off the hood. "Wetter'n hell out there," she grumbled.

"I thought this storm hit because you prayed for rain yesterday," said Meg.

"Thought they mighta pumped some of that sass out of you along with the dope."

"No," said Meg truthfully, "I think they added some."

"Wunnerful." Doreen hung up the slicker, tied her apron around her waist, and sat down at the butcher block. "Got time for coffee," she suggested. "Only one room is still occupied. Baumer."

"*Everybody* left yesterday?" said Quill.

"Pret' near. It was the ambl'ance comin' and goin' that done it, I think. When it come for that one"—she pointed an accusing finger at Meg—"lady in one-o-six said if they were tryin' to kill the cook now, it was time to leave."

Quill braced herself. For the past four days, Meg had met prophecies of financial disaster with the sunny confidence of a high-caliber chef cooking for the most influential of captive audiences: the food critic from *L'Aperitif*.

"John will think of something," said Meg. "If not, we can always purchase Harvey Bozzel's rewrite of 'Rock Around the Park' and depend on advertising to bring the customers back."

"That's 'clock,'" said Doreen loftily.

"No, it's not," said Meg. "It's sung by the Chili Stompers on the Three Bean label. Quill sang it to me in the hospital. I told her I'd heard it before."

"Sass," grumbled Doreen.

"Wait a second," said Quill. "What about our four-star review in *L'Aperitif*?"

"Now that you know who Edward Lancashire really is," said Meg airily, "I don't have to keep up the charade anymore."

"You thought Edward was the food critic from the very beginning!" said Quill. "You cooked your brains out for that guy!"

"You've got to be kidding." Meg scowled. "I knew the second meal I created that he wasn't any gourmet critic. The man's a peasant. I was just keeping your spirits up by going along with your delusion."

"Admit it, Meg. He had you going."

There was a suspicious tinge of pink in Meg's cheeks, but she said obstinately, "I knew all the time."

"You did not!"

"I did, too!"

"Good to be home," said John Raintree as he came through the dining room doors. Myles was with him. Both men were soaked. "Not as quiet as your jail though, Myles."

"Has it ever been?" Myles shook the water from his raincoat and hung it on the peg near the back door. He came up to Quill and stood close.

She looked up at him and touched his cheek. "You're soaked. Meg's got coffee on. You both should have something hot." Myles settled into the rocker, declined the expresso with a grimace, and accepted a cup of the Melitta drip.

John sat on the stool next to Doreen. "Quill, I'm not much good at thanks . . ."

"Neither is she," Meg said briskly. "What we want to know is how all this came down while I was getting my stomach pumped."

"Marge and Doreen," said Myles.

"Marge?" said Quill. "Doreen?"

He shot her an amused look. "What I'm about to tell you is not true. It's a guess. If it were true, I'd have to make a few arrests, for illegal hacking, unlawful entry into private data, and violation of several interstate banking laws." He stretched his long legs in front of him. "I gather that after your visit to the diner, something clicked in Marge's brain."

"It did?" said Quill. "I told her Mavis always referred to herself as a modern-day Scarlett O'Hara. Marge got this funny look in her eye."

"It would have helped Eddie a lot to know about Scarlett O'Hara," said Myles. "Even her son didn't know where Mrs. Hallenbeck hid her money, although he guessed that Mavis was concealing it for her. After you left, Marge hared off to solve the mystery of the missing three hundred thousand. She walked over to Mark Anthony Jefferson's bank. The two of them got on to the phone and into the computer, and they tracked down information that turned most of Eddie's guesses into evidence. Mavis Collinwood, as Scarlett O'Hara and with a fictitious social security number, had close to four hundred thousand dollars in a checking account in Atlanta. The only authorized signatory to the account was Amelia Hallenbeck. Incidentally, six payments averaging twenty thousand dollars each had been paid into the account by various hotel and motel insurance companies over the past eight months. This cross-checks with the information Eddie had from the Insurance Index about fraudulent claims the women had been making."

"So he knew Mrs. Hallenbeck was guilty!" said Quill. "He never said a word to me."

"He was pretty certain she was behind the tainted-meat scandal," said Myles. "And Quill, Eddie wasn't here to solve the murders. He worked for the son. His job was to stop the trafficking in the meat. And I don't blame him for keeping undercover. Confidentiality is the core of his business. Without it, he wouldn't get another assignment."

"Confidentiality," Meg said sarcastically. "Try *deceit*. Try ripping people off. Try *bogus*!"

"I *knew* you thought he was from *L'Aperitif*," said Quill. "Ha!"

Myles rapped the arm of the rocker for silence. "May I continue? Then Marge and Mark turned the computer on to Keith Baumer. They called the American Express Traveler's Cheque operations center in Salt Lake. Mark, in his capacity as bank vice-president, convinced the Fraud Unit there of the urgency of the situation. The Fraud Unit gave them Baumer's address, and the name of the bank where he'd bought his cheques. Marge thought there was a strong likelihood the cheques would have been purchased at the bank where he had a checking and savings account, and she was right."

"And?" said Quill. "Baumer was in on it. I knew it!"

Myles shrugged. "My guess is he's guilty of something. Just what that is, is anybody's guess. His savings account showed regular deposits of amounts varying from three to five thousand dollars, ever since he left Doggone Good Dogs. But I have no official knowledge of this. Baumer doesn't appear to have committed any crimes here. I don't have jurisdiction anyway, so there's no way for me to follow up. I did suggest to Eddie that he have breakfast at Marge's diner this morning. It may be that Baumer was a co-conspirator with Mrs. Hallenbeck—and that Eddie can prove it after he talks to Marge. But the money must have come from somewhere else."

"What do you think, Myles?" said Meg.

Myles hesitated. "I believe that Mavis was blackmailing Baumer, just as she was blackmailing John and Tom Peterson. I don't believe in coincidence. Baumer, Marge, John, and Tom were all connected through Mavis. There are some people who are natural catalysts. Mavis was a catalyst for disaster."

"You put dough into the oven, and heat turns it to brioche," said Quill. "Mrs. Hallenbeck was the heat. Mavis was the yeast."

"Come again?" said Myles.

"Meg." Quill gestured at her sister "She said murder's like a recipe. The same set of ingredients don't guarantee the same dish. Everyone who came into contact with Mavis ended up with a motive to murder—but only one killed her."

"Thank you, Dr. Watson," said Meg.

"*You're* Watson," said Quill "I'm Holmes. If I'd had a little more time . . ."

"But it was Doreen, there, who provided the hard evidence in the case," John interrupted loudly.

"You did?" said Quill. "Doreen, how clever of you!"

"That there Willy Max," grumbled Doreen. "*I* din't call him."

"She got Dina to call the phone company and check the outgoing calls," said Myles. "Tracked the call to Rolling Moses to Mrs. Hallenbeck's room."

"Old witch!" said Doreen. "Lied and made me out a fool. Searched her room proper. Found the makin's of them stupid drinks Mavis liked."

"The mint juleps?" said Quill. "Of course! She fed them to Mavis before they walked down to the Pavilion."

"Tied the glasses and the bottles up in a Baggie and turned them over to Davey," said Myles. "Andy Bishop had them tested for Seconal right there at the hospital. I sent the glasses on to the state lab for fingerprinting. I expect that both Mavis' and Mrs. Hallenbeck's will appear all over them."

"So that's the link to the murder in the Pavilion," said Meg.

"Only piece of hard evidence we have," admitted Myles, "and it's circumstantial. There was such confusion the day of the play that no one remembers seeing Mrs. Hallenbeck going around to the back of the shed, much less pulling the hood over Mavis' face."

"Did she confess?" asked Meg.

Quill winced. Myles reached up and covered her hand with his. "Yes. She did."

"What'd she say?" Meg persisted.

Quill answered the question in Myles's eyes with a reluctant nod.

"There's nothing wrong with her intellect. That sets her apart from most murderers I've known." He grimaced. "Almost all of them are borderline intelligence. Of course, my experience has been with street crime. But she shares one characteristic with them. She's proud of the result. Confessions are easier than the public thinks. Most killers can't wait to tell you, once they know we know."

"So she boasted about it?" said Doreen.

"She wouldn't talk to me with witnesses present and until she was sure I wasn't wired. When she knew, for certain, I couldn't do anything with the confession, she told me she'd decided to kill Mavis as soon as an opportunity presented itself—a decision she'd made before she met you, Quill.

"That first night, she and Mavis had planned an 'accident' on the balcony, and as we suspected, Mrs. Hallenbeck tried pushing Mavis over the edge. Mavis was a lot younger, and a lot tougher, and Mrs. Hallenbeck lost that round, as we know.

"After the rehearsal at the duck pond, she took a walk while the others were making plans for the dinner that evening, and removed the bolt from the front loader of Harland's tractor. 'No one really pays attention to the old,' she said. 'We're overlooked, ignored, discounted. I just took advantage of that.'

"She shrugged Gil's death off as an 'unfortunate circumstance.' She knew her next good opportunity would come at *The Trial of Goody Martin*. She poured doctored mint juleps into Mavis. When Harland came around to the front of the stage, she nipped around the back. Mavis was passed out on the sledge. She pulled the hood over her face, hid the dummy, and came around to the bandstand in the space of three minutes."

"It was so *chancey*," complained Meg.

"She said she'd try until she did it," said Myles.

"That ought to help you sleep better, Quill," said Meg. "Good grief."

"Pretty single-minded," said John. "But then, she always was."

Quill sipped at her coffee and said nothing.

"She did give me enough evidence to convict Tom Peterson on several counts of Federal violations." He looked at his watch, "Couple of the boys should be pulling up to that warehouse now."

"And Mrs. Hallenbeck?" said Quill. "Where is she now?"

"It's done," said Myles. "They picked her up this morning. She'll be there until she passes on to whatever justice there is."

"Wow," said Meg. "Now if I just had some people to eat what I cook, things would be back to normal."

"You just wait," said Quill optimistically. "We've never been sunk for long. You the gourmet chef, me the efficient manager . . ."

John cleared his throat. "I haven't had much of a chance to go over the accounts, Quill, but I understand that we've been pretty free with donations lately."

"Donations?" said Quill.

"He means the two checks to the volunteer ambulance fund, the free brandy and *crème brûlée* for the Chamber the night of the dress rehearsal, the full buffet breakfast on the house, for forty-two, Monday morning, the bar bill for the volunteer firemen, and not to mention the fact that we've got no hope of collecting from Mrs. Hallenbeck," said Meg. She grinned. "Maybe we can put a percentage of it on Baumer's bill. Sort of a P.I.A. surcharge."

"P.I.A.?" said Myles blankly.

"Pain-in-the-ass," explained Doreen. "We talk about it, but we ain't never done it, yet."

"Baumer's a P.I.A. candidate if there ever was one," said Quill, "except that he should be charging *us*. I let his wife into his room so she could sue him for adultery with Mavis. Meg poisoned him with various noxious substances, and he got exorcised by Willy Max and the two Creeps for Christ. I can't believe the guy stuck it out this long."

"Leastways Meg can still cook," said Doreen practically. "Long as the kitchen's open, we got people wantin' to eat."

"Well," said Quill, "it could be worse. I thought maybe Marge had made that phone call to the D.O.H., but she obviously didn't, since we haven't seen anything of them."

There was a double tap on the dining room doors. A thin, unhealthy-looking guy in a polyester suit pushed the doors open. He carried a clipboard and wore a New York State badge reading "Department of Health."

"Until now," said Quill, feebly.

"You!" said Meg, "get out of my kitchen." She ran her hands through her hair. It began to flatten ominously.

"Look, lady, I get a call, I gotta show up."

"I got rooms to clean," Doreen said, "Well, two, anyways." She trotted out of the kitchen.

"I'll give you a call later, Quill," said Myles hastily. He disappeared out the back door.

"Rats deserting the sinking ship," Quill yelled after them.

Meg advanced on the inspector, a wooden spatula in one hand. "I've got the cleanest kitchen in Central New York," she said through gritted teeth. "I hire the best *sous* chef in six states. I use the finest ingredients you can buy!"

"Meg—" said Quill.

"GET YOUR CLIPBOARD OUT OF MY KITCHEN!"

"Excuse me, sir," said Quill.

She nodded to John. John took Meg by the right arm, Quill the left. They dragged her to the dining room. "Just keep quiet, Meg. Everything's going to be fine." Quill forced Meg into a chair at one of the tables and sat down next to her, keeping a firm grip on her arm.

Meg slumped over the table and groaned. "I can't believe that Marge did this! She's a fellow cook! She's a member of the clan! I'll wring her fat little neck."

"Maybe it wasn't Marge," said Quill. "It could have been Maureen, the paramedic. Or her pal, Doyle."

The guy from the D.O.H. poked his head around the door. He held up a small white card. "How often do you use this recipe for zabaglione?"

Meg threw the sugar bowl at him. The inspector ducked. The bowl shattered against the doorframe and powdered the inspector with white snow.

"I gotta lot of questions," he said severely, and disappeared once again.

"I see you have company," said Keith Baumer.

Quill blinked at him. He looked different somehow. Cleaner. Less shabby. More . . . elegant. The baggy blue suit had been replaced by a beautifully cut double-breasted blazer and cream flannel trousers, the ash-covered ratty tie by a tasteful silk cravat. His weekender dangled from one shoulder.

"Just stopped in to say goodbye." Baumer extended his hand. Quill took it, reluctantly. Baumer clasped it and wiggled his middle finger suggestively against her palm. "Wanted to thank you for the interesting stay."

Quill, mindful of the courtesies incumbent on innkeepers who strove for professionalism (and of the fact that they were finally going to see the last of Baumer), shook her hand free, but said politely, "I sincerely apologize for the last few days, Mr. Baumer. I'm afraid you didn't find us at our best."

The kitchen door banged open. The man from the D.O.H. came out with a second recipe card in his hand. "This recipe for mayonnaise . . ." he said. "Oh! Mr. Baumer! How are you, sir?"

"So *you* called them in," said Meg. "It figures."

"At least it wasn't Marge," Quill whispered. "Just keep your lip buttoned. After Baumer leaves we can explain all about him to this guy. Maybe he'll give us a break."

"And your name?" said Baumer to the man from the D.O.H., with a hearty "my man" attitude that set Quill's teeth on edge.

"Arnie Stankard."

"It's a pleasure, Arnie."

"The pleasure's *mine*, sir."

The two men shook hands.

"Stoolie," muttered Meg in disgust.

Baumer lit a cigarette and flicked the match on the floor. "Mayonnaise, zabaglione, and don't forget the Caesar salad, Arnie. Ladies? It's been an experience." He strolled out.

"Arnie," said Quill, as soon as Baumer was out of earshot. "I don't know where you met that man, but we need to explain him to you."

"You mean you know?" said Arnie. "I'm kinda surprised that you do. He always makes such a big deal of traveling incognito. Usually poses as a grungy salesman. Quite a boost for your restaurant, being visited by the food critic from *L'Aperitif*."

L'APERITIF, October issue

from the review column, "Fair's Fare"

Traveling through Central New York is normally a joy in summer. Red-painted barns nestle between neatly bisected fields of rye, and the streams and rivers of this glaciated country flow swift and clear. In past years, come traveling time, those in the culinary know headed straight through this delightful country for the Inn at Hemlock Falls.

L'Aperitif should have taken a detour.

Two years ago, on our first visit to the Inn, Master Chef Margaret Quilliam put on a bravura performance, delivering the Best of the Basque in the most unlikely of places, a rural farming community. Alas! Like the notorious California Chardonnays of '87, Quilliam's early promise has flowered into a disappointing maturity. Although the simplest of American fare—pancakes, omelettes, steaks—remain competently cooked, the complexities of the truly sophisticated chef have eluded the kitchen. The *Pot au Feu* is a trifle bland, the bread textures prey to the vagaries of a succession of beleaguered *sous* chefs, the sausage which made the Inn's reputation, overripe.

(The recent visit of the New York State Department of Health to Quilliam's kitchen is *not* germane.)

It is with regret that we remove our starred rating from the Inn at Hemlock Falls; it is with hope that our demotion is only temporary. We'll return next spring to this delightful part of New York State, to see if Ms. Quilliam has regained her genius for food in the *L'Aperitif* tradition.

The Inn At Hemlock Falls
4 Hemlock Avenue
Hemlock Falls, New York
Fare Score: 0

NEWSWEEK, November issue

Sentenced, for bribery: **Keith Baumer,** 56, food critic for the gourmet magazine *L'Aperitif.* Convicted of accepting a $5,000 bribe in exchange for a favorable review of the trendy restaurant Chien Cous-Cous, Baumer received a suspended 10-day sentence, pending restitution.

TV GUIDE, November issue

60 Minutes—Mike Wallace interviews super PI Edward Lancashire on Doggone Good Dogs and gourmet mag scandal.

ZABAGLIONE À LA QUILLIAM

Per serving:
one tsp. superfine sugar per egg yolk
one tsp. marsala per egg yolk

1. Beat egg yolks into a thick, even consistency, adding a stream of sugar and wine.
2. Place custard over boiling water; beat it until it foams and thickens. AVOID CURDLING!
3. Serve warm over chilled berries or as is; if creating at table-side pour into crystal sherbet glasses that have been kept at room temperature.

Equipment:
copper bowl; wire whisk

A DASH OF
DEATH

To my sisters, Cynthia and Whit

ACKNOWLEDGMENTS

For their support in the technical areas of this book, I would like to thank Beth Martin, M.D., of the Hematology Department at Strong Memorial Hospital in Rochester, New York; Tom Flood of the Finger Lakes Paint Factory; Chad Sheckler of Refractron Technologies; and Ann Logo, O.T. Any errors in their fields of expertise are due to my inability to understand.

For their personal support, I'd like to thank Miriam and Rachel Monfredo, and Nancy Kress.

THE CAST OF CHARACTERS

THE INN AT HEMLOCK FALLS

Sarah Quilliam	the owner-manager
Margaret Quilliam	her sister, the gourmet chef
John Raintree	the business manager
Doreen Muxworthy	the head housekeeper
Dina Muir	the receptionist
Kathleen Kiddermeister	a waitress
Helena Houndswood	a guest and famous TV personality
Dwight Nelson	Helena's dresser and makeup artist
Tabby Fisher	Dwight's girlfriend, Helena's hairstylist
Makepeace Whitman	a guest and director of the Friends of Fresh Air
Mrs. Whitman	his wife

MEMBERS OF THE CHAMBER OF COMMERCE

Elmer Henry	the mayor
Harvey Bozzel	president, Bozzel Advertising
Howie Murchison	town attorney and justice of the peace
Freddie Bellini	director, Bellini's Funeral Home
Miriam Doncaster	the public librarian
Marge Schmidt	owner, the Hemlock Hometown Diner
Betty Hall	her partner
Esther West	owner, West's Best dress shop
Dookie Shuttleworth	minister, the Hemlock Falls Church of the Word of God
Mark Anthony Jefferson	banker, Hemlock Falls Savings and Loan

| Harland Peterson | president, Agway Farmer's Co-op |
| Norm Pasquale | principal, Hemlock High School |

. . . among others

THE SHERIFF'S DEPARTMENT

| Myles McHale | sheriff of Tompkins County |
| Dave Kiddermeister | a deputy |

EMPLOYEES OF PARAMOUNT PAINT

Dawn Pennifarm	a bookkeeper and supervisor
Rickie Pennifarm	her husband
Sandy Willis	a supervisor
Roy Willis	her husband
Connie Weyerhauser	a supervisor
Kay Gondowski	a supervisor
Dot Vandermolen	a supervisor
Hudson Zabriskie	the plant manager

CHAPTER 1

"If it is Helena Houndswood, you gotta bite the bullet, blow her cover, and nail her to the wall." Harvey Bozzel, Hemlock Falls' premier (and only) advertising executive, passed a careful hand through his thinning blond hair. "Anything else is suicide, business-wise. It's a war, Quill, and the profits go to the general who takes the hill. You get me?"

Quill, bemused, wasn't sure she got it at all. Confronted with what she hoped was a temporary lull in July and August bookings at the Inn she owned with her sister, Meg, Quill called Harvey for help. Harvey demanded an immediate "strategic planning session with all managers of customer-contact personnel." Quill dutifully rounded up Meg (the Inn's gourmet chef), John Raintree (the Inn's business manager), and Doreen Muxworthy (their head house-keeper). All four of them now squeezed together on the couch in Quill's office, facing Harvey like ducks on a shooting range.

In preference to an immediate response, Quill glanced sideways and reflected on the four pairs of feet planted on her Oriental rug. The fiftyish Doreen opted for comfort; a brand-new pair of Nikes poked out from beneath her faded print dress. These were in definite contrast to Meg's battered and much smaller pair. Quill's own sandaled feet were tucked next to John's long legs. John looked the same summer and winter: tasseled loafers, sport coat, tie, dress shirt, and chinos; only his coppery skin and coal-tar hair saved him from looking like a clone of every other MBA from downstate schools.

"So we get a grenade in there," said Harvey into the silence.

"Do you really think Helena Houndswood will feature the Inn on her TV show?" Quill asked doubtfully.

"T'uh!" said Harvey, rolling his eyes to the ceiling. "Do I not!"

Not sure whether this was a "yes" or a "no," Quill opted for the appearance of comprehension and gave Harvey a decisive nod.

Meg shot Quill an amused look and locked her steely gaze onto Harvey's moist brown one. "Bullshit, Harvey. The woman's hiding out. She registered as Helen Fairweather, private citizen, not Helena Houndswood, TV star. Hasn't shown up in the dining room. Sits in the bar in a dark corner. Walks in the rose garden in a big veiled hat. Makes mysterious calls on that cellular phone. If Quill asks her to do a show on location here, she's going to throw a major hissy fit. The woman has immured herself for a reason." Meg crossed one leg over the other and rotated her dangling foot. As slender as Quill, she was a full head shorter. She was wearing her usual chef's gear: black leggings, sweatshirt, and brightly colored socks. Meg's sock color varied according to her mood. These were yellow. Quill wasn't certain what yellow signaled; it was a new pair.

"What's *immured* mean?" said Doreen.

"Entombed," said Meg.

Doreen sucked in her cheeks and widened her beady eyes. This maneuver—enhanced by gray hair frizzed around an exceptionally high forehead—increased her resemblance to a cockatoo. "Whoa! I shoulda guessed! Her face is all swole. They had a show about celebrity terminal diseases on *Geraldo*."

"She's not sick, Doreen," said Meg. "She's recovering from a face-lift. Or liposuction. Or collagen injections. Whatever it is that celebrities do to keep on looking twenty-eight."

Quill rubbed her temple with one forefinger, pushed the skin up, and turned inquiringly to her sister.

"No," said Meg.

"No?"

"Well, you are the older sister. But you're not that much older. And don't tell me carrot-colored hair is aging because I've heard that one before."

"It's auburn," said Quill, greeting this familiar family argument as a splendid diversion.

"Well, strawberry-colored hair," Meg conceded. "Does fruit-colored hair sound better than vegetable-colored hair? I think not. Anyhow, thirty-three-year-old women don't need face-lifts. We can't afford it anyway."

"We could afford the Caribbean, couldn't we? It's cheaper."

"We can't even afford a twenty-year-old lifeguard. And they come *really* cheap. Doreen'll throw sea salt in your bathwater."

"I wouldn't have to pay a lifeguard. Central New York is full of muscled volunteers that'd love to join me in the tub. Harvey can run an ad. In the personals column. That's cheap."

Harvey cleared his throat uneasily.

"Speaking, of affordability," said John Raintree, "Harvey's on the clock. We need to settle this. We've got a cash-flow problem, and we've got to decide how to solve it." Tall, quiet, with a chiseled nose and textured skin that reflected his three-quarters Onondaga blood, John kept the Inn from widening into a wholly unstable orbit. Without John, Quill thought, not only would things fall apart and the center fail to hold, the general ledger would be a total mess. After four years in the business she wasn't entirely sure about the differences (if any) between accounts receivable and accounts payable.

Contrite, she made an effort to stick to the business at hand. "Do you think I should ask Helena Houndswood to film her TV show—"

"Tape her show," said Harvey fussily.

"*Tape* her show here? I just thought Harvey could place a few ads in the travel magazines. Maybe do a mailing to travel agents. Things are bound to pick up."

John rubbed his forehead, for him a rare and extravagant gesture of worry. Although she knew what was coming—she'd heard it all before, which was why she'd called Harvey in the first place—Quill's stomach sank. "It's June," he said. "And we need cash. Spring bookings were lean. The only receivable due is the forty-five-hundred-dollar check from the Paramount Paint people, for the Bosses Club lunch meetings and the employee banquet last quarter. Payroll's six thousand dollars a month, Quill—and you know as well as I do that New York State will shut you down if you don't pay the help. Bookings are down forty-five percent from last year. For the rest of the summer, all we have is the monthly Chamber of Commerce meetings, and two weeks of reservations for the Friends of Fresh Air."

"Nobody told me about them," said Meg. "Friends of what?"

"It's an environmental group," said Quill. "The director and his wife are coming in today. The rest of the group will be in tomorrow. Fifteen rooms, twenty-eight people. It's on the bulletin board, Meg."

"I seen it," said Doreen, "it's the note marked FOFA twenty-eight."

"Fish on Friday," said Meg. "I thought we were having twenty-eight dinners of fish on Friday."

"That'd be FOF28D," said Quill, who was experimenting with a new shorthand system. "And it'd be in the meals column, not the rooms column. I explained that at our last meeting."

"What the heck am I supposed to do with my order for two crates of cohoe salmon?"

"Mousse?" Quill suggested.

"Pâté," said Meg.

"Terrine."

"Aspic."

"Ugh. I hate aspic." Quill made a face.

"Aspic it is," said Meg firmly. "'Cause honeychile, aspic the meals around here."

Quill groaned. Meg burst into laughter.

"Them two'd cavort if the Devil himself called at the front door," said Doreen to nobody in particular. "I like this-here idea Harvey has about war."

"You would," said Meg.

Doreen had a propensity for whacking those who infringed on her value system, which, like those of the very best dog trainers, was direct and unambiguous. She'd developed a bucket-to-the-knees, broom-handle-to-the-midsection technique that owed a lot to old Bruce Lee movies. She was, Quill thought fondly, pretty agile for a fiftyish widow with a tough life behind her.

John cleared his throat. "The Friends of Fresh Air represent a nice piece of business for June. We could use a lot more just like it for July and August."

"What's coming in for July and August?" said Meg.

"Nothing."

"Nothing?"

"No guests and no cash," said John firmly. "Just the check from the Paramount Paint people. Income from the Friends of Fresh Air won't be in for another sixty days since they've all paid by credit card. We'll have to go into our line of credit. And unless I can show the bank significant business third quarter, they're going to be difficult about it."

"Nothing," said Meg. "Oh, God. It's my fault, isn't it. It's all my fault."

"Meg, it's not your fault," said Quill.

"Your business is off forty-five percent?" said Harvey. "Was I right or was I right? I told this whole town that canceling History Days last year was going to be a public relations disaster. And just look at what's happened. The Inn at Hemlock Falls is the third largest employer . . ."

"We are?" said Quill.

"Well, sure," said Harvey.

"But the Qwik Freeze plant and the Paramount Paint people . . ."

"Oh, them," said Harvey, "they've got hundreds. But who is there between them and you?" He addressed the ceiling again. "I told you. I told you Meg's losing that three-star *L'Aperitif* rating was bad news. Bad news. It's a good thing you called me in. You shouldn't have waited. It's probably already too late."

Meg raked her hands through her short dark hair, turned deep red, and started to sputter like a teapot on the boil. Harvey blinked simplemindedly at her. Although the events of the prior year had descended on them like a brakeless tractor-trailer on a downhill slope, everybody in the room (except, apparently, Harvey) knew that Meg was convinced the poor review from *L'Aperitif* was her fault.

Watching Meg eye Harvey, Quill held her breath. On her good days Meg had a full quota of the passionate irrationality common to genius; barely controlled, but tolerable. On red sock days her wrath was volcanic and limited to verbal eruptions. On black sock days she dented things: walls, pots, although up until now, never people. Quill wondered if yellow socks meant that Harvey was going to catch one up the side of the head.

"Shut up, Harvey," said Doreen. "The magazine sent a letter of ab-ject apology, and the critic went to jail. They gave the rating back. Says so on the plaque in reception."

Meg settled back against the couch and said merely, "So there, Harvey, you jerk."

"Let's get back to the point," said John. "You're pretty sure that Helen Fairweather is Helena Houndswood, Quill?"

They followed his gaze to the window. Quill's office was on the ground floor and overlooked the rose garden. Scented Cloud, Quill's favorite hybrid tea, sent tendrils of perfume through the open window. A slim figure in a straw hat dripping with chiffon strolled down the graveled path that wound among the thickly flowered bushes.

"Them fancy trousers she's wearing'll turn green with grass stains," said Doreen in her foghorn voice. "I thought this Helena Whosis was a high muckety-muck about gardens. She don't look like no gardener that I ever seen. You know, she could be one of them celebrity copycats. They had a show about that on *Geraldo*, too."

Quill got up and closed the window. Sound drifted well on the humid June air.

"Not only does she *look* like Helena Houndswood . . ." Meg began.

"Could be a celebrity look-alike," Harvey interrupted with authority. "There's a lot of that sort of thing around."

"Din't I just say that?" demanded Doreen.

". . . but Dina Muir in reception told me her gold card is imprinted 'Helena Houndswood.' "

"Oh," said Harvey. Having temporarily lost the upper hand, he frowned at Doreen in minatory way. "She's *the* authority on beautiful living," he instructed the uninterested housekeeper. "She's from a very exclusive background, but she's as down to earth as you or me. Her closest friends call her Hank, not Helena. She publishes those coffee table books. Big expensive ones with four-color plates. And she's written about gardens, table settings, interior design, cooking, and weddings. Her television show has a forty share." He leaned forward and jabbed his thumb in Doreen's direction. "That's eighty million households. She tells America how to live the beautiful life. And when America listens, eighty million households *buy*. If Quill talks her into sponsoring the Inn on her show, you'll have thousands of people beating down the doors."

"We only got twenty-seven rooms," Doreen pointed out.

"Think of the campaign I could write for you guys. Think of the money I'd make." He leaned back and shut his eyes. "Wait. Wait. It's coming to me. I've got an idea . . ."

They waited expectantly.

"Houndswood . . . or wouldn't she?"

"Wouldn't she what?" said Meg.

"Live the Beautiful Life at the Inn at Hemlock Falls."

Quill sighed. "It seems kind of tacky to me."

"Well!" said Harvey with a huffy air. "This is a preliminary stab at the creative, of course. Naturally I'd need time to come up with something a little more focused."

"I didn't mean your campaign idea, Harvey. I meant asking her to use the Inn in her show. She's here under an assumed name, which means she wants her privacy."

"That one," sniffed Doreen, "is in a snit 'cause no one knows who she is, if you ast me."

John stirred a little on the couch. "Why do you say that?"

"No reason." Doreen shrugged. "Just a hunch is all."

Quill and John exchanged a significant glance.

"You didn't try and sell her stationery?" asked Quill. "Doreen, we've talked a lot about *not* pushing your businesses on the guests." Doreen's enthusiasms, ranging from Christian evangelicalism to marketing Nu-Skin, were short-lived but fervent. Her latest assault on the bastions of the entrepreneurial was peddling expensive stationery. Quill had six variations in size, color, and rag content in the lower drawer of her desk. She'd made these purchases with a sense of relief. Doreen had been flirting with selling nursing home insurance, and stationery seemed a safe—even useful—alternative. At the time she'd reasoned that there'd be no unpleasant consequences to, for example, one's long-term debt load (Nu-Skin) or one's physical person (Church of the Rolling Moses). Now, Quill wasn't so sure. "Doreen?"

"Thought she might use some of that-there Creamy Ivory Geranium-Scented Notepaper." Doreen stuck her lower lip out belligerently. "With the Embossed Bookman sheriff type."

"Serif," said Harvey, "not sheriff, serif."

"Whatever," said Doreen.

"So did she order some?" asked Meg.

"Wanted *me* to pay *her*. Ast if I could afford her, with this smirky kinda look on her swole-up puss. 'You kiddin' me?' I says to her. 'Why'n the heck would I pay you for?' 'Well!' she says in this hoity-toity way. 'You obviously know who I am. Do I have to spell it out for you?' 'Guess so,' I says back. 'Beat it,' she says. 'Stuff it,' I says back."

Incredulity made Harvey pink. "You told Helena Houndswood to stuff it?" He turned to Quill. "She's torpedoed the whole thing. Ruined it. Absolutely. Right down the tubes."

"Not necessarily," said John. "Ms. Houndswood's obviously practiced at the endorsement process. I think a lot depends on the quid pro quo."

"Cheek," said Doreen darkly, reliving the moment, "that's what I call it." A cheerful smile split her angular face. " 'Course, if she's lookin' to be em-murred soon, it sorta explains the cheek. Dee-pressed, most likely."

"Aagh," said Meg, "she's not sick, Doreen."

"There's not much to offer her," said Quill. "I mean, we can't afford the kind of prices she commands."

Meg spread her arms wide in an all-encompassing gesture. "Look at this place. It's possible that I'm the greatest cook in the known universe without a four-star rating, but it's definite that you're the greatest decorator of Inns. It's gorgeous, Quill. The woman'd be nuts not to want it as background for her TV show."

Quill twiddled her thumbs. The Inn dripped with charm, from the Tavern Bar with its polished mahogany floor and wain-scoting to the reception foyer with the original cobblestone fire-place and flower-filled Chinese urns. Each of the guest rooms was uniquely decorated from the blue and yellow Provence suite with its wrought-iron balcony and Adams-style fireplace to the spare and lovely Shaker suite. The singles and doubles were draped in hard-to-find patterned muslins, chintzes, and linens. All the rooms were dominated either by expansive views of the perennial garden or the hemlock groves and the waterfall. The building itself sat on a granite ledge overlooking the sweep of Hemlock Falls, flanked on two sides by flower and herb gardens and backed by a grove of hemlock trees. No matter what her mood, Quill could always find part of the huge old place that gave her pleasure.

"She drinks sherry in the bar every afternoon, doesn't she?" asked Meg. "So she must have seen your paintings. Ten-to-one the woman already knows who you are."

"Was," said Quill. "I haven't picked up a brush in a long time."

"A mere hiatus," said Meg airily. "Once a celebrity, always a celebrity."

"Meg! I was mentioned in *Art Review* once, and that was when I quit the business. That hardly qualifies me as a celebrity."

"It might," said John. "Even I knew who you were when you hired me, Quill. It's likely she might. And there's Meg, of course. The two of you are well-known in your own way. I think you ought to feel her out."

"Ugh," said Quill. "Ugh, ugh, *ugh*! I hate stuff like this."

"Then you girls just leave it to me," Harvey said. "Hank and I both talk the talk, if you get my drift. I'll give her just a smidgen of some pretty powerful ways I can boost her image. Maybe even see if she wants to go national with a 'Houndswood or Wouldn't She' blitz. Plus, and here's a real important thing, gals, I can reassure her Meg's not on the skids, foodwise."

There was a short silence.

"Not a bad idea, Harve," said Meg, through her teeth. "Not a bad idea at all. Of course, Quill might stand a better chance. Just because she's a woman—sorry, Harvey—'girl.' If Ms. Houndswood—sorry again, Harvey—'Hank'—has just had a face-lift, she might not want to talk to a man. Just yet. It's kind of a girl thing, Harve. If you get my drift."

"Um," said Harvey uncertainly.

"Now, *foodwise*, Harve," Meg continued, her voice rising, "let me tell you something *foodwise*."

"Stop," said Quill. "I'll do it. I'll talk to her."

"Fine," said Meg, suddenly cheerful. "When?"

"Well." Quill thrashed a bit, feeling like a fish which had successfully avoided the bait until the third cast. "When's she checking out?"

"She booked for three weeks," said John.

"But there's no time like the present, Sis."

"Don't call me Sis. I hate it when you call me Sis." Quill sighed. "I don't have the time. I have to collect that forty-five hundred dollars from the Bosses Club. I dropped Dawn Pennifarm a note asking her to bring it with her."

"We're that cash short?" said Meg, startled. "Since when have we started harassing customers for payment?" She jiggled one foot nervously. "Does this mean you're going to hassle me about kitchen supplies again? Are you insisting I cancel the salmon?" She raked her hands through her hair. "You know I can't cook if I have to worry about budgets. I hate worrying about budgets."

Quill glanced at John. "Over to you," his look said. "Well, we do need the money, Meg. We're not hassling the Bosses Club exactly, but John and I talked it over, and we decided to be firmer with slow payers, the Paramount people in particular."

"They're very slow pay," John repeated, deftly picking up his cue. "Hudson Zabriskie claims the company's having a slow quarter and wants to discuss a lower-cost lunch menu."

Meg scowled. "But the same quality, I suppose."

"Of course," said Quill, "they appreciate great food. We can serve soups and stews instead of meat entrées. They *love* your cooking, Meg. It's why they come. If they didn't care, they'd be down to Marge Schmidt's diner like a shot. Anyway, I need to pick up that check and talk to Hudson about revising the lunch budget. That's a little more urgent than this TV thing."

"Talking to Hudson shouldn't take more than three or four hours," said Meg with cheerful sarcasm. "They don't call him the Bloater for nothing. And what's more important, Quill? Losing ten percent on their lunch costs or, as Harvey says, angling to have eighty million American households beat down our door? Talk to Helena Houndswood first, then tackle Zabriskie and pick up that check from Dawn."

"And I have to tour the west end of town issuing tickets for people who haven't fixed up their businesses for Clean It Up! Week." Quill brightened with an idea. "Tell you what, Meg. You take on Clean It Up! Week and I'll talk to Helena Houndswood."

"Clean It Up! Week is a crock. The Chamber of Commerce has no business telling perfectly respectable citizens how their storefronts should look. They're a bunch of fascists anyhow."

"From the way you're talking, anyone would think Mayor Henry's Mussolini. All it is—all it's *ever* been—is a polite reminder to people to keep their buildings neat."

"Who's on the list?" asked Meg suspiciously. "West end of town? That's Nickerson's Drug . . ."

"And you like Nicole Nickerson."

". . . and the post office. Aaah! Vern Mittermeyer! That lizard! Last time I went to the post office, he kept me waiting thirty minutes to buy stamps. I'd love to whack him one over a Clean It Up! Week violation. What's the Chamber want him to do?"

"Repaint the trim."

"Good luck," said Meg scornfully. "I'll bet he said it wasn't in the budget . . ."

"Ah, Quill," said John.

"It doesn't have to be in the budget. Connie Weyerhauser arranged for Paramount to donate three gallons of Crimson Blaze."

"Quill," said John. "In the interests of civic tranquillity . . ."

Quill caught his eye. "Never mind, Meg, I'll take care of it. I'll take care of all of it."

"The Bosses Club meets until five. It's eleven o'clock right now. Talk to Helena immediately. Get it over with. You'll feel better."

Crossly deciding that Meg had the tenacity of a shorter-than-average pit bull, Quill gave up. "All right. Okay. I'm going." She put her hand on the office doorknob, then turned around and looked at her staff. Meg, John, and Doreen nodded encouragement. Harvey, eyes closed, was murmuring "Hounds*wood* . . . could, should, would, hood," his habit when searching for rhyming words.

"Excelsior!" Meg gestured toward the rose garden.

"I'm going, dammit."

Quill's office was located behind the reservations desk in the front foyer. As she closed the office door behind her, she automatically surveyed the area, checking to see that fresh flowers had been placed in the large Chinese urns that flanked the cobblestone fireplace (they had), that no stray luggage had been left on the polished oak floor (it hadn't), and that no guests had been cast forlornly adrift, waiting for service. The foyer was depressingly empty, except for Dina Muir, the Cornell student who worked as a receptionist part-time.

"Any messages?" asked Quill with hope.

"Just Sheriff McHale. Wants you to call him back to confirm your dinner date tonight at ten-thirty." Dina's hair was cut short and framed wide, innocent brown eyes. They widened even farther at the change in Quill's expression. "Is anything wrong?"

Myles. Quill closed her eyes. She thought of her studio in Manhattan, now a Chinese delicatessen. "Do you know if Helen Fairweather is still in the rose garden?"

"You mean Helena Houndswood? Oh, God." Dina slapped a hand over her mouth, removed it, and said, "She swore me to secrecy. Nobody's supposed to know she's here. I found out because of the credit card. Isn't she gorgeous? The TV show is *fab*-ulous. She just knows everything about how to live right. She was in the rose garden, but she just this minute went into the bar. You won't tell her I told you who she is? I mean, I gave my blood oath that I'd keep it a secret. I only told Nate and Meg, of course. And now you. Rats. Stars like she is just get hounded to death, she said. Now you look even worse. Are you sure nothing's wrong?"

"If you absolutely had to sit down, would you choose a rock or a hard place?"

Dina grinned. "Which is Sheriff McHale?"

"My mother would say a rock. A positive brick. A safe harbor in the storms of life." Quill picked up the desk phone and punched in Myles's number. "Hey," she said, when he answered.

"Quill"—Quill was a sucker for deep, manly voices, and there was no question that the six-foot-three, broad-chested Myles McHale had one—"about dinner tonight."

"Yes, Myles. I'm not sure . . ."

"I'm making a run to Syracuse on a missing persons. I don't know when I'll be back. I'll need a rain check."

There was a silence. Quill knew he wouldn't ask about the other. He'd asked once, and he'd wait until she made up her mind. She wondered how long he'd wait. Lots of people waited until they were drawing Social Security to get married. "So," she said brightly, "who's missing?"

If he was impatient with her, she didn't hear it in his voice. "It's not who as much as what. Hudson Zabriskie claims there's a cash shortage at the plant. And the bookkeeper didn't show up for work this morning. Hudson's always been able to put two and two together to make five, so the two events may not be related. But we'll see."

"The Bloater? The guy from Paramount Paints?"

"Yeah."

"It's not Dawn Pennifarm, is it? The bookkeeper?"

Another silence, that of a sheriff being circumspect. Quill rolled her eyes at Dina then gave him a verbal nudge. "Myles?"

"Might be," he agreed cautiously.

"Hell." Dina's eyesbrows rose. Quill gave her love to Myles and hung up the phone.

"There *is* something wrong," Dina said sapiently.

"A rock, a hard place, and the deep blue sea," Quill murmured. "Helena Houndswood's in the rose garden you said?"

"She's not in the rose garden," Dina said. "The Lounge, I think."

It was not cowardly, Quill decided as she headed out the front door, to take a few minutes in the rose garden. Dina might have mistaken the TV star's destination. Besides, she needed time to plan the attack.

The rose garden was only a quarter of an acre, and it took Quill less than five minutes to determine that Helena Houndswood wasn't there.

The air was moist and cool from the nearby waterfall. Quill inhaled with delight. Water roared over the lip of the granite gorge with a muscular rush that sent spray as far as the koi pond in the center of the garden. Quill strolled down the path to the pond and pulled a few wild chamomile from the lavender beds surrounding the basin. Sunlight sparkled on the water, reflecting tiny shards of light from the scarlet-silver carp. Quill snapped the stem of a blousy tulip and poked gently at the fish. One of the seven turned and nibbled at the stem, its open mouth like a baby bird's. Quill chased the fish with the tulip stem until the vigorous rapping of knuckles on glass roused her. She glanced toward the sound. Meg, John, Doreen, and Harvey stared accusingly through her office window. She sighed, waved the dripping tulip at them in a gesture of surrender, and went to the Tavern Bar. She'd ask Helena Houndswood if she'd feature the Inn on her show, get turned down, march into the Bosses Club meeting and demand forty-five hundred dollars from Hudson Zabriskie and get turned down, call up Myles McHale on his car phone and turn *him* down, and then go live in Detroit and sell real estate.

Maybe, thought Quill, Helena Houndswood would be surrounded

by adoring fans, or her agent, or on the phone, so clearly occupied with something else, it'd be rude to interrupt. Maybe she wasn't even there.

At first the Tavern Bar looked empty, except for Nate the bartender. Quill liked the room, which was situated on the northwest corner of the building, separated from the dining room by thick plaster and lathe walls. Her eye traveled around the bar appreciatively, moving from the teal walls, to the brass and mahogany bar, to the floor-to-ceiling windows at the west end.

Helena Houndswood, arbiter of the Beautiful Life, role model to millions, was sitting in one of the easy chairs drawn up to the windows overlooking the hemlock grove, sipping a glass of sherry, her cellular phone at her ear. She was alone. She looked cross. Quill sighed and proceeded across the mahogany floor with an air of confidence she was far from feeling.

CHAPTER 2

Dina was right, Helena was blond-haired, blue-eyed gorgeous, although much smaller than she appeared on television. Her thinness was that of the dieter for whom denial was a religion. Her straw hat lay next to the chair. The swelling around her eyes and chin had ebbed, leaving no bruises. From Quill's limited knowledge (one blind date with a plastic surgeon) she guessed that Meg had been right about the collagen injections and wrong about the face-lift.

Helena, ignoring Quill's approach, folded the cellular phone with a snap and began examining one of Quill's acrylics, the heart of a Kordes Perfecta hybrid tea. There was a slight frown on her face. Quill cleared her throat. She raised her exquisite eyebrows and said coldly, "Did you want something?"

Her voice was soft and low, which may have been an excellent thing in a woman, Quill thought, if it hadn't been so repelling.

"Ms., um, Fairweather, I'm Sarah Quilliam, one of the owners here. Do you have a moment?"

One eyebrow went a little higher. The expertly glossed lips turned down in a charming, rueful pout. "You know who I am, don't you? Or if you don't know, you're determined to find out." She extended a slim hand. The nails were perfect. "I would have thought celebrities were rare in this backwater. But then, I'm constantly amazed at the reach of my books and my show. How do you do?"

Quill shook her hand. "We get very few celebrities here, Ms. Houndswood, but we're all great fans. May I sit down for a minute?"

"Call me Helena. Not Hank, please. Since that article in *People* came out, every pretentious little bastard in the country calls me Hank. I hate it when people call me Hank." She waved a hand in the direction of the chair on the opposite side of the table.

Quill sat down and folded her hands in her lap. "Are you enjoying your stay? Is there anything you need to be more comfortable?"

Helena ran one hand through her moussed hair. "The food is close to terrific. The interiors are tasteful. The grounds are absolutely B plus. I am amazed. Amazed and charmed."

Quill worked this through and decided if you discarded the "amazed" part, it amounted to a compliment. She took heart. "It's really my sister's cooking that's made our reputation. Meg has a three-star rating from *L'Aperitif*." She took a deep breath. "We think we have a broad appeal. To . . . to . . . the same kind of people that watch your show, for instance."

The clear blue eyes narrowed. The frown deepened. "Let me guess. You think it might be a nice backdrop for the show. *Quelle surprise*, as we say in the Big City." Helena returned to her indifferent contemplation of Quill's acrylic, tilting her head to one side, an art gallery mannerism Quill had never figured out. What did a painting offer better sideways than it didn't straight on?

"If you like the Inn . . ." Quill began.

"Oh, it's not bad. This, of course"—she waved her hand at the painting—"is rather nice. It's the largest collection of hers I've seen. Even the galleries don't have as many. Of course, her output wasn't what you'd call prodigious to begin with . . ." She smiled at Quill's expression of surprise. "You know, I don't believe you realize what you have here. No, you don't. How charming!" She leaned forward and patted Quill's knee. "That, my dear, is a Quilli . . ." Her eyes narrowed. The fluty vowels dropped into a flat midwestern twang. "A Quilliam," she finished, "and you're Sarah Quilliam. Of course. How delightful." She withdrew her hand. "I should have known. I'm sure I did know, actually. I mean, the place reeks of your taste." She measured Quill with a long look.

"So. This is where artists of talent end up when they quit the rat race? Why'd you do it? I mean, you were getting terrific press. And the price on your work's gone up. A lot. Rising fame scare you or something?"

Quill couldn't think of anything to say. Helena answered the question herself. "The stress got to you. God, I can relate to that. The pace. The writing. The cameras. Even the goddam lights." Absently she smoothed her upper lip, which didn't help the puffiness at all. "Worried all the time about the fucking media. The fucking ratings. And of course, now there's the fucking china contest."

Fucking, thought Quill, must be a part of the famous down-to-earth charm. "The china contest?"

"It's a beautiful life," said Helena obscurely.

Quill, wondering if this referred to a Capra remake she knew nothing about, said "a-*hum*" with a great deal of authority.

"The winner is going to be featured on the show in three weeks. Actually"—she cast a swift appraising eye over the bar—"I was already thinking of doing it live from here. Great background. You wouldn't mind, sweetie, would you? That's what you were after, wasn't it?"

"Yes," said Quill, dizzy. She swallowed, pinched her own knee hard, and looked wildly around for some support. She signaled Nate the bartender with a "thumbs-up," and mouthed "wine" at him. He looked at his watch in surprise, pointed to Helena with a raised eyebrow, and at Quill's nod, poured two glasses of sherry and brought them over.

". . . and of course it's utterly, utterly confidential, dear, but the winner's from Hemlock Falls."

"I'm sorry," said Quill, "what?"

"Do listen, sweetie." She looked up as Nate set the second sherry next to her empty glass. "I didn't order that."

"On the house, Miss Houndswood."

"Good. Another when this is gone, then."

Quill, engaged in mental gymnastics, finally recalled that Helena's TV show was called *It's a Beautiful Life*. Not only that, an old isuse of *Architectural Digest* had something about an *It's a Beautiful Life* design competition for tableware. She choked on the sherry. She remembered, now. The prize was a million dollars. The contest had banned professionals. No members of the Artist's Guild. No architects. Nobody who'd been paid for professional design work. "The winner's from *here*? From Hemlock Falls?"

"Yep. It's not you, is it, sweetie? We'd have to work something out, you know. No pros. At least, not that my fucking public could find out about."

"No," said Quill evenly, "it's not me. The rules were pretty clear, weren't they?" Immediately regretting her flash of annoyance, she said politely, "Can you tell me who it is? Or will the winner be announced on the show?"

"No. No. No. The winner has to be notified. The contract's got to be signed. A sample table setting is being manufactured by little gnomes somewhere even as we speak. There's a hell of a lot to do, frankly, which is why I came up so early." She passed her hand over her upper lip. "I've just been . . . gathering my resources before buckling down to it. So, yeah, I can tell you who the winner is. I'm sure you know her." She dug into her purse and withdrew a Filofax. "You know, it's quite exciting really. *It's a Beautiful Life* is by, for, and about the crème de la crème." Quill, hearing the sudden passion in her voice, was careful to maintain a neutral expression. "You wouldn't believe some of the Names who submitted drawings. Right from the Old Hundred."

"You mean the Four Hundred?" corrected Quill absently, and at once realized her mistake.

Helena paused a beat, looked pointedly at Quill, and resumed evenly, "Four Hundred. As I said." She dropped to a confiding tone. "The selection was agonizing. Of course, I did it myself. Who, I asked myself, is the right sort to be the winner? Not only must the design be tasteful, elegant, *and* discreet, but it must be beautiful. And the winner must be beautiful in the Houndswood tradition." She grasped Quill's wrist. Her fingers were cold and slightly sweaty. "I spent bloody *weeks* at it. And do you know what was the best tip-off? Of course you do. I mean, I spent an entire show on it just last year."

"What?" asked Quill.

"Stationery."

"Stationery?"

"Stationery. The Beautiful Life is beautiful in all details. The well-bred woman is a woman of elegance of dress, manner, and mind. And what is the first line of defense against an intrusive world? Elegant stationery."

Quill looked at Helena's empty sherry glasses. "Sure," she said warily.

"Anyhow. Here's our winner. I'll show you the design first." She produced a large manila envelope from her purse and handed it over.

Quill opened it with care. Inside were watercolor drawings of a china setting. The design was lovely; a delicate tracery of perennial herbs twined around an exquisitely rendered rose-breasted grosbeak, its chest a cloudlike drift of violet suffused with pink.

"These are wonderful," said Quill.

"You'd know, wouldn't you?" There was a peculiar desperation in her voice. "I mean, *you* can tell crap from genuine talent. If anyone's got an eye it's you. It's genuine, isn't it?"

"Genuine?" said Quill, bewildered. "If you're asking if there's real talent here, yes. There is. It's an amateur talent, that's clear. It's not . . . I'm not sure just how to express it. It's not a *unified* work. My guess is that it's a student's effort. Not a young artist, necessarily, but someone who's learning from somebody. You can see that there's another mind at work besides the artist's. I don't teach, but if I did, I would take whomever did this on as a student. It's marvelous."

"And you could tell if, say, the person who won really did the drawing. Or if it was taken from somewhere else."

"I suppose if I looked at the artist's other work, I could make an educated guess. Do you suspect fraud?"

"Oh, no, no, no, no. I just have to be careful."

"These are just terrific," said Quill. "The design's incredible. It looks like a million dollars."

"I hope it's worth a hell of a lot more than that. I share in the royalties." She gave Quill a candid grin. "We figure a first-year gross of half a million in sales, with growth somewhere in the region of one, one point five million, maxing out around two. If we're lucky, it'll be a backlisted design, and the royalties will roll in for a good long time."

"Backlisted?"

"Like Royal Crown Derby, or Wedgwood, or any of the biggies. Classic china's big business."

"And someone from Hemlock Falls won? This is wonderful."

Helena handed Quill the contest entry. "Here's the name. Don't forget, sweetie, you're one of the first of the locals to know. You owe me one."

The entry letter was written on stationery with a high rag content. The color looked like Creamy Ivory. Quill held it to her nose. It smelled like Scented Geranium. She looked at the embossed name and address: Bookman serif type, Doreen's best-selling stationery. No! thought Quill to herself, and grinned. A momentary vision of Doreen with a million dollars and a star turn on *It's a Beautiful Life* made her toes curl with pleasure. Too bad Doreen couldn't draw.

"Elegant, isn't it?" said Helena anxiously. "The stationery? As I said, the Beautiful Woman's first line of defense against decaying standards. You know the winner, of course."

Quill unfolded the letter and read:

Constance G. Weyerhauser

The Hall

Hemlock Falls, New York

She gave an involuntary expression of delight. "This is fantastic. Helena, this is terrific. I can't think of anyone more deserving."

"Too much to hope it's the lumber people, I suppose."

"No" said, Quill, "it's not the lumber people."

"And you must know Constance."

"Yes," said Quill, "I know Constance. She may not be quite what you—"

"Where the hell's the Hall?" Helena interrupted. "Somebody's got to notify her so we can get the damn contracts signed. My people want to tape it. Get the first reaction on tape so we could run it on the show. Can you imagine anything tackier? I mean, what woman of taste and discretion would stand for it?"

Quill knew several. Among them Constance Weyerhauser. "Somebody? You aren't going to do it?"

"Look, sweetie. Since you know her, what about arranging an introduction? Let her know about the win . . ."

"You're sure you don't want to tell her?" said Quill. "You've put so much work into this."

Helena's eyelids flickered. "No," she said. "I'm sure she'll want to have some time to reflect on this privately. She may not even want to be on the show. Which is *fine*. Just *fine*. All we are contracted to do is feature the china. We don't have to feature the person." She hesitated, then said, "Frankly, emotion's so *sticky*, don't you think? I mean, control and discipline are important parts of the Beautiful Life."

Quill, who'd thought until now that emotion was as much a part of a beautiful life as food and sex, opted for a noncommittal "mm," then wondered if she ought to consider the advantages of asceticism. Except that she couldn't see any advantages to asceticism if she had to give up Myles McHale or her sister's cooking. On the other hand, maybe she would paint more. Painting well required concentration. Focus. The paring away of what Helena Houndswood would undoubtedly call nonessentials. Like Meg. And the Inn.

"Sarah?"

"Yes. Sorry. I was thinking." A second thought occurred to her: Helena had arrived at the Inn Sunday evening. This was Wednesday. What if she'd already asked about Constance Weyerhauser, which would have been only natural. And if she already knew about Constance and her daughter . . . somehow, Quill didn't place much stock in Helena Houndswood's compassion. On the other hand, if she wanted Quill to prepare Connie a little bit . . . "Shall I see if Connie can be here about seven o'clock?"

"We'll have cocktails. I've got my lawyer and producer joining me at eight-thirty for dinner. Look, it's what . . . lunchtime? I'm desperate for a bit of a nap and then some fresh air. I'd love to see your village. It's delightful. I'm going to take a walk to your post office to deliver a package to my publisher this afternoon." She made a *moue* of mock distress. "Galleys, I'm afraid. The deadlines in this business are lethal. Why don't you come with me? You can show me all the most adorable peeps."

"Peeps?"

"Views. Sights. Pretty places. I'll go up to my room and change. There's a good chance I'll be recognized, so you can protect me from the ravening hordes."

"We'd be happy to get the package to the post office for you. There's no need to . . ." Quill hesitated, ". . . expose yourself if you don't want to."

"The price of fame." Helena laughed dismissively. Clearly, her enforced seclusion was beginning to wear.

"I've got quite a bit to do," Quill apologized. "There's a customer group I have to check on about a rate reduction, and a few other things"—like, she thought, that bloody forty-five-hundred-dollar check—"and I'd love to have a little time to spend with Connie Weyerhauser. It's going to mean so much to her. Are you sure you don't want to tell her yourself?"

Helena shrugged.

"You know, this is just like those old TV shows with the happy endings." Quill looked directly at her. "Connie's black. She has a young daughter who's been in and out of the hospital. Cerebral palsy. This is going to be just the best thing that's ever happened to Connie and her daughter. They're wonderful people."

"Sick kid on the show?" Helena wrinkled her nose attractively. "As the kids say, 'not.' You see? A really sensitive woman wouldn't want the publicity. You sound her out. See if she's the sort of person who prefers anonymity. You tell her we'll be *glad* to offer it. Delighted."

"I really don't think it's appropriate for me to talk with her about that," said Quill, by now convinced Helena had known about Connie and Barbara. "It isn't her race that bothers you, is it?"

"Who, me? Absolutely not. And I resent the insinuation. Call her. Just make sure she's here at seven or so. And I'll meet you in the lobby at three o'clock. That should give you plenty of time to run all your little errands."

"Helena, I really have to pass on this. I think you should tell her, and I don't have the time today to walk to the post office."

She raised an eyebrow in inquiry. "Really? Then maybe you can give me some idea of where we should tape the show. Maybe the Inn isn't the best place to shoot after all."

Quill counted to ten and swallowed hard. At least she could check

Vern's progress on repainting the post office building, which would cross another item off her To Do list. "About three o'clock, then."

"Good girl." Helena patted her arm, then walked briskly out of the room. Nate, coming to the table to clear the empty glasses, said, "So, boss. What's she like?"

"Subtle," said Quill. "Very subtle. Nate, did she ask you anything about Connie Weyerhauser?"

"Black gal works at the paint factory? Nope. She going to give us some PR?"

"She's going to shoot her show here."

"No kiddin'?"

"I've got to tell everybody. And Nate. You know Connie Weyerhauser fairly well, right?"

"Sure. I bowl same night as she does down to the Hall. Good gal." He thought a minute. "Hell of a bowler."

"The Legion Hall, you mean. She's had some wonderful good luck. Meg in the kitchen?"

Nate looked at his watch. "They'll all be there. It's lunchtime."

When Meg and Quill had decided to purchase the Inn five years ago, the kitchen had been in the most urgent need of remodeling. Quill had determined to save the brick floor and the hearth; Meg had taken over from there. A huge Aga dominated the center of the room, flanked on three sides by double-wide butcher-block and stainless-steel counters. Birch shelving ran the length of the north and east walls; the south wall was composed of windows overlooking the vegetable gardens. Quill entered through the swinging doors from the dining room. Doreen, John, and her sister had pulled stools up to the counter and were eating soup. They put their spoons down and stared expectantly at her.

"Lunch," said Quill with a casual air. "I'm starved." She sat next to Doreen. One of Meg's *sous* chefs brought her a large bowl of gazpacho and a small loaf of sourdough bread.

"Well?" demanded Meg after a moment.

"Yes."

"Yes!? She's going to use the Inn?!"

Quill nodded. "That's not all. You guys keep this quiet until I tell her, but you know Connie Weyerhauser?"

"She's a member of the Bosses Club. Line Supervisor, third shift at Paramount," said John. "Heck of a bowler, I understand."

"She's got that sick kid," said Doreen. "I work with her down to the clinic once in a while. You know, they got that volunteer program helpin' 'em exercise."

"What about Connie?" said Meg.

"She's won a million dollars."

"You're kidding!" screamed Meg.

Quill explained the design contest, to general congratulations.

"So she's gonna be on the show, too?" said Doreen. "Cripes!"

"Has Helena met her yet?" asked John cynically.

"Um," said Quill. "She says she hasn't. But she knows she's black. And she knows about Barbara. I told her, but I'll bet she found out before. She wants me to tell Connie about the win. Assure her she doesn't have to actually appear on the show."

"It can't be a problem," said Meg. "Not in this day and age."

"Right," said John. "So you're going to tell Connie now?"

"Have they finished lunch?"

"Ayuh," said Doreen. "Went right back to meetin'. That bookkeeper Dawn Pennifarm ain't there, though. I ast 'em. Said she din't show up for work this morning."

Quill's bright mood clouded. "Damn. That check. It's possible we're going to have some problem with that. Myles said Hudson thinks Dawn's taken off with some company money."

"I don't believe it!" said Meg indignantly.

"Let's not jump the gun," said John. "Quill, would you like me to talk to Hudson?"

"Nope. I can handle it. Who's manager here anyhow? I'll talk to Hudson. Hudson's in the meeting, isn't he?"

"Oh, yeah," said Doreen, "spouting his usual hoo-hah."

"Well, he'll be able to give us the check," said Quill confidently. "Meg, Helena wants to plan a small party for Connie about seven o'clock."

"How many?"

"Let's make it for seven people. She'll want to bring her husband and daughter."

"Seven at seven it is. You're going to stand by, I take it."

Quill looked at John, who smiled sourly. "Yes," she said, "I think I should."

Hudson Zabriskie, general manager of Paramount Paint, was slouched against the wall outside the conference room gazing dolefully at nothing in particular. He was exceptionally tall, a fact usually unnoticed because he slouched. It wasn't the "I'm-going-to-knock-my-head-on-the-ceiling" slouch of, say, a basketball player, it was more of an anxious hunch. Just why Hudson hunched like that nobody knew. He had a very nice wife who ran a tailoring business, a good job, and attended Dookie Shuttleworth's Hemlock Falls Church of God with every appearance of spiritual satisfaction. Doreen thought Hudson's nerves rose from the management skills required by Paramount Paint's female workforce. When Quill, too indignant even to shriek, had taken exception to this theory, Doreen had quoted neurological studies (courtesy of a dogged perusal of an article in *Newsweek*) confirming women were more verbal than men. The Bloater, Doreen said, couldn't make any situation clearer, even if the plant were ablaze and all he had to holler was "Fire." Women, said Doreen with satisfaction, din't put up with that kind of crapola. Especially the tough cookies at Paramount Paint.

Hudson greeted Quill like a balky engine on a cold day: "Hello, hello, hello, Quill. Didn't expect to see you today."

"I'm so glad I caught you," said Quill. "I have just a couple of things. Some *really* good news for Connie, and a small request—John thought that we might be able to pick up that quarterly check."

Hudson jumped like a startled fawn. "That's Dawn Pennifarm's job. She's not available."

"Doreen did mention Dawn had to miss the team meeting today. Is someone taking over from her while she's . . . she's um . . . away?"

Hudson gave her a hunted look. "I am. How much was the check for?"

"Forty-five hundred?" said Quill.

"Forty-five *hundred*? Oh, God. Oh, God. This is terrible news. Just terrible. I'll take care of it. Don't do a thing." His mustache trembled. "There's nothing else, is there?"

"Well, there's some terrific news that's going to cheer everyone up. Do you mind if I pull Connie out of the meeting?"

"Connie Weyerhauser? Right now?"

"Honestly, Hudson, I wouldn't interrupt if it weren't the most marvelous news. Really."

"The team's achieving consensus," said Hudson. "Excellent training, excellent. It's given me a real strategic perspective."

"Is it okay to interrupt the meeting?" Quill repeated patiently. "Should I wait until a coffee break?"

"I'll go in with you. They should be finished just about now. They're in there," he said unnecessarily. "Your new conference room. Great remodeling job. New York's pleased."

"John will be delighted to hear it."

Although it had started as a tavern more than three hundred years before, at various times in its history, the Inn had been a sanitarium, a Home for Wayward Girls, and, because of its proximity to Seneca Falls, an occasional safehouse for the underground railway run by the abolitionist Glynis Tryon. It was John who'd suggested a new incarnation to attract lucrative corporate accounts: the addition of a conference center. The old ballroom had been successfully converted to accommodate business meetings. Double pocket doors slid open into the hallway. Inside, on the wall opposite the doors, was a large cabinet which concealed a VCR, a white board, a bulletin board, and a cork board. The white board was on display as Quill and Hudson joined the Bosses Club.

Four women sat around the polished conference table. The board was filled with exhortations in black and red marker: BOSSES BUST ASS WE'RE A LEAN MACHINE. A series of square boxes connected by arrows was labeled: PARAMOUNT PAINT PRODUCT DELIVERY PROCESS.

A woman Quill didn't know looked up with a ferocious scowl as they walked in. "We've finally figured out what you meant, Hudson, you asshole." Harshly dyed black hair was pulled uncompromisingly from her face. Years of cigarette smoking had carved deep grooves on either side of her thin-lipped mouth. "Siddown, and we'll tell you how we'll pull it off."

Hudson sat. Quill stood in the doorway.

"Sit with us, Quill." Sandy Willis, lead supervisor for one of the production lines, greeted Quill with a smile. She was thin, with an intense, cheerful demeanor that Quill had always found appealing. "It's good to see you again. I think you know everybody except our newest member, Dot Vandermolen. She's just been promoted. Dot. This is Sarah Quilliam."

"Congratulations!" Quill said as she sat down.

The black-haired woman grunted.

"Just give us a second, Quill, okay?" Sandy turned to her team-mates. "Dot, let's not get too insulting. Why don't we take another coffee break and cool off. Then we can fill Hudson in on our decision."

"I just want this son of a bitch to know we can cut the remake stats to below half percent. But that means no layoffs, right, Hudson?" Dot drew furiously on her cigarette, and just as furiously stubbed if out. "I figger it's my responsibility to the guys on the line to go over that whole file, there"—she pointed at a stack of manila folders—"and see they're getting a fair shake."

"We're in synch, we're in synch"—Hudson nodded—"but, ladies, and this is a large *but* . . ."

"Like yours, Hud," said Dot.

The three other women looked shocked for a moment, then there was a chorus of laughter.

Hudson, who did, thought Quill guiltily, have a large squishy sort of rear end, pulled on his pencil-thin mustache with short, agitated jerks.

"We're going to come awfully close to the strike days of ten years ago if we can't guarantee no layoffs," said Sandy.

"Absolutely," said Hudson. "No question. You've got my word on that, Sandy."

"I hate to say anything, Mr. Zabriskie." Kay Gondowski, round, sweet-faced, and hesitant, cleared her throat a little nervously. Her voice was almost inaudible. "But didn't you say that last year? I mean, I'm not sure, but I know we got that three percent gallonage increase for you, and you let five people go four months later."

"Kay's got a legitimate issue," said Sandy firmly. "It's verifiable, too. Dawn's got those minutes from last year."

"But Dawn's not here," said Hudson swiftly. "I've told you ladies how important New York feels attendance is. Now Dawn's a very good example of what I was about to tell you. She's a regular member of this team, she's in a responsible position, and did she bother to call with an excuse when she missed her shift this morning? Has anyone even heard from her? I think not."

"Connie?" said Sandy. "You're backup for Dawn. You've got those files? It'll show those layoff figures."

Connie was a large woman with a rich, slow voice. Unlike her teammates, who preferred bowling jackets and jeans, Connie wore a calf-length skirt and print blouse. Small gold earrings gleamed against her dark skin. She pulled a computer printout from a large accordion folder. "Here they are. You were right, Kay. Last Year To Date. Production up twelve percent; employment down fourteen percent."

"There!" said Dot vindictively. She jerked her chin at Quill. "What dy'a think of *that*?"

"Quill's not interested in our little battles," said Connie peaceably. "But I'll bet I know what she *is* in here for. That check, right?" Connie thumbed methodically through the file. "Check for four thousand five hundred sixty-three dollars and eighty cents?"

"Yes," said Quill gratefully.

Connie's brow furrowed. "Sorry, honey. Just got the stub for it. No check at all." There was an uneasy silence around the table.

"Oh, dear," said Quill. "Well, it doesn't matter now. Connie, could I talk to you outside a minute?"

Sandy shrieked and bounced in her chair. "Look at her! Look at her! See that big shit-eating grin? We've won! I knew it! We've won a million bucks!"

CHAPTER 3

"You *all* won it?" Quill said.

Connie, smiling so hard Quill thought her face would split, nodded majestically. "The whole Bosses Club!"

"Whoop!" screamed Sandy Willis, leaping onto the conference table. Her tennis shoes beat a firm tattoo on the mahogany surface. She danced her way down to the end and back, pausing midway to wiggle her rear end in Hudson Zabriskie's astonished face. He had turned pale, then red, then pale again at the news.

"I get it, too, don't I?" said Dot. "You said I was part of it, didn't you?"

"Sure," said Sandy, rather shortly. "We all get it."

"Shee-it!" shouted Dot, then muttered fiercely, "I'm going to quit my *job*. I'm going to quit my *job*. I'm going to . . ."

Kay Gondowski burst into tears. Quill searched in her skirt pocket for a Kleenex and handed it over.

"Everybody settle down," said Connie. "C'mon, guys. Sit! Sit! Sit!"

"Woof!" said Sandy, grinning hugely. She heaved herself off the table and settled into a chair.

"We're rich," wept Kay.

"Okay. Quiet," Connie ordered. "Nobody quits anything until we figure this all out."

"Let's buy the factory!" shouted Sandy. "We'll give everyone a raise!"

"And send Hudson to hell, to hell, to hell," Dot chanted, punctuating each *hell* with a blow of her fist.

"A million dollars," sobbed Kay.

"Yes!" shouted Sandy, shooting her fist in the air. "A million dollars!"

"Split five ways," said Connie. "We figured that out, remember? That's two hundred thousand each including Dawn and Dot, here. We haven't got it, yet. We wait until we get it, and *then* we talk about quitting. We can invest it at the bank. I talked to Mark Anthony Jefferson, just asking him, you know, and he said two hundred thousand dollars invested at six percent is twelve thousand dollars a year."

"Twelve thousand dollars a year," sobbed Kay, "for free."

"Taxes," said Hudson suddenly, "you ladies forgot about taxes. There's absolutely no way. No way at all. Nobody can live on twelve thousand dollars a year." He smoothed his mustache.

"The mixers on the line do," said Dot sharply, "We've been telling you all along, Hud, they ain't paid enough."

Quill cleared her throat. "You *all* won?" she said again. "How did you do it? I've seen the design. It's just gorgeous."

"Kay watches *It's a Beautiful Life* every week," Connie explained. "She told us about the contest six months ago. We're all on the bowling team at the Legion Hall Tuesday nights. So every Tuesday night for a month—"

"I bought us a pitcher of beer," said Dot. "Remember that. Every Tuesday night since I joined. You said I could be in on it, too. And we brainstormed on how to win that million bucks." She shot a conciliatory look at Hudson. "Just like you taught us in team training."

"We pooled our money for a sketch pad and watercolors," said Kay so softly Quill could barely hear her. "And we put our heads together and came up with this design. Dawn drew it."

"And drew it and drew it and drew it," said Connie, chuckling. "Whoa, but that girl wanted some plumb ugly stuff on the saucers."

"The teacup shape," said Sandy. "We fought about that for weeks!"

"We used Connie's stationery because it was so classy," Kay confided in her near-whisper.

"I've got to call my girl, Barbara," said Connie, "and my Roosevelt. And my grandmother. Whoo!" She shook her head, unbelieving.

"We're supposed to meet her at seven o'clock?" asked Sandy. "Helena Houndswood?"

"In the Tavern Bar," said Quill. "I've asked Meg to make some hors d'oeuvres. On the house."

"Helena Houndswood," breathed Kay. "She's so beautiful!"

"We'd better go and get cleaned up," said Sandy. "We can't meet Helena Houndswood dressed like this." She indicated her bowling jacket, jeans, and baggy T-shirt with a stagily elegant sweep of one hand. There was a general scraping of chairs. Hudson Zabriskie held up his hands. "Ladies, ladies, the shift doesn't end until five-thirty . . ." A chorus of dismay made his mustache jump. "But this time, I'm making an exception. Just give me another hour, here, and then you can all go home and get ready for tonight. I may even join you, if you'd permit it."

"Sure, Mr. Zabriskie," said Connie briefly, "whatever you like." She gave Quill a hug, then turned to her teammates. "We'll dress up a bit, guys. Like for the bowling banquet."

"Whoop!" shrieked Sandy. "Let's slam through the rest of this stuff."

"I'll see you out, Quill," said Hudson, gnawing a fingernail as the door slid closed behind them. "New York's going to be upset. Very upset. I'm not sure how HR will react to this."

"HR? I don't quite . . ."

"Human Resources. There'll be a lot of publicity. Things were going very, very well at the plant. Extremely well, since I took over. Just two more quarters and New York is going to be pleased. Very pleased. But this!" He flailed both hands in the air.

"Everything is going to be fine," said Quill diplomatically.

"Productivity's bound to be affected. Of course, I've handled situations like this before quite well, but still . . ."

"And I'm sure you'll handle it well, again." Quill drew a deep breath. "I'm really sorry, Hudson, but I've got to ask you for that check."

"Dawn will be back tomorrow," he said. "Next day at the latest. I can't authorize what would be a duplicate payment." He rolled an eye at her, then took a sudden, intent interest in the wainscoting. "She'll, be back to collect her winnings. I mean, once word about this gets around . . ."

Quill debated with herself. Myles never got angry, precisely, but he was bound to dry up as a source of information if she told Hudson she knew that Dawn was missing, apparently with the Inn's operating capital for the month. Tiny beads of sweat had appeared at Hudson's temples. He suddenly seemed very . . . short, thought Quill. And she'd bet half that missing check that "New York" didn't treat him any better than his employees did. "Let's not worry about this now. Not when the Bosses Club's had such terrific news. Maybe I can stop by the plant tomorrow and we can straighten this out."

"I'm sure we can work something out," Hudson said uncertainly. He shifted from one foot to the other.

Quill glanced at her watch, then touched his shoulder. "I'll see you this evening, then."

A pleased expression lightened Hudson's face. "I wouldn't shirk that duty, Quill," he said earnestly. "The girls really need me tonight. You realize I've been used to dealing in some large arenas. It's not technically in my job description, but that's never stopped me. So I guess I'll be back for this . . . she's ah, here, is she?"

"Ms. Houndswood, you mean? Yes, I'm supposed to meet her in

the lobby at three, which means I *really* have to go, Hudson. I'll see you tonight." She shook his hand and fled.

She reached the lobby as Helena Houndswood drifted down the stairs in a cream-colored walking skirt and cotton gauze blouse. "That's gorgeous," said Quill, without envy.

"You like?" Helena cocked her head and whirled gracefully. She adjusted yet another straw hat—this one covered with ecru silk roses—then drew a thick manila envelope from the oversize handbag she carried. "My galleys. Guard them with your life." She followed Quill out the front door. Outside, she threw her arms wide and inhaled sharply. "Marvelous! Marvelous! And that view! It's idyllic. Relaxed. Unstressed. The Country Life. You know . . . I'm getting the germ of an idea for a book, here." She stopped short, frowning. "Helena Houndswood presents—It's a Beautiful Life on the Farm!"

"Of course," said Quill weakly. "Um, Helena, about Connie Weyerhauser . . ."

Helena gave her a sharp sideways glance. "So. You reached the lucky winner?"

"Yes. They were thrilled."

"What do you mean, 'they'?"

Quill explained.

"Why the hell didn't they put all their names on the contest entry, then? Did you say one's called Gondowski, for God's sake? And a—what do you call it now? 'A person of color.'"

"Paramount's very proud of its diverse workforce."

"Jee-sus! Oh, for God's sake, Sarah, get that look off your face. I'm thinking of my audience. I'm no fucking bigot."

Quill bit her lip, hard.

"Five winners. God, that'll be a field day for that fucking studio lawyer. The fees'll be tripled. How the fuck did it happen? Why didn't they put *all* their names' on the entry?"

"Well, I asked them that. Apparently Connie'd bought this new stationery from . . . well never mind who . . . and they'd seen your show on how stationery was the first line of defense against a vulgar world—" Quill broke off, aware that this wasn't getting anywhere. "Helena, they're so excited about this. You can't imagine what it means to them."

Helena said enigmatically, "Quite the little Girl Scout, aren't you?'

Quill told herself she wasn't going to lose her temper, suggested they begin their walk, and pointed out what she hoped were interesting features of the gardens surrounding the Inn as they walked down the gentle grade leading to the village. "The roses, of course, you've seen. I'm not really sold on the hybrid teas, as you noticed . . ."

"Nor I," said Helena agreeably. "So tacky, don't you think? Rather *nouveau riche*. Or perhaps I should say sterile, in the face of the vitality and vigor of the Old Roses."

Quill, finding no possible response to this, went on. "Mike, our lawn guy, suggested the plantings here." She indicated the sweep of dwarf dahlias lining the driveway to the Inn. "They turned out well, don't you think?"

Helena bent over a clump of yellow pom-pom dahlias and mused, "Unusually early for daisies, isn't it?"

"Actually they're both dahlias," corrected Quill cheerfully, then immediately regretting the lapse, said, "The British Dahlia Society's registered more than twenty varieties, which is a lot to keep up with, of course. Mike forces them in the greenhouses out back."

"All twenty?" asked Helena sweetly. "How clever of you."

The village lay at the foot of the Inn, curving around a bend in the Hemlock River. They walked through the heavily wooded park, passing the bandstand and the statue of General C. C. Hemlock, who had founded the village three hundred years before. From the statue it was less than five minutes walk to Main Street.

The Chamber of Commerce, and through them the zoning boards were clearly dedicated to civic pride; most of the buildings on Main were of cobblestone, carefully restored and meticulously maintained. The rest were white clapboard trimmed in black, in keeping with the town's Colonial heritage as interpreted from the village building code. Along Main Street's flank, huge baskets of scarlet geraniums swung from the wrought-iron street lamps. Black painted planters filled with early blooming marigolds and purple pansies flanked wrought-iron benches underneath. There were some advantages, Quill thought, to the Chamber's fierce dedication to such civic activities as Clean It Up! Week.

"Marvelous," murmured Helena, frankly, peering up and down the street. "I envy you this life, Quill. I can see exactly why you left SoHo. This is so unpeopled."

The current population of Hemlock Falls was three thousand four hundred and twenty-six, and on any given day of the week perhaps ten or twelve citizens were out shopping, gossiping, or running errands. If Helena was out looking for an audience, thought Quill, she'd just have to accept that this was it. She caught sight of Esther West, standing in front of her dress shop in a print dress splashed with scarlet begonias talking animatedly to a customer. Neither of them looked toward Quill and her companion. Quill waved. Helena swept off her hat. The famous mane of golden hair gleamed in the afternoon sun.

"Charming, charming, *charming*," Helena projected. "We've got to get all this on tape for the show. We'll bring in some extras, of course. Preppie couples—awful word!—and a few Golden Retrievers. Darling, we're going to put you on the map." She ran a hand through her hair, gesturing widely. Esther still hadn't noticed them.

Directly across the street from the dress shop, Elmer Henry, mayor of Hemlock Falls, emerged from Marge Schmidt's Hemlock Hometown Diner, Harvey Bozzel on his heels. The two men stopped in their tracks. Elmer was wearing two BOOST HEMLOCK FALLS buttons on the lapel of his shiny polyester coat. Harvey grabbed Elmer by the arm and whispered in his ear, then started toward them at a dog trot, dragging Elmer behind him like a bashful barge. Esther and her customer turned to watch where Harvey was headed. Esther's jaw dropped. She shrieked.

Helena glanced casually at her watch. "God. Here they come. We'd better get going. Where is this post office of yours? I've got to get my package off."

She matched Quill's brisk pace down the sidewalk, the mayor and his entourage puffing in her wake.

The post office—a defiantly modern building—stood in the middle of the historic district, at the corner of Main and Maple, across from the Hemlock Falls Savings and Loan. One of Vern Mittermeyer's postal workers had sanded the flaking red trim and was in the middle of repainting.

"That looks wonderful, Lloyd," Quill said as they approached the front door.

"Might look good. Don't paint so good." He waved a loaded brush at the window ledge. "Spots something awful, this stuff."

"Excuse me," said Helena. "We'd like to get in?"

Lloyd pursed his lips. "Now, it's a good thing you stopped by, Ms. Quilliam. You're a painter, right? You know what's wrong with this stuff?"

"Excuse me!" Helena edged rancorously past the open can of Paramount Crimson Red, her skirt dangerously near the dripping lip.

"I'm not that kind of a painter," Quill said to Lloyd. "But it does look a little thick."

"It don't stick right. Stinks, too. Guess that's why they give it to the post office. Vern's always said folks don't app—"

"Sarah!" said Helena in a dangerous tone, "I'm *late*."

Quill pushed the door open for her.

The post office hours were listed in large black letters on the glass: HOURS 8:00 to 12:00. 1:00 to 5:00. Below this, in aggressive red marker, was hand-lettered: ACCORDING TO POSTAL CODE 2.134 NO EXCEPTIONS! THIS MEANS YOU.

Helena turned to Quill with a raised eyebrow.

"Vern Mittermeyer's postmaster," said Quill, knowing this was an inadequate explanation. "He's very . . . dedicated."

"Sweet," said Helena. "Look, it's quarter to four, already. I've got to get back and change for that seven o'clock cocktail party." She looked behind heir. Harvey, flanked by Esther and a pregnant customer, was less than a block away. Elmer puffed a few steps behind.

"Vern shouldn't keep you too long," said Quill dubiously.

They went into the building, the door swinging shut in Harvey's face. He pressed his face to the glass. A circle of moisture formed beneath his nose.

Quill saw with relief that only one customer stood at the counter. "Eloise!" she said loudly. "How have you been? Helena, this is Eloise Nicholson. Eloise has lived in Hemlock Falls for . . . how long is it?"

"Eighty-nine years!" said Eloise proudly. "I was born here. I haven't seen you for the longest time, Quill." She adjusted the hearing aid under a fluffy white curl and tottered forward on her cane. "How is your dear sister?"

"She's just fine!" shouted Quill. "And how are you?"

Pleased, Eloise planted a foot on either side of her cane and took a breath to respond. Helena looked at the clock on the wall and pressed past Quill to the counter. "I need to send this overnight to Manhattan."

"Gotta get in line," said Vern, nodding to an undefined space behind Eloise.

Helena thrust her famous profile next to his and put the package under his nose. She tapped the return address meaningfully with a buffed fingernail. "I'm on deadline, here," she said.

Vern eased from one skinny hip to the other. "Next!" he shouted at Eloise.

Eloise blinked. "I'll be just a moment, dear Quill." She turned, set her large plastic handbag on the countertop, and rummaged through it.

Helena rapped the counter sharply. "Will you take this while she's finding her mail, please?"

Vern blinked at her slowly, like a particularly malevolent turtle. "What'cha got there, Eloise?"

"My rebates, Mr. Mittermeyer." Eloise emerged from her purse triumphant, a thick sheaf of pink envelopes in her hand. Quill recognized Doreen's Pink Morning sixteen percent rag content stationery from the budget line.

Vern cast a beady eye over the envelopes. "Need the ZIP codes."

"Then you can take this while she gets them," snapped Helena.

"Eastman Kodak Company, Rochester, New York," said Vern, squinting at Eloise's first envelope. "Gotta look that up for ya." He turned, pulled a thick volume from the shelf behind him, thumbed through it, then read, "One-four-six-oh-four."

"One-four-six-oh . . . four?" Eloise wrote as she spoke.

"Ayuh." Vern took the envelope, shuffled to the out-of-town mail bin, dropped it in, and shuffled back to Eloise. He picked up the second envelope. "Procter and Gamble," he read aloud.

In the ensuing minutes Quill discovered that Eloise had coupons for a disproportionately large percentage of the Fortune 500.

". . . Chicago, Illinois," finished Vern, finally, "oh-oh-two-six-seven. That'll be it, Eloise." He cast a severe look over Helena's head. "Next!"

Helena stepped forward.

"He'p you?"

"This is to go overnight to Manhattan," said Helena between her teeth.

Vern looked at the clock. "You gotta come back tomorrow."

"What?"

"You gotta get overnights to Manhattan in before four o'clock," Vern said. "Otherwise it won't get there until Friday. This is Wednesday, see? You mail it today, it ain't gonna get there until Friday."

"And what if I mail it tomorrow morning?"

"Thursday?" said Vern. His face brightened perceptibly. "Oh, it'll get there Friday, for sure."

Helena's face turned a dangerous shade of pink.

"Take the package, Vern," said Quill.

"If I mail it now," said Helena, "it won't get there until Friday."

"Right."

"And if I mail it tomorrow?"

"Oh, it'll get there Friday, all right," said Vern.

The dangerous shade of pink deepened to emergency mauve.

Quill pulled the manuscript from Helena's unresisting fingers. "Vern," said Quill. "We want this package to get there Friday. How should we do it?"

"Friday?" Vern thought this over. "Couple of ways to do that. Two-Day Priority. Or you could come back tomor—"

"Two-Day Priority," said Quill. "That's exactly what we want. Thank you, Vern. Helena, there's an amazing crowd of fans outside. Why don't you take care of some autographs and I'll get this sent off?"

"Is there a back way out?"

"Well, yes, but I thought—"

"My fans?" Helena didn't laugh, precisely, it was a sound more like the high-pitched squeal of an old Chevy rounding a sharp bend at high speed. "Fuck them." She slung her heavy handbag over her shoulder "No. I want a place to dump this bastard's *body*. Is there one of those big trash bins out back? That'll do just fucking fine."

"Oh, my," said Eloise, pleasurably offended.

Quill guided Helena to the door and pushed her into the waiting arms of the crowd. Eloise thumped out after her.

Vern snapped his gum and gazed incuriously at Quill. "He'p you?"

"How much is that, Vern? For Two-Day Priority."

"She shoulda sent it Monday."

"What?"

Vern gestured at the large red, blue, and white sign under the clock. "Tells all about it on that sign."

"She was in here Monday?"

"Lookin' for the Hall. What Hall, I says to her. You mean the Legion. Thought it was some mansion. I says to her, I says, you mean the Le—"

"Nine-ninety for a one-pound package," Quill read from the Priority Mail sign. "Here's ten. Keep the change."

"Baltimore don't allow us to keep the change," said Vern doggedly.

Quill grabbed the dime. Then pushed her way out the front door and into the small crowd on the sidewalk. Eloise, balancing on her cane, was clearly in the middle of a story involving the "F" word, famous actresses, and overnight Express Mail. From the look on everyone's face, it was a hit. The actress in question was nowhere in sight.

"Up the hill and through the woods," said Elmer Henry, in response to Quill's question. He stuck out his chest and lowered his head to form a third chin. "Quill, could you approach the young lady to appear at the Chamber meeting tomorrow? It'd guarantee us a pret' good turnout, and you know how the members have been missing meetings lately." He leaned forward and whispered. " 'Course, if what Eloise says here is true . . ."

A backfire from somewhere near the park obscured his whisper, and Quill said, "Pardon, Mayor?"

". . . 'fuck'!" shouted Elmer, to his constituents' consternation and his own alarm. 'This bidness of the language . . ." he trailed off uneasily.

The ensuing discussion seemed endless. Quill waited patiently for a tactful opening; at the first opportunity she promised to do her best, then said, "Could you guys excuse me? I've got . . ." Quill stopped, not sure what she'd got. "My hands full," she finished.

She walked down Main to the park road intersection, trying to arrange pieces of the puzzle. Why would Helena have lied about meeting the Bosses Club? *Had* she met the Bosses Club? She stepped off the curb into the street and jumped back as a large red pickup truck turned the corner with a shriek of its overinflated tires and a second backfire. Quill had seen the driver before: Rickie Pennifarm, Dawn's husband.

"Hey!" yelled Quill, waving her hand. "Rickie. Stop!"

He shot a bloodshot gaze over his shoulder and gunned the motor.

What she should do, thought Quill, was go back to the Inn and follow Rickie to his trailer and see if he knew anything about the forty-five hundred dollars John needed to make payroll. Quill walked back through the park wondering if Helena Houndswood's lies mattered and guiltily acknowledging that she'd far rather untangle Helena's odd behavior than go bill collecting. The Bosses Club's preference for polyester and home perms didn't fit Helena's notion of the Beautiful Person living the Beautiful Life. But so what? She couldn't change the facts: the women had won the contest, and even Helena couldn't take the money away from them. What she could do was make life pretty unpleasant for everyone in the next three weeks with snide comments, outrageous behavior, and obnoxious demands.

Quill passed the statue of General C. C. Hemlock and stopped at the entrance to the footpath through the birch woods. The sky's blue was past celestial, she thought, green scents spiraled through the sunny air, and she was heartily sick of Helena Houndswood. A walk through the birch trees would put things in better proportion.

The woods were silent, except for the cracking of twigs beneath her feet. It was cool without the direct rays of the sun, and Quill rubbed her arms, suddenly oppressed by the quiet. A black fly snarled past her ear, then another. Gradually the tide of silence was overcome by insect whine. Quill stopped to look for the source. She'd walked into black flies once before, and they had a sting to rival hornets. A thick cloud clustered at the base of a bodelia bush. She stepped back onto a discarded pile of plastic. The color was familiar. She picked it up and shook it out. A bowling jacket, soggy with moisture; the embroidered name on the pocket read *Dot*.

Quill frowned at the blood on her hand. Then froze. And for a long, icy moment refused to look at the mass of flies and what they fed on.

CHAPTER 4

"Are you sure you're all right?" John sat next to Quill on the couch in her office, an arm companionably around her shoulders. Meg was curled in the chair behind Quill's desk. Doreen leaned against the closed door, arms folded. "Do you want a little more brandy?"

Quill shook her head and set the snifter on the coffee table. "No, I shouldn't have had that bit. I was just so cold."

"Horrible," murmured Meg.

"Sher'f comin'?" asked Doreen.

"Myles is still in Ithaca. Dave Kiddermeister's in charge," Quill said. "He said he had everything under control." She ran her hands through her hair. "Dave thinks it looks like a hunting accident."

"A hunting accident? In June?" Meg slung her feet on the desktop. "Bullshit."

"Folks after woodchucks this time of year?" observed Doreen. "Hard to mistake a person for a woodchuck. On t'other hand I din't know her. This Dot."

"Not a lot of people did," said Quill "She lives—lived—in a trailer out near the paint factory. A husband, Dave said. The boys are grown and have left home. One of the other deputies knew the family. Not very popular, I guess."

"Well, it's too bad," Meg said briskly, "but I don't know what we can do about it. And you look a little less ghastly than when you came in, so I'm getting back to the kitchen."

Quill frowned "Just like that?"

"Sorry. But I didn't know Dot Vandermolen from Adam. I'm

concerned about you, of course. It must have been awful, seeing the body."

"Well, it was. But that's not the most awful part."

"What could have been more awful than finding a corpse with its head blown off?" said Meg.

"I don't think it was an accident."

"You mean murder?" Meg's eyebrows lifted. John groaned. "Who would want to kill Dot what's-her-name? Vandermolen."

"I don't know anything about Dot Vandermolen personally," said Quill. "But the woman just won two hundred thousand dollars. And she was very aggressive. And besides . . ." Quill trailed off. Helena Houndswood had passed through the park not ten minutes before Quill found Dot's body. The "backfire" Quill'd heard when she was in front of the post office had obviously been the shots that had killed her. But if Dave Kiddermeister thought it was a hunting accident—were the backfire noises she heard rifle shots? Where would Helena get a rifle? She'd been carrying an overlarge handbag. Did they make rifles that collapsed like umbrellas? Quill frowned and pulled at her lower lip.

"Besides what?" asked John.

"I did see Rickie Pennifarm driving away from the park," Quill admitted. "In that brand-new Bubba truck he owns with the lifts and the giant tires . . ."

"And the gun rack," finished Meg. "There you are, then. Did you tell Deputy Dave?"

"Yes. But why would Rickie Pennifarm want to shoot Dot?"

"More for him and Dawn," said Doreen. "Don't have to split that million five ways."

"1 don't think so," Quill said. "I mean, the money would go to the heirs, right? Not the rest of the group."

"Not necessarily." John tapped his pencil against his lip with a thoughtful expression. "Sometimes those contests aren't assignable. We could check that out. Why don't you ask Helena, Quill?"

Quill got to her feet. "I'll leave that to Myles," she said virtuously. "In the meantime, I'd better make sure Helena understands it'd be inappropriate to have the party now. John, do you know if they make rifles that collapse like umbrellas?"

"That what?" A suspicion of a grin lightened his face. "That *was* a large bag she was carrying," he agreed.

"You think Helena had somethin' to do with this?" Meg ran one hand through her hair. "Jeepers, Quill."

"I'm just going to talk to her about the party—and maybe a few other things. Under the circumstances, I'm sure Helena will want to wait a few days for the Bosses Club celebration."

"Bet she won't," said Meg.

"Of course she will. Even Helena Houndswood can't ignore this."

"Wanna bet?" Meg followed her sister to the door. "You just let me know *instantly* if we've got a party tonight."

"There won't be a party tonight," said Quill. "Where is she?"

"Outside," said Doreen briefly. "Went down to the wood to talk to Deputy Dave. Pokin' her nose in, I call it."

Quill overtook Helena at the dahlia border. Her complexion was its usual porcelain perfection. She was observing the dwarf pom-poms with critical respect. "Do you know," she said as Quill came up, "I had a fan call in to one of my flower specials last year and absolutely insist that these adorable little things were part of the daisy family?" She slipped her arm confidingly through Quill's. "Doom, death, and disaster, I understand."

"It's horrible," said Quill shortly.

"Hunting accident, according to that bovine deputy. I went down there of course—can't keep the reporter out of this little girl—and he found the bullet casing. It's a what? A two-seventy caliber. Deputy thought someone was hunting out of season."

"It was a rifle wound?"

"Apparently. Now. About the party for these tacky little winners . . ."

Quill stared at her. Helena wasn't carrying her handbag. It hadn't been large enough to conceal a rifle. She was still wearing the long, full skirt and loose overblouse. Could she have tucked the rifle inside her clothing, somehow? Swiped it from Rickie's truck and replaced it? Would Rickie let her borrow the rifle to murder Dot?

"These little fits happen often, sweetie?"

Quill blinked. Helena snapped off a dahlia and stuck it in the brim of her hat. "It's almost twenty to six. Your little party is set up for seven, *n'est-ce pas*? I'm going to need the time to recharge myself to meet these—how many women did you say? Just three, now, right? Can you be a doll and take care of them for me, if I'm just the teensiest bit late? I need a good long soak in that marvelous whirlpool tub of yours. I feel quite—not fresh."

"You're not thinking of going ahead with the party?"

"Let me remind you, sweetie, I've got exactly three weeks until airtime. I didn't know this Dot. I'm dreadfully sorry for the accident, of course, but time and TV wait for no man. And I've got a lot to do to shape those women up. No? You think I'm wrong to go ahead? Tell you what. You call those girls and offer them a choice; party tonight to celebrate their win, or a suitable time for mourning somebody they didn't seem to like very much anyway from what the deputy tells me. The less notice that's taken of this the better."

"Perhaps I can find another location for the party," said Quill, a little stiffly.

"You're serious!" Helena laughed. "Get real, sweetie. Where else is there in this burg?"

"There's a Marriott on route fifteen. I'm sure they'll be glad—"

"Come on. Both of us have stepped over worse on the streets of Manhattan. And you really want to send all this money to a competitor? Look. We'll go top flight. Okay? I'm always looking for delicious new ideas for the show. Tell what's her name, Meg, that I'll think about a cooking segment on the shoot. Maybe. Just maybe."

Rage made Quill dizzy. She turned abruptly and left to find Meg. She, John, and Doreen had abandoned the office for the dining room and some hot tea.

"That woman," said Meg, after Quill had given a clipped, angry account of Helena's demands, "absolutely boggles the mind. So we've got a cocktail party for how many? Kay, Sandy, and Connie? I'd better check the supplies."

"Do you think they'll show up?" said Quill. "Sandy and Connie and Kay. And what about Dawn?"

Doreen gave a cynical snort.

"It's just awful to have Dot's death pass totally . . ."

"Unremarked?" suggested John. "Why don't we do something for Dot's family? A donation from the Inn for the funeral?"

"You think we should go ahead with this, too?" Quill said.

"Short of throwing her out—and the revenue for the rest of the year with her—I don't see what else we can do."

"I do," said Meg. "We'll go ahead with this party, but we'll sabotage the food. A little cayenne in the *crème brûlée* . . ."

"No!" shouted John, Quill, and Doreen together.

"Let's go ahead," said Quill reluctantly. "At least she wants you to go all out, Meggie."

"All out? In less than two hours? Dammit, I knew I shouldn't have canceled that salmon. How am I supposed to go all out without any salmon?"

"All of it?" said Quill. "What are the environmentalists going to eat? The Friends of Fresh Air?"

"What about them?" Meg began to rake her hands through her hair, an ominous sign.

"Environmentalists don't eat meat, Meg. At least, I would expect that they'd eat more fish than meat. They suck fish up like vacuum cleaners. Everyone knows that. Why did you cancel all the salmon?"

"Because you made me!" Meg shrieked untruthfully. "I've got shrimp and haddock. That's it." She pulled a pen from John's breast pocket and began to scribble on the tablecloth. "Quennelles of scampi and haddock?" she muttered. "Are you kidding? When are they coming?"

"Two of the FOFA people have already checked in," said John calmly. "Makepeace and Abigail Whitman. He's the director. Ten more couples are arriving this evening."

"You'll just have to send them down to Marge Schmidt's," said Meg. "I can't do environmentalists and Helena Houndswood, too."

"They did ask for nonsmoking rooms," said Quill. "Doreen, you made sure . . ."

Doreen set her teacup down with a smack. "I'd just like to know how come everyone's in a state of the jimjams. I know my job, don't I? I don't suit, I can always get a job down to the Marriott on route fifteen. They got a better health plan, anyways." She scowled. "And no fancy actress throwing her weight around."

"Let's not let her get to us," said Quill. "It's going to be much worse if we start whacking each other. Doreen, if you could find out from Mr. and Mrs. Whitman if any of the group is vegetarian, I'll call the supplier and reorder the salmon."

"You stay out of my kitchen!" Meg jumped up, slammed through the dining room doors to her stove, only to reappear seconds later. "They won't deliver without a check. Did you get that money? Is there any money in this place? Or do I have to screw the delivery boy to get fresh fish!" The double doors banged shut.

Quill put her head in her hands.

"Them yellow socks," Doreen observed. Then, "Time that one had a date, if you ast me."

Quill peered at her through her fingers and refrained from saying that nobody had. "Maybe we should close up for a week?"

"I'd rather not," said John. "That's disaster plan B. In the 'How did you like the play, Mrs. Lincoln' vein—did you get that check from Hudson?"

"No," said Quill. "Dawn Pennifarm didn't show up for the Bosses Club meeting. There was a check stub in her bookkeeping files, but no check. Hudson said he couldn't reissue a check without knowing what happened to the first one. I think we've got trouble. Do either of you know Dawn Pennifarm very well?"

"That husband Rickie of hers is a no-good," said Doreen. "Seen him at the Croh Bar much more'n I should." She chewed on a lump of sugar, reflectively. "Mean son of a gun."

"Do you suppose she just left town with as much money as she could scrape together?" said Quill. "I didn't know her very well, but she was a pretty angry person. A lot like Dot Vandermolen, as a matter of fact. Little younger."

"Word is Dawn's been at the battered women's shelter more than once," John observed.

Quill hesitated. John was a member of A.A., and loath to betray any of its members. "Has Rickie been part of your group?"

John moved the sugar bowl to the exact center of the table. "I don't think the homelife is too good."

Quill, who knew John better than anybody else, decided this was as far as he'd go with a yes.

"And Dawn sure don't have much of a job at that there factory," said Doreen. "I worked there once, you know. Back some ten years ago. Awful, the fumes and all. OSHA come in twice time I was there to shut the joint down."

"It's gotten a lot better since Hudson's taken over," said John. "Paint manufacturing's tough. A lot of the solvents they used to use in oil-base have been banned."

"Not exactly a desirable career," said Quill. "Dawn sounds like a woman with lots of reasons to leave town."

"But she won that million bucks," said Doreen. "She'd stick around for that."

Meg poked her head through the swinging doors. "They're bringing the salmon right up. They'll wait for the cash for a week or two. And guess what? They've got crab!" She disappeared. Quill hoped, for the last time. Once Meg got down to cooking, her temper became serene, if not sunny.

"I won a million bucks, I'd belt that Rickie good and stick around to pick it up." Doreen crunched a second lump of sugar.

"They didn't know about the win until today," said John.

Quill shoved the sugar bowl left of center. "It's possible," she said, "that Dawn knew two days ago."

"But the only one who knew about the win before this afternoon was Helena Houndswood," said John.

"Exactly." Quill sat back in her chair and folded her arms. "There's more. Helena took the same path I did back to the Inn this afternoon, John. She wasn't more than ten minutes ahead. Let's say that Dawn isn't missing Let's say she's . . . well, permanently out of the way. Let's say that . . ."

"No," said John "No. No. No! Put it *out* of your mind, Quill. We've got problems enough without this. Helena didn't even know Dot Vandermolen by sight. If anyone's responsible for anything, it's Rickie Pennifarm."

"But why would Rickie shoot Dot?"

"That's not our problem, Quill. We've got a host of others. Let's not borrow any more. And speaking of borrowing—I'm going to have to do something about cash flow pretty soon. I need a decision from you about whether to get personal loans from the bank, or delay payment to suppliers, or close, the Inn for a week or two."

"Problems with the bank. Bodies in the bushes. Witchy actresses. Decisions. Yuck! I'm moving to Alaska." Quill tugged furiously at a strand of her hair and bit it. "You're right. Involving Helena in this doesn't make sense. I must be losing my mind."

John covered her hand with his. "I don't mean to be intrusive, Quill, but maybe this marriage business with Myles is getting to you a little. Have you talked to Meg?"

"No."

"Time to stop takin' care of her," said Doreen gruffly. "She should be takin' care of herself. Does all right on her own if you ast me."

Quill shook her head. "She's still mourning Colin. I can tell. Sometimes I think if he'd had an illness, she would have coped with it better. She would have had more time to think what life would be like without him. But the car accident was so sudden. And they were so happy. It was awful."

"She'll marry again," said John.

"Both of you should," said Doreen. "Fix all this up."

"How would marriage fix all this up?" Quill demanded indignantly.

"Reg'lar sex life," said Doreen. "Good for ya."

"I've *got* a regular sex life!" She moved restlessly in her chair. "It's not just Meg that's keeping me from a decision about Myles. My own marriage wasn't a perfect romance ending in sudden death, John. It was grisly, day-to-day awful. And he wasn't a bad guy. I'm not certain I want to jump into that kind of contract again. We're doing well, here, aren't we? I mean, it's taken a pile of work for all of us to make the Inn successful. I'm proud of it. We've done it together. We're happy the way we are. Why change it?"

"I suppose we'll pull out of this slump—assuming the bank gives us the line of credit," said John.

"That's the accountant in you," said Quill. "I made sure you were properly gloomy about business forecasts when we hired you. Who wants a cheerful business manager? You're in charge of doom, death, and disaster, and I'm in charge of keeping the guests happy and the staff comfortable . . ."

"Quill?" Dina Muir, her hair ruffled, approached the table at a run. "There's about fifty people in tuxes and stuff milling around the lobby. What am I supposed to do with them?"

"Fifty people?" Quill looked at her watch. "Good grief, it's almost seven o'clock. It's not the Bosses Club, is it?"

"And their husbands, kids, mothers-in-law, cousins, plus half the Chamber of Commerce. You'd better come quick."

The lobby was as jammed as Bloomingdale's the day after Thanksgiving. Quill surveyed the crowd in astonishment. The front door opened. Helena Houndswood, still in her rose-covered hat and floating skirt, drifted into the room. She stiffened. The crowd surged forward. She jammed the hat over her head and ran upstairs.

"That was her!" breathed Sandy Willis. "See, Roy, I told you! It's really true!"

"You're early," said Quill. She looked around the room. "All of you."

"Not all of us," Sandy said. "We keep calling Dawnie, but she hasn't shown up. And Kay's not here yet." She glanced at Quill, then quickly away. "You heard about Dot?"

It seemed to Quill that the massive crowd quieted a little. "Yes. I'm sorry. I know that Helena insisted on the party, and you must feel just awful about it."

"Yeah. Well, to be perfectly honest, that's not real true, you know what I mean? Thing is, none of us knew her all that well. And she kind of horned in the china contest, once she joined the bowling team and the Bosses Club. Dave Kiddermeister said it was a hunter or something?"

"Myles hasn't done an investigation yet," said Quill carefully "He's in Ithaca."

"Dave's good at his job. Looks like a hunting accident, probably is a hunting accident. That's what everybody else thinks. And Quill. Nobody wants this to drive Helena Houndswood away. You know what I mean. I mean, it's not like it was on purpose or anything. Just an accident."

There was a murmur of agreement among the crowd, like the threat of a tidal wave on a sunny afternoon at the beach. Quill thought of Elmer and Harvey and Esther West chasing Helena Houndswood down the street that afternoon. Single-handedly, the actress had transformed the nice neighborly citizens of Hemlock Falls into raging opportunists.

Sandy tugged at the skirt of her evening dress. "Anyway, it's okay that we're early, isn't it? And we look okay, don't we? We weren't sure that she wouldn't have the TV cameras right here, and everything, so I called the girls and told them to really put on the dog."

"You look fine," said Quill.

Sandy's advice to dress up had been interpreted in varying ways. Connie herself was in pale blue chiffon, with a lace top, capped sleeves, and a full skirt that came just below her knees. Her satin shoes were dyed pale blue to match. Sandy had opted for basic black, with a scoop neck that revealed the sharp lines between a deep gardening tan, the pale tops of her freckled breasts, and more than a hint of her underwire bra.

Several perfumes fought the air: Evening in Paris, which Quill hadn't smelled since she was eight years old; Obsession; the room-deodorant smell of Liz Claiborne. The Bosses Club was augmented by husbands and boyfriends (mostly sport coats and string ties) and the Chamber of Commerce, Elmer Henry a self-important bulge in their center. A number of ruddy-looking people in hiking shorts and T-shirts lettered FOFA: WE'RE THE FRIENDS OF FRESH AIR! added to the general confusion.

Feeling somewhat like a border collie ordered to "herd them ducks!" Quill set about the task of sorting the Bosses Club into the conference room and the interlopers from the village into the dining room. She turned the FOFA members over to Doreen to show to their various rooms. John took the husbands, boyfriends, excited relatives, and Hudson Zabriskie into the Tavern Bar, "just," Quill explained to Sandy's husband Roy, "until Ms. Houndswood can meet the winners. She's only expecting the Bosses Club, you know."

"They all split the cash, equal," said Roy anxiously. "She knows that, don't she?"

"Quill'll take care of it," said Sandy, pressing close to his side. "She and Helena are practically best friends."

"Tell Nate to run a house tab, Roy. Sandy, I'll see your team in the conference room in about ten minutes. We'll serve you dinner there. I'm going to check with Meg to see everything's all right."

Quill walked into the kitchen, slapped her hand on the counter, and said, "Whiskey for me. Fresh horses for my men."

"How's by you, Colonel?" asked Meg cheerfully. She twitched pieces of mint leaves gracefully into place on a plate of cucumber-caviar toast rounds.

"Fine. Just fine. Nobody seems to miss Dot, much. I mean, there's a few comments of the 'shame about the body in the woods, but where's Helena!' variety, but no one's crying in their beer, that's for sure. They're all too worried Helena's going to leave town. Harvey even asked me if he thought the Chamber should write an official letter of apology for the disturbance. Can you believe it?"

"You look like a game hen confronting the ax. Have a glass of sherry. It'll settle you."

Quill sank into the rocking chair near the cobblestone hearth and accepted a glass of the Spanish Pale Dry Meg kept in a cupboard. "Let's put a lock on the kitchen door."

"A large German shepherd would do just as well."

"The way the day's going, it'd bite all the guests and we'd get sued and have to give up the Inn and move to Detroit."

Meg set the cold food aside and started filling delicate shells of pastry with a mixture from her pastry cone. She began to sing, words she'd made up to the melody of Chopin's Polonaise: "Vic-tor-ri-ous! (you bet) and the food it will be glorious (I'm set) . . ."

Quill, rubbing the back of her neck, felt some of the accumulated agitation of the day slip away. "You're not having a hissy fit over all the guests?"

Meg gestured backward with her wooden spoon. "I called in the *sous* chefs. First time all summer. And the salmon's here. And the crab."

"So everything's hinky."

"And I've got a new dish. What do you think?" Meg handed her a plate of plumply browned pastries. "Spinach and *herbes varieux*."

"*Herbes varieux*? Old herbs?"

"Various herbs. We are getting on in years, aren't we, that we've forgotten all our French. Time for a face-lift. Just ask Helena for the name of her doctor."

"They're terrific." Quill bit a second one in half. "She'll love them."

"La Helena's in the bag. That fourth star is just around the corner." She switched to "When You Wish Upon a Star," stopped, and said suddenly, "You don't think she might feature some of the cooking in the show?"

"*Et tu*, Margaret?"

"If you mean by that am I going to suck up to Helena Hounds-wood just because she's an arrogant, unfeeling celebrity show host . . . you bet your butt. I need my reputation back, Quill."

"You never lost your reputation," said Quill. "You've always been terrific. And some bitchy TV person who doesn't know a dahlia from a daisy has nothing to do with who you are or what you can do."

"Thank you, Doctor. You know where that kind of attitude got me in the past. Maybe it's time I sort of soft-pedal things a bit. Think about you for a change, instead of me."

"Has John been talking to you?" demanded Quill. "He couldn't have, he hasn't had the time." Her sister in a penitent mood was unsettling. "I mean, come on, Meg. You're a great chef. I expect volcanic temper tantrums from you. I expect red sock days and béchamel flying through the air at regular intervals."

"Well." Meg fiddled a bit with the pastry cone, then turned and slid the tray into the broiler. "Is somebody going to tell me how many reservations we've got? These hors d'oeuvres are going to be ready in about six seconds, and I've got to do a quick estimate of the specials."

"John'll come in with the count." Quill got to her feet. "I'll carry some of that stuff in to the Bosses Club, if it's ready. Or do you think we should wait for the star to descend? She went up to change clothes again."

"How many times is that today?" said Meg, clearly fascinated.

"I counted once this morning, once this afternoon, and a third time for cocktails. She's booked the dining room at eight-thirty for dinner. For four. I wonder if she'll change a fourth time for that?"

"Bet you she does," said Meg.

"Nobody can take that many showers in a day."

"A dollar fifty says she does."

"Done." They shook hands. A timer rang, and Meg slid the cheese puffs out of the oven. "I'll take these in to the Bosses Club, Quill. I want to congratulate them in person. Why don't you slip into something more . . . you know . . ."

"You don't like this?" She glanced down at her challis skirt.

"It's a little . . . small town."

Quill stamped up the stairs to her suite of rooms defiantly determined to look small town.

She decided on a calf-length black skirt, a lavish white silk blouse, and high strappy sandals which looked so sophisticated that she got cross and had another glass of sherry. She drained it with a flourish. Everyone, she decided grandly, if a little vaguely, deserved what they were going to get.

"This is wonderful," said Helena with apparent sincerity to the gratified winners some thirty minutes later. "You all are marvelous. I'm just so sorry I can't stay for the dinner Sarah's arranged for you and learn all about you right now! You all worked together to win the prize? I am just so impressed, I can't even begin to tell you. This is *fab*-ulous."

"All of us," said Sandy Willis. "Dot, too, of course." There was a short—very short—moment of silence between the women, whose starstruck gazes hadn't left Helena's face from the moment the actress had arrived at the conference room in a Diane Freis cocktail dress. "And don't forget Dawn and Kay. They're part of it, too. I'm sure Kay is going to be along any minute. She was that excited to be here."

Quill poured herself a glass of sherry and brooded. Where *was* Kay?

"Nobody answered at her house," said Connie. "Roosevelt and I drove by on our way here and her trailer was dark. Her car was gone."

Quill, startled, hadn't realized she'd spoken aloud. "She's a widow, isn't she?"

"Cancer," said Connie, nodding grimly. "Got him last year. He was only forty-six. Smoked like a chimney. Sons are grown and out of the house."

"Kay and Dawn were that close," said Sandy. She swallowed the last of a grapefruit and vodka drink Nate called a Fuzzy Navel. "Maybe Kay took out after Dawn, and that's why she's not here. Say—what happens if Dawn or Kay don't show up at all?"

Nobody answered this question. Helena had a brightly interested, concerned look that Quill thought as phony as a two-dollar bill. Except the Federal Mint had issued a two-dollar bill, hadn't it?

She set the sherry bottle down with a determined thump and brooded darkly. Myles would know about the two-dollar bill. And about what had happened to their forty-five hundred dollars. And whether Rickie Pennifarm had murdered poor Dot. Except Myles was in Ithaca. Or Syracuse. On the other hand, it looked very much like Myles McHale standing, no, looming in the doorway to the conference room "Hey," said Quill. He looked terrific. She walked unsteadily out to the hall.

"Hey, yourself," said Myles. "I hear you discovered a body."

"That was no body. That was Dot Vandermolen." She blinked at him. "Or Dawn Pennifarm. Or Kay Gondowski. They're all gone. Are you back to investigate?"

"The investigation can wait a bit. Dave did a credible job. And you were a good witness. You saw Rickie's pickup truck leaving the area near the shooting a few minutes before?"

Quill nodded and kept on nodding. "Heard the rifle shots, too, I think. But then, so did the mayor and Harvey and Esther. I don't know about Eloise Nicholson. She's pretty deaf. But you're back." She stopped nodding, not entirely certain why she'd started. "You don't think Rickie did it?"

"Dave's already got most of the force looking for him. He'll pick Rickie up eventually. We'll see when Dave brings him in. I'm back here to investigate Dawn Pennifarm. She's now been officially missing for more than seventy-two hours."

"She's run off with our money," Quill mourned. "And that's not all. The Bosses Club won a million dollars. The Inn's going to be on TV. Kay Gondowski's missing. And I don't like . . . certain people."

"Not me, I hope."

"Nope. Not you. Not good ol' gorgeous you. Certn'ly not you." Quill hiccuped.

Myles leaned forward, brushed her cheek with his lips, and inhaled. "Bad day?"

"Certn'ly not!" said Quill indignantly. "Well, moderately bad."

"Why don't I get you some coffee, and we'll talk about it."

"There's a whole fresh pot in the conference room." Quill leaned against the wall and closed her eyes. Time passed. Myles wrapped an arm around her and gave her a warm mug of coffee. She sipped at it, leaning into him. "That sherry must have hit me," she admitted. "It was just three little glasses. I think."

"That's quite a collection in there." Myles nodded toward the conference room. "Who's the blonde?"

"For the fourth—and last—time today," said Quill. "It's Helena Houndswood. Murderess." She explained. It took two more cups of coffee. By the third cup, her head had cleared. "So what I'm worried about is Kay. Honestly, Myles, you don't know Helena. She should have gone ballistic over these winners. And you went in there twice. And what was she doing?"

"She was quite pleasant," said Myles. "But then, some murderesses are."

"Quite pleasant. You see? I thought so," said Quill. "And if you don't call that suspicious, I don't know what you call suspicious." She squinted at him. "What do you think happened to Dawn Pennifarm? Do you think she took off with a bunch of payroll receipts from Paramount, and our forty-five hundred dollars? Or do you think Helena Houndswood paid her a tidy little sum on the side to disappear. And Where's Kay? Tell me that!"

"One thing at a time, Quill. I haven't had time to look into Dot's death. As far as Dawn Pennifarm is concerned, we don't have charges on her. Hudson doesn't know if any money's missing or not."

"He doesn't know?"

"He claims that Dawn Pennifarm was 'empowered' to handle the bookkeeping, and his orders from New York are to let the employees make decisions pertinent to their job descriptions. He saw monthly numbers and didn't get involved in the day-to-day accounting. He won't know if there's a shortage until Dawn's backup gives him a report."

"That's Connie," said Quill. "She's Dawn's backup."

"As far as Dawn herself is concerned, I checked with the women's shelter. Bebe Cardoza said she came to some kind of crisis point last week during one of the group therapy sessions. My guess is that she headed for Detroit to her sister's. With or without your money."

"Dawn wouldn't have left now," said Quill instantly. "Not without her two hundred thousand dollars."

"You're assuming she knew about winning the two hundred thousand dollars, Quill. From what you've just told me, no one knew until today."

The look on Myles's face was all too familiar: wariness that she was sticking her nose into his investigations; slight amount of exasperation; amusement. Quill's frown turned into a scowl. "Dot's dead. Dawn's gone. And Kay is missing. None of this has anything to do with Rickie Pennifarm. If it does it's because of Helena Houndswood and that million dollars. Don't look at me like that."

Myles raised an eyebrow.

"That 'what does the little woman have in her pretty little head now' look. Miss Kitty," she added obscurely.

"You're too young to remember *Gunsmoke*. What do you mean, Kay is missing, too? She's an hour overdue for a cocktail party."

"One of the most important things in her life! You should start thinking about the possibilities here, Myles."

"I don't think anything until I have some facts. And you don't think about this at all, Quill. You're licensed to run an Inn, not the Tompkins County Sheriff's Department. Connie Weyerhauser's here, isn't she? I need to talk to her. Bebe Cardoza said if Dawn had talked to anyone about where she was going, it'd be Connie."

"It's what, seven forty-five? We're serving dinner at eight o'clock for the Bosses Club. Helena's got a party coming in at eight-thirty, so they should be breaking up pretty soon. This was a sort of combination celebration and introduction. I'll take you in now, if you don't mind dealing with Helena. She's"—Quill hesitated—"a little difficult."

Helena was not difficult at all, which irritated Quill profoundly. "God, he's *gorgeous*," she whispered to Quill, after Myles had skillfully extracted Connie from the group. "Lucky old you . . . unless it's not what you'd call an exclusive relationship? Don't answer that. I'll be crushed if it is. Be a doll, make my excuses to these girls, will you? I've got to run up and change for dinner. My producer's due in for a meeting, and the poor lamb will be frantic if I'm late. You might see if he's checked in, by the way, and let me know. The lawyer, too, the schmuck. And tell that good-looking sheriff to stop by the table around nine-thirty or so, will you? My nose tells me something's going on with this Dawn person. We'll want a teensy bit of brandy in that nice dark Tavern Bar of yours. You'll arrange that? Girls!" She clapped her hands suddenly. Sandy and Connie fell worshipfully silent. "Tomorrow morning. Ten A.M. sharp. Makeup session. Eleven-thirty we'll have a chat with the lawyer people and get all that icky business stuff out of the way."

"Tomorrow morning?" said Sandy.

"Yes, darling. We don't want the grass to grow under our feet."

"We gotta work," said Sandy. "Line's changing over to latex."

"Well, of course, but the . . . what is it . . . paint people can do without you for a few hours. I'm sure there's other workers who can handle whatever."

"Line's changing over to latex," said Sandy desperately. "And with three of us gone . . ."

"What she means is that we've been running oil-base for the last two weeks and we have to shut down, clean the ball mills and the mixers, and get them ready to make latex paint," Connie said. "It's a complicated job, and you can't do it without the supervisors. We're the supervisors. You know, the Bosses Club."

"We'll quit," said Sandy.

"We're not doing anything until we get the money settled," Connie said. "Here's what we do, Sandy. We tell Hudson to schedule the changeover third shift."

"He won't pay overtime," warned Sandy.

"Who cares?" said Connie. "We're rich!"

"I do," said Quill. "You guys will be exhausted. You won't get any sleep."

"We wouldn't anyhow," said Sandy, grinning. "Makeovers? New clothes? Two hundred thousand bucks? Whoop!"

"Whoop!" added Connie, with her rich laugh.

"We're going to sit with the guys in the bar until dinner's ready," said Sandy. "You want to join us, Quill? The drinks are on us!"

"Bring them back here for dinner in about twenty minutes," said Quill. "That will give Kathleen time to set up. I'll join you as soon as I can."

"You'll have to excuse Sarah, girls," said Helena, "she's got to do some things for me. Check on those other arrangements for me, will you, Quill? And don't forget the hunk."

"Don't forget the hunk," Quill repeated gloomily in the kitchen

some minutes later. A walk through the herb gardens at the back of
the Inn had cleared her head of sherry fumes. She'd come into the
kitchen by the back door to a scene of cheerful activity. The *sous*
chefs simmered sauces and grilled fish. Meg herself chopped meat
at the long butcher's block, whacking the bits in time to Figaro's
aria from *Il Barbiere.* The only Italian she remembered from the
solo was "bravissima Figaro," which made it repetitive as well as
tuneless. She abandoned the aria for nursery rhymes. "Ooooh . . ."
Meg sang, in response to Quill's summary of Helena's interest in
Myles. "I went to the Animal Fair. The birds and the beasts were
there . . . And what became of the hunk, the hunk, the hunk . . .
No. Wait! I've got it!" She stopped short and gesticulated wildly,
the meat cleaver in her left hand. This precipitated obvious anxiety on the part of the youngest *sous* chef, a Russian exchange student at the Cornell School of Hotel Management. Meg crouched
double, raised her left shoulder, dangled her left hand, and shuffled
sideways across the slate floor. "Hunk, Dr. Frankenstein? What
hunk!" She straightened up. The Cornell student eyed the meat
cleaver in alarm. "Remember? *Young Frankenstein*? Mel Brooks?
Quill! Snap out of it! We're going to be on TV! The world will see
our marvelousness. And the bookings will come rolling in . . ." Her
face brightened as she was reminded of yet a third song. Andrew
Lloyd Webber suffered next: "And the boo—o-okings kept rolling in from every side. Evita's pretty hands stretched far and they
stretched wide . . ."

"In one of her fits, is she?" said Doreen, stomping through the
swinging doors that led from the dining room. Simultaneously she
and Quill bent over to look at Meg's socks.

"Argyle," said Quill.

"Figures," said Doreen. They straightened up. "She needs to go
on those there friendly fresh-air hikes. Best thing for her. Clear her
head. Get right up near to God and Nature."

"So they're all settled in?"

"Ayuh. They like it fine. Anyhow, they need a bunch more
rooms for next week. Said it's one of the best places they bin. They
ast me to join 'em." Doreen smoothed her apron with a pleased
expression.

"Uh-oh," said Meg.

Quill, foreseeing the end of the stationery, which had been so uneventful, commented that the FOFA people had seemed very nice in a tone wistful with hope.

"Don't know about nice," said Doreen in a considering way. "Don't know that folks been persecuted like them are nice. Brave, more like."

"Persecuted? Hikers?" shrieked Meg. "Pooh!"

Doreen gave it as her opinion that them Quakers weren't as peaceful as they made out.

"You mean they're the 'Friends of Fresh Air' as in the Quakers are called the Friends?" said Quill.

"Ay-uh."

"But the Quakers are pacifists," said Meg. "And I thought the FOFA people were environmentalists or something."

"Yes, ma'am," said Doreen, "and you know about farmers. Them farmer Quakers just persecuted them Friends of Fresh Air right out of the church." There was a familiar, fanatical gleam in Doreen's beady eyes.

Meg and Quill exchanged a look. Meg's said, "Don't ask."

"What's this about farmers and environmentalists?" asked Quill.

"Horseshit," said Doreen.

"I beg your pardon?"

"Manure," said Meg. "I heard part of this while you were occupied with the Bosses Club. Manure disposal, to be precise. I was at the Heavenly Hogg's Farm today to order sausage, and you wouldn't believe the hassle over proper manure disposal. Mickey Dooley was telling me all about it."

Quill's sherry intake had left her with a monster headache. She remembered Doreen's entrepreneurial track record. She briefly mourned the demise of the stationery business. "Doreen."

"Yes'm?"

"Are the FOFA people here to stage a protest over Hemlock Falls' farmers' manure disposal practices?"

"No'm."

"They aren't going to march down Main Street waving signs about slurry control?"

"No, ma'am."

"All that's happening is that they absolutely love this place and want to book more rooms for the next week?"

"Yes, ma'am. If there's room. Thing is, they like that the TV people are gonna be here. On account of they're celebrities."

Quill eyed her, frustrated.

"Star magic," said Meg. "See? It's working already, I told you, didn't I?"

"Yes," said Quill, "it's great."

John came into the kitchen.

"My God," said Meg, "he's smiling."

"What is it?" said Quill. "Dawn Pennifarm showed up with the check?"

"Almost better than that." John swung a long leg over a stool and sat down. "We're totally booked for the next six weeks. Between the Houndswood TV people and FOFA, we're full. No Vacancy. Full House."

Meg performed a drumroll with her wooden spoons. "So soon, John?"

"I got a call from the Golden Pillar people . . ."

"That huge travel agency?" said Meg.

"They've heard she's staying here, and reserved half the rooms for the fall season. Once word gets out, they said, their clients are going to come down in droves. And"—he paused impressively—"*L'Aperitif* called. They want to review us for that fourth star." Meg screamed. "But not until early next year. Come with me and just take a look at the dining room, Quill. All of you."

They followed John to the double doors. Doreen pushed them open a crack. The room was jammed. Helena Houndswood sat at the table in the center of the room, directly under the crystal chandelier. The light gleamed on her golden hair. There were three men with her; the lawyer and the director, Quill guessed, and the third, broad shoulders straining his old tweed sport coat, was Myles "Hunk" McHale.

"Will you look at that," marveled Doreen, "sitting jawing at the table just like she was anybody ordinary and not a stuck-up actress with a swole upper lip. Wonder what the sheriff thinks?"

Helena leaned forward and spoke into Myles's ear.

Myles threw back his head and laughed.

"Stop that," ordered Doreen, "bad for ya."

"Stop what?" said Quill.

"Grinding your teeth," said Meg.

CHAPTER 5

With John right behind her, Quill pushed through the swinging doors. Meg's manic mood should have tipped her off; the dining room was full to overflowing and a riot of noise assaulted her. Extra tables had been tucked into the corners of the room. She had chosen mauve, cream, rose, and pale yellow to complement the view of the falls and enhance the enjoyment of Meg's food, but the room's usual quiet serenity was gone, swallowed up by bodies, food, and chatter.

Their waiters swirled around the room like skaters on a pond, trays held high over the diners' heads. Peter Hairston, one of the Cornell graduate students without whom Quill couldn't have staffed the Inn, gave her a high sign and pointed at Helena's table, miming "wine." John, whose knowledge of wines precluded the need for an official *sommelier*, threaded his way deftly toward Helena Houndswood's table and struck up a properly serious conversation with a slender, harried-looking man with a bald head. The producer, thought Quill. And she owed Meg a dollar and a half; Helena had changed for the fourth time into a little black dress that was very black, very little, and exposed a lot of gorgeous bosom. At Helena's left, a man with gray hair and a square, florid face was eating his way through what looked like Meg's latest experiment in starters, crab profiteroles. The lawyer. The fourth person at the table was, of course, Myles McHale, with the slight smile that always jolted Quill's heart. They were seated at table seven, the one with the most sweeping view of the gorge and the waterfall. Helena's teeth gleamed wolfishly white under the chandelier.

Most of the prominent citizens of Hemlock Falls were crowded at the surrounding tables, at a respectful distance. Their faces, thought Quill crossly, resembled the carp in the pond outside: bulging eyes, mouths open, rubbery lips. Elmer Henry sat with his wife, Adela, and Esther West. Howie Murchison, the town attorney and justice of the peace, shared a table with Harvey Bozzel and a blond cashier from the SuperSaver. It was hard to tell whether the blonde was with Harvey or Howie. Quill wondered briefly at Claire Murchison's absence. Even the Reverend Dookie Shuttleworth sat at a table for six with two of his deacons and their wives, Dookie conspicuous for his completely bewildered expression. Quill spied Marge Schmidt and Betty Hall, partners at the Hemlock Hometown Diner, at a table for two against the north wall. Marge waved a beefy fist. Quill waved back and threaded her way through the crowd, murmuring greetings. People were excited in a repressed, self-conscious way: elaborately casual attitudes (knees carelessly crossed, elbows on the table); overly careful speech ("Please pardon us, Ms. Quilliam, can we move this chair out of your way a little bit?"); and a great deal of attention to hair and clothing ("This old thing? I've had it in the closet for years, Elmer. Of course you've seen it before. Comb your hair, dear. Not at the table! Go to the men's room.").

"Good grief," said Quill when she reached Marge and Betty's table.

"Hook a chair for Quill from Norm's table, Betty, willya?" At Norm Pasquale's protest, Marge's heavy jaw thrust forward in instant belligerence. "Stuff it, Norm, you ain't using it." Quelled, Norm sank into silence. Marge extended a pudgy hand, and Quill shook it warmly. "How's it goin'?"

"Okay, I guess," Quill said. Aware of the dubiety in her tone, she grinned suddenly at Marge, who grinned back.

"Looks a bitch, from here," said Marge. She shot a penetrating look at Helena Houndswood from under a beetling brow. Her massive checks rotated slowly, and she swallowed the last of Meg's country pâté with a small burp. "Good business, though."

"Very good," Quill agreed. "For the whole town, I should think. She's going to feature the village on the TV show, you know."

"No kiddin'."

"John says that these production crews usually have the crew meals catered. We thought you two might be interested. You won't mind if we mention you to them?"

"Hell, no." Marge chuckled. Even Betty smiled faintly, drawing delicately on her cigarette, then carefully stubbing it out. "Things pickin' up for you, then."

"I hope so."

"Good. We could use a few more a them brochures of yours near the cash register. Running a little low."

"Thanks." Quill straightened the crystal salt and pepper shakers. Marge and Betty's Hemlock Hometown Diner was *locum* for any and all town gossip. Most of the men and women from the surrounding farms had breakfast there at least one day a week—and all the businesspeople in town lunched there. "So what have you heard?"

"Heard about Dot."

"Did you know her, Marge?"

"Nope. Came into the diner once, maybe twice. No more'n that. Piece of work, though, wouldn't you say, Betty?"

Betty, who was as thin as Marge was fat, examined her lipstick in the bowl of her soup spoon. "Not as much of a troublemaker as that Dawn Pennifarm. But I wouldn't call her a good old girl. Not by a long shot. Does anyone know who did it, that's what I want to know. Didn't think Dot was neighborly enough to make enemies."

Quill thought this through for a moment and decided it made sense. "Kept to herself, then. So the town thinks . . . what?"

"Accident," said Marge laconically. "Now, about this million bucks." Marge was clearly unimpressed with the sum involved; as one of the richest residents of Tompkins County, she didn't need to be.

"Yes," said Quill, with the distinct feeling that Marge wasn't changing the subject.

"Kinda oiled her way into that china contest," said Marge. "From what I hear."

"Sandy told you?" said Quill. "Was she upset about it?"

Marge nodded, her chins folding and unfolding like a fan.

"Million split four ways, now. Very nice for 'em," Betty agreed.

Marge dusted her hands briskly together. "You heard Dawnie's gone missing?"

"Myles just put out an APB this evening."

"And for Rickie, too, I hear." Marge regarded her with a sapient eye.

Quill took the bull by the horns. "Do you think something funny is going on?"

"Where's that no-good son-of-a-bitch husband of hers? That'd be my guess."

"Buffalo," said Betty.

"Buffalo?" said Quill.

"Been there a week. Got back today I guess, in time to shoot Dot. He was in for breakfast last Sunday just before he left. Got fired from the Qwik Freeze for mouthing off. Looking to find work in Buffalo, he said." She picked a flake of tobacco off her tongue. Marge grunted. "All that ol' boy's looking for is trouble. Thanks, honey."

Kathleen Kiddermeister, one of the Inn's more reliable waitresses, placed a steamed artichoke in front of Marge and a plate of cold asparagus in front of Betty. Marge daintily stripped an artichoke leaf and tasted it. "Tell Meg this is good, but she's a little heavy with the comfrey."

"I will, thanks." Quill knew that Marge was a good cook, and had an even better palate. Meg had said once that if Marge ever went into gourmet, instead of what the diner owner referred to as "Four Square American," she'd hang up her wooden spoon. "So you think Rickie's behind this."

Betty breathed on her soup spoon and polished it with her sleeve. Marge ate another artichoke leaf. "Tell you what I think," Marge said flatly. "It might look like that ol' Rickie done away with Dawn and shot Dot in the woods this afternoon. Might look like that. But Rickie can't hit the broad side of a barn on a cold day in Juneau. So, I'd say if he done Dot, it was an accident. Ain't nobody proved he done Dawn, neither."

"I'll tell you what," said Quill, her gaze drifting to Helena, who had one scarlet-nailed hand on Myles's knee, "I don't think Rickie's involved, either." Quill rose and replaced the chair at Norm Pasquale's table with a word of thanks. The high-school bandleader and his wife didn't respond. They were gaping at Helena Houndswood, along with the rest of the diners. Everybody had been seduced, except, Quill thought, for good old pragmatic Marge.

"Be seein' you at the Chamber meeting tomorrow?" said Marge.

"Yes. Lunchtime."

"Elmer didn't tell you? We thought we'd come around ten. Conference room's available, ain't it?"

"Sure," said Quill. "Have we got that much business to discuss?"

"TV people'll be here," Betty explained. "Whole town's going to want to see what they do with the girls."

"Makeover," sighed Marge. She belched, patted her ample stomach, and fixed her little turret eyes on Helena Houndswood. "I hear she can make the plainest old girl look just like her. I hear that she ain't even all that cute when they take the makeup off, and all." She sighed, a little wistfully. "She's sure got that Myles goin', though, don't she?"

"Does she? I'm afraid I didn't notice," said Quill with an assumption of carelessness and decided that she really needed an aspirin from the reception desk. She walked by Helena's table with a gracious, rather queenly air, and nodded casually to Myles. He waved one hand in her direction without taking his eyes from Helena's face.

The aspirin was in its usual place at the reception desk, which was without its usual receptionist. Quill, aware of irascability, found Dina lurking in the kitchen, one eye between the crack in the swinging doors. "Can you believe Ms. Houndswood's dress?!" she said as Quill ushered her back to the lobby. "I mean, have you ever seen anything more fabulous in your life? It's just—"

"Fabulous," agreed Quill. "Dina, I know you want to look at Helena Houndswood, but you really shouldn't have left your post. You know our rule about the phones."

"But I was looking for you!" said Dina indignantly. "There's been these weird phone calls."

"Weird? You mean obscene calls? You're okay, aren't you?"

"Oh, mouth-breathers." Dina dismissed this with an airy hand. "No. I mean weird. Some guy who sounds drunk out of his mind asking if Dawn Pennifarm's here. That's the bookkeeper that's run off with all our money, isn't it? I said no the first time, and then he called back, and called back, and I finally decided I should talk to you or John about it, and that's why I was in the kitchen, it wasn't because I'm, like, some starstruck kid who hangs around backstage."

"If it's Dawn's husband we'd better get some help. Is Myles still slobbering . . . where's Sheriff McHale?"

"Right in there with Her," breathed Dina. "Didn't you see?"

"Oh! Yes. Come to think of it, I did see him at her table." Dina's cynical expression, Quill felt, was unbecoming to her tender years. "I'll go see now. In the meantime, would you check with Mr. Whitman for me? He told Doreen he wanted more rooms for next week. Make sure you cross-check with John about how many TV people are going to be here, so we don't overbook."

"Yes, ma'am," said Dina. "Can you believe all the business she's brought in? It's simply *fab*—"

"Dina!"

"Yes, ma'am."

Quill looked at Dina's fresh and innocent face. She thought of Meg in the kitchen, ebulliently cooking her way toward fame and fortune. She thought of Myles "Hunk" McHale flirting like any starstruck fool. She was, she thought, jealous.

"Dina," she said, "I am such a jerk."

"No, you aren't."

Quill squinted at her.

Dina patted her arm. "Myles thinks you're the absolute nuts. *I* think you're the absolute nuts. She's just . . . famous. Everybody gets a little wonky around somebody famous. She'll leave, and it'll be all over. You'll see."

Quill drew a deep breath.

The phone rang.

"Don't answer that!" said Dina.

"Don't answer the phone?" said Quill. "You think it might be the guy after Dawn?"

"Let me get on the extension first. I'll go into your office. Then Myles'll have corroborating evidence."

"No. *You* get Myles and I'll try to keep him on the phone. Then he can hear for himself."

Dina raced out of the foyer. Quill picked up the phone.

"Quill?" A lost voice. Thick, foggy. Slow. A woman's voice. "Quill? Can you help? I need help."

"Kay?" shouted Quill. "Kay, where are you?"

Tires squealed out front. A shotgun blast splintered the front door. A hornet bit her temple. The phone flew out of Quill's hand. She shouted, surprised. Blood ran down her cheek and drenched the white silk of her shirt.

There was an eclipse of light; an interval with time suspended. The first and only time she'd had an anesthetic was at fourteen, when she'd had her wisdom teeth extracted. She felt like that now, a little buzzy, remote, aware of the room and the people in it at a distance.

She felt as though she'd slipped into a parallel dimension.

"No hot soup," said Quill.

"She's dee-lirious," said a familiar voice. "Get an ice pack."

Doreen.

Quill's cheek was crushed against a hard fabric-covered surface that moved up and down. She had a warm hat on her head. She blinked. The surface was Myles's chest; the hat his hand cupping her head.

It started to rain.

"Doreen, put that ice down," said her sister. "She's not delirious, she's been shot."

Angry voices shouted beyond the shattered front foyer. Myles's chest was replaced by her sister's. The floor shook with pounding feet.

Quill sat up. Her head was clearing. Her stomach lurched. "May I have some Alka-Seltzer?" she said.

"The ambulance is coming. Can you just lie back and take a couple of deep breaths?" Meg's voice held a note Quill had only heard once before, the night the highway patrol called to tell her Colin had been in the accident that had killed him.

"Meg, I'm fine." She peered at her upper arm. Her silk blouse was stained red. Her head hurt. She looked up at Meg. "What the heck *happened*?"

Meg's face was pale. Her hair stuck up in spikes. She smiled anxiously. "Somebody blasted the front door with a shotgun. It looks like you got in the way."

"Dissatisfied guest?" Quill sat up.

"Very funny. Just sit there, Quill. Andy Bishop's coming and so's the ambulance. Myles said don't move."

Quill frowned. Her head hurt like the dickens. "There's something I have to remember. Just before this happened?"

"Shock," said Doreen in gloomy satisfaction.

"This is so embarrassing," said Quill. "I'm fine."

She got unsteadily to her feet, Meg holding her firmly. The foyer was as jammed as it had been earlier when everyone had shown up at once to see Helena Houndswood. Doreen, John, and Meg surrounded her; beyond them seemed to be everyone who'd been within hollering distance of the Inn: Elmer and the rest of the Chamber of Commerce members; the FOFA people; Helena and her lawyer and producer.

"Nuts," said Quill. She looked helplessly at John, who promptly and tactfully began to move people back to the dining room.

"I don't care what the sheriff said, you go upstairs and lay down," said Doreen fiercely. Then, to Meg, "You take your sister up to her room, missy. I'll go get the first-aid kit and be right on up." She peered at Quill's temple. "Guess I'll bring the sewing kit."

"I guess you won't!" said Meg, startled. "Why don't you stay here and tell Myles where we are?" She walked behind Quill up the stairs, arms extended protectively, until Quill told her crossly not to be an ass.

"So what happened?" asked Meg, once they'd reached the privacy of Quill's rooms.

Quill explored her forehead with tentative fingers. Her hand came away sticky with blood. "I thought you could tell me."

"Let me see that." Meg grabbed her arm. "Ugh. Looks a mess." She went into the bathroom. Quill heard the sound of running water. Meg re-emerged with a damp towel and began to sponge off Quill's temple. The color was back in her cheeks.

"Ow!" said Quill. "That stings."

"Just shut up. Andy'll be here in a minute. If you were a Rock Cornish game hen, I'd put a few stitches into you myself, but since you're not, I'll wait for him."

"Meg, there's something I have to remember. It's important. What happened exactly?"

"Well, it's no use asking me. *I* don't have the foggiest idea of what happened. I heard this 'boom!'—then Dina started to scream and I ran into the foyer along with half the population of the village and there you were sitting on the floor with this confused look on your face and blood all over your head and neck."

"I thought I'd been stung by a wasp."

"There was blood all over the wall behind you. We'll have to repaint. Anyhow, I went over and tried to make you lie down. Myles thundered in behind me along with a bunch of guys from the Lounge." Meg began to wave her arms dramatically, the towel a pink-stained flag. "He pulled his six-shooter—"

"It's a thirty-eight," said Quill dampingly.

"Whatever, and raced to the front door, yelling, 'Get down!' It was thrilling. He looked out the front door, holding the gun up just like in the movies. He looked back at you—simply *haggard* with despair, as Esther West might say—and I said, 'She's alive!'" Meg snapped the towel with relish. Quill ducked out of the way. "He was back in a few minutes, minus the handcuffs in his belt, I should add, and came and picked you up like a baby. Then you came to and said you wanted soup. What kind of soup? I'll get you some."

"I wasn't unconscious," said Quill indignantly, "and I didn't want soup. I said 'no hot soup.' I remember everything except what happened right before and after I was shot."

A sharp knock sounded at the door, and it opened almost immediately.

"Doc Bishop," said Meg, "and his handy little black bag." They grinned at each other. Andy was fair, with the tight-knit slender build of a tennis player. He'd opened a family practice in Hemlock Falls soon after the sisters opened the Inn. He was single, and for a few years there'd been a succession of pretty office nurses until he hired the stolid wife of an auto mechanic who'd settled in with a firm hand and a gimlet eye. Quill, noticing Andy and Meg notice each other, had a flicker of hope.

"Wow," said Andy, examining her temple with light sensitive fingers. "You were lucky. I came through that front door and wondered if I'd brought enough catgut." He set his bag on the floor and pushed Quill gently into an arm chair. "I'm going to clean that up and give you a shot of Novocain. This is going to take a stitch or two."

"Is there a bullet in there?" Meg asked with what Quill felt to be ghoulish interest.

"Nope. She's lucky," said Andy. "It was a rifle, with two-seventy caliber bullets. Rickie Pennifarm hunts deer, I guess, when he isn't hunting his wife. And no, there are no bullets in there."

"Dawn Pennifarm's husband shot me?" said Quill. "Did he shoot Dot, too? Is he crazy?"

Andy drew on a pair of plastic gloves and selected a syringe. Quill winced at the sting of the anesthetic. "Do you know what happened?"

Andy broke open a packet of catgut and threaded a needle. "Count backward from ten." The *snick* of the needle made a sound like a small bite into an apple. Quill made a face at her sister. "Myles had Rickie handcuffed in the patrol car, and the weapon in custody. He's waiting for Deputy Dave to take Rickie off to the slammer, then he'll be up. My guess is Rickie thought Dawn was here, although everyone downstairs is saying he wanted to get rid of you because you were a witness to his getaway from Dot's murder this afternoon. Maybe he thought Dawn was Dot in the woods today. I heard Dawn was missing, and that Rickie was slamming all over town looking for her. What do you remember about tonight, Quill?"

"Nothing," said Quill. "And it's driving me crazy. I know there's something important, but all I can recall is dragging Dina back from the kitchen to her post at reception. It's the oddest thing, Andy; after that, the next thing I remember is my wisdom teeth."

"No hot soup!" said Meg in triumph.

"Retrograde amnesia," said Andy. "Often happens after an accident. Your memory will come back in a couple of days. And besides, Dina should remember. She was there." He knotted the catgut, snipped it off with a pair of surgical scissors, and swabbed the wound with a piece of cotton. "Not too bad, if I do say so myself."

"There was a phone call," said Quill with an effort. She yawned suddenly.

Andy snapped on a penlight, looked into her eyes, and suggested a good night's sleep. "I've got some Demerol, if you need a painkiller."

Quill shook her head. She felt fine. "I don't think I need anything." She yawned again, convulsively. "I'm just so sleepy all of a sudden."

"Shock," said Andy briefly, "no biggie. Get a good night's sleep and don't get that wet until I take the stitches out. Anything else I can do for you? Cissie Axminister's dilated four centimeters, and I should get back to the hospital. Labor," he added unnecessarily. Outside, the ambulance wail rose to a shriek and died abruptly. "I'll head those guys off, Quill. Meg, are you coming downstairs with me?"

"I'd better wait until Myles gets here."

He left, with a swift, intimate smile for Meg.

"Oh, ho," said Quill, "blows the wind in that quarter?"

"He's asked me out a couple of times for coffee," said Meg with a shrug. "I told you that."

"You told me you gave him a 'heck, no.' He looked like he'd gotten a 'well, maybe.' "

"Well, maybe," said Meg.

Andy had left the door slightly ajar. Myles pushed it aside and walked in. There were lines in his face Quill hadn't seen there before. Quill got to her feet and, to her astonishment, began to cry.

"Shock," said Meg wisely, patting her back. "Maybe I should pour you a glass of sherry."

Myles held her, carefully. "She just needs some sleep."

"Did you lock Rickie up?" asked Meg. "Did you find out what happened from Dina?"

"Dina's had a fit of hysterics. Says she can't remember a thing. I collared Andy downstairs to give her a sedative. And Rickie's on his way to jail."

Quill blew her nose into Myles's handkerchief, cleared her throat, and said in a rather foggy way that she couldn't remember anything, either, but she'd be damned if she had hysterics.

"Did he shoot Dot, too?" asked Meg.

"It's possible." Myles touched Quill's bandaged temple. "Dina did say that there's been a series of phone calls to the desk from a man who sounded like Pennifarm." He set Quill back in her chair, took her bathrobe from the back of the bathroom door, and wrapped it around her shoulders. "Did you take any of the calls?"

Quill shook her head. "I don't remember."

"Andy said her memory would be back in a couple of days," offered Meg. "Any leads on Dawn at all? I think you should borrow my meat mallet and pound the truth out of that little creep. I'll bet he shot both Dawn and Dot and tried to get Quill."

"I think we should hang on a bit until we've collected all the facts. Connie Weyerhauser said the whole Bosses Club knew that this was the week the win would be announced. Dawn was sure they were going to win. Connie said she was planning to use the money to move out of Hemlock Falls and away from Rickie. She doesn't think that Dawn would have gone anywhere far, just yet. If Rickie scared her off, Connie's convinced she's hiding somewhere near here. Who knows? Now that Rickie's in custody, she may come out of hiding."

"She's not at the battered women's shelter?" asked Quill.

"No. And her sister in Detroit hasn't heard from her. Connie did suggest checking with Kay Gondowski. Kay still hasn't shown up for the celebration, and it's what . . . nine o'clock . . . but Kay lives alone, and Connie thinks she would have helped hide Dawn from Rickie."

"If that's what happened," said Quill. "Myles, don't you think it's very odd that two of the winners of this contest have disappeared in as many days and a third one's been shot!?"

"Yes," said Myles.

"What about Sandy and Connie?" demanded Quill. "Are you putting guards on them, or something? I mean, what if I'm right and Helena Houndswood is approaching each one of them in turn to pay them off so they won't embarrass her. And if they won't accept a payoff . . ."

"You might be right," said Myles equably. "It's just as likely that we're dealing with separate instances. We have a reasonable explanation for all the events except Dot's murder. Rickie says he didn't do it. Said his pickup ran out of gas near the park. He left it there and walked to the gas station. When he came back he claims someone had fired his rifle and replaced it in the gun rack."

"And you believe that?" Meg demanded.

"That gives Helena Houndswood means, motive, and opportunity," said Quill. "She was in the woods exactly at the time Dot was murdered."

"So were the rest of the Bosses Club," said Myles. "Hudson finally let them go at four-thirty."

Quill stared at him. "You've got to put a tail on Helena, Myles, before the whole Bosses Club ends up in the ravine."

"Oh, come on," said Meg. "The woman's a TV star, Quill, and you don't climb to the top of her profession by letting a little setback like the Bosses Club throw you for a loop."

"You don't know her," said Quill sleepily, "she's bananas on the subject of the crème de la crème and the New York Four Hundred and all kinds of things." This time when she yawned, her jaw almost broke.

"What happens to the million dollars if there's only, say, one member of the Bosses Club left?" asked Meg.

"I checked with Helena's lawyer at dinner," said Myles. "The money's not assignable."

"And that means . . . ?" asked Meg.

"And that means it's like a tontine; the survivor takes all."

Quill put her head in her hands. "Then that might mean . . . Connie?! Or Sandy?! I don't believe it."

"You need to follow Andy's advice and get some sleep." He picked her up out of the chair easily.

"I'll get back to the kitchen," said Meg. "Is there anything I can do, Quill? Do you want some soup? No? Then I'll see you in the morning." She left, closing the door quietly behind her.

Quill submitted to being put to bed by Myles with reasonable grace. He stood looking down at her, his face shadowed behind the circle of light cast by the nightstand lamp.

"You don't think Sandy or Connie has anything to do with this, do you?"

"Go to sleep, dear heart."

"You never call me dear heart," said Quill sleepily.

"Not since the last time you were shot."

"You're the least sentimental man I know."

"Would it help, Quill, if I were more sentimental?"

"No," said Quill, "it'd help if you'd appreciate how good I am at detecting and let me help you solve your cases."

He snapped off the light. "I'm going back to headquarters. Andrew thought I should sleep at my place tonight. I can sleep on the couch, here, if you need me, Quill."

"No," said Quill, "I'll be fine."

She woke in the middle of the night, and said into the empty darkness, "Kay?" as though she had been called, and getting no answer, went back to sleep.

CHAPTER 6

Quill woke suddenly just before the morning alarm, urgency and a sharp headache both propelling her out of bed. For an entire year after she and Meg had purchased the Inn, she'd had dreams of missing the opening of a new show, nightmares of searching the crowded streets of New York for a gallery address she could no longer remember. The same feeling nagged at her through a hasty bath and a close inspection of her head wound. It felt inches deep and a mile wide. She peeled the bandage back and saw a neatly stitched incision about the size of a tarragon leaf. She searched irritably through her closet for a loose-fitting blouse that would be comfortable and cool enough for what promised to be an unusually warm June day, then hurried downstairs to the reception desk. Maybe Dina was in, her hysteria gone. Maybe she remembered what Quill had forgotten. Dina wasn't at her post, but the director of the Friends of Fresh Air was. Makepeace Whitman and his wife were flushed and sweaty from an early morning hike. Quill introduced herself and apologized for failing to greet them when they'd arrived. "But I see you've already made yourself familiar with the grounds. Did you have a good hiker?"

All the Friends of Fresh Air had the indefinable air of Renaissance saints, Makepeace and his wife in particular. They were both blond and slender. Their skins glowed with a well-scrubbed pink Quill associated with babies. They smelled of mint and rosemary.

"We saw the sun come up over the gorge," said Mrs. Whitman in her soft voice. "The light was purely of the Lord's making."

They linked hands.

"The air's magnificent here," said her husband. "Very little taint of the city."

"We saw a rose-breasted grosbeak," said Mrs. Whitman. "Exquisite!"

Quill thought of the china. "They're rare," she said, "but they're beautiful birds."

"Disappearing before the advance of man and the gasoline engine," said Makepeace with disapproval, "as are many of God's creatures of the air and earth."

"Yes," said Quill, "I'm so sorry."

"We simply bathed in the sunshine," said Mrs. Whitman, "and we feel so refreshed."

"You must be hungry, then. Would you like me to make arrangements for breakfast? If you don't want to eat here, there's a very nice diner in town."

"Bacon"—Makepeace shook his head—"and sausage, no doubt. These small-town diners. It's a constant wonder to me that places as close to nature as Hemlock Falls should have diners. Do you have a full range of yogurts?"

"If we don't have what you like, just ask, Mr. Whitman. We'll be happy to get it for you. Are the arrangements all right? Is there anything we can do to make you more comfortable?"

They exchanged a limpid blue gaze.

"This actress disrupts things," Makepeace complained.

"That disturbance last night . . ." said Mrs. Whitman, "and the hunting accident."

"Disruptions in the natural flow," her husband concluded. "Very distressing."

"Miss Houndswood is here for her television show," said Quill. "The disruption will be for a while, I'm afraid. As for last night . . ."

"Gunshots!" said Mrs. Whitman. She shuddered. "*Not* what we expected."

"I'm so sorry," said Quill. "But our sheriff's very capable, and the man is in custody. It's possible he was responsible for both incidents. It must have been very upsetting. Are you from a farming community yourselves?" She thought of the Amish. "Pennsylvania?"

"Queens," said Mrs. Whitman.

"Queens, New York?" said Quill.

"Last night," said Makepeace reprovingly, "was not at all conducive to the healthful contemplation of nature's glories."

"No. I suppose not. If there's anything at all I can do for you . . ."

"Perhaps maps?" suggested Makepeace. "Of hiking areas well away from the polluting areas?"

"Maps? We would be glad to provide maps."

"And if my wife and I could alert the rest of our group as to where these television cameras might be—"

"Oh, that won't be for weeks yet," Quill assured him.

"We would like to know, just in case," said Mrs. Whitman. Her blue eyes drifted to the ceiling, and she repeated dreamily, "Just in case. One never knows about these people."

"I'll see what I can do. If you'll excuse me. Our receptionist's just come in, and I need to speak with her. About those maps." Quill gave Dina a small wave of recognition and stepped aside as the Whitmans went up the stairs.

"That's the cleanest couple I've ever seen," Dina observed as she watched them leave. "How are you doing? You sleep okay? Does you head hurt? Jeez . . ." She examined it with frank curiosity. "It looks *awful*."

"I'm fine," said Quill. "It was just a scratch. Dina, what do you—"

"Just a scratch? You get half-killed by a maniac with a shotgun and you call it just a scratch? Did you see the wall! Gross!' She pointed at the speckles of blood on the cream paint.

"There's more blood on the wall than there was on me," Quill said. "It'll need repainting, though. Maybe you could mention it to Mike when you see him. He's mowing today, but tell him the lawn can wait. Dina, what do you remember of last night?"

"It was horrible. Horrible!" She settled behind the reception desk with a thump. "I had nightmares all night. Like one of those tapes on an endless loop, you know? I kept seeing it over and over again in my mind. Like when I saw that Freddy Kreuger movie a few years ago and just could not get that scene with the cheerleader out of my mi—"

"So you remember what happened?"

"Sure! Freddy's got these steel knife fingernails—"

"I mean about the shooting."

"Remember! I'm going to replay this for the rest of my—"

"Tell me exactly what happened."

"You don't remember? Did you hit your head when the blast knocked you over? You mean you have amnesia?"

"It's kind of amnesia, but Andy Bishop said it will go away after a few days. I can't recall a thing except finding you in the kitchen. And I have the most awful feeling that something important happened after that."

"You got shot," said Dina with a kindly, let-me-help-you expression.

"I know I was shot. What happened before I was shot?"

"Well, we came back here. And you were saying how you hated Helena Houndswood and everything . . ."

"I was?" Quill flushed guiltily. "Did I say anything really awful?"

"Not in so many words. But you were kinda—jealous like—you know? Specially since she was sucking up to Myles, and I guess he wasn't feeling too bad about that himself . . ."

"We came back here." Quill placed herself in front of the desk. "And you sat down . . ."

"And I sat down, and I told you not to answer the phone."

"Not to answer the phone?"

"Yeah. And that's what you said. 'You don't want me to answer the phone?' And I said, 'Rickie Pennifarm keeps calling and making the most gruesome threats, and then hanging up,' and you said, 'Get Myles.'"

"What kind of threats?"

"Oh, you know. Like, 'Is Dawn Pennifarm there? You better find her. I have to talk to her.' Drunk," said Dina with relish, "drunk and crazy, and then he tried to kill her and ended up almost killing you."

"So he called . . . how many times?"

"Oh, I don't know. Five. Six maybe. And then he called one last time and you picked up the phone and I went to find Myles. What did he say? More threats, probably."

"I can't remember any of this." Quill ran her hands through her hair. "Not a bloody thing. You say I picked up the phone . . ."

"And then I heard this gigantic roar, of his pickup truck, you know, and then like a wheelie, you know, the tires squealed, and then 'Blam!' this gigundous blast shook the door."

Quill walked over to the front door and pulled it open. The edge of the frame was splintered with buckshot. The door itself was intact. "Was the door open?"

Dina frowned. "Yeah. It must have been. I leave it open summer nights because it gets so warm in here. So the gunshot blasts through the foyer and you scream 'I've been shot! My God, I've been shot!'"

"I did?"

"Well, maybe not those exact words. I would have, that's for sure. And I came running back and you were passed out on the floor. That must have been when you hit your head," said Dina kindly.

"I didn't hit my head. And I'm pretty sure I just sat down. I didn't fall." She frowned with the effort of recollection. "I had the phone in my hand, you say?"

Dina nodded vigorously. "Talking to that crazy Rickie Pennifarm."

"How could I be talking to Rickie Pennifarm? He was outside blasting the doorframe with his deer rifle."

"Jeez. That's right." Dina looked genuinely puzzled.

"So if I wasn't talking to Rickie Pennifarm because he was outside in his pickup truck, who was I talking to?"

"Beats me."

"Who put the phone back on the hook?"

"Gosh, Quill. I have no idea. Somebody must have, though. I mean the lobby was full of all these people in about sixty seconds, and Sheriff McHale was holding on to you looking like he was going to *kill* who'd ever done it, and Meg was practically fainting . . . and everybody was screaming and everything. It was," she said with satisfaction, "a real mess."

"This doesn't sound right," said Quill.

"I'm not saying my memory's perfect," said Dina indignantly, "but I saw what I saw."

Quill pulled at her lower lip. "I hope Andy's right. I hope this comes back to me." She shook her head. "I'll go nuts if I try to force it, or start to remember things that didn't happen at all."

"I have to give a deposition, you know," said Dina. "You have to give two. One about finding that Dot Vandermolen, and the other about getting shot. Myles said I was too upset to take a statement right then and there, so both of us have to go down to the sheriff's office this afternoon and tell Deputy Dave what happened. Do you think you'll remember who it was on the phone by then?"

"What time are we supposed to be there?"

"Myles said the sooner the better. He said as soon as I felt calm enough to go down, I should. He said to let you sleep. But here you are—up and around and everything. I'd feel calmer if you went with me. But I've got to do my shift this morning, so I was thinking maybe this afternoon. But we can go together, Quill, can't we?"

"Of course we can. I've just got to get through the Chamber of Commerce meeting."

Quill ate a quick breakfast and methodically went to all the staff present to ask who'd hung the phone up the night before. She was met with blank incomprehension, earnest efforts to remember— and no answers. By ten o'clock, when the Chamber members began to arrive for the ad hoc meeting, the sense of unease was a steady presence in the back of her mind.

She was, for once, prompt for a Chamber of Commerce meeting, in the hope that since everyone at the meeting had been gawking in the foyer the night before, at least one of the more civic-minded citizens might have a clear recollection. "Nope," said Elmer Henry, when he met her outside the conference room. "Don't recollect at all."

"Hear Myles has got Rickie Pennifarm in the lockup," Elmer continued as they walked into the conference room. "Can't believe he had the gonads to shoot the sheriff's girlfriend. Always was a bozo, that boy."

Quill wondered if Rickie Pennifarm would have been less of a bozo in Elmer's eyes if he'd shot, say, a passing tourist. She settled into her accustomed place between Miriam Doncaster, the town librarian, and Esther West.

"He really wasn't aiming at you or anybody else, you know," Elmer said reassuringly. "He just wanted to get Dawn's attention."

"I heard that three men had to hold Myles back from thrashing Rickie within an inch of his life," Esther said with suppressed excitement. She adjusted one of her mother-of-pearl earrings and hitched the buckle of her white patent leather belt one notch tighter. "I heard Myles was simply *wild*."

"You've been checking out too many bodice rippers," said Miriam. She cocked a wise blue eye in Esther's direction. "Mysteries are a lot less heated. The new Monfredo came in yesterday. I'll put you on the waiting list." She winked at Quill. "How are you feeling, Quill? Andy Bishop said it was only a flesh wound."

"It's fine," lied Quill, whose head hurt like the Devil. "Miriam, do you remember seeing the phone off the hook last night?"

Miriam squinted with the effort of recollection. "Yes."

"Did you see anyone put it back on the hook?"

"Yes. Mrs. Whitman. She said she was Mrs. Whitman. I asked her about her T-shirt. You know, it had the FOFA logo."

"Mrs. Whitman? The Friends of Fresh Air Mrs. Whitman?"

"That's right. She tried to recruit me. Quill—about these FOFA people . . ."

"Did she say anything into the receiver?"

"I don't remember."

Quill, making a mental note to ask Mrs. Whitman who'd been on the line, relaxed a little. Now she was gelling somewhere.

Harvey Bozzel swept in, wearing his best suit and carrying a new leather briefcase. He smiled whitely in the general direction of the assembled Chamber members, then dropped a confiding hand on Quill's shoulder and whispered, "Is she coming?"

"Who? You mean Helena?"

"I thought you were going to ask her to attend the meeting this morning. Remember? We took a meeting on the street yesterday. Near the post office."

"Took a . . . ? Oh. No, Harvey, I didn't get a chance to ask her. Besides, she's upstairs with the Bosses Club. They're having their first makeover."

"Dawn didn't show up, did she?" said Esther. "I hear she hasn't turned up yet. There's talk of dragging the river."

"Who's talking about dragging the river?" demanded Elmer.

"Why, down to Marge's this morning," said Esther. "Everybody is. Marge, wasn't everyone talking about looking for Dawn Pennifarm in the river?"

"No funds to drag the river," said Elmer, "lessen we get some volunteers. And what do they want to drag the river for?"

"Dawn Pennifarm," Esther said. "And I hear Kay Gondowski's gone missing, too. They already found Dot, of course."

"Talk was Rickie mighta put the body in one of them refrigerators down to the dump," said Marge. "Nobody said nuthin' about the river. For Dawn or for Kay. Kay's not in the river anyhow. She's just so shy she run off to her son's in Cohocton. Bet you even money she'll be back this morning."

"Bodies in the river?" said Harvey Bozzel. "There's a story here, folks. This has got Hemlock History Days beat six ways from Sunday."

Elmer rapped his official gavel and stood up: "This meeting of the Hemlock Falls Chamber of Commerce is now in session."

"Mayor?" said Harvey, getting to his feet. "May I say something?"

"We got the old order of bidness, the minutes, and then new bidness," said Elmer. "You wait a bit, boy."

Harvey nodded wisely, then turned to the members with an expansive gesture. "First, I'd like to say that the turnout for today's meeting augurs well for community spirit and public relations!"

Elmer whacked the gavel. Harvey ignored him.

Quill glanced around the conference table. Chamber members she hadn't seen for years had come to Elmer's ad hoc meeting: Harold Pearson from Qwik Freeze; Cornwallis Nugent from Nugent's All-Ways Insurance; Chris Croh from the Croh Bar. She hastily wrote: Harvey talks: ASK???, then listed "Attendees: THE USUAL, plus," and began to transcribe names.

". . . minutes, Quill?" said Elmer.

"What?" Quill looked up; thirty members of the Hemlock Falls Chamber of Commerce were studiously ignoring a red-faced Harvey and staring at her.

"Elmer asked Harvey who died and left him king?" Miriam summed up in a rapid whisper. "Then he slammed his gavel again, told Harvey to shut up, said the Helena Houndswood show was new business, and it wasn't even on the agenda, and asked for last week's minutes."

Quill flipped hastily through the notebook, cleared her throat, and peered at her undecipherable notes.

"Just the agenda, Ms. Secretary," said Elmer formally.

"'Tabled for June discussion,'" Quill read aloud, "'paint and pound.'" She blinked. "I'm sorry, Elmer, that must be a note to myself. I can't remember what 'paint and pound' is for."

"Town cleanup," said Elmer, who had long ago adapted to Quill's self-admitted peculiarities in matters of shorthand. "Clean It Up! Week. Matter of civic pride. The town's gotta look good. Specially since we may be on TV pretty soon. Matter of civic importance."

There was an expectant silence. Elmer had finally brought up what was on everyone's mind.

"Timely, very timely," agreed Freddie Bellini, the funeral director, cautiously.

"This is a progressive village," Elmer reminded Freddie sternly. "Now, we got the Dump Day to schedule, and the report from the Assessment Committee. We'll get to more important things in the proper way. Procedure, you see. Revrund Shuttleworth, you're the chairman of the Assessment Committee. What's your assessment?"

Everyone relaxed slightly with the assurance that the Helena Houndswood TV show would be addressed in due course.

Dookie, with his gently fuddled air of hearing only celestial voices, had been elected to the position of Assessment Committee chairman by popular acclaim. "Since nobody," Marge Schmidt had opined, "was about to kick a man of God in the butt for telling them to clean up their crap." The acceptability of the Assessment Committee chairman was vital to the success of the Hemlock Falls Clean It Up! Week, such well-known cantankerous and thrifty souls as Vern Mittermeyer being in favor of the patched and paintless school of building maintenance.

Dookie got to his feet. "Brethren?" he said, with a large-minded, if tentative, assurance that there were no goats among his sheep. "Let us pray."

There was an abrupt ducking of heads.

"Lord, give us strength to accept the human challenge presented by Clean It Up! Week. Amen."

"Amen," the members echoed.

"You may sit," said Dookie, although nobody was kneeling. "Lord, these are the souls who have heard your call to clean up . . ."

"It was my call, Revrund," said Elmer, "just to set the record straight."

"First to clean it up, Lord, is your servant the mayor, at the town hall, to keep the grass trimmed, the Dumpster repainted, and the parking lot free of coupons, flyers, and other detritus. How's that going, Mayor?"

Elmer flushed to his third chin.

"Next, Lord, your servant Esther West, to keep more seemly dresses in her shop window. Ladies' underthings, Lord, were meant to be concealed and not revealed. Have you changed your display, Esther?"

Esther adjusted the shoulder pads of her cotton pique jumpsuit with a "tsk!" of annoyance and a muttered, "Heck, no."

Quill listed the malefactors with absentminded determination, finishing with Dookie's request to ask the Lord's servant Vern Mittermeyer to complete the repainting of the post office trim with dispatch. "Hopefully, a dispatch greater than his record of attending to the mail," hissed Esther in Quill's direction.

"About this repainting of the post office," said Vern Mittermeyer heatedly. "The damn paint's no good. Splotches awful. The budget's been cut all to hell this year. The town wants a contractor to repaint, they gotta see to it themselves. Might not be in the regulations, anyhow."

"Nothing in the municipal budget for Federal buildings," said Elmer promptly. "I know what you earn as postmaster, Vern Mittermeyer, and you can afford to buy a couple of gallons and paint it yourself, easy."

Vern, with all the outrage of a Shakespearean asked to do a bump and grind, said it was against Federal regulations.

In the ensuing acrimony (a familiar feature of Chamber meetings, and for which Quill had a special written "time out" symbol in the minutes), she reflected on the whereabouts of Dawn Pennifarm and Kay Gondowski.

Quill furiously doodled a rose-breasted grosbeak, entwined with rosemary and thyme, a check for $4500, and an extremely unflattering caricature of Helena Houndswood, with the mayor and Harvey kissing her feet.

A ripple of applause broke her concentration.

"You got that, Quill?" said Elmer. "Make a note to send a formal thank-you."

"Um. Yes." Quill raised her eyebrows frantically at Miriam, who obliged her with a smile.

"Paramount Paint donated four gallons of Cardinal Crimson Latex Exterior Paint for the use of the post office. Everyone voted to thank Hudson without letting him know Vern doesn't like it. They don't want to be rude."

Quill scribbled, then said in a low tone, "Miriam, you'd be so much better as secretary than I would."

"Uh-huh," said Miriam promptly. "No way."

Quill wrote: Bribe Miriam to take this lousy job! Then she drew a picture of Meg piling desserts in front of Miriam at lunch.

Elmer expanded his considerable chest with a deep breath. Everyone came to attention. It was clear they were going to finally come to the point. "We got a lot of bidness to cover, folks, so do I hear a motion to table the rest of the reading of the minutes from last week?"

"I so move," said Howie Murchison. The town attorney was looking a little strained, and more rumpled than usual. Miriam leaned over and said *sotto voce*, "Claire left him last week. For an insurance salesman." Quill raised both eyebrows. That explained the blond cashier last night at dinner. Miriam raised her hand and said loudly, "I second," and sent Howie a sympathetic smile.

Quill wrote: Howie DATE Miriam? and scribbled a pleased looking Miriam at the altar, with an equally happy looking Howie.

"Order of new bidness," said Elmer. Harvey raised his hand, waited for Elmer's reluctant, but acknowledging nod, then leaped to his feet.

Quill sighed, flipped her notepad open to a new page, and scrawled the date and time.

Harvey cleared his throat. "Folks, the first order of new business should concern us all. One of our leading citizens was attacked at her place of business last night. We all know who"—he gestured largely in Quill's direction—"and we all know *what* happened. I'm issuing a call to action. A call to the men of Hemlock Falls to form a coalition for the protection of our women. I move to create a Victim's Fund, the first proceeds of which should go to pay the medical bills of our hostess."

Quill doodled a smiley face on her official minutes pad, then added a pair of horns and a pitchfork. She scribbled a little Harvey figure on top of the pitchfork.

"No need to suck up to Quill so's she'll get Helena Houndswood to this meetin'," Marge said with deadly, if elephantine, accuracy, "from what I seen in the dining room last night, the sheriff's got more influence with that there Helena than her. And what medical bills are you talkin' about, anyways? Andy Bishop said it was only a flesh wound. She's right here, healthy as a horse."

Quill drew a little Marge figure in flames under the pitchfork.

"Golly," said Miriam into her ear. "Those sketches are good."

Quill gave a guilty start.

"Important thing is," Marge boomed on, "how are we going to get in on this Helena Houndswood thing?"

There was a chorus of "yeahs" and one "right on," this last from Harvey, nothing if not firm in the belief that majority rule made the world safe for profitability.

Elmer rapped his gavel. "The floor is now open for discussion on more new business."

Harvey's hand shot up. "This remarkable turnout of the membership of the Hemlock Falls Chamber of Commerce," he said solemnly, "is here, I am sure, partly in tribute to the bravery of Miss Sarah Quilliam." He began to clap. The Chamber joined him, mostly, Quill knew, because it was a conditioned reflex. Quill turned pink.

"Although a newcomer to our ranks"—(Harvey had moved to Hemlock Falls two years after Meg and Quill bought the Inn, which made Harvey a flatland foreigner if anybody was)—"she has dedicated herself to the interests of our town without hesitation. So I know she will heartily support our next endeavor to make Hemlock Falls as well-known as Rochester, New York, in this great land of ours."

Elmer looked impressed. Miriam, who clearly had doubts whether anyone cared about Rochester except for George Eastman—and he was dead—dropped Quill a wink.

"What endeavor you got in mind, Harve?" asked Elmer with interest.

"A show," said Harvey simply. "A show to replace our late—and much lamented—Hemlock History Days. A show which will demonstrate to people of all kinds the dignity and commercial viability of our community. A show which will demonstrate the desirability of living and working in Hemlock Falls to those not fortunate enough to live and work here. A show, ladies and gentlemen, which will bring new blood to Hemlock Falls."

Esther, who'd written and directed the annual pageant for Hemlock History Week, gave an excited squeak. Dave Shoemaker, who sold real estate part-time, exchanged an interested look with Matt Crawely, general manager of the Wal-Mart.

Harvey reached under his chair and set an A-frame on the table with a great flourish. "Citizens, I bring you one of the most important ideas—conceptually speaking—that Bozzel Advertising has had in the past decade." He flipped the first frame of the pad up:

THE LITTLE MISS HEMLOCK FALLS
IT'S A BEAUTIFUL LIFE
TALENT AND BEAUTY PAGEANT

and underneath:

YOU'LL FALL FOR US

"This is it, guys," said Harvey enthusiastically. "We have a beauty pageant for all female residents of Hemlock Falls under ten. And we get the coverage for it on Helena Houndswood's show!"

There was a buzz of excited comment.

"We get our finest citizens to act as judge—like you, Mayor, and maybe some others—and the little ones dance, sing, whatever, and dress up in their best. And we get the kid who wins to show all the folks out there in TV land what a great place this is to live and work. Norm—we'll take the viewers to the school to show 'em how weapon free the schools are and whatnot. She'll shop at the Wal-Mart. Maybe get a couple of dresses at Esther's shop, West's Best, right, Esther? Go to Bellini's Funeral Home to show folks where grandma and grandpa are buried—we can fake that a little bit, Freddie. Go down to Marge and Betty's diner for Saturday breakfast. I *mean*"—Harvey leaned forward and thumped the table dramatically—"we can hit every high spot in this town!"

"Little Miss Hemlock Falls." Elmer, the father of three girls, eight, ten, and twelve, nodded thoughtfully. "I like this, Harve. I like this."

Esther was almost blue with excitement. "Only I think ten is a little young. Maybe we could get a teenage contest going." (Esther's daughter was sixteen.) "They have," Esther explained earnestly to a frowning Harland Peterson (one six-year-old granddaughter), "a little more poise at that age."

"Harvey," protested Quill, "I don't think this is—"

"We can work up something very tasteful in white satin," said Freddie Bellini.

"The children's book room at the library?" asked Miriam, Quill's second-to-last hope.

"Miriam!" said Quill. "Harvey! Mayor!"

"And of course, since Ms. Houndswood is already planning to shoot the winners of the china contest right here at the Inn," said Harvey rapidly, avoiding Quill's outraged gaze, "Quill's the one with the inside track. I move that Quill form a one-woman delegation to approach Ms. Houndswood about having the pageant featured on the shoot."

"Shoot?" said Elmer. "You want to include Rickie blastin' Quill's front door?"

"No, no, no," said Esther, who owned the *Complete Guide to Television Production* in videotape, "he means the camera shoot."

Elmer rapped the gavel once again. "Quill? You want to say something."

"Guys," said Quill, "a little girl's beauty pageant is just an awful idea. I mean . . ." She faltered to a stop. "Reverend Shuttleworth," she said. "Don't you find the idea of a beauty pageant for little girls exploitative? I mean . . ."

An expression of mild surprise crossed Dookie's face, which may have been occasioned by the fact that he had been addressed at all. He opened his mouth.

Noreen DeVolder, owner-operator of the Hemlock Hall of Beauty, snapped her gum with authority and interrupted to volunteer free hair and makeup for the girls. They'd look, she said, like little angels when she and the gals got through with them.

Harvey gazed from Quill to Dookie and back again with a thoughtful expression. Suddenly he snapped his fingers and sat forward in his chair. "We'll have to get the whole choir in the background as the winner shows the folks at home where she goes to church. The Reverend here needs to let the folks at home know that this is a godly town."

Dookie closed his mouth.

"A prize, perhaps, for most spiritual, eh, Reverend?" said Elmer, on whom no flies rested for long. Dookie nodded, without, Quill thought, a great deal of comprehension.

"Well, Quill?" said Harvey. "You want to go on up and ask her now?"

"Ask her now?" Quill repeated dumbly.

"Yay!" said a couple of members from the far end of the table.

"Sandy Willis says the two of you are like that," said Harvey, crossing two fingers. "Or, folks, we can form a delegation, maybe me, the mayor . . ."

The thought of a Chamber delegation descending on the Shaker suite made her head throb. "I'll go up and talk to her."

"When?" demanded Harvey. "She goes for this, and I know she's going to, there's a lot of planning to do."

Maybe, thought Quill, she could nip this in the bud right away. "I'll be back as soon as I can." She put the minutes pad in front of Miriam and fled.

Quill found Helena calm in the midst of chaos, ruling over the Shaker suite with a well-groomed iron fist.

"Poor you! Kiss-kiss!" Helena greeted her like Charles de Gaulle greeting the Germans in 1944. "Meet the minions. That's Tabby Fisher, doing Connie's hair, and Dwight Nelson, putting all those pretties onto Sandy. People? Sarah Quilliam, the artist. You remember her, took SoHo in a storm of oils about six years ago, then left for parts unknown. Did that dishy sheriff catch the guy who tried to murder you? Tab, the poor girl got shot at last night. And then there was a body in the bushes to boot. Just like home, *n'est-ce pas?* And no, dear ones, it wasn't an art critic, whatever you may think."

"Sawyourstuf's great," said Tabby laconically. No question

where Tabby was from. Her brightly hennaed hair stuck up in sophisticated clumps at the back of her head. She wore a white bodysuit, with no bra, a tunic embroidered GET STUFFED in scarlet thread, black leggings, and purple ballet shoes. Intricate gold chains swung from each ear, brushing her shoulders. Dwight's provenance screamed Manhattan, too: his earrings were silver ankhs and his face only slightly less pale than Tabby's. Quill felt a sudden, urgent nostalgia for Soho.

The two remaining members of the Bosses Club looked fabulous. Terrified, but fabulous. Dwight fussily draped fabric swatches over Connie's stiff shoulders, murmuring delightedly at the effect of a bronze almost the color of her skin, then scribbling on a small notepad hung around his neck. Sandy sat upright and immobile in a straight-backed chair as Tabby dabbed blusher on her cheekbones with careless expertise. Her brown-blond hair had been highlighted a soft gold. She sat on the edge of the couch near the mullioned windows of the Shaker suite, taking occasional, shallow breaths, as though normal body movements would destroy the effect of her makeover. Tabby's magic had taken ten years off Sandy's face.

"My gosh!" said Quill.

"What d'ya think?" said Sandy anxiously.

"I think you look fantastic. You both look wonderful!"

"Maybe we could take some pictures?" Sandy's voice was timid.

"I'll call downstairs and see if John can find a camera," said Quill. "This looks like so much fun."

"It's like a *dream*," breathed Sandy.

"Lord, don't wake me up," said Connie.

Sandy gave her a determined punch in the shoulder. They both broke into nervous giggles.

Quill made a quick call to John for camera and coffee. "Herbal tea for me, sweetie," said Dwight, frankly eavesdropping, "and maybe the teensiest glass of some wine. White. The sulfides in reds are murder for my head."

Quill completed the call and sat next to Helena. "They're awfully good," she commented, with a nod in Tabby and Dwight's direction.

"Um. The little bastards charged me double for coming up here to the boonies," said Helena, clearly bored. "You'll agree this called for drastic measures."

"Not really." said Quill. "We're not real downtown here—and do you really think that matters to your audience? I mean, it's a national show—you've viewers in the Midwest, the South, the Northwest. Not everyone wants to look like a *Vogue* insert."

"Aren't we Citizen Sarah this morning," Helena drawled. "Actually, my producer said the same thing. I'll tell you, after one look at this crew, I'd decided to cancel the show."

So it did bother her. The bowling jackets and the home perms. The Wal-Mart makeup. The question is, Quill thought, did it bother her enough to get rid of Dawn Pennifarm and shoot Dot Vandermolen? In the middle of the cheerful activity of the Shaker suite, it didn't seem likely. Unless there was another motive—one she hadn't discovered yet. "And you think your producer's right?"

Helena shrugged. "Doesn't matter, does it? I'm committed to do this damn thing. Unless they all miraculously disappear like this Dawn person seems to have done. I should hope." Her voice rose: "Sandy, darling, I ask you. Is that fantastic or is that fantastic. Thank Tabby, like a good girl."

Sandy shyly surveyed herself in a hand mirror. "My husband is going to shit a brick."

"And Kay?" said Quill.

"Kay?" The indifference in Helena's tone made Quill's palm itch to slap her.

"Kay Gondowski. The shy one."

"Oh! The one with no cheekbones whatsoever. Here's a treat for you. Connie? Tell our Sarah about Kay."

"She called last night," said Connie. "Said she was petrified to face the cameras. Asked Sandy and me to get her money and set it up in an account. I already talked to Mark Anthony at the bank, and he says she's got to have a signature card. Kay said she'll call either me or Sandy back tonight, and I'll ask her to send us one."

There was a tap at the door. Kathleen Kiddermeister wheeled in a cart, and there was a rush for coffee and wine. Helena yawned and beckoned to Tabby. "Either you or Dwight's *got* to do something instantly about my hair."

Quill sat on the couch next to Connie. "Did you talk to Kay yourself?"

"Yes, Quill. I did."

"How did she sound?"

Connie smiled warmly. "Scared."

"But you're sure it was Kay?"

"Who else would it be?"

And that, thought Quill, is the sixty-four-thousand-dollar question. A memory tugged at her, and she shook her head to clear it. "Kay told you to set her money aside for her, and she'd claim it later?"

"Look," Sandy interrupted. "You gotta know Kay, all right? This is one shy lady. That husband of hers ups and dies on her, and do you think I could get her to go down to the Croh Bar Saturdays just for a couple of laughs? No way. This is a lady that likes to sit, knit, and watch TV. Don't surprise me at all that she's ducked out of this."

"Have you talked to Myles about this?"

"God, no, Quill," Sandy flushed guiltily. "Who had time?"

Quill was silent.

"Myles found out anything about Dawn yet?" asked Sandy after a strained moment.

"No. Not yet. But he's good," said Quill confidently. "I'm sure something will turn up soon." She hesitated, then asked, "What do you guys think happened to Dawn?"

"Well, Connie knows her best, and she's clueless."

"But you all must have some theory."

"Sure. That no-good son-of-a-bitch Rickie. The whole town thinks he hit her over the head or blasted her with that damn shotgun and dumped her body in the river." She frowned. "You know what they say—don't pray for it 'cause you might get it? Well, it's a little like that. I'm not lying when I tell you, Quill, there's a third of a million for each of us if Dawn doesn't show up, with Dot and all. Isn't that a hell of a thing?" She shook her head. "You asked me last week if anything could have broken the Bosses Club, I would have laughed in your face. We were tight. Dookie Shuttleworth's always on about how the love of money is the root of all evil. I guess he might be right. My God! You hear that?"

The door to the Shaker suite burst open. Harvey Bozzel, Elmer Henry, Dookie Shuttleworth, and Esther West flooded in, if, Quill thought, four people could constitute a flood.

Harvey waved a camera like a cheerleader at the head of a parade. "Somebody call for a photographer?" Sandy jumped up with a shriek of joy.

John closed the door behind them, raised an eyebrow at Quill, and sat next to her on the couch.

"You think this is hilarious," said Quill.

A muscle twitched in John's cheek.

"You can't pull that silent man of the plains act with me, John Raintree. You're laughing your head off."

"I did try to stop them," he said. "You've heard about the Little Miss Hemlock Falls Beauty contest?"

"They voted to do it?"

"So the mayor tells me. It was a unanimous vote."

"Even Dookie?"

John thought a moment. "I believe that Dookie was under the impression he was voting for a guided tour of the church, conducted by the child our citizens voted most spiritual."

"Harvey," said Quill. "That bozo."

They watched Harvey.

"Oozing charm from every pore . . ."

"He oiled his way across the floor," John said, "I can't remember the rest."

"Dum-de-dum-barbarian," said Quill. "Which doesn't fit because he isn't Hungarian, and what did Lerner have against Hungarians anyway?"

Harvey snapped Connie and Sandy's picture rapidly, three times in succession. Then he gave a patently artificial start of surprise and maneuvered Sandy into taking photos of himself posing with Helena, shaking her hand, standing next to her, and finally with his arm around her, which she shook off with the ease of an expert. The moments dragged on. Dookie engaged in a serious conversation with Dwight; Elmer, reduced to incoherence by Tabby's braless bodysuit, stared at the floor and talked beauty pageant to the clearly indifferent makeup artist; Quill and John sipped coffee.

Observing the twitch under the actress's left eye, Quill bet Helena would clear the room of Hemlockians in under twenty minutes.

John refused the bet. "Ten or less."

"You've got to admire her technique," Quill added. "I couldn't empty a room like that to save my life."

Harvey (although he reappeared at the door twice before his final exit) was the first to go, followed by Sandy and Connie, still moving as if their new looks would shatter at a cough. Dwight fluttered his fingers at Dookie and beat a swift retreat with Tabby. Only Dookie remained in innocent incomprehension, maintaining an amiable flow of conversation with Helena, until Quill, grumpily responding to John's encouraging eye, finally took a hand.

"I was just telling Ms-ah-urm that her colleague may be oddly dressed, but he has a most Christian interest in his fellow man."

"Although none at all in his fellow woman," said Helena nastily. "Has he offered to 'make over' the boys choir at the church? Now, if you'll excuse me, Reverend."

"It is past eleven, Dookie," said Quill.

"Already!" Dookie cast an anxious glance at the ceiling. "I'll be down at the jail, Quill, if anyone should ask for me."

"He does a great deal of good work with the prisoners," said Quill defensively as Dookie made his gently aimless way out the door. "You might lay off a little bit."

"You tell your citizens to lay off me," Helena snapped. "Beauty contest? What fresh hell is this?"

"You mean the beauty contest?"

"Didn't I just say that? Christ! That clodhopper mayor and that *sleazy* asshole of an excuse for an ad man—" She broke off and looked pointedly at John standing silently at Quill's elbow. "Is there something I can do for you?"

"John's the general manager here, and what concerns the Inn, concerns him," said Quill. "And we need to talk about arrangements for your crew during the shoot."

"I'll be liaison for the beauty contest," John volunteered with a suppressed grin. "I hope to learn a great deal from you."

"Don't even think about sucking up to me, sweetie. You're dealing with a grand master. You, Quill, or your office boy here, are to tell those crazies that in no way, no how is any Little Miss Hemlock Falls Beauty Pageant going to appear on my show. Never, in this life or the next. And you tell that geek in the gray flannel suit—"

"His name is Harvey Bozzel," said Quill evenly, "and he has

the village interest at heart, Helena. His ideas can get a little out of control—"

"A kid's beauty contest? My God!"

"It is a little vulgar," Quill admitted, "but properly managed, it might not be too bad. I mean, it doesn't have to be awful. This is a nice place to live, and your audience would like to see happy kids just like anyone likes to see happy kids."

"I don't," said Helena with finality. "I don't like kids. Kids are not part of a Beautiful Life. Kids—"

"Have a talent for upstaging you?" suggested John.

Quill held her breath. Helena turned bright red. Glared at John. Noticed, Quill hoped, that he really was an extremely good-looking man.

"Nobody," said Helena, "upstages me. Not the cutest little bastard in the world."

"You can't see fresh-faced children in the rose garden here at the Inn?" urged John. "Drinking milkshakes at the Hemlock Hometown Diner? Playing ball by the edge of the falls?"

"I'm way ahead of you, pal." Helena crossed her arms in front of her chest and rocked back and forth on her heels. "I'll think about it."

"You will?" said Quill.

"Maybe a few shots—no audio, just background—of kids reciting their own poetry?" John suggested. "Or a ballet class? Or band recital?"

"No horrible little boys lipsynching street rap," said Helena.

"Certainly not," said John. "If you have the time, I could show you some of the places in the village that'd make interesting footage."

Helena looked up at him. She smiled. Took his arm. "Hey, why the hell not?"

Quill, standing in the middle of the Shaker suite, began to feel like a fifth wheel. "I'll just go see how the lunch trade is doing," she said.

Helena turned and regarded her with a steady look. "Tell your mayor I'm thinking about it. But I'm telling you, I get one two-foot Liza Minnelli in an icky little tux, and the deal's off."

CHAPTER 7

"My granddaughter," said Elmer Henry proudly, "sings 'New York, New York' so that you can't tell the difference from that singer what's-her-name."

"Liza Minnelli," said Quill. "I'm pretty sure that isn't what Ms. Houndswood had in mind."

She'd had no trouble rounding up those Chamber members who had volunteered to be on the Little Miss Hemlock Falls It's a Beautiful Life Talent and Charm Contest Committee. Elmer and Harvey were waiting in the lobby to enlist Helena Houndswood's attendance at all (or any) meetings pertaining to the show. Helena herself slipped out through the kitchen with John to tour the village. Quill invited Elmer and Harvey into her office for a candid chat.

"She don't want us to say 'Beautiful Life' in the contest title, then?" said Elmer.

"I'm afraid not, Mayor. It's sort of a trademark of hers, you see, and while she's agreed to have the winners host a little tour of Hemlock Falls, she won't do any judging or feature the contestants. She won't sponsor it."

Elmer's belligerently expressed opinion was that if Hemlock Falls preteens were good enough for the village, they were good enough for the nation.

"That is not it," said Harvey with great authority. "She's thinking a whole new concept entirely." He rocked back in Quill's chair, contemplating the northwest corner of her ceiling. "I had a little chat with her this morning while we were taking the meeting in the Shaker suite. And I can't tell you what transpired, but it's going to be big. I mean really big. So here's what we do. We go ahead with the contest categories . . ."

"'Little Miss Personality,'" said Elmer, consulting a scrawled piece of paper from his vest pocket. "'Best Little Talent' and 'Little Miss Hemlock Falls' herself."

"Yessir," said Harvey in satisfaction. "Prizes to be offered by Frederick Bellini's Funeral Home and Peterson's Buick."

Quill found her patience wearing thin. "Harvey, if the town really insists on doing this, don't you think we should open it to little boys, too?" Neither man looked at her, which told Quill they'd discussed the possibility that she would bring it up.

"Women's lib," said Elmer. "Well, I guess we got to consider you feminists. Now, I'm all for women's lib, Quill, or I should say"— (this with heavy jocularity)—"*Ms.* Quilliam, but I don't know as how we could get the town to support a beauty contest for boys. Now, if we had a category like Best Little Fisherman, or Best Little, I dunno, some more boy-like thing . . ."

"Best Little Bow Hunter?" Quill heard herself say. "Best Little Sport with a Shotgun? *Best little penis?*"

"Oh, my God," said Elmer.

"It's the gunshot wound," said Harvey. "Saw a lot of it with 'Nam."

"Harvey, you were never in 'Nam," said Elmer, "not even close."

"I didn't say 'in' 'Nam, I said 'with' 'Nam."

"Ayuh. You know what you need, Quill? A nice cup of coffee or something."

Quill went into the kitchen to get a nice cup of coffee or something.

"I'm losing it," she told her sister. "It's the gallery business all over again. One-way trips to remote mountain areas are starting to look attractive."

"Explain," said Meg.

Meg demonstrated the proper degree of outrage over the Little Miss Hemlock Falls Beauty Contest, loyally endorsed Quill's proposed category, and immediately began preparing cappuccino as a restorative. "I'm surprised you haven't fizzed out before this, Quill." She frothed the milk, blended in the coffee, and added cinnamon and chocolate. "There. Put your feet up. Think soothing thoughts. Are you thinking soothing thoughts? Maybe you and Myles should try to get away for the weekend. We can handle things here just fine."

Quill twitched in her rocking chair: "Every time I try to think soothing thoughts, I end up against that damn brick wall. Why can't I remember what happened last night? Where's Mrs. Whitman? I've got to talk with her about what she heard when she hung up the phone."

"On a hike, of course. What's this about hanging up the phone?"

"At the reception desk last night. Dina said I was on the phone when Rickie blasted the front door. I just can't remember who I talked to. I have this feeling it's important." She bit her lip. A tendril of memory came back. "Someone asking for directions?"

"Hanging up the phone is sort of an automatic response," said Meg. "I doubt that Mrs. Whitman would remember doing that last night. I certainly wouldn't; not with all the fuss."

"Dot's dead. Dawn's disappeared. Kay didn't show up for the party last night. It's all very suspicious."

"You were just like that as a kid," said Meg. "Remember that old couple that moved next door to us when I was in kindergarten? You told me that they were feeding a whole bunch of little people that lived in her basement. And you got me to sneak over with you at eleven o'clock at night to get evidence. Because she was carrying all kinds of fresh vegetables down there and you said it was to feed the little people. That's what you said to me then—'Meg. Something very strange is going on. Mrs. Nussbaum is feeding vegetables to the little people living in her basement,' and it turned out she was canning tomatoes!" Meg waved one finger in the air. "Now, the thing about Mrs. Nussbaum, Quill, is that you never did turn in that volcano project at school. The whole reason you made up that story about Mrs. Nussbaum was because you were afraid to put vinegar and soda together to make a bubbly little explosion. There's a word for what you do. Sublimation or something. Maybe avoidance. No. Displacement. That's it."

"You've been talking with a tennis-playing physician."

"No, really, Quill . . . Well, maybe a little. The question is, what's the real problem here? I mean, aside from the Horrible Helena and your flesh wound and the usual manic goings-on?"

"You have beady little eyes," said Quill.

"Come on, Quill. Give. Think about it."

"Myles wants to get married." She bit her lip. "I didn't mean to blurt it out like that. It just goes to show you how frazzled I am."

"Hm."

"You're not gasping with astonishment."

"Why should I gasp with astonishment? He loves you. In a lot of ways he's a traditional kind of guy. Why shouldn't he want to marry you?" Meg tugged affectionately at her sleeve. "Is that what's been making you edgy for the past couple of weeks?"

"It'd mean changes."

"Changes," said Meg. Her face clouded. She looked around her kitchen. She handed Quill a cup of cappuccino. The cup rattled in the saucer. "What do you want to do?"

"I like things the way they are. It's the 'or what.' "

"What or what?"

"What happens if I say no? Do we continue on the way we are? Or does Myles run off with a brunette? Or with Helena Houndswood? If I say yes . . ."

Meg cleared her throat. "You could build a little house near the rose garden." She smiled.

"Put up the trellis. Build a picket fence."

"So what are you going to do?"

"Nothing. Something. I don't know if I want to get married again. You know what life with Daniel was like. It's all too much to deal with."

"Maybe displacement is therapeutic. Don't think about it. If you don't think about it, your subconscious will solve the problem all by itself. Think business. Business is good. Helena Houndswood shows up and everyone's making reservations. All these New York types gossip, Quillie. Word-of-mouth like that is terrific for the Inn. Things are going to be terrific. Another couple of months and we'll be rolling in cash."

"You want to think about business? Great. John says we have cash-flow problems. We can't wait a couple of months for cash to come in."

"So business is something you want to displace. Especially thoughts of immediate business. Especially when young Dawn's on the lam with that check." Meg took a large sip of Quill's cappuccino. "Okay, so the more I think about it, the more a certain degree of stress is inevitable in the following weeks. So here's what you do. Instead of thinking there's little people in our basement, or worse than that, two more dead bodies in addition to the one that's already there, and that Helena put them there, focus on a real problem that we can solve. What's happening with the Bosses Club? Who killed Dot and why? Where's Dawn Pennifarm and that forty-five hundred dollars? Men and money problems will make junkyard dogs of the best of us. And you, Quillie, are the least snappish person I know. But here you are saying outrageous things to the mayor and Harvey and growling at the Chamber people. So here's the plan, Stan. We talk to Connie and Sandy. We talk to everyone who saw Dawn last on Monday, including the Bloater. We even talk to Marge Schmidt, because she has all those connections at the bank, and she can maybe find out what Dawn's finances are. And whether she's got a secret stash of cash."

Quill retrieved the remains of her cappuccino, gulped it, and set it on the butcher's block with a thump. "That's exactly what we can do. I'll start with Rickie Pennifarm. I'll forget Helena. You're right, her involvement doesn't make sense."

"The Gourmet Detective."

"Artist as Gumshoe."

They shook hands.

"So what do we do first?" said Meg. "We make a list. Except that I've got the Chamber lunch to fix, so we'll have a—what do you call it?—strategy session this afternoon."

"Dina and I have to give statements about last night at the sheriff's office after lunch. I'll interview Rickie Pennifarm then. But I've got free time now. I'll make a preliminary list, and we'll go over it tonight."

Quill decided that the best place for detecting was outside, in the rose garden, where the sun, fresh air, and blue sky would provide a calm center in the middle of any psychic storms. Mike the groundskeeper had built a gazebo overlooking the falls and surrounded it with Blaze, a reliable floribunda climber in the sometimes tough growing conditions of Central New York. Quill settled back on the cushioned bench under the roof and watched the water through a spray of crimson blossoms. She kept a pocket-sized pen and note-book with her—for sketches, comments on Inn matters, requests from guests she encountered during the day—and she pulled it out and flipped through to a clean page. She'd asked Myles once about the success of his investigations; she knew his record of convic-tions as a detective in Manhattan was a goal for the New York police statewide. Crimes formed a pattern, he'd said, and each had its set of solvability factors. The point was to answer who, what, where, when, why, and how with proven facts. The trick was never to make assumptions, or operate on gut feel. Which was why, she, Quill, should stick to Inn management as a career.

She did a quick cartoon sketch of a wild-haired Quill marching side by side a Myles with an oversize sheriff's badge. Underneath the sketch she wrote:

VICTIM:
Dot Vandermolen

MEANS:
Rifle 270-caliber bullet. Kept in pickup truck with access to all suspects listed below.

OPPORTUNITY:

Rickie Pennifarm	(seen leaving by reliable eyewitness)
Sandy Willis	
Connie Weyerhauser	(all in vicinity of the Inn
Kay Gondowski	at the time of death)
Hudson Zabriskie	
Helena Houndswood	
Dawn Pennifarm	(????)

After a moment she added "X"? since part of solving any mys-tery had to take into account the occasional random tramp beloved by inept village constables in the English countryside.

Quill sat and considered motive. The truth stuck out like a red flag on a ski slope. Every single surviving member of the Bosses Club benefited when a member died. And no one in the Bosses

Club liked Dot. That left almost all of the suspects with a motive, including Rickie Pennifarm, who may have thought that the more members of the Bosses Club he killed, the more money would be left for Dawn.

On the other hand, Hudson Zabriskie, far from having a motive, had lost a supervisor at a critical moment in production. At least, that was what Quill surmised from his distracted behavior. And the surviving members of the Bosses Club must know that they'd be suspects.

IMPORTANT she scrawled in capitals, Dawn's disappearance linked to Dot's death?

She had a lot to ask Rickie Pennifarm, if she could get into his jail cell and talk to him while Myles was away.

She turned to Dawn Pennifarm herself.

Who: Dawn Pennifarm, age 32. Supervisor at Paramount Paint ? years. Married, Rickie Pennifarm ? years, no children.

Then she wrote WHY? She thought a moment. What else did she know about Dawn? She'd been to Hemlock High School, as had almost all the workers at Paramount. She was tough. She was mouthy. She was a good worker, according to Sandy (who was loyal to the Bosses Club) but not according to Hudson Zabriskie, her ultimate boss (who was loyal to the much invoked "New York HQ").

Quill added the caption SOLVABILITY FACTORS and then wrote: Did she need money? Did she have debts? Did she have a record?

Then: WHAT REALLY HAPPENED? Fact: disappeared Monday. Assumption: $4500 of Inn money PLUS? Paramount money? That Dawn disappeared *with* the money, Quill figured was an assumption. And how, Quill thought, did Kay's disappearance fit into all of this? Her head started to throb. Quill wrote INTERVIEW SUBJECTS and listed: Rickie Pennifarm; Hudson Zabriskie; Sandy Willis; Connie Weyerhauser.

"Quill? You busy?" Connie Weyerhauser stood outside the gazebo railing. "My husband and Sandy's husband are in at lunch talking with Howie Murchison about how we get the money. I left them to it. Just give me the check, I said. I'm going for a walk. You men figure it out and just give me the check."

"I'm glad you came out. As a matter of fact, I've been wanting to talk to you. Come up and sit down."

Connie hauled herself up the one step and settled at the far end of the bench.

"You look terrific," said Quill. "That makeover must have been so much fun."

"It lasted?" Connie patted her bangs carefully. "I've never done this before in my life. None of this seems real. I'm just hoping I can do it at home. I looked at all the makeup Tabby had in her cart. . . . Maybe I can buy a cart like that when I get my money. Barbie'd love it."

"How is she?"

"Oh. You know. The doctors . . ." Connie sighed. Her face shuttered closed. "They tell you one thing and then they tell you something else. There's a clinic for C.P. children in Buffalo. I was thinking maybe about taking her there, once I get the money. They have cures for all kinds of things these days. Dawn always said there was one kind of medicine for rich people and another kind for the working poor. Actually, there's three kinds, the third is for minorities. I was thinking now that I'm going to be rich, I could find out more about a cure."

"But you've got health insurance through the factory," said Quill. "Isn't her treatment covered?"

"Oh, yes. But Dawn always said there are treatments they don't want you to know about because of how expensive they are. The company doctor just says there's nothing we can do. I believe there's an operation somewhere that can get Barb out of the wheelchair." There was a terrific urgency in her deep slow voice. "Maybe in Switzerland. You read about all kinds of cures in Switzerland. And Mexico."

"Cerebral palsy's pretty tough," said Quill, a little helplessly.

"You're telling me, girl?" Connie sighed. "Would you behave any different?"

"I think I'd probably do exactly what you're doing; look for something to help until I know that there isn't anything more I could do. The trick is knowing when to stop. When you've done all you possibly can. That'd be a tough one for me."

"That's so." Connie smiled. "And then this happens. I thought I'd done all I could, but now look. All this money, Quill."

"Dot's share is added to yours, then. And Dawn's if she doesn't turn up."

Connie moved restlessly, her gaze shifting. "I don't know what got into Dawn, running off like that."

"Did you see Dawn the day she disappeared?"

"Monday, you mean? Sheriff asked the same thing. We knew Helena was here, you know, so we were all excited about that. Didn't talk about anything else at break time."

"You knew Helena was here! This was on Monday?"

"We discovered she actually got here on Sunday. She got off the train with twenty pieces of fancy luggage, didn't she? And the station's right next to the Croh Bar. Rickie called and told Dawn. He'd stopped in at the Croh Bar, as usual. He was supposed to be in Buffalo, looking for work. I told Dawn that man was no good, and now look what he's done." She glanced at the bandage on Quill's temple. Quill waited for the expected inquiry. It didn't come. "He called Dawn right up at their trailer, then she called each one of us."

"So you knew you won Sunday afternoon?"

"Well, we didn't know for sure." Connie chuckled. "Dawn wanted to come right up here to the Inn and demand to know. But Sandy said we had to vote on it. So when we went to work on Monday, the Bosses Club voted to wait a few days, see what happened. We were a little scared to call on someone as famous as she is."

"So what did Dawn do on Sunday? Did she go see Helena?"

Connie, Quill discovered, had dimples. "Sheriff's gonna be upset, you keep on poking around his investigations."

"I'm not . . ." Quill began with dignity, "well, maybe . . . I just . . ."

"As far as I know, Dawn did what she was supposed to do that day and nothing else. Monday, we worked the seven to three shift, like always. After, Dawn had to go to the Qwik Freeze for a bench-marking meeting, so I assume that's just what she did."

"To Qwik Freeze for a what?"

"You know, benchmarking." Seeing Quill's bewildered expression, Connie said, "Let's see if I can make it simple. When one business has a good process for doing something, another business visits to ask about the process. This better way of doing things is installed in their own business. The Monday second shift at Qwik Freeze has a worker rotation process, and Dawn, as one of the Bosses Club team, was supposed to talk to the workers to see how satisfied they were with the arrangement. It's part of our Paramount Quality program, to go to different operations and benchmark processes they perform better than we do."

Quill, somewhat fuddled, made a surreptitious note INTERVIEW QWIK FREEZE and said, "So Dawn went to Qwik Freeze . . ."

". . . to benchmark employee satisfaction with their rotation shifts," said Connie.

Quill decided not to write this down. She sent up a fervent hope that benchmarking had nothing to do with the investigation. "So did she go to Qwik Freeze?"

"She left the shift early and headed in that direction."

"The Qwik Freeze plant is right next to yours, isn't it? You're on that little crossroads between ninety-six and route fifteen."

"Mr. Zabriskie calls it the Hemlock Falls Industrial Park," said Connie. "Far as I can tell, it's two plants close together. Lord, Quill! Look at the time. I have to pick up Barb from the adult care center. You'll excuse me. And I forgot that I came out here for a reason; Doreen wants to see you."

"Thanks."

Quill found Doreen stacking clean towels in the large linen closet next to the kitchen.

"So. There you are," she said. She counted the towels by two, under her breath, recorded the number on the clipboard on the inside door, then laid one calloused palm on Quill's forehead. "Huh!" she announced. "Thought so."

Quill felt her forehead herself. "You mean I have a fever? I don't have a fever."

Doreen locked the closet door with a deliberate click of the key and said with an air of disapproval, "Mayor thought you might. From that there gunshot wound. Told him I thought you was dee-lerious, saying strange things about this beauty contest. Ast me to give you some aspirin." Quill felt her cheeks go warm. Doreen withdrew a bottle from her apron pocket. "So do you want some? You look flushed."

"No. Thanks."

Doreen stuck the aspirin bottle back in her pocket and jiggled it. "Is that why you wanted me? To give me aspirin?"

"Nope. It's this-here beauty contest."

Quill ran her mind over Doreen's family. She had a daughter with two young boys. Rowdy ones. "Your grandkids want to enter the contest? I told the mayor and Harvey that we should let little boys enter, too—"

"It ain't that. It's Mr. Whitman. The Fresh Air folks. They're fixin' to protest." Doreen sucked in her lower lip. "They ast me to let you know, they don't think it's fittin' or proper for young bodies to be paradin' out in dressy clothes and makeup. S'not fitting for young girls, is Mr. Whitman's message."

"The Friends of Fresh Air want to protest the beauty contest?"

"Right."

"I thought they were environmentalists," said Quill. "Not that I don't agree with them about beauty contests . . . I mean, I'm not violently opposed or anything, but golly, Doreen."

"Your body's part of the environment, too."

Doreen's logic, Quill admitted, was irrefutable, if a trifle unorthodox. But then, how orthodox were renengade Green Quakers? "I'm not too certain how I can help, Doreen."

"Mr. Whitman thought maybe that there Helena Houndswood might give him and his group a bit of time on the TV show. Say a few words about how Hemlock Falls is to be left natural."

"I see," said Quill, who was sure she did. "Well, you tell Mr. Whitman. No, I'll tell Mr. Whitman that it's a free country and he can protest up Main Street and down again for all I care, but I'm *not* going to help him and his group get airtime on *It's a Beautiful Life*."

"You think maybe that's not all they want?" said Doreen anxiously. "They ain't sincere?"

"I'm sure they're sincere," said Quill mendaciously. "But I'm also positive that anyone who gets within fifty yards of Helena Houndswood becomes absolutely addled and starts thinking TV stardom immediately."

"Addled," said Doreen with satisfaction.

"Don't tell Mr. Whitman he's addled. And for goodness sakes, don't give him aspirin for it, or call the funeral home, or do any of the things you do that drive me *crazy*, Doreen. I suppose you want to be on TV, too."

"No, ma'am," said Doreen with a sniff, "but I know somebody who does. Somebody who's right here in front of this linen closet."

"I don't want to be on Helena Houndswood's TV show!" Quill calmed herself with an effort. "I'm sorry, Doreen. I didn't mean to shout, I don't know what's gotten into me these days. . . ."

"You started the whole thing," said Doreen. "Astin' her to put the Inn on and all."

"You and John and Meg and that rat Harvey made me!"

"You can't make a body do what she doesn't wanna do," said Doreen virtuously. "Mr. Whitman even says you shouldn't keep the body from doing what it wants to do because it's unhealthy. Mr. Whitman says . . ."

Quill foresaw days, if not weeks, of "Mr. Whitman says." "Stop!" said Quill. Doreen stopped. Quill found herself with nothing further to add and went in pursuit of John to discuss his walk with Helena. He was, Doreen called after her, sitting in the Lounge drinking sherry with That Ms. Houndswood.

John stood up as she joined them and pulled out a chair. "Did you get any lunch?"

"No. Not yet."

"I'll ask Nate for some soup. You look a little flushed. Mayor thought you might be starting a fe . . ."

"I am absolutely *fine*," said Quill. "Helena, how's the day going?"

"The usual. Squabbles among the staff. They find the Bosses Club hopeless. They are, of course." She was dressed in pale green, a fitted jacket over a long floaty skirt.

"That outfit is just terrific."

Helena flicked a dismissive eye over Quill's challis skirt and cotton blouse. "Well, one does like to keep up."

John handed Quill a bowl of onion soup and resumed his seat.

"God. That looks terrific," said Helena. "Your sister's pretty good, isn't she? It smells great."

"Would you like some?" asked Quill politely. "We can—"

"No, no." She patted her nonexistent stomach. "I'm on nine hundred calories a day. I don't know how you keep so skinny. I've seen you eat like a horse."

Quill, deciding she spent far too much time decoding messages, ignored the possible insult and asked if the Inn was to her lawyer and producer's liking.

"Marvelous," said Helena promptly. "It's inspired my next book."

"The Inn? Really?"

"The Inn. The village. The country life. What is the dream of every upper-class American? The life of a gentleman farmer. A beautiful farmhouse, centuries-old, filled with antiques. Velvet green pastures and an adorable red barn. A few of those lovely fluffy sheep in the barn. A sleek, gorgeous horse that one can ride through green fields A herd of crimson and sunshine-yellow chickens peacefully walking about the front lawn. One of those friendly-looking cows with the big brown eyes. Fresh milk. Fresh butter. That thick lovely cream. Delicately browned omelettes from farm-fresh eggs. The pictures will be wonderful."

"Manure disposal," said Quill suddenly, remembering the potential for altercation between the farmers and the Friends of Fresh Air. "I don't think farming is all that easy a life, Helena. Besides, the farmers I know work like dogs."

"This is gentlemen farming," Helena corrected her. "All the latest equipment combined with an understanding of what it really means to live a Beautiful Life can make farming a pleasure, not a business."

"The reality may be quite different," said John, with such a sober expression Quill knew he was amused. "I worked on a farm when I was growing up here in Hemlock Falls, and it's not as easy as it looks."

"Nothing ever is," said Helena soberly, "which is why I've had my lawyer make arrangements to try it myself."

"Try it yourself?" said Quill.

"You looked amazed." Helena tossed her head and laughed in a way someone had probably told her was delightful. "You should know—my audience does—that what I write, I write from real life.

So Harvey rented that lovely parcel down by the waterfall for me for a month. I move in tomorrow morning."

"You mean the Peterson house?" said Quill. "That's been empty ever since Tom Peterson went off to jail last year. His wife moved to Syracuse with the children."

"One of Hemlock Falls' oldest families, I understand," murmured Helena, "and quite wealthy."

"Well, yes," said Quill, "except that he made all that money by selling rejected shipments of meat to third-world countries."

"Every great family has its black sheep." Helena waved this aside. "I've looked the house over this morning, on my walk. It's lovely. Harvey is making the arrangements to move me and the animals in for a month. My guess is that this book will be another best-seller."

"The animals?" said Quill.

"The sheep, the cow, the chickens. Everything, My publisher will take care of all the expenses, naturally. A small John Deere tractor. A Land Rover. All the accoutrements for a Beautiful Life on the Farm. As I said. When I write, I write about what I know. What I've directly experienced."

"Are you going to have help?" asked Quill, fascinated in spite of herself. "I mean, I don't know much about farming, but those animals take a lot of care, not to mention the manure dispo . . . well, never mind."

"I will have advice, of course. I've put Harvey on retainer. He has offered to provide anything I need to support my research."

Quill, doubting that Harvey knew the difference between a chicken and a guinea hen, suppressed the pleasurable thought that Helena would no longer be drifting about the Inn with her predatory eye on Myles "Hunk" McHale. On the other hand, it was going to be harder to keep tabs on her in case she had an undisclosed motive for murder.

"You're moving out tomorrow?" said Quill. "We'll have to keep in touch."

"Thank you, darling. I'll have you and that marvelous sheriff over for a farm-style meal. But drop in anytime."

"I certainly will," said Quill.

Helena glanced idly over Quill's shoulder. "There's a little person waving dramatically at you from the doorway."

Quill turned around. "Oh, dear."

Dina marched up to the table with a shy glance at Helena. "Quill," she said urgently. "The deposition!"

CHAPTER 8

Quill made sure she had her investigation book, brushed her hair, and swept on some blusher, then met Dina at the car. On the road she gave Dina a quick rundown on her plans to investigate Rickie Pennifarm.

"You and Meg're going to do what?" Dina's eyes widened and she turned in the passenger seat to shake her head at Quill. "Did you talk to the sheriff about it?"

"I don't know why everyone seems to think I should check out every little discussion with Myles." Quill signaled a left turn onto Main Street and pulled her battered Olds through the intersection. "All I want to do is talk to Rickie Pennifarm by myself for a few minutes. If you can keep Deputy Dave busy, he probably won't even notice."

"The sheriff notices everything," said Dina. "I don't think this is going to work."

"Myles won't be there. He's in Ithaca. Rickie's essential to the solution of the case. He's a solvability factor."

"Solvability factor," muttered Dina.

"But unless you distract Dave Kiddermeister, he's not going to let me in to see Rickie."

"And how am I supposed to do that?"

"You know, flirt."

"Flirt?"

"Flirt. Bat your eyelashes. Sit on his desk and adjust his tie. Cross your legs and let your skirt creep up over your knee. V. I. Warshawsky does it once in a while, even though it's against her principles. And if V. I. can do it, so can you."

"I'm a doctoral student, not a private investigator. And I'm wearing jeans. Besides, Quill, my generation doesn't flirt."

"We need that forty-five hundred bucks. Rickie's probably the only one who knows what Dawn did with it. We need it to pay your salary. Your generation spends money, doesn't it? To eat?"

"Right. Jeez. Well, okay."

"You'll distract him?"

"Do my best."

Dina subsided into a glum silence. Quill drove to the end of Main Street and paused at the entrance to the parking lot. The Hemlock Falls Municipal Building was a large wooden structure dating from the upper third of the nineteenth century and prey to the chief architectural sin to which those decades were heir: Carpenter Gothic. Even unadulterated Carpenter Gothic made Quill's teeth itch; but, like an uncertain lady experimenting with hair dye, the municipal building suffered from the contribution of strong solutions to a style which had been problematic from the start. It stood, a proud eyesore, at the end of Main Street.

Quill parked at the rear of the building in the space marked Official Sheriff's Business Only, responding to Dina's nervous query that they *were* on Official Sheriff's Business Only. "Besides," she said, "I told you Myles isn't here."

"So Deputy Dave is going to take our depositions?"

"Probably. You can handle him with one hand behind your back and a bag over your head. Just don't call him Deputy Dave. He hates it." Quill led the way through the labyrinth of dark corridors, low ceilings, and splotched linoleum to the door marked SHERIFF'S OFFICE AND COUNTY LOCK-UP, knocked, and walked in. Dave Kiddermeister (Kathleen's younger brother) immediately rose to his feet. The word for Dave, Quill thought, was dewy: he was blond, with a bleached Scandinavian fairness, young, and he perspired a lot. He blushed frequently, too, a distinct disadvantage when apprehending Saturday night revelers at the Croh Bar. Dewiness inspired invective. A desert sunset pink spread up to his hairline as Quill and Dina came in. He rose, stuck his thumbs in his belt, and frowned in a sheriff-like way.

"You ladies ready to give a statement about the incident of the night before?"

Nervousness made Dina bridle. "No, Dave, we're here to plead a parking ticket. And thanks for asking about Quill—she's just fine. And thanks for asking about me. I'm just fine, too."

The desert pink deepened to red. "Sorry, ma'am. Ms. Quilliam. How's your head? Doc Bishop said it was—"

"Only a flesh wound," said Quill. "No problem."

Dina circled the small office like a cat with sore feet. "So, is he here?" she whispered.

"The alleged perpetrator of the murder and the assault? Yes, ma'am."

"Ick." Dina settled into one of the plastic chairs with a shudder. "I don't hear him or anything. What's he doing?"

"Just sitting there, ma'am," said Dave. "You know, waiting for the sheriff and all." He looked thoughtful. "Got a hell of a hangover, pardon me, ladies."

Quill patted her skirt pocket to make certain she hadn't forgotten the investigation book, and wiggled her eyebrows at Dina.

"Dep . . . Dave," said Dina huskily. She rose to her feet and swayed in a seductive manner across the room. "I can call you Dave, can't I?"

Dina perched on the edge of his desk and crossed her legs, revealing fluorescent green socks. She smiled at the deputy, who grinned back.

Quill sidled toward the cell block door. "I'd like to see Rickie for a moment, Dave. Just to see how he is."

Dave's grin disappeared and his thumbs went back in his belt. He shook his head. "Can't do that, ma'am. Not allowed. On'y friends and relatives."

"Well, I'm a friend."

"You're the victim, ma'am."

"That's an even better reason," said Quill, who thought that Dave's view of which role was more important would have been significantly affected if he were the one with an inch-long wound in his skull. "Did Sheriff McHale say specifically that I couldn't talk to Rickie?"

"Well, no, ma'am, can't say as he did, but like I told you, on'y friends and rel—"

"Helena Houndswood asked me to give him a message about the money from the contest . . ."

Dave took his thumbs out of his belt, dropped one shoulder, and lowered his head confidingly, the universal Hemlockian response to getting a good piece of gossip. "It's true then. They really won a million bucks? And that actress, Helena whatsis . . ."

"Helena Houndswood," said Quill. "Yes. She's staying at the Inn, you know. As a matter of fact"—Quill raised her eyebrows slightly to increase her air of innocence—"she wanted me to see Rickie, too. Just for a minute. It's possible she's considering . . . just considering, Dave . . . bringing the cameras in here to do a short segment on crime in Hemlock Falls. It's by no means a sure thing, but it's a possibility."

Dave looked around the office. "A TV crew, here? You mean like those True Cop Stories TV shows?" His cheeks, Quill noted, had achieved an interesting shade of mauve.

"But, Quill," Dina said, "Helena's TV show is about—"

"The biggest thing to hit this town in years," interrupted Quill solemnly. Dina closed her mouth and fluttered her eyelashes.

"We'd look pretty good next to those cops from Miami, I guess," said Dave proudly, "and Detroit. No flies on us here in Hemlock Falls."

"I guess you might call me a scout," Quill said, thinking, well, he might. He'd be wrong, but he might. "So I'll just take a few seconds, no more than that, to feel him out about this." Still talking, Quill marched confidently up to the steel door labeled LOCK-UP, slipped through, and left Deputy Dave to Dina's wiles.

The county lock-up consisted of two steel barred cells with concrete floors that made Quill think of a dog pound. The air was sourly humid with cigarette smoke. Rickie Pennifarm was the lock-up's only occupant. He sat hunched on a horizontal gate covered by a mattress, dressed in soiled blue jeans and a red flannel shirt. Rickie was scrawny and small, with a straggling brown beard and mean little eyes. He inhaled the last of an unfiltered cigarette, stubbed it out carefully with his booted foot, and dropped it in the toilet.

"Mr. Pennifarm?" said Quill.

"Yeah." He got up and advanced to the side of the cell facing her. "You a lawyer?"

"Am I? No. No. I'm Sarah Quilliam."

"Yeah?" He squinted at her. "I guess you are. I seen you around. Oh!" His snigger trailed off into a cough. "You're the one I winged. Din't mess you up much, looks like."

"Not too much."

"So. What can I do you for?" He leered at her.

"We're looking for Dawn. You really don't have any idea where she is?"

"Fuck, no. You think I woulda shot you up if I knew where she was? Hell, I thought she was at that party spending the money she won, just to spite me. That bitch's got no sense of gratitude."

"When's the last time you saw her?"

"What, you the fucking sheriff's deputy? No? Wait. I got it. You're the one fucking the sheriff."

Rickie's laughter at his foray into wit left Quill unmoved. She'd had some pangs of conscience about her proposed method of interrogation; she abandoned them. "Helena, I mean Helena Houndswood, the actress, is up at the Inn making arrangements about the million dollars. If Dawn's disappeared, of course, you're her husband—"

"Fuckin' right!" He grabbed the bars with both hands. "Dawnie comes into a million, it's my million, too. I mean, I'm her fuckin' husband, for christsake."

"Well, it's not a million, you know. It's one fourth of that. Connie, Kay, and Sandy all share in the prize."

"One fourth," said Rickie. "Son of a bitch. That's a lot of money, right?"

"It's increased, of course, since Dot Vandermolen passed away."

"No kidding? Four-way split?"

Quill, increasingly sure that Rickie was innocent of at least Dot's murder, decided to spare him the effort of calculation. "Two hundred fifty thousand dollars."

"Two hundred fifty fucking thousand dollars. Yes!" He pounded his thigh enthusiastically. "So. Look. I may need a little advance. For my defense and all. You get this Helena Houndswood to come and see me? Maybe bring some of it in cash?"

"I'll ask her," said Quill, "but I'd like to ask you some questions first."

"Little trade-off, right? Fire away."

"When did you last talk to Dawn?"

"Sunday morning. Told her I was headed off on to Buffalo, looking for work. Lost my fuckin' job at the fuckin' Qwik Freeze on account of—"

"So you left her at home?"

"Yeah. Stopped at Marge's for some breakfast."

"And then you went to the Croh Bar."

"Couple of pops for the road," he said, his lower lip at a belligerent angle. "So what?"

"And you saw Helena Houndswood come off the train?"

"Yeah. Man, that's some babe." He shook his head. "Looks smaller than on TV, you know. Saw her, figured Dawnie oughta know. I mean, shit. What's the broadie here for 'cept to fork over the bucks? And I wanted what's owed me."

"You were broke, is that it?"

Rickie scowled, immediately defensive. "Who the fuck told you that? They're a goddam liar. I'm as good off as anyone in this shitheel town. Hell, I paid my truck off two months ago, and that trailer's practically paid off, too. We got enough, not that the bitch is any too free handing it out." He flexed his fist absentmindedly. "Guy needs some beer money, he should get some beer money. No damn wife of mine's gonna say no, either."

"Could Dawn have had a separate checking account?"

His mouth tightened into a mean line. "Could be. Wun't put it past her. We put our paychecks in the same damn account. She makes eleven twenty a hour; I was making fifteen. She'd wave that checkbook at me once in a while, bitching about my takin' out beer money."

"There must have been some opportunities to find extra money at Paramount. I mean, she was the bookkeeper. You know, Rickie . . ." Quill glanced behind her. The steel door was closed. She took a breath and plunged in. "If you know about something Dawn did—maybe if you even helped her to some extra money, if you talked to Sheriff McHale about it, things might go better for the both of you. I mean, if she's hiding out because she maybe took off with some extra funds from Paramount and is afraid to come back to claim her winnings, or something . . ."

"You mean I could get that money faster?" Rickie's little pig eyes glittered. "If Dawn was like, a thief, she maybe couldn't collect that million bucks. It'd come to me?"

"No, no no," said Quill, "that's not what I meant. What I meant is you could sort of throw yourself on the mercy of the court by confessing before the court had to go to all the expense of an investigation. They go more lightly on people who confess up front, I think."

"Yeah? I could use some lightening up, that's for sure. I mean, what kind of fucking fool shoots the goddam sheriff's fucking girlfriend? And now they think I shot up some broadie I don't even know. Although," he said with a conciliatory air, "I di'n't mean to hurt nobody. Least of all you. Anyways, I'm standing here to tell you that Dawn never thought about being a thief. Not Dawnie. An out-and-out slugger bitch, yeah, no question. Whacked me more'n once with the fry pan, coming home too late from the Croh Bar. Whacked me another time, she finds out I been drawing a little extra from the checking account for beer. Besides," he said with a very peculiar kind of dignity, "we have our plans, Dawnie and me. I mean, we have our disagreements, no question about that, but I was going to Buffalo for a better job. We was going to start saving for the kid, and then she ups and disappears on me. Bitch!" He pounded one fist into the palm of his hand. To her amazement, Quill saw tears in his eyes.

"I didn't know you had children," said Quill. Myles, she was convinced, had no idea, either, and she had a sudden chilling vision of toddlers left in the Pennifarm trailer overnight with no one to take care of them. "Is anyone taking care of them? Can I check on them for you?"

"No kids. Not yet, anyhow. Dawnie has a bun in the oven. Not that she thanked me," said Rickie bitterly. "Said she don't want no drunk for a father. She thought maybe I'd fuck it up or something."

"You mean Dawn was pregnant," said Quill.

"Yeah," said Rickie proudly. "Our first. Three months along."

Quill threw another involuntary glance over her shoulder. "About yesterday, Rickie."

"What about it?"

"I found . . . the body, you know. Dot Vandermolen."

"So?"

"I guess the bullet that winged me might have come from that rifle?"

"So fucking what? I didn't do it. I wasn't anywheres near that place. Sure the truck was there, but I keep that Remington right where it's supposed to be, see? In the gun rack in the back. And so what if some damn fool comes along and borrows it? When I get my hands on that bastard . . ." His lips curled back from his teeth. "And I got an alibi. I was down to Frank's, getting gas in a can. No matter what that fuckin' sheriff thinks I done, I didn't do that stupid bitch."

"Dot," said Quill. "Dot Vandermolen."

"I run out in the woods!" raged Rickie, his hands white-knuckled on the bars. "I run outa gas in the fuckin' woods and I walked off down the fuckin' road to the fuckin' gas station and I didn't fire no rifle!"

"I see," said Quill.

Quill concluded the interview with a few vague promises to give Helena Houndswood the opportunity to offer Rickie an advance on his two hundred and fifty thousand, and returned to the office. Dina was leaning over Deputy Dave's shoulder, looking at his gun. She greeted Quill with a cry of relief.

"Rickie claims he was getting gas?" said Dina. Quill had added her short and unremarkable statement to Dina's, and they were driving back to the Inn. "That's pretty thin. What about Dawn? You think he killed her, too?"

"I don't think Rickie's killed anyone. For one thing, he talks about her in the present tense. Even though my gut feel says Dawn's dead, and he's the likeliest suspect, I still don't think he did it. Being married to Rickie—and she was pregnant by the way—it gives her even more of a motive to take the money and run. But it doesn't make sense. Why make off with our forty-five hundred dollars when she was convinced that two hundred thousand dollars had gotten off the train with Helena Houndswood? On the other hand, with his pickup truck parked right there, and unlocked, *anyone* could have picked up that rifle. And there were a lot of people in the woods that day. Sandy. Kay. Connie. Helena herself." Quill brooded, and absentmindedly turned right under the sign on the intersection that said NO TURN ON RED.

"Uh, Quill," said Dina.

"What? Oh! Was that red? Darn." Quill braked. A horn sounded. Quill waved at Elmer Henry in his 1980 Seville. Harvey was seated next to him. Neither man waved back.

"Uh, Quill!"

"What, Dina?"

"You probably didn't drive too much being from Manhattan and everything, but we shouldn't be sitting in the middle of the road like this."

"Oh. You're right, of course. Sorry." Quill shifted into Drive and mused on. "Unless Helena did it. Killed Dot and bought Kay and Dawn Pennifarm off."

"Helena Houndswood!" said Dina, scandalized. "Why?"

"Dina. You've met Dawn. And the rest of the Bosses Club. I don't know if you'd met Dot, but she was a pretty tough cookie. Suppose you're Helena Houndswood with a reputation for appealing to the crème de la crème, and here the china contest winners turn out to be Dot, Sandy, Connie, Kay, and Dawn. Now. You find out who they are. You realize that Connie is well spoken and attractive, but she's black. And don't you tell me that racism isn't alive and well and thriving from Manhattan to Tacoma. She's clearly not a candidate for Helena's screwy notions of who gets to lead a Beautiful Life. Ditto Sandy Willis, for separate reasons. Kay Gondowski and Dawn are intimidated into keeping their mouths shut, and they leave town. But Dot . . ."

"A shouter?" said Dina. "An activist?"

"And almost as mean as Rickie Pennifarm himself. If you were Helena Houndswood, wouldn't you try and do some damage control?"

"Wow," said Dina thoughtfully. "No offense, Quill, but it's just an opinion, right? I mean, you don't have any proof."

Quill parked in front of the Inn's main door. "I'll get proof. But not before I've identified the solvability factors and eliminated the nonessential facts. This will lead me to a logical conclusion."

"These solvability factors," said Dina, "you've mentioned them before."

"They're facts that lead to the solution of the crime," said Quill. "You collect all the facts pertaining to a crime, and then you determine which are the ones that lead to the solution, and those are the solvability factors."

"How do you determine which fact is the right one?"

"Analysis," said Quill firmly. "Are you getting out?"

"You're not coming in?"

"No."

"I think everyone from the Chamber's left. I mean, the only ones who were really mad at you were Miriam and Harvey and Elmer and Howie."

Quill stared at her. "Really mad at me? Why?!"

"The Chamber minutes."

"The Chamber minutes. Oh, dear," said Quill guiltily. "I have this kind of weird shorthand, Dina, and it was probably impossible for Miriam to interpret them."

"They interpreted it just fine. The drawings were real clear, I guess. So were the captions. You're awfully good, Quill, as an artist I mean."

Harvey on the pitchfork. Marge in flames. Quill slid down in the driver's seat: the matchmaking note about Miriam and Howie Murchison. "They saw it? All of them?" she said after a moment.

"Yep. So I can see why you might want to stay away from the Inn for a while. Miriam's waiting for you."

"I'm not afraid to go into my own Inn," said Quill, which wasn't the literal truth. "I'm going to Paramount to talk to Hudson Zabriskie. I'm gathering evidence."

"Jeez," said Dina. "The Bloater. See you in a couple of days, then."

"Very funny."

Dina got out, then leaned in the open window. "You know, I was thinking that maybe I could solve this with you and Meg? It was kind of fun, being a femme fatale with Deputy Dave. But I don't know, Quill, Rickie Pennifarm is like the scum of the earth. And Hudson Zabriskie . . . I mean, ick! Nice guy, but we're talking geek city."

Quill decided a modest smile was in order. "Not everyone," she said, "has the motivation to be a detective, Dina. Which is fine."

"And besides, it takes time." Dina sighed heavily. "The orals for my dissertation are up in three months. Keep me up on your progress, though, right?"

"Right."

The drive to Paramount was short. Quill kept an eye out for Harvey and the mayor, stopping carefully at every red light. She pulled into the employee parking lot and sat for a moment, wondering who had the Chamber minutes now, and if the Chamber members would consider a free eight-course gourmet meal as sufficient apology. "Never apologize, never explain," somebody had once said, which Quill thought perfectly ridiculous: she was going to have to apologize all over the place if she wanted to keep any friends. "Head wound" or "post-traumatic stress syndrome" might do as an explanation. Quill tried to think of Famous Detectives who'd used "head wound" as an excuse for rudeness, and failed utterly. "Order and method," said Quill aloud. "Use those little gray cells." She took out her Interview book, recorded the substance of her interrogation of Rickie Pennifarm, adding a note: Take Miriam shopping? Call Howie and grovel? Bag Harvey! Then listed the next set of Things To Do.

1. Where was Hudson at the time of Dot's shooting?
2. Verify Dawn's last seen/last day activities?
3. GET MONEY!

Quill had never been inside the Paramount Paint Factory, although she'd passed it innumerable times and it was hard to overlook. The building was long and low, the size of several football fields end to end. Each section of aluminum siding was painted in a different Paramount exterior color, beginning with Cryst-All White, through the red-yellow-green-blue-violet of the color palette. The Qwik Freeze plant a quarter of a mile away was bigger and employed more people, but Paramount loomed a lot larger in the town's collective imagination. Although when she thought about it, this may have been because of Hudson himself and not the startling appearance of the factory building. Hudson was widely popular despite his esoteric dyslexia, perhaps even because of it; frequently, the only rational response to Hudson's linguistic vagaries was a genial, uncomprehending nod. Hudson never made any real enemies because no one could tell if he was voicing an unpopular opinion or not. More to the point, as a subsidiary of a Fortune 500 company, Paramount pay scales and benefits were better than Qwik Freeze, whose local farmer-owners were notoriously thrifty. Hudson benefited from the halo effect.

Quill went through the front door and into the reception area. There was no one at the front desk, but a large sign read VISITORS WELCOME! PLEASE SIGN IN! with an arrow pointing downward to a visitor's book. Quill wrote her name, then pushed a bell labeled RING FOR ASSISTANCE, and sat down to wait.

The reception area was furnished in what Meg called Business Plastic: bucket chairs and teetery end tables with fake geraniums resting on an exceptionally clean linoleum floor. The walls were off-white, and displayed Paramount's "COMMITMENT TO QUALITY," an award for "EXCELLENCE IN EXTERIOR LATEX" and a plaque for the U.S.A.P.M. Race for the Rainbow First Prize for a paint called Crimson Blaze, displaying a virulently orange-red paint sample.

"You sap 'em," said Hudson, coming through a door marked NO ADMITTANCE. "Two years in a row."

"Hi, Hudson," said Quill.

Hudson veered aimlessly to the plaque. "Dutch Boy couldn't touch it," he said with visible pride.

"U.S.A.P.M. The United States of America Paint Manufacturers," said Quill with sudden insight. "How wonderful, Hudson. It's an important prize, I take it."

"Without question." Hudson smoothed his mustache. "My process, you know. Leadless. Nothing to do but promote me, they said."

"How in the world did you get that marvelous orange-red without using lead oxide?" asked Quill. "It's amazing!"

"Teamwork," said Hudson. He beamed. Quill noticed he had a very nice smile. "The Bosses worked under my leadership. Enormous savings, not using lead. OSHA's happy. UMC's down. New York's delighted with me, just delighted. No contaminants, you see, at least, not that we can tell."

"What did you use instead of lead oxide?" Quill's professional curiosity was aroused.

Hudson looked at her helplessly. Quill made a mental note to ask Connie Weyerhauser whether Hudson knew anything at all about the process that had brought them to the attention of New York.

"Well, it's wonderful," said Quill. "I'm sorry to interrupt your workday, Hudson, but I thought maybe I could pick up that check?" She stopped herself, aware that she'd rushed her fences. Nothing made Hudson more hopelessly twitchy than the mention of money. Hudson was oblivious, contemplating his plaque.

"Trying to get the color of fire," said Hudson, complacently observing the framed sample of Crimson Blaze. "You're a painter, too, they tell me. Of course, pictures are different, but paint's paint."

"Artist's colors *are* a bit different," said Quill diplomatically. "The process—"

"The process! How right you are! Paint is *not* paint, Quill. Why, there's a very well-known oil-base manufacturer, and I'm naming no names, mind you, but I'd swear they'd put their label on anything! Soybean substitute!" Hudson snorted in patent disgust. "Very few people really understand paint, Quill. People who really understand paint, really love paint, who know about the value of paint to our culture, know why I'm so concerned about the cost of our lunches. Would you like to see the improvements I've brought to the Hemlock factory?"

Great detectives, thought Quill, frequently conducted their investigations along unobvious and seemingly irrelevant lines. Look at Miss Marple. "Sure," said Quill.

Hudson barged through the NO ADMITTANCE door rather like a golden retriever begging for a walk, treading backward to face Quill waving his arms back and forth like twin tails. "It all begins," he said seriously, "with the exoskeletons of tiny creatures who died hundreds of thousands of years ago." He inhaled, choked, and apologized, "Sorry. I got so excited I swallowed my spit."

Quill was disarmed. She followed him meekly through the factory, which was huge, noisy, and very clean. Quill heard about diatomaceous earth, cut out of the Adirondacks in ten-ton chunks and thrown into Paramount's sixteen-foot-wide, sixty-foot-long ball mills, to be ground to the consistency of talcum powder, then mixed with calcium carbonate, mica, and zinc oxide, the latter, Hudson told her sternly, an expensive mineral that certain companies skimped on. Not Paramount, which was, if Quill didn't mind a little jest, paramount.

Hudson was rather endearingly fond of oil-based paint. "They'll ban it eventually, you know," he said wistfully. "If I hadn't come up with my orange-red process, we'd have to be obsolescing the whole line in five years. It's a pity."

Quill, who loved the fiery depths of color, agreed, but added practically, "Latex is much safer."

"Latex!" Hudson's scorn was clear. "Let me tell you about latex! More expensive, but will customers pay for it? Absolutely not. So the profit margin's lower. I have to work that much harder, which I don't mind, of course, not at all. Terrible coverage. Awful stick. Fades. Disgraceful. Nothing," continued Hudson earnestly, "will touch your basic oil-base."

"Hmm," said Quill, for lack of a comprehensible response. Cursed with a memory only erratically retentive, Quill later found herself able to quote the properties of "hiding" pigments like titanium dioxide (which gives paint its quality of coverage), zinc oxide (which makes dried paint hard), and how "certain manufacturers who shall remain nameless" cheated on the quality of oil-base paint by using the lowest-grade linseed oil—sometimes achieving the nadir through the use of a soybean substitute.

"You would think," she said to Meg that evening, "that I could remember stuff like your recipe for ratatouille, or the combination to the office safe, but no, my brain stores the fact that pigment is seventeen point six percent of paint."

"I gather that the rest," said Meg solemnly, "is solvents."

"Hamlet, sideswiped." Quill settled back into a rocker next to the kitchen fireplace. "Actually it was kind of interesting. Those ball mills are filled with fist-sized stones. The mill rotates, the rocks tumble, and ten-ton chunks of rock are reduced to the consistency of talcum powder in about eight hours. I was thinking a little teeny ball mill would be fun in the kitchen. You know, you could grind up spices and whatnot."

Meg, who was grinding nutmeg to a powder with a mortar and

pestle, stopped and gave her sister a dubious look. "Aside from genius ideas about innovative kitchen equipment, did you get the money?"

"I didn't get the money."

"Why didn't you get the money?"

"Because Hudson talked so much about mineral spirits and kerosene and how his process for making oil-based orange-reds is leadless that I didn't get a chance. He claims that he won't know if the money's missing until he talks to the bank, and I asked him to talk to the bank, and he picked up the phone and then started to fill me in on how stones from Normandy are the only ones you can use on a ball mill without cracking. Which I thought was pretty interesting, by the way." She ignored Meg's eye-rolling and said, "I did, however, pin him down about Dot and where he was at the time of her murder. He gave Kay Gondowski a ride home from the Inn. So she's his alibi. If she shows up." Quill frowned, the faint memory troubling her. "I think he thinks Dawn stole the money. But he waffled. And he clearly doesn't want to pay up, which is why he's saying he's not sure, and he has to call the bank. But he thinks she took it. He said he's suspected her for a long time of petty thieving. There's *always* a certain amount of small stuff in a business, but lately, Hudson said—well, he didn't exactly say it, but I gathered as much—that there'd been a lot of complaints about money missing from the women's locker room. The workers all have to wear white lab coats and change their shoes and shower off. They have a locker room for men and women, and the women's locker room has been where the thefts have occurred. The Bosses Club will be crushed if Dawn's a petty thief. So, in fact, will Rickie Pennifarm, who thinks his sweetie is incapable of it. But that's what it looks like, at least. Hudson also thinks Kay and Dawn just up and quit. Hudson said he's already received budget approval for five new supervisory positions from New York. He says Connie and Sandy are going to quit, too."

"Hudson didn't tell us anything very useful, did he? You're awful at pinning people down," Meg observed without rancor. "On the other hand, you're pretty good at caricature, from what Miriam Doncaster tells me."

"Uh. That."

"It's great when you squirm. If they haven't burned the min-

utes book, I'd love to see it. So Dawn seems to have done a permanent bunk. Maybe we don't need the forty-five hundred as much
as John thinks we need the money. The Inn is stuffed full, Quill.
The dining room's booked through the weekend. Nobody from the
Chamber, of course, since there's a temporary boycott due to your
minutes book. I take it you didn't leave your Investigator's Book
lying around for Deputy Dave to find and marvel at?"

Quill pushed the rocker into motion, to avoid a descent into ado-
lescent behavior involving phrases of the "Shut up, stupid," "Who's
stupid?" "You're stupid" variety. "Well, maybe Hudson wasn't all
that useful. But Rickie Pennifarm was. Now, here's what we know
from Dawn's creepo husband." She summarized her conversation
with Rickie Pennifarm, gratified at Meg's horrified expressions
of sisterly concern: "You talked to this guy alone!" Then, "How
could she stand being married to him!" Then, thoughtfully, "So
they weren't broke."

"But she's pregnant. And it makes sense to me that she grabbed
money from everywhere she could to get away."

"God!" Meg shuddered. "What a father the kid's got to look
forward to." She emptied the nutmeg into a glass bowl, opened the
freezer, and pulled out a large beef tenderloin. She dumped it into
the Cuisinart and watched the meat pulverize with a thoughtful
expression.

"So what do you think?" asked Quill.

"Steak tartare's a big seller when the dining room's full."

"No, I mean about the investigation."

Meg added salt, pepper, and a dash of vinegar to the glass bowl,
turned off the Cuisinart, and dumped the beef into the spices. She
began to shape the meat with her hands. "Rickie's alibi is tissue
paper. He could have shot Dot by mistake before or after he went
to get gas. It looks like Dawn Pennifarm has run off with as much
cash as she could pull together. When she hears about the million
bucks, she'll probably be back. If she's lucky, Rickie'll be sent up
the river for twenty years for murder." Meg nodded in the direction
of the newspaper folded on the countertop. "There's a paragraph
in *USA Today* about the win. She'll see it. And she'll come home
with some story or other. It looks like the case is closed, Sherlock."

"But what about Kay?"

"Connie heard from Kay, didn't she?"

"So she said."

"It's consistent with Kay's character. That she'd take off and hide."

"What's consistent, Meg, is that all these women are connected to Helena Houndswood, who has every reason in the world to buy them off."

"Bullshit." Meg thumped the beef.

"I take it that means you don't think Helena Houndswood is behind the planned disappearance of the Bosses Club one by one."

"I never did think that. You thought that. What I thought is that we could find Dawn and get our forty-five hundred dollars back. Now I think we have to wait until Dawn finds us."

Quill leaned her head against the rocker back and closed her eyes. "Helena is leaving tomorrow. Although it's just down the hill to the Petersons' old house. If there's anything funny going on, it's going to be harder to keep an eye on her."

Meg shaped the finely ground beef into a large ball, covered it with cheesecloth, and put it in the cooler. "I don't know a thing about what's-this-he-called-it retrograde amnesia, but that whack on the head seems to have given you a *thing* about Helena Houndswood."

"I don't have a thing about Helena Houndswood. I have a thing about one woman dead and two women missing after winning more money than they've ever seen in their lives."

"Then we should be looking at Connie and Sandy as suspects, right? I mean, they have the most to gain." Meg wiped her hands on a kitchen towel. "God, my hands are cold after handling that meat."

Quill stiffened.

Meg turned to the sink and rinsed her hands in warm water. "And I don't believe Connie's capable of hanky-panky. Sandy, now, she's a possibility . . . except that there's a logical explanation for both incidents. Tell you what, let's try displacing stress with some good old sex. Much more fun than detecting, sex. I was thinking that maybe you and Myles and Andy and I could go to Syracuse next Friday and have dinner somewhere else, for a change. . . . Quill, are you all right? What's the matter?"

"That's what Kay said. 'God, my hands are cold.' Meg! I remember! It was Kay I was on the phone with when Rickie shot up the front door. Kay Gondowski!"

CHAPTER 9

"That's all you remember? 'My hands are so cold'?" Myles was dressed in a rumpled tweed sport coat and a blue workshirt. He slouched against the kitchen fireplace, his evidence case at his feet.

Quill nodded. The bullet wound itched. She rubbed it with a tentative finger. "That's it. It's a funny sort of memory, like an electrical short. Sort of sputtery. I've tried and tried to remember more, but I can't."

"But you're sure it was Kay."

"Positive."

It was after eleven. The kitchen was deserted except for the four of them. Quill sat on one side of the long counter, John and Meg on the other. Quill had sent most of the young staff home; the sole remaining diners were a young couple on a tour of the Finger Lakes who'd gotten lost on their way to Canandaigua.

Meg fiddled with a plate of salmon sandwiches she'd made while they waited for Myles. "You said you found some evidence at Kay's house? But no Kay?"

"No Kay. I did find this. Recognize it?" Myles set the evidence case on the counter and removed a sheaf of manila files.

"It looks like the minutes of the team meetings for the Bosses Club," said Quill. "I saw it yesterday in the conference room."

"In whose possession?"

"Connie's. Connie Weyerhauser." Quill paged through the file. There was an incredible amount of paper; page after page of notes, accounts, printed material from various government agencies. "She was Dawn Pennifarm's backup on the team."

"It was Connie who told you Kay called her to say she'd left town because she was too frightened to show up."

Quill, uneasy, nodded reluctantly and attempted a diversion. "Boy! Look at all the stuff you have to do to handle lead oxide!" She pulled out a Materials safety handling sheet from OSHA. "Masks for the workers, gloves, vents. No wonder the Bosses Club leadless process is saving so much money."

Myles refused to be drawn. "John, I'd like you to take a look at how Dawn handled purchasing."

"The general ledger's in there?" said John with a frown.

"Just the inventory accounts."

John spread the files on the counter, took a pencil from his pocket, and began to leaf slowly through the pages.

"So did Rickie Pennifarm confess to killing Dot yet?" demanded Meg. "That alibi of his is pretty shaky, if you ask me."

"I tend to believe it," said Myles. "It's the airtight alibis that bother me. Frank Talbot sold Rickie five gallons of gas yesterday afternoon sometime between five and five-thirty. He doesn't remember precisely. Rickie was drunk, he said, and wanted a ride back to the truck, which Frank wasn't inclined to give him."

Meg made a noise indicative of disbelief. Quill bit her lip.

"Hm," said John. "Well, well, well. Myles. How would you feel if your supplier charged you two thousand dollars a ton for iron oxide?"

"I don't know," said Myles. "Bemused?"

"Suspicious." John looked up, a faint grin creasing his face. "That's red clay, basically. A pigment. According to the Bosses Club, it's the ingredient that replaces lead oxide to get that orange-red color. It's cheap, I know that. Nowhere near two thousand dollars for a ton."

"Iron oxide?" said Quill. "To replace lead oxide as a pigment?"

John ignored her. "There's a second inconsistency. The proportion of pigment versus solvent is roughly one to five. But the amount of iron oxide ordered is far more than the gallonage for the whole factory. At least on paper."

"Where's the iron oxide shipped from?" said Myles.

"The wholesaler's address is Queens, New York," said John.

His brow furrowed. "Queens. Now where have I seen that address before?" He raised his eyebrows. "By God! Makepeace Whitman!"

"The Fresh Air People!" said Quill. "You're joking! The guy wholesales clay?"

"Well, somebody has to," said Myles, amused. "I don't suppose it's inconsistent with his interest in fresh air. Everyone has to have a hobby. John, if you had to guess, what would you say is going on here?"

"Embezzlement," said John. "Not on a huge scale. Don't hold me to this, but . . ." He withdrew his pocket calculator from the breast pocket of his sport coat and rapidly punched in numbers. 'If I extrapolate from this one month, April, somebody pulled three or four hundred dollars out of Paramount. Multiply this by twelve and it's a little less than four thousand a year."

Quill opened her mouth. Myles held up his hand to forestall her comment. "It's not enough for Hudson Zabriskie to be involved, Quill."

"That's not what I was going to say," said Quill indignantly.

"Well, it's what I've been thinking. Hudson's responsible for the Bosses Club, and for the P and L at the end of the year. What do you think, John?"

John shook his head. "No way. It wouldn't make sense for Hudson to engage in this kind of petty theft. He makes well over a hundred thousand a year. . . ."

"He does!" gasped Meg.

"How do you know?" asked Quill.

"Benchmarking," said John. "Most of the large businesses in town share salary figures. It gives an idea of how much we have to pay local employees."

"Bench, what?" asked Meg.

Quill patted her arm. "I'll explain to you later."

"So it's not worth Hudson's time. Certainly not worth the risk. But it might be worth the Bosses Club's. The women's wages average a little less than eleven hundred a month, and an extra three or four hundred pays a lot of groceries. On top of that, it's unlikely that this scam would survive an audit. And Hudson's way too smart for that."

"A hundred thousand a year," marveled Meg. "He's such a dope!"

"He's a dope running a subsidiary of a Fortune 500 company." John shrugged. "What can I say?"

"Have you bench whatis chefs' salaries?" Meg demanded. "Quill . . . a hundred thousand a *year*?!" Quill opened her mouth again. "You were going to say that I'm not worth a hundred thousand a year," said Meg furiously. "Well, I'll have you know that a good chef in Manhattan is worth five times that. Ten times that!"

"That's not what I was going to say," said Quill. "And you're priceless, Meg. John, that iron oxide . . ."

"I took a cursory look at the figures," said Myles. "Do you agree that both Dawn and Connie Weyerhauser may have been involved?"

John paged through the figures again. "It's a good guess."

"Sufficient grounds for an arrest?"

John nodded. "I can work up a paragraph for you for a warrant."

"Myles, no!" Quill clenched her hands. "This is absurd. There's no way that Connie Weyerhauser could be mixed up in this!"

"I know you're upset, Quill—"

"If you pat me on the head," said Quill through gritted teeth, "I'll hit you."

"Quill," said Meg. "Settle down. Look at the facts. Connie left the Inn at four-thirty, just before Dot was killed. You told me yourself that Dot was threatening to look at those files. Worse yet, every time a member of the Bosses Club drops out of the picture, Connie gets another piece of that million dollars. It's a pretty strong motive."

"I suppose you're going to tell me she stuck Kay Gondowski in a refrigerator somewhere," said Quill, stiff with anger. "And that Sandy Willis is next."

"I didn't think that either Kay or Sandy had access to these files," said Myles. "But I'm wondering why Kay had them. And yes, I'm concerned about both the women. Which is why I'm going to pick up Connie now."

"Wait!" said Quill. "What about Helena Houndswood?"

"What about Helena Houndswood?" said Meg, exasperated. "Honestly, Quill."

"She was in the woods at the very minute Dot was murdered,"

said Quill. "And she could have passed right by Rickie Pennifarm's truck, swiped the rifle, and killed Dot."

"Except she hadn't seen any of the Bosses Club at that point," said Meg. "How would she know who to shoot?"

"That's where you're wrong," said Quill. "I have proof that she knew about the Bosses Club the Sunday she came into town . . . well . . . not proof exactly, but a strong suspicion. *And* she said she was going upstairs to take a hot bath, and she lied about that— she was out, probably shooting Kay Gondowski. And she's got a motive, Myles. She thinks these women could end her career. I know she does. And besides . . ."Quill stopped suddenly and folded her arms, determined not to discuss the puzzle of the iron oxide until she solved it herself.

"Besides what?" said Myles.

"Nothing."

"Stubborn," said Meg. "It's just like that time with Caroline Addison, Quill."

"It is not like the time with Caroline Addison."

"What about Caroline Addison?" asked Myles.

"They don't want to hear about Caroline Addison," said Quill.

"I do," said John.

"Caroline Addison—" said Meg.

"Meg!"

"—was the meanest, rottenest waitress at the country club when we were in high school. Quill and I waitressed at the club in the summers. And the deal was, all the waitresses put their tips in a big jar, and we split it at the end of each shift. Caroline never put in any tips, and we all said that it was because Caroline kept hers and then took some of ours, but no, Quill didn't believe it. She said we should leave Caroline alone because it would be just awful for Caroline to have to admit nobody gave her any tips because she was a rotten waitress. It would be even worse to accuse her of being a thief. Which she was. Instead, Quill started giving her little hints about how to be a better waitress, and Caroline got pissed off and socked her. So I socked Caroline. And we all three got fired. But that's Quill. Stubborn in defense of the helpless. Caroline Addison was about as helpless as a rattlesnake.

"And Myles, the same thing is happening here. Quill likes Connie. She feels sorry for Connie because she has a daughter with C.P. and a hard life. I do, too. But it looks very much like Connie's in the middle of this, Quill. And you don't like Helena Houndswood because she's not an underdog. She's an upper dog. She's about as upper dog as you can get." Meg, seeing Quill's expression, continued rapidly, "And now she's really mad at me, so I'm going, going, gone to bed." She backed out of the dining room doors and disappeared.

Quill picked up the salmon sandwiches with a purposeful air and aimed them at the sink. The plate landed on the rinse side with a crash.

John put the Bosses Club files into a neat stack with a grin.

"Where is Helena?" asked Myles with a conciliatory air.

"Harvey took her to Ithaca to look at tractors," said Quill shortly.

"Tractors? Why would she want a tractor?"

"She's moving into the Peterson house for a month. She's going to write another book. Farming: It's a Beautiful Life."

Myles gave a shout of laughter. John bit his lip.

"I'm serious," said Quill, smiling in spite of herself. "She's going to get a horse, a cow to milk, some pigs. And some chickens."

"Chickens!" John nodded at Myles. "I was there. It's true." John burst into outright laughter.

"What's wrong with chickens?" asked Quill. "I sort of like chickens."

John shook his head, helpless.

"It'll be interesting," said Myles. His smile died. "I'm leaving now, Quill. I'll check in with you later."

"You're going to arrest her?"

"I've got probable cause, Quill. And I have one dead woman, and two missing. And a fourth to worry about. Sandy Willis. Every time a member of the Bosses Club disappears, Connie benefits that much more. No, I'm not sure. But I've got cause to wonder."

John, murmuring vague excuses, went to bed and Quill was left glaring at Myles alone. "Please wait, Myles. You have to talk to the Whitmans, right? And where are you going to get an arrest order this time of night? You'll have to go to Ithaca and raise a judge and by the time you get back it'll be morning. Why not wait tomorrow?"

"Quill, I . . ."

358 Claudia Bishop

She reached over and drew his hand to her cheek. "You're wrong about this. I know you're wrong. Come up to bed with me."

He put his arms around her and rested his chin on the top of her head. "You're right, I suppose. A few hours isn't going to make any difference. And Judge Anderson is going to be a little more receptive to the warrant if I catch him during chambers." He drew back and took her chin in his hand. "You go on up. I want to give one of the deputies a call."

"You're going to have Connie's house watched," said Quill.

"Give me twenty minutes."

"Okay," said Quill. "Okay."

"What is so funny about chickens?" Quill asked Myles sometime later. She lay with her head against his chest, both of them propped up in bed, looking out the window at the summer moon.

"You've never raised chickens?"

"Of course I've never raised chickens. I was brought up in Connecticut. In the suburbs. You've never raised chickens, either, Myles, have you?"

"I knocked around a bit after college. Spent some time in Central and South America. Worked in a lot of places for my keep. Poultry farm was one of them. Chickens are . . ." He paused, and silent laughter reverberated in her ear. "Messy. Very stupid. There's nothing meaner than a chicken. People who raise chickens eat a lot of chicken. Not out of necessity. Out of revenge."

"Oh, ha, ha." Quill sat up and drew her hair off her neck. "You never told me that before."

"You never asked." He stroked her cheek. "If I'd known about this compelling interest in chickens . . ."

"I don't mean chickens. I mean about Central America. You just don't . . . talk to me, Myles. I find out things about you by accident. From other people." The atmosphere in the darkened room changed. She felt him withdraw. Quill tried to keep her tone light. "I never knew a thing about your stellar career as a SuperCop in Manhattan, for example, until your partner . . . what's his name . . ."

"Billy Nordstrum. Smilin' Bill."

". . . Came to visit and you two started reminiscing and I discover you're some kind of legend in Manhattan." She continued: "I don't know anything about your first marriage, either."

"You could talk to my first wife, I guess."

"Myles! That's just the point." She got out of bed and walked out onto the balcony, water mist rising from the falls cupping the stars and shrouding her view of the moon. She folded her arms around herself and shivered slightly. Myles moved through the darkness, and embraced her from behind, burying his face in her hair.

"It's an ordinary story, you know. Most failed marriages are."

"That's not true. You know that's not true. Failed marriages tell a lot about people."

"All the more reason to talk to my first wife."

"You're serious. Is it that hard to tell me yourself? I feel . . . awkward . . . asking you. I'm afraid you don't trust me. I feel as though I should be doing more to prove you can trust me."

Myles was silent for a long moment. "You're such a gentle woman, Quill. For all your fierce defense of your stray lambs and black sheep."

She reached around and jabbed him in the side. "Gentle, huh? Of all the condescending, fat-headed things to say . . . Do you think I can't take it? That's an insult, Myles, and pretty damn chauvinist. The fragile little woman bit! I thought you were past that."

The phone rang, cutting through the two A.M. quiet with a shrill insistence. Quill moved quickly into the bedroom, stubbed her toe, and knocked the phone off the stand. She picked up the receiver with a muttered "Hell!" to hear Deputy Dave blushing over the wire. "Uh . . . Sher'f there, Ms. Quilliam? Sorry to disturb you, but it's an emergency."

She handed the phone to Myles, then switched on the light and stood watching his face. He listened silently, then said, "Give me twenty minutes," and hung up. He looked years older.

"Bad news," said Quill.

"Sandy Willis. Automobile crash on fifteen."

"Myles! No! Is she all right?"

Myles shook his head.

"She's not dead? Oh, Myles. Oh, this is terrible! Roy? The children?"

"Roy's at home with the kids."

Distractedly Quill began to dress. "There must be something I can do. You must let me help."

"There is. I'm going to the scene to relieve David. I want you to go over to the house and talk to Roy. Find out why she was driving on route fifteen alone at two in the morning. Wait there for me, and then I'll take him over to the morgue. He'll have to do the identification."

"Me?" said Quill, dismayed. "You want me to help with the investigation by interviewing Roy within an hour after his wife's been killed?"

"I know he'll be upset," said Myles quietly. "Sometimes that's the time to get the truth out of people. You've got a way with people, Quill. And I need the facts. There's been one too many coincidences involving the Bosses Club."

Myles took off in his car with efficient, quiet speed. Quill followed him down the drive and out onto the highway at a more sober pace.

Sandy and her family lived on East Lane, a one-street-long development a half mile from the Paramount plant. The plant had opened in the late twenties, just before the Depression, and five stone and lathe houses had been built for the plant managers and supervisors at the cul-de-sac; in the booming fifties, more than a dozen one-story ranches built by one of the enterprising Petersons extended the length of the street. Another handful of cheap, prefabricated houses had been added during the decade-long boom of the eighties. One of the latter had a patrol car parked in front. The mailbox read WILLIS.

Quill pulled the Olds to the side of the road and sat for a moment, gathering the courage to go in. Lights shone in every room of the house, spilling out onto the lawn. The house was sided with aluminum clapboard, alternating with brick facing in front. A tricycle was upended on the sidewalk, and the lawn was unevenly mowed. But there were flowers in homemade planters on either side of the short sidewalk, and cheerful print curtains at the windows.

Quill went up the short, concrete walk to the door. Daisies and marigolds bloomed from wooden half barrels on the porch. She rang the bell and waited. Roy Willis jerked open the door. He was in jeans, barefoot and bare-chested. Behind him, Quill heard the wail of a young child. A second child, who sounded somewhat older, scolded in a singsong voice: "Timmy's face is dirty, Timmy's shirt is dirty, Timmy's butt is dir—"

"Quiet!" Roy yelled, turning back to the living room. He swiveled back to Quill, regarding her mutely.

Quill stepped inside. Dave Kiddermeister stood uneasily by the television set, his Stetson in his hand. He was pale. He greeted Quill with a relieved smile. A toddler, no more than two years old, Quill guessed, lay on a tattered blanket in the middle of the carpeted floor, crying and waving his legs in the air. A little girl of perhaps five or six stood next to him, holding a Barbie doll by the hair in one hand, and sucking her thumb with the other. Both were in pajamas. Roy picked his daughter up and cradled her in his arms, his eyes fixed on Quill's face.

Quill cleared her throat. "If you'd like," she said without preamble, "I can help you get the kids back to bed."

"He needs changin'." Roy indicated his son with a jerk of his chin. "Sandy should have been home by now. It's her night. We trade off nights for changing the baby, see. On account of we work different shifts, is why I do it."

Quill glanced at Dave. He shrugged helplessly and said in a low voice, "He can't seem to understand about the incident, ma'am. I told him. Took a swing at me and then ran around and got up the kids. Called me a liar."

"Well, you are a liar!" shouted Roy. "You're a goddam liar!" Both children burst into tears. Quill sent Dave to find clean diapers, picked up the toys scattered on the couch and floor, then lifted the baby onto one hip. Dave reappeared with a box of Pampers and a washcloth. "I can do that, ma'am," he said.

At Quill's doubtful look, be smiled. "Seven kids in my family, and I was the oldest." Quill surrendered the baby, then gently took the little girl from Roy's arms.

"Are you sleepy, honey?"

The child nodded.

"Can you tell me your name?"

"Brenda."

"Can you show me where your bedroom is?"

Brenda gestured with the Barbie doll. "Up 'tairs."

Quill carried her upstairs to a tiny bedroom decorated with colorful posters and a handmade quilt on the small bed. "Mommy did it," Brenda explained. She wriggled and Quill set her down. She ran to a gaily painted box and flung open the lid. "You wanna play Barbie?"

"Not right now. Aren't you sleepy, Brenda?"

"I'm waiting for Mommy. I can play until she gets home to put me to bed."

Sandy must have a sister, thought Quill, or a mother. Someone needed to be here. "Do you have a grandmother, Brenda?"

"Grandma June."

"Does she live around here?"

"Yes," said Brenda, then, "no."

Dave must know, Quill thought.

She got Brenda to lie down, "just to *pretend* to go to sleep," and went quietly downstairs. Roy sat slumped on the couch. Dave was waiting by the front door, his hat firmly in place. "The little guy's asleep," he said, "and I have to get back to the . . ." He darted a glance at Roy, who sat staring at nothing.

"Brenda said there's a grandmother. Her name is June."

Dave nodded. "Sandy's mother. She lives over to Trumansburg. Ought to be here in another twenty minutes. You'll wait with him, because I've got to get back to the . . . you know."

Dave left. The silence in the room was profound. Quill found the kitchen and made coffee. Feeling cowardly, she stalled until the machine stopped perking. She carried the carafe and three mugs back to Roy, and set them on the coffee table. He took the filled mug without looking at her.

"June will be here soon," said Quill.

Roy nodded.

"She . . . um . . . worked tonight? Sandy? The three to eleven shift?"

Roy nodded a second time. "Got home about a quarter to twelve." Tears began to run down his cheeks. Quill's throat filled.

"She came home? She went out again?"

Roy's gaze shot to the telephone on the TV set.

"She got a phone call?"

The tears rolled silently down his cheeks and splashed onto his bare chest. Quill blinked rapidly and lowered her head. It was hard to look at him. Stories about great detectives rarely told you how hard it was to look at people in trouble. "Do you know who the call was from?"

"Kay."

"Kay Gondowski?" Quill set her mug carefully on the table. "Do you know what she wanted?"

"Sandy," he said simply, "Sandy was laughin'. Told her she was a scaredy-cat. 'You ol' scaredy-cat, you,' she said. And then she told her about the makeover and all, and how good Kay was gonna look after Dwight got hold of her." The tears ran down his cheeks. His grief was simple. Uncomplicated. He breathed with a sound like a sea bird calling from a long way.

"Did she go out to meet Kay?" asked Quill carefully. "Did she say where Kay was?"

"Sandy said Kay got scared. Just took off in that old Plymouth of hers and drove instead of coming to the party last night. Stopped at some motel and liked to froze to death 'cause she didn't bring no clothes to sleep in. Wanted Sandy to bring her some stuff. Sandy said okay, tell me where you are, I'll come get you." Roy's voice rose higher and higher, and the words began to spill out of him like the water spilled over Hemlock dam. "Sandy said isn't it just like that girl to get scairt of good fortune and run right off. Sandy said only Kay Gondowski would win two big ones and run off like some rabbit. That was Sandy, you see. She always knew everything about everybody. She always could tell what people were gonna do and then she could tell them how to get it right. Sandy said she'd bring Kay back here to stay with us for a while and that was Sandy all over. 'I'll take care of it,' she said. 'Don't you worry, I'll take care of it.' She put a nightgown and sweater and a toothbrush in a plastic bag to take to her." He was sobbing. Quill bit her lip hard and pinched her knee.

The doorbell rang, and Quill bolted for the front door. It opened as she grasped the handle, and a woman who looked like Sandy would have twenty years from now walked into the room. Behind her was Myles.

"Roy!" she cried. "Oh, Roy! My little girl."

Myles drew Quill outside and shut the front door behind her. Quill drew three deep breaths.

"Rough in there," Myles said after a moment. "Are you all right?"

Quill nodded, grateful for the cool air.

"We'll give them a minute. Did you learn anything?"

Quill steadied her voice with an effort. She moved away from him and looked out over the lawn until she felt more in control. "Kay called her about midnight."

"Kay Gondowski?"

"Told Sandy she was at a motel outside of town. Sandy went to get her. What happened, Myles?"

"Did she tell Roy which motel?"

Quill shook her head. "Was there another car?"

"Yes. A red Ford Cortina. This year's model. It's a rental car. We found it abandoned about a quarter mile down the road. It was set up to look like a hit-and-run. I've got Syracuse running a computer check. You're sure Roy doesn't know the name of the motel."

"It can't be too far from here," Quill said, after she summarized her talk with Roy Willis. "I mean, the night of the party, I got that call from her about what . . . a quarter to nine? So assuming that she had checked in at a motel, she should be two to three hours from here. Good grief, Myles, how are you going to check all the motels within an eighty-mile driving distance? This time of year thousands of people are vacationing in the Finger Lakes and taking the wine tours."

"That's what APBs are for," said Myles absently.

"You told me APBs are no substitute for legwork."

"They aren't. But I haven't got the manpower. The county mounties will help, but I can't count on it." He'd been speaking almost automatically, his mind elsewhere. He seemed to come to a decision; his gaze sharpened and he took her chin in his hand. "Why don't you go home and get some sleep."

Sandy's mother opened the door. She held Roy by the elbow. Her eyes were wet. "Roy says he's got to go with you?"

"Just down to the county hospital for a while," said Myles.

"You'll bring him right back?"

"I'll bring him right back."

"Is there anything I can do?" asked Quill. "Would you like to go with him, June? I'll be happy to stay with the children."

"Don't want to see her," said Sandy's mother. "I can't. Roy'll do it. He's tough." She patted his arm. He looked dully at her, then without a word went down the narrow sidewalk to Myles's car and got inside.

Quill got into the Olds and drove home.

When Quill looked at the Inn, she saw it through colors composed of paint from an infinite palette in her head; her mind's eye edited for the rightness of composition. Every view could be made perfect in her mind. There had never been a time when her painter's connection to the Inn had failed her, when she saw shapes and atmosphere that could not be translated into a painting in her head. Until now.

The Inn was alien ground to Quill when she walked up the drive to the front door. On summer nights the moon was high, bathing the grounds in silver light, and the sounds of the peeper frogs by the river were a musical undercurrent to the rushing water. Tonight, the building and the gardens were shrunken, diminished, the colors flat. She unlocked the front door and went inside, circling through the dining room, the kitchen, the Lounge, the conference room, waiting until the place lost its strangeness and became familiar again. On her second slow wandering through the foyer, she found herself noticing small irrelevant details in an effort to push back the guilt she felt. She blamed herself for this. If Myles had gone to arrest Connie . . . would Sandy be alive? Quill blinked back tears. Mike the groundskeeper had sanded the front door and filled in the gunshot holes with spackling compound. The splintered edge of the reception desk had been glued in place. He'd even found time to refill the giant Chinese urns with roses, purple spar, and early lilies. Quill switched on the overhead lights and sat on the couch by the cobblestone fireplace. The cream-colored wall by the staircase had been repainted. Spotches of blood showed through. Quill shivered and closed her eyes.

"You okay?" Meg appeared at the top of the stairs. "I heard you and Myles leave a while ago." Quill sat up and wiped her cheeks with the back of her hand. Meg was dressed in a long purple T-shirt with a bunny logo. Her feet were bare. She padded downstairs and sat next to Quill. "Out for a midnight snack?"

"Mike did a good job in here," Quill said.

"It's a good start." Meg surveyed the wall critically. "I know he repainted that wall. But the blood shows through."

"Blood eats through paint. He'll have to sand it off. Otherwise, it'll be a constant reminder of my flesh wound."

Meg smiled faintly. "How come *you* know so much?"

"I'm a painter," said Quill. "Just ask Hudson Zabriskie. Paint is paint. He's a painter, too, he says."

Meg slipped an arm around her shoulders and hugged her. "My sister the artist. So what happened? You look grim."

"Sandy Willis was killed in a hit-and-run tonight. Myles asked me to go over and see Roy."

"You're joking. Oh, my God. That poor woman." Meg jumped up and began to pace up and down the foyer. Her bare feet slapped on the wood floor. She looked angry. "This is crazy. It's too much coincidence. Way too much coincidence. What's Myles going to do about it?" She made a face. "He doesn't think Connie's behind this, does he?"

"He can't. He just . . . can't. They found the other car at the scene, and he's checking that out. Roy said Kay Gondowski called the house and asked Sandy to come and get her; that's why she was out so late. Kay supposedly said she was checked into a motel. Myles is going to put an APB out on Kay. Meg!" Quill lowered her voice to a whisper. "Helena Houndswood rented a car, right?"

"Right."

"What kind?"

"A red one."

"No! Was it a Ford Cortina?"

"It was red! How should I know a Ford Cortina from a Porsche? Now, monkfish from lobster, no problem."

"What time did she get in tonight?"

Meg shot a glance upstairs. "I don't know," she said in a low voice. "I went to bed when you guys did, about eleven-thirty. She wasn't back by then."

The front door opened. Quill jumped. John walked in, a pair of jeans hastily pulled on over his pajamas, his sockless feet encased in well-worn tennis shoes. "Quill?" he said. "I wondered why all the lights were on."

"It's not all the lights," said Meg. "It's just the foyer lights. Keep your voice down."

"It looks like all the lights from my apartment."

"That's all you can see from over the carriage house is the foyer, and stop worrying about the utility bills, John."

John settled onto the coffee table. "I know you, Meg. All that irrelevant chatter means something's up. What is it?"

Helena Houndswood appeared at the top of the stairs. She was in a brocaded bathrobe. Her feet were in slippers. Her hair was uncombed. She rubbed her eyes and yawned. "What the hell's going on down there? Is it a party?"

"Quill," Meg hissed, sliding next to her on the couch. "She's in full makeup. Nobody goes to bed in full makeup."

CHAPTER 10

"The whole story sounds incredibly suspicious to me," said Meg. "I don't believe a word of it. Helena's tame lawyer claims he dropped the rental car off in the Hertz lot and used the Jiffy thingummy . . . ?"

"The Rapid Return," said Quill. "Let's not talk about it for a while, okay, Meg?" Quill admitted to herself that she was tired and confused, and didn't want to discuss the events of last night at all. Meg, on the other hand, not only looked as though she'd had a full night's sleep (which she had, barring her late-night discussion with Quill) but was in one of her talkative, chatty moods. Mikhail, the Russian *sous* chef, had made sour cream and caviar scrambled eggs. Quill took a bite and attempted a diversion. "I think we ought to put these on the menu."

"He's pretty good with a skillet," Meg agreed. "So the lawyer uses the Jiffy thingummy and hops the late train to New York City and somebody steals the Cortina out of the lot and runs into Sandy and kills her? And Myles buys this bag of baloney? Sure! And now poor Connie's locked up."

"She couldn't account for her whereabouts at the time Sandy was killed. She claims Kay called her, too. That Kay gave her the same story she gave Sandy. When she got to the hotel—it was the

Dew Drop Inn, Meg, if you can believe—she woke up the owner to find out why nobody answered her knock at room five, and he said it was because nobody had checked into five all week. When Connie came home, the deputies were waiting for her and they took her."

"Is Connie sure it was Kay on the phone?"

"She said if she hadn't thought it was Kay, she would have stayed in bed with Roosevelt where she belonged." Quill, with the memory of Roy Willis's bewildered face in her mind's eye, was guilt-ridden. She tried a diversion. "Any idea when the *L'Aperitif* people will be by to review?"

"Oh, not till the end of the year," Meg said dismissively. "You've been right about La Helena all along, Quill. I admit it. She could have imitated that little voice of Kay's. When I came downstairs this morning, she had acres of luggage in the foyer, and you wouldn't believe how she sucked up to me about the food. 'The best of the best, darling,' she said. 'I'll be up a couple of times a week for dinner. Couldn't live without it.' Couldn't live without it? Then why is she moving out?" Meg twirled her fork indignantly. "A murderer *and* insincere."

"She's moving to the Petersons' farmhouse this morning. She probably doesn't want to cook for herself since she's committed to feeding the chickens and the horse and the cow."

"Yes, but now? With the TV show coming up in two weeks? Of course," Meg answered herself, "she doesn't have to lift a finger to do the show. She's got all those 'little people' to do it for her. All she has to do is show up and chat. That woman chats at the drop of a hen's egg. I think she's leaving because she's heard about how we solved that murder last year and she wants to escape your eagle eye."

"She's got an excellent alibi for last night," Quill said. "Harvey swore on a stack of King James Version Bibles that they'd been in Syracuse until well after midnight."

"Harvey," said Meg with disgust. She poked at the potato soufflé on her plate. "There's too much cheese in this. And Mikhail used milk instead of cream." She jabbed at it until it deflated.

"Harvey's an idiot," Quill said. "But he's a good-hearted idiot. I don't think he'd lie to cover up a murder, Meg."

"Not a murder. Vehicular homicide." She swallowed a piece of sausage and screwed up her face, "Somebody in there went ballistic with the sage. I've gotta get back." She jumped out of her chair. "My guess is Helena got tanked up—how else could she stand six hours straight of good old Harvey?—smacked into Sandy, and coerced that tame lawyer of hers to help her out of it. And she could get Harvey to lie about the time she returned. You know she could. I think you're right. She killed Dot and did something awful to Kay and Dawn, and now, poor Sandy. So I say, go ahead and nail her." She paused with her hand on the swinging door to the kitchen. "But not until after the TV show. She wants to feature my soups."

"My sister the cynic."

"Your sister the realist. At least she's out of your hair, and mine. Although I have my doubts as to how long she's going to stick at gentleman farming. Andy says she has no idea what she's getting into." She pushed her way into the kitchen and came back out. "Where's the activity sheet?"

Quill, thinking of her "X" suspect, was vaguely aware of Meg's insistent finger in front of her nose. She wondered about Kay Gondowski. If Connie were convicted of a capital crime, she couldn't benefit from it—Kay would take the entire million.

"Quill! The activity sheet!"

"Oh, God. I forgot."

"How am I supposed to plan the meals today without an activity sheet? You know I can't run a decent kitchen without the activity sheet! And will you ditch that goofy new format you developed? I liked the old one: number of guests, meetings, lunch, dinner. Real simple. Now! Now! Now!"

The doors banged shut. Quill ate the rest of her eggs, drank her grapefruit juice, and gave serious consideration to the missing Kay Gondowski. There was a hot brioche, made from dough Meg had prepared two days before. She ate that and surveyed the dining room. There was an independent witness to Kay's existence. Mrs. Whitman. Six of the tables were occupied by the Friends of Fresh Air. They had the flushed, sweaty look of people who'd been up at the crack of dawn, marching through the hills and moraines of the countryside surrounding Hemlock Falls. Their Friends of Fresh Air! T-shirts came in sizes ranging from small to, if the lady crunching her way through a mammoth bowl of granola mixed with yogurt represented a clue, extra-extra-large. Makepeace Whitman caught her eye and gave her a modest wave. His wife smiled. Maybe she ought to try the natural look, Quill thought: Mrs. Makepeace's gilt hair was drawn back in a modest bun. Her large blue eyes glowed with health. Her cheeks were blusher free and delicately pink.

The kitchen door banged open. "Well!" Meg demanded, hands on hips.

"The only meeting today is a subcommittee of the Chamber. The Hemlock Falls Clean It Up! Committee."

"And?" said Meg dangerously. "Reservations? Dinner? Lunch? *Tea?!* How full are we? And conventions at the Marriott? Are we going to be hit with an overflow? *Quill!*"

"*Meg?!*" Quill shouted back. "I'm going to finish my breakfast first!"

"Okay," said Meg.

"Okay," said Quill. They grinned at each other. Quill got up and made her way to the Whitmans' table.

"Toxins," said Makepeace Whitman, by way of greeting.

"Yes," said Quill, with every appearance of comprehension. "I hope you had a good walk this morning? The weather is just beautiful."

"Pollutants," said Mrs. Whitman, her mascara-free eyelashes pure and silvery in the June sunshine, "affect the neurotransmitter fluid in the brain."

"Leads to all sorts of instability," said Makepeace agreeably. "Your . . . sister . . . is it? Would she like to join our group?"

"The sun just flushes all the toxins out of the system," added Mrs. Whitman. "It's God's way of purifying our bodies."

"I know it may not look like it," Quill said, "but she's actually in a pretty good mood. Did you enjoy your breakfast?"

"Wonderful," said Makepeace. "The cooking is marvelous. We understand that Helena Houndswood is going to feature the Inn on her show. As a matter of fact, I was going to speak to her about our group. Do you think she could find time to talk to me? Perhaps I could invite her for tea?"

"Or one of our lectures," said Mrs. Whitman. "A very dear,

dear friend and supporter, a veterinarian, is giving a lecture on our feathered sisters and brothers at four."

"Birds," said Makepeace helpfully.

"Ms. Houndswood has moved to a farmhouse in town for a month to write a book," Quill said, "so I'm afraid I won't be seeing much of her, if at all. If the opportunity arises, of course . . ."

Makepeace Whitman pressed her hand in an understanding way. "You and your sister must be relieved," he said sympathetically. "I could tell from the outset, Ms. Quilliam, that your heart and mind are more in tune with nature than one might suspect. Ms. Houndswood, alas, represents much that's artificial and frivolous about our society. Whereas, you! Perhaps you would like to join us."

"May I sit down?" asked Quill, whose thoughts had been diverted by Whitman's *whereases*. "I mean yes, thank you, I'd love to join you for a moment."

"Indeed!" Makepeace pulled out a chair, and courteously stood while Quill sat down. "Any questions you have, we'd be glad to answer."

"There's two. Not about your environmentalist movement, which I think is wonderful, but about the night before last, when the shooting occurred."

"Oh, yes." Mrs. Whitman drew back as if confronted with Styrofoam.

"You hung up the phone at the reception desk? When it was off the hook?"

"I believe I did."

"Did you hear anything? You know, put your ear to the receiver?"

"Oh, no!" said Mrs. Whitman. "I would never do that."

"It's just the usual reaction," said Quill, "and I don't believe you were listening in, or anything like that, it's just that it would be very helpful if you could identify the voice on the end of the line."

"I never listen to the phone. I never use the phone."

"You don't?" asked Quill politely.

"Electricity," said Mrs. Whitman, "just pours out of the receiver. It's why I hung that phone up. It's very bad for the brain."

"Oh," said Quill.

"There was a second question?" asked Makepeace Whitman. "We have some literature on our group. . . ."

"Iron oxide," said Quill. "Does your company ship iron oxide to Paramount Paints?"

Mrs. Whitman shrieked, "No! You promised!"

Makepeace Whitman flung his spoon furiously into his yogurt plate.

Mrs. Whitman sobbed, "You swore! You swore you would stop the rape!"

"Now look what you've done," hissed Makepeace. "A perfectly legitimate business and . . . dear. Dear." He patted his wife's hand. She bared her teeth at him. "We use very gentle backhoes. And we replace as much as—"

"Tearing great gouges of earth flesh from Her sides!" screamed Mrs. Whitman. "You bastard!" She shoved her chair back and ran from the room.

Mr. Whitman, with a despairing look at Quill, ran after her.

Meg poked her head out of the kitchen doors. "What the heck was that!"

Quill, conscious of the shocked diners, carefully picked up the dirty dishes from the Whitmans' table, carried them to the doors, and thrust them into her sister's hands. "Sometimes," she said, "investigations can get a little rough."

"A little rough? It sounds like you ran them over with a bus."

"Never mind." Quill pushed Meg into the kitchen, letting the doors swing behind them. "Meg, I've got to break into Paramount Paints tonight. After the plant is closed."

"Is Myles going to like that?"

"He's not going to know anything about it. Are you with me?"

"Sure. Why can't we go now?"

"We can't let anyone know. Just act normally."

"Okay. Normally I'd want the activity sheet. Will you get it for me, please?"

Dina was sitting at the reception desk, looking woeful as the last of Helena Houndswood's luggage was carried out the door to the Inn van. Mike the groundskeeper was sanding the bloody spot from the wall, a bucket of paint beside him. Mike was short, dark, and Italian, a gardener and a son of a gardener, he'd said when

Quill hired him three years before. "It's in the blood. Us Sicilians were born to garden. It's like, genetic."

"I'm glad Mike's doing this," said Dina by way of greeting. "That blood spot was giving me the creeps. Like that scene from *Macbeth*, you know?"

"Is she gone yet?" asked Quill.

"Ms. Houndswood? She walked down the hill about twenty minutes ago. Peter's taking the luggage down. It's not going to be the same without her around here."

"She's not all that far away," said Quill gloomily. "Have you got the activity sheet?"

"Yeah." Dina tugged it from beneath a pile of papers. "It says you're supposed to be, like, in a meeting?"

"Me? Here. Give me that. Hemlock Falls Clean It Up! Week," Quill read. "Bozzel, Henry, Shuttleworth, Schmidt, Doncaster, Quilliam. Ten A.M. I'm not a member of the Clean It Up! Committee." She frowned. "Harvey isn't, either."

"They changed it," said Dina. "It's now the Clean It Up! Beauty Pageant Committee."

"Oh, damn."

"One good thing, though."

"What's that?"

"They aren't mad at you about the minutes book anymore."

"You sure?"

"Yeah. They think that they have to suck up to you so Helena Houndswood will keep the beauty contest winners on the show."

"That's ridiculous."

"That's what I told them," Dina said earnestly. "Harvey was all for getting you off any committee where you took notes. And Miriam said she hoped you went and gained twenty pounds. 'Wait a minute,' I said. 'You're talking about my boss. She's a great person. You don't have to suck up to Quill just because she and Helena are like best friends,' I said."

"What did they say?" asked Quill anxiously.

"Harvey said he'd forgotten that you and Helena were so close, and maybe they should be careful of how they treat you."

Quill thought about this for a moment. If Harvey had lied to save Helena Houndswood, wouldn't he be cocksure about the TV show? Did Helena even need Harvey to establish an alibi? She'd been so tired by the time Myles had finished questioning Helena last night that she hadn't gotten Sandy's time of death straight. Maybe she could weasel something out of Harvey.

"Quill?" said Dina insistently. "So you see? It worked out okay. You can go sit in that meeting and they'll be nice as pie. They're meeting right now. You'd better go."

"Dina," said Quill, "you don't have to defend my honor. Really. As a matter of fact, I'd rather you didn't ever again."

"It's the least I can do," said Dina. "You're the best boss I've ever had."

"But I'm not Helena Houndswood's best friend! And I don't *want* to be on any more committees!"

"They're even going to let you take notes again," said Dina. "How's about that?"

"I take terrible notes. That's what started this whole mess in the first place. Here's what we do. Esther West is just dying to be on the Beauty Pageant committee, right?"

"She is?"

"Of course she is. She loves things like this. Remember how much she enjoyed directing the Hemlock History Week play? Call her, Dina. Tell her the Beauty Pageant committee is meeting right now, and to get on over here in, say, about an hour. That'll give me time to talk to Harvey, in a subtle way. Then Esther can take my place, and I can get down to investigating this properly."

"Why? I thought you were going to give investigating up. That's what you said when I saw you before breakfast. So you've decided not to give it up. Why not?"

"Lots of reasons," said Quill vaguely. "Just see if you can find Esther, okay? If she's not at her shop, try her at home. And if she's not at home . . . I don't know what to do if she's not at home."

"Maybe Sheriff McHale could put out an APB?"

Quill contemplated her receptionist for a long moment. Dina's brown eyes were clear and innocent. She even had a dimple. She was getting a Ph.D. in limnology. Quill decided that a doctoral student in fresh pond water ecology was probably naive about such matters as APBs. "It's not quite that important, Dina. But I'd really truly appreciate it if you can get Esther to this meeting. If you can't, about eleven o'clock come in and tell me there's an emergency."

"Got it. You don't want to be on this committee. So what kind of emergency shall I make up?"

"Anything short of a kitchen fire. It'd be pretty obvious to those guys that we're not having a kitchen fire."

"I'll think up a great one if I have to," Dina assured her. "But I'll get Esther here, too."

Quill went to the conference room wondering if the Cornell Management School for Labor Relations had a course in Quelling the Imaginative Employee.

"Hey, Quill!" Harvey exclaimed as she walked into the meeting. "You're looking terrific this morning."

A chorus of enthusiastic "hellos" and "good to see yous" came from the members of the Clean It Up! Beauty Pageant Committee. Quill nodded to Marge, Miriam, Elmer Henry, and Dookie Shuttleworth as she sat down in the chair Harvey drew out for her.

"Can I get you some coffee?" Harvey asked solicitously. He went to the sideboard where Kathleen had set out the coffeemaker and mugs, as she always did when there was a Chamber meeting. "We decided that you and Meg shouldn't have to put out for free coffee for us, so Elmer put out a little cash jar." Coins clanked as he rattled it. "It's a quarter."

Marge snorted, "She ain't going to pay for her own coffee, Harvey. Sit down, Quill."

"I appreciate being invited to sit in on the committee, guys, but—"

"We'd like you to be secretary," said Elmer heartily. "Take all the notes you want. You can draw all the pitchers you want, too." He thrust a notebook into her hands and proffered a pen.

"Really, Mayor. Thank you very much, but—"

"You're a little late, but that's okay," said Harvey generously. "I'm the chair of this committee, by the way, so when I say it's okay that you're late, it's okay."

They waited, expectant. Quill sighed. Sat down. Opened the notebook. Wrote CI/Beu/Comm at the top of the page, then Members: and rapidly sketched flattering caricatures of Dookie, Marge, Harvey, the mayor, and Miriam.

"Lovely," said Miriam, leaning over Quill's arm.

"Is there a first order of business?" asked Quill.

"Haven't gotten to it yet," said Harvey somberly. "We were discussing the car crash last night."

"Awful," said Marge. She blew her nose furiously. "Betty and me both liked Sandy. That little shit of a husband is still in the slam, though, right? So he didn't do it. Sure like to find the sucker that whacked her."

"Dreadful, dreadful," murmured Dookie.

"They say," said Quill cautiously, "that Helena Houndswood's car was involved."

"Stolen out of the lot," said Harvey. Quill watched him closely. He was as pompous as ever, but there was no trace of guile or deceit in those protuberant eyes. "I was with her all evening, you know, finding a John Deere tractor in Syracuse. We stopped for dinner at a little place I know of, there. Got back after midnight."

"You took her car," said Quill.

"Mine's in the shop," said Harvey. "Would have been glad to drive, but . . ."

"That old Caddy of his ain't fancy enough for her," said Marge Schmidt shrewdly. "What, Quill, you think old Harve here was involved with killin' Sandy?"

Quill saw the change in Harvey's face the moment the penny dropped. "Hit-and-runs happen in every town, in every state in these United States," said Harvey indignantly. "Kids, usually, driving stolen cars. That's what Sheriff McHale thinks, and that's very probably what happened. Tragic, but an inevitable part of driving in America. And for your information. Quill"—he leaned forward, his self-importance temporarily forgotten—"Helena's lawyer took the late train back to the city when we came back and left the car in the lot. My guess is some kids were waiting in the bushes, just hoping for something like this to happen, and as soon as the train left the station, they broke open that Rapid Return box, stole the keys, and were off like a flash. You should see that box. Smashed all to hell."

Clearly, no one had heard that Myles had arrested Connie Weyerhauser. It wouldn't be long before word got out, or, Quill figured, for gossip to indict, try, and condemn her.

Harvey sat back in his chair, the flush on his face subsiding.

"I'd like to get to the first order of business—Elmer, you have that gavel?"

"Subcommittees ain't allowed to use the gavel," said Elmer promptly. "It's the mayor's gavel."

"The gavel should be for committee heads," said Harvey persuasively. "Now, I know you keep it with you at all times, Mayor. . . ."

"Kids, my foot," said Miriam, who'd been in a brown study since Harvey had put forth his car theft theory. "I heard that Sandy got a phone call from the killer just before she went out. Did Myles say anything to you about it, Quill?"

Quill hesitated. Myles seemed to have relaxed his rigid rules about her participation in his investigations. And he hadn't said to keep what she knew confidential. On the other hand, maybe the confidentiality was implied.

"I heard she and Roy had a fight over the money," said Marge. "Sandy slammed out of the house to cool off."

"What did I tell you, Mayor," said Harvey loudly, "no one's paying attention to the next order of business."

"Gavel's not going to help you, boy," said Elmer. He dug into his mayoral briefcase. Reluctance in every line of his body, he handed the gavel to Harvey, who promptly smacked it loudly against the table.

"For heaven's sake, use the rest," said Miriam. "You'll wreck the finish. Somebody said you were over there last night, Quill. At Roy's."

"Just to sit with the kids while Myles took Roy to the sheriff's office."

"This meeting will come to order!" Harvey beat a tattoo on the table with the gavel.

Miriam leaned close to Quill and whispered, "They don't think Roy had anything to do with it? Did he tell you who called Sandy?"

Quill decided that, one, Roy would probably tell anyone who asked about Kay Gondowski, and two, that she was behaving as badly as Harvey over the gavel. "Kay Gondowski called her, Miriam. Apparently she'd gotten so flustered at the idea of all that money and attention, she just left town to give herself some breathing space."

"Kay Gondowski caused the wreck?" said Elmer. "My God, what's the town comin' to!"

"What does Kay say about it?" demanded Marge. "She say she made that phone call?"

"I don't think Kay's shown up yet," said Quill.

"If this meeting isn't called to order, I'm calling off the Beauty Pageant and you can just handle Clean It Up! Week all by yourselves," said Harvey loudly. "We've got important issues here."

Dookie *tsked*. Marge scowled. Miriam looked at him with exasperation.

"These things are important, Harvey," said Quill. "You're right. But it's natural to be concerned over Dot, and Sandy and Kay. And Dawn Pennifarm, too. I mean, these are the women who made all this possible, in a way. Helena Houndswood wouldn't be here if it weren't for the china contest, and if she weren't here, we wouldn't even be considering a beauty contest."

"I don't see that that follows," said Harvey. "No, I don't see that at all."

"All three of these girls were members of the Bosses Club, right?" said Marge.

"Yes," said Miriam.

"They split the money equal?"

"Yes," said Quill.

Marge crossed her arms over her considerable bosom. "And what happens to the money if there's only, say, one winner?"

Quill doodled on the pad.

"The heirs get it, or what?"

"The money's not assignable," said Miriam. "It's like a tontine."

"Like a what?" demanded Elmer.

"A tontine. The survivor gets it all."

There was a long silence.

"How'd you know that? About not being assignable," asked Marge.

"I had a discussion with Howie Murchison over it," said Miriam primly. "I just happened to drop by his office—he'd invited me out for coffee—and happened to mention it."

"Hell," said Elmer. "Pardon me, Revrund. So all these gals have a motive to knock each other off."

"Maybe we'd better get back to the agenda," suggested Quill. "The sheriff's handling all this."

"Question is," said Harvey, "does he have enough manpower? I happen to know—this is in strictest confidence—that he's put in a request for three more men in next year's budget."

"That's not in strictest confidence," said Elmer. "Town budget proposal's published in the *Gazette*. Everybody know Myles needs more men."

"Maybe we could help," said Miriam.

"I don't think Myles . . ." Quill began.

"Just a minute, Quill." Harvey put his hand up authoritatively. "We have a motion before the committee."

"We do not," said Quill.

"Hang on. Hang on. A concept's coming to me." Harvey got up and paced around the room, hands thrust in his trousers pockets, head down. He flung his head back, closed his eyes, then opened them. "I've got it. We'll form a citizens' committee. There's all kinds of national precedence for a citizens' committee. A committee to Stop Crime. Composed of tireless volunteers from the community, this band of citizens cries Stop! Stop the crime. The violence. The rape of our women."

"Well, now," said Elmer, "I'm not sure that a citizens' committee is legal."

"Isn't nothing illegal about it, Mayor." Marge explored a back tooth with her tongue and looked thoughtful. "We look for the bodies, for example. They get volunteers to search for the bodies all the time, with missin' kids and so on."

Harvey, who'd been circling the conference table like a large dog in search of a hydrant, clapped a hand on Marge's shoulder. "True, Marge. That's very true. There's a lot of publicity about it. National publicity."

"Screw the publicity," said Marge. "I want to find out who did this. We find out if anyone seen Kay. The last time they seen Dawn, and where she was headed. Whether anyone saw Sandy on route fifteen last night. And like I said, we search good and hard for the bodies. This has gotta stop." She lowered her chin and looked around the table, unsmiling.

"We will find out what has happened to these three women," said Harvey in a radio voice. "With Myles as understaffed as he is, it can only help. We are the Citizens Against Rampant Crime. C.A.R.C. cares."

"You don't think we should . . . um . . . check with him about it, first?" said Quill.

"Mayor?" said Harvey. "I'd like to authorize you to contact Sheriff McHale about permission to support the sheriff's investigation through the medium of my citizens' committee, because C.A.R.C. cares."

There was a respectful silence.

"I'll do it," said Elmer, "I'll get hold of him right now. I can use the phone in the hall, Quill?"

"Of course. But, Elmer . . ." Quill chewed her lip. "Could you maybe not mention my, um, involvement? I wouldn't want him to think that I was . . ."

"Horning in on the investigation like you done before? Don't worry about a thing, Quill. I'll be real tactful." Elmer walked majestically out of the room, preceded by his belly.

"Might as well get some business done while he's gone," said Marge in a practical way. "About those assessments for Clean It Up! Week. How's everyone doin'?"

"Clean It Up! Week's at the end of the agenda." Harvey frowned. "Next item on the agenda is contest rules for the Little Miss Hemlock Falls contest."

"Any kid who wants to can enter," said Marge promptly. "How are we doin' on Clean It Up! Week? We want the town to look good for that TV show."

Harvey thumped the gavel. "I've drawn up a complete list of agenda items. While the mayor is carrying out my instruction, we are scheduled to discuss the beauty contest categories and the dress code, and establish the panel of judges, and time limits of the entertainment. You can't accomplish anything without pre-work, Marge. And then there's the budget."

"What budget," said Elmer, returning.

"For the expenses," said Harvey. "As chairman of this committee, I think it only right that we get a professional job done and that we retain a professional firm."

"And what professional firm would that be, Harve?" asked Marge with spurious interest.

"There are excellent firms in Syracuse," said Harvey, with an air of disingenuousness, "and of course one or two in Buffalo. Why don't you leave the selection up to me?"

"Why don't I put a fox in my henhouse?" said Marge. "Well, Elmer, what'd the sheriff say?"

"Says fine with him," Elmer said unhappily.

Quill sat up abruptly. "Fine with him? He really said that?"

"Thought maybe Harvey could arrange to have some C.A.R.C. posters printed, too." Elmer sat down, clearly disgruntled. "Thanked me for coming up with a civic-minded idea."

"He did?" said Quill.

Harvey cleared his throat modestly and raised his hands in a deprecating way. "No charge for this idea, folks, unless we take it national."

"Asked me to work up a schedule for the search. Wants a twenty-four-hour rota, concentratin' on the swamp."

"The swamp?" said Miriam. "Does he have any reason . . . why the swamp?"

"Said it's as good a place for a body as anywhere else."

"Does Myles think we'll find a body?" demanded Marge.

"Well, no," Elmer admitted, "no, he didn't. Said it's good idea, though, on the off chance that Harvey here is the right. The citizens' committee of Harvey's . . ."

"Actually," said Harvey, "if you don't mind. It was Miriam's idea, Quill. I'd like that in the minutes. That Miriam thought of this, not me."

"The heck it was my idea," said Miriam. "C.R.A.P., sorry, C.A.R.C., the citizens' committee was your idea, Harvey, and I'm certainly not going to slop around in a swamp at two A.M. for bodies which our own sheriff doesn't expect to be there. Maybe we should vote on this."

"All in favor of Harvey's idea to search the swamp for bodies say 'aye,' " said Elmer, grabbing the gavel and whacking it on the table.

"Aye," said Dookie, into the quiet.

"Nays?"

The "nays" carried it.

"All right, then," said Elmer, "we get on with the agenda." He took the agenda from Harvey's hands. "Okay. Any progress from the citizens who're sp'osed to Clean It Up? Courthouse is comin' along good. Only thing left that I can see is the post office. Quill, you go along and encourage Vern to finish up. You can tell him, official, from the mayor about the pride we all have in this town, and how it's their civic duty to make a good showin' on Helena Houndswood's TV show. All in favor?"

They were unanimous, except for Quill, who was glumly sketching Vern Mittermeyer throwing cans of Paramount paint from a flying buttress she'd placed atop the post office. There was a little tiny Quill on the ground, ducking the spatters.

"Motion carried," said Elmer with satisfaction. "Now we're gettin' somewheres. Beauty contest, next. Harvey? We ain't budgeting a nickel for advertising. Got that? This is a volunteer town, and we're doing a volunteer beauty contest. Anyone here have any experience with beauty contests?"

Quill looked at her watch: three minutes after eleven. No Esther. And no Dina. She raised her hand. "Esther West has had a lot of experience running town productions," she said. "I move to have Esther West appointed to this committee."

"Absolutely not," said Harvey. "This pageant needs a professional touch, and with all due respect to Esther, she's never run a project as complex as this one before. Why, she'd want to direct it and everything. And I can just see the faces on those guys from the Helena Houndswood show when she drags out that *Complete Guide to Television Production* video. I mean, she's a great gal. A great gal. But anyone who's learned all there is to know about TV from a tape out of a catalog . . ."

"Be a lot like somebody learning about advertising from *The Complete Encyclopedia of Advertising Terms and Expressions*," said Miriam with a wink at Quill.

Harvey fidgeted in his chair. "Professionals use reference works," he said earnestly. "I'll admit that . . ."

"Quill?" Dina appeared at the conference room door, frantically waving a slip of pink paper. She'd removed what little cheek blusher she used and powdered her face to a pale beige. She leaned against the doorframe, panting slightly. "Please. Disaster has struck!"

Quill got up from her chair, avoiding Miriam's skeptical eye. "I was afraid this might happen," she said with an apologetic smile. "It's probably going to take a long time. Miriam, could you take over the notes?"

"I'll take the notes." Esther marched into the room, her eyes sparkling. "Thank you so much, Quill, for inviting me to be on the committee. I'm so sorry I'm late, Harvey, Mayor. But I didn't hear about it until just now." She waved her handbag excitedly. "I ordered the *Complete Guide to the Miss America Beauty Pageant*, and I was just down to the post office. It came overnight mail. It's got some terrific ideas."

"Vern paintin' right along?" asked Elmer alertly.

"Nope. He's cursing a blue streak," said Esther. "Didn't see too much progress."

"Well, Quill's goin' to stop by there today and push him," said Elmer. "Right, Quill?"

"And I'd better get to it," said Quill cheerfully. She excused herself and went out into the hall.

"Was I dramatic enough?" asked Dina.

"Oh, yes," said Quill absently.

"It's just a phone message from Sheriff McHale," said Dina, handing her the pink piece of paper. It was damp and slightly crumpled. "So what do you think? I figured if I just left, like, mysterious, then it might be more impressive. Were you impressed?"

"I'm impressed," said Quill. She took the slip of paper.

"I'm back to thinking maybe this detecting business is all right. You know, first seduction, now mysterious lady in black. Except that I'm wearing jeans."

Quill read the note: "If you're not on swamp patrol, what about an early dinner?" She stuck the note in her skirt pocket and moved down the hall to the back of the Inn, Dina following.

"So, since I'm back on the scent, what's next?"

Quill said "nothing," figuring a bit of subterfuge was in order if she was going to plunder the Paramount office that evening.

"Nothing?"

"Nope. Investigation's temporarily suspended. I have to run to the post office. If the sheriff calls, looking for me"—Quill paused, one hand on the back door—"tell him I'm in the swamp."

She stepped outside into the vegetable garden and let the door slam behind her.

A dirt path curved around the side of the Inn to the falls, and from there through a copse of beech, hemlock, and crepe myrtle to the village. It would take her to the west end of Hemlock Falls, without passing through the birch woods, where Dot had been killed.

Quill walked past the Peterson place and paused to look over the fence. The farmhouse had originally been part of a forty-acre parcel that Norm Peterson's father had deeded over to the town thirty years before. About five acres were left; a portion of the lot was taken up by a charming cobblestone farmhouse, trimmed in white, and a small hay barn, painted the traditional red. About three acres had been left fenced for pasture. A brown and white cow (which Quill recalled was a Guernsey) grazed peacefully next to a nervous looking horse. Quill clucked and held out her hand. The horse, which was brown and big, dashed up to the fence, reared, whinnied, and dashed away again, its eyes rolling. Quill wondered if Helena could ride. In the farmyard she heard the clack and squall of a herd of chickens and caught a glimpse of a large straw hat trimmed with purple flowers of some kind. It was Helena herself, moving among the chickens, flinging some sort of grain to the ground. A loud and angry "Fuck!" floated through the air.

Quill grinned to herself.

A few more minutes' walk took her to the west end of Main.

Quill rounded the corner of Main and Maple to find Vern slowly at work sanding and painting the red trim. An open bucket of Paramount Paint's Exterior Latex Crimson Red sat beside him.

Quill said hello. Vern grunted. The weather was fine for June, although a bit warm. Sweat rolled down his face, which made him look like a damp turtle instead of a dry turtle.

"How is it going, Vern?"

"This paint stinks."

"I've never minded the smell of fresh paint myself," said Quill, "although I know it bothers some people. The red's nice and . . . and . . . bright."

"Nice and screwed up, you mean," said Vern. "That Hudson's allus going on about how fabulous his paint is, right?"

"He does like his paint," Quill admitted in the vernacular. "How do you mean screwed up? Lloyd was having problems, too."

"Looky here." He stepped back from the window frame. "See what I mean? It stinks."

Quill peered closely at the frame. The red paint was mottled, stippled on the sanded wood. She frowned. "Did some sawdust get into the can, maybe?"

"Just opened her up," said Vern. "I sanded first, *before* I opened her up."

Quill looked into the can. The surface of the paint was smooth, unmarked . . . She looked back at the window frame. She looked at Vern. There were no cuts or bruises on his skinny arms or freckled hands.

Who would have thought the old man would have had such blood in him?

"Hey," said Vern. "You can't faint on federal property." He grabbed her arm. "Siddown. Get your head down." He pushed Quill onto the bench under the lamppost.

She took several deep breaths. Her vision cleared. She straightened up, her breath harsh in her throat. Vern didn't move. Just looked at her, eyes like a lizard's in the sunlight. Quill shivered.

"Stop," she said. "Stop painting right now."

CHAPTER 11

"What d'ya mean, there's blood in the paint?" Vern let Quill sit on the hard plastic chair inside the post office ("Can't stop you, I guess"), and after a silent communion with the postal gods, brought her a glass of water. Quill examined the glass as though it were a foreign object and set it on the floor beside the open paint can.

"Vern, did you cut yourself when you were painting? Did some of it get into the can?"

Vern examined his freckled, paint-spattered arm with deliberation. "Broke off the nail opening the lid." He offered a grimy forefinger for her inspection. "Gotta file a disability claim. Might not," he added generously, "depending."

Quill started to ask how freely the finger had bled, and stopped herself. There was no way Vern's finger could account for the amount of blood disfiguring the coated trim. And besides, Lloyd had had the same problem two days before. A horrible possibility was growing in her mind. She shivered.

"Can't change the temprachure in here," said Vern belligerently. "Set by the guv'mint. You cold, you go outside."

"Lloyd said this paint came from Paramount?"

"Picked it up myself, on Tuesday. Connie Weyerhauser gave it to me. Part of an overrun on Crimson Blaze, she said. No charge." He shifted his wad of gum from one cheek to the other. "'Course, now I see why it come free. Like I said at the Chamber meetin', this stuff stinks."

Maybe Vern meant it literally. Her heart quivering, Quill leaned over and inhaled. There was, unmistakably, a faint coppery odor underlying the fresh scent. Abruptly she got up and moved away, as one might from a dead animal in the road. She should call Myles. Except Myles was out scouting motels for Kay Gondowski, and she'd undoubtedly get Deputy Dave, and the whole town would be engaged in frantic speculation by nightfall.

"Would you like me to return the paint for you, Vern?"

"Eh?"

"You know, take it back. Get you another—what, three gallons?"

"Not of the Paramount stuff, thank you very much. They're not an approved United States guv'mint supplier anyways."

"What if I took this and we bought some Dutch Boy, or something. From Nickerson's."

"Ain't in the budget."

"I'll tell you what. If you can give me a ride back to the Inn, we can stop at Nickerson's and have them put the paint on the Inn account. You can choose any paint you want. I'll just take this back to . . . I'll take it with me. That is, if you can leave the post office."

Vern threw his thumb over his shoulder. "Lloyd's on duty. It's my day off."

Quill, who had recovered herself a little, smiled and said it was civic-minded of Vern to come in on his day off.

"Ah, that's okay," said Vern expansively. "Gotta file for overtime, of course."

Some thirty minutes later Quill, appalled by the cost of three gallons of name-brand exterior latex paint, was in the kitchen. The cans of Paramount Crimson Blaze stood on the newspapers spread on the floor. Meg and Doreen had been in the kitchen testing various recipes for gazpacho when Quill had come in. All three of them now stared at the cans in horrified fascination.

"There can't be a body in the paint can," said Meg after a moment. "I'll tell you why. Those ball mills you described to me—they're filled with special round rocks all tumbling together to break up the chunks of mineral?"

"Yes," said Quill. "You can put a three-ton chunk of diatomaceous earth into a ball mill, and about sixteen hours later, you get stuff the consistency of talcum powder."

"But minerals are dry and brittle. Bodies aren't. I'll show you what I mean." She went to the huge built-in refrigerator and pulled out a raw Rock Cornish game hen. "See?" she said, wielding it aloft. "Guts included." She dropped it into the Cuisinart and turned the dial. The hen spun around, blades chopping futilely at the rubbery skin. Meg switched it off. "You get goo. And not very good ground-up goo, at that. These are sharp blades, too, not rocks."

"You freeze the meat before you chop it, right?"

"That's my point," said Meg in exasperation. "Now if the body were frozen, I'd say, yeah, maybe this is a unique, first-time ever, one-of-a-kind way to dispose of somebody, but come on, Quill. You think somebody stuffed Dawn Pennifarm into their home freezer, hauled her out, took her into the plant in the dead of night, and dumped her in the ball mill?"

"The Qwik Freeze is right next door," said Quill. "You tell me."

Meg's eyes widened. "God!" She ran her hands through her

hair and circled the kitchen in agitation. "God! Somebody shut her in the nitrogen room at the Qwik Freeze, spun that dial down to twenty degrees below centigrade, and froze her stiff."

"It's possible, then."

"Oh, yeah. I mean, they handle tons and tons and tons of green beans that way, flash frozen. God."

"You bin watching too many Terminator movies or what?" said Doreen. "No body parts in that paint can that I can see. You'd get little bits and pieces. Teeth and such like."

"You haven't seen what those ball mills can do," said Quill stubbornly. "But we can drain it through a sieve and find out."

"You drain it through a sieve," said Meg.

"See? You both think I'm right. You think that Da . . ." Quill stumbled over the name. "Somebody might be in there."

"All the saints!" said Doreen obscurely. She knotted her apron firmly around her waist, went to the cupboard and removed a sieve, then selected a large stockpot.

"Not that one," said Meg. "You're not going to ruin a perfectly good stockpot with red paint. Not in my kitchen."

"For god's sake," said Quill. "We can buy another stockpot from Nickerson's. I'll get it myself."

Doreen took the stockpot, the sieve, and the open can of paint to the sink. Meg and Quill stood at each shoulder as she carefully poured the paint through the sieve.

"Smooth as paint," said Doreen in satisfaction, "I told you."

"That doesn't mean anything," said Quill. "The paint's sieved before it's canned."

"They check it for contaminants, don't they?" asked Meg. "If there'd been anything in the paint that's not supposed to be there, they would have found it at the factory."

"It's all automated. And they check for dirt, not blood. Maybe they wouldn't find it. Maybe the person who put the body into the ball mill runs the quality assurance line. I don't know."

Meg gazed at the counter, picked up a spoonful of gazpacho, gazed dubiously at the tomato-red color, and set it down again. "Baloney."

"Those ball mills can reduce an automobile to metal grit in about a day," said Quill impressively.

The three of them drew a little closer together.

"Maybe you should put the paint back in the can, Meg," said Quill in a hushed voice.

"You put it back. You brought it here."

"And their shoes!" said Doreen, rolling her eyes skyward, in apparent reference to the aforementioned saints. She upended the stockpot and poured the red liquid back into the can. She set the can inside the pot, and placed the sieve upside down over the lid. "Somethin' weird in that paint can, I'll tell you what it is— rodents."

"Rodents?" said Quill.

"Mouse. Or a rat." Doreen stuck out her lip and shook her head. "You two get crazy ideas, I'll tell you. All kinds of stuff gets into food, don't it?"

"You could be right," Quill admitted.

"Din't raise two kids and outlive three no-good husbands without bein' right," Doreen grunted.

"Let's put the whole thing in a box and cover it up and call Myles," said Meg.

"That shows *some* sense," said Doreen scornfully. "I got boxes in back." She marched out of the kitchen.

"So the question is, 'What bloody man is that?' " said Meg, "unless it's What bloody rat is that?"

"Rodent," said Quill gloomily. "What if we're crazy?"

"What if we're not? What if that's where all the missing women are ending up? Is that why you wanted to break into Paramount tonight?"

Quill blinked at her. She'd forgotten the iron oxide. She said aloud, "What's iron oxide got to do with the body in the paint can?"

"Earth to Quill!" said Meg. "Non sequiturs not appreciated. What about the iron oxide?"

"Well, I tried to tell you last night, but you were too anxious to bring my youthful defalcations to the attention of Myles and John."

"People without defalcations in their past are boring, boring, boring," said Meg airily. "So tell me now."

"For one thing, I doubt very much you can use it as a pigment substitute for lead oxide. Not without changes in the mixing process. I think that iron oxide is just plain old rust, isn't it?"

"Beats me."

"Anyway, it didn't sound right to me. And then when John found that the address for the supplier was the same as the one for Makepeace Whitman, I asked him about it."

"Makepeace Whitman supplies minerals to Paramount Paint?"

"Well, he's got to do something for a living. And his wife had a really peculiar reaction when I asked him about it."

"Which was?"

"I told you. Peculiar. Something about raping the earth. Which would make sense if Makepeace were engaged in a business that polluted, but iron oxide isn't a pollutant. At least, I don't think it is. My courses in paint chemistries were oriented more toward how to make colors than how the stuff is manufactured. But Paramount has those material safety sheets that OSHA makes you post? I wanted to get a look at them."

"Why do we have to break in to do it? Why not just go down there and ask them?"

"Because if something funny is going on, and women are being murdered, you don't just walk into the place where the funny stuff is happening. How many times have you read a Gothic novel and thrown it across the room because the heroine was so stupid she went into the basement? And everyone up to Chapter Seven had told her, 'Don't go into the basement!' There's too many questions about Paramount Paint just to walk in there and ask to see the files. Why should Hudson give them to us anyway? It's none of our business. Now there's even more of a reason to break in tonight. Who knew about the embezzlement from the inventory invoicing? What does Makepeace Whitman know about the orders for iron oxide?"

"You're going to end up proving Connie Weyerhauser's responsible," said Meg. "Are you ready for that? Nobody else has a motive and an opportunity both."

"Kay Gondowski does," said Quill. "And let's not forget Helena Houndswood. And if the iron oxide's a red herring, I just want to get the question cleared up. I don't know at this point whether it's a solvability factor or not."

Doreen came back into the kitchen carrying a large wooden box marked Moët & Chandon. "This'll do." The housekeeper placed the stockpot and the remaining two gallons of paint in the box and hefted it. "Storeroom? Or you gonna take it down to the sher'f's office?"

Quill hesitated.

"Storeroom," said Meg. "By the time Myles gets back into town, we'll have the whole thing nailed down."

Doreen shook her head and lugged the box to the storeroom. She set it down with a loud thump and returned, her lips thinned to a stubborn line.

"Now"—Meg dusted her hands briskly—"first job is to find out whether there's a body in the paint can, right?"

"Right," said Quill.

"Second job is to break into the paint factory and find those sheets you were talking about."

"Materials safety handling sheets. Like the one that was in the Bosses Club file which described how to handle lead oxide."

Doreen gave a loud snort, sat at the counter, and picked up her soup spoon.

"You're going to eat that stuff with a soup-colored corpse in the same room with us?" demanded Meg.

"Perfectly good soup." Doreen swallowed and considered, "Might be the last I get if you two end up in jail for breaking and entering."

"The third job," said Quill, ignoring Doreen, "is to talk to Connie Weyerhauser."

"You think Deputy Dave is going to fall for Dina's mysterious-woman-in-black act again?" said Meg. "I don't. I think he'll throw you right out of the jail."

"She's not in jail," said Doreen. "Howie Murchison sprung her. She's at home. Warn't enough evidence to keep her in."

"There you are," said Quill. "I'll go talk to Connie, and you call Andy Bishop."

"Me call Andy Bishop? Why?!"

"Because he can test the contents of the can."

"I don't want to call him. You call him. I'll go talk to Connie Weyerhauser. If I call him, he'll think I'm encouraging him."

"You don't want to encourage him?"

"Yes. No. I don't know."

Doreen took her empty soup bowl to the sink. "Rest of the world like you two, we wouldn't have any kids." She put her hands on her hips. "I got more important stuff to do than lookin' for rodent parts. You need me for anything else?"

"You don't want to be in on this investigation, Doreen?" asked Quill.

"Told the Friends I'd go on a hike with 'em this afternoon. Fresh air'll do me good. 'Sides, if I know you two, you'll be crawlin' around Paramount in the middle of the night lookin' for bodies and findin' rodents, and I like my sleep, thank you very much. You let me know what happens." Doreen hung her apron on its peg. "I think you should tell Sheriff McHale. You two want to go banging round that there factory, it's all right by me."

"Doreen? Before you go?"

"What, Quill?"

"Could you find out, just sort of casually, how the Whitmans came to choose the Inn for their FOFA convention?"

"I know that already. What d'ya wanna know for?"

"It could be important."

"I ain't betraying the Friends," said Doreen with dignity. "You'll know in due course, says Mr. Whitman, due course. So I say, that's for me to know and you to find out. Ha."

"Doreen," said Meg. "If you know how they heard about the Inn, you're duty bound to tell us. And you'd better tell us."

"You din't ast me *that*. You ast me if I know why they chose this-here Inn. How they heard 'bout us is different."

"Well, how'd they hear about us, then?" said Quill.

"Beats me." Doreen shrugged. She left, banging the back door shut.

"I'm going to push gazpacho up her nose," said Meg.

"If there's a link between the iron oxide, the embezzlement, the murders, and Makepeace Whitman, Connie should know. Or at least be able to point me in the right direction."

"Do you think she'll talk to you?"

"I'm going to try. In the meantime . . ."

"All right, all right, all right," Meg grumbled. "I'll call Andy." She went to the wall phone, picked it up, and hung it up again.

"What if Doreen's right? You read all the time about insects and whatnot that get into food. Why not into paint? Three parts rodent hair per million or whatever."

"Call Andy. That's the only way we're going to know for sure."

Meg lifted the phone and hung it up again. "What if you were right from the beginning? What if it's Helena? Let's say the iron oxide is the red herring. It was Helena Houndswood's car that was implicated in Sandy's death. The day Kay Gondowski disappeared, Helena said she was going to sit upstairs in the hot tub, and we both saw her come into the Inn at six forty-five, dressed in the clothes she'd worn that afternoon. And she passed Rickie Pennifarm's pickup truck just before Dot was killed. And none of this started happening until she rolled into town on Sunday. Sunday, let me remind you, was the day Dawn Pen—"

"Who's to say these things are all connected? Call Andy," said Quill inexorably. "I'm going over to see Connie. I'll be back in a few hours."

The phone book listed Connie and Roosevelt Weyerhauser's address in a section of Hemlock Falls not far from Sandy Willis's home. Quill debated on whether or not to call, then decided she would have a better chance of talking to Connie if she could see her face to face.

The Weyerhauser home was a small, stucco and beamed cottage dating from the twenties. The yard was neatly mowed. A wheelchair ramp had been built to the front door. Quill parked in the street and walked up to the house. A curtain on the front window twitched closed. She pushed the doorbell. The front door was plain leaded glass, and it was hard to see through the ripples. There was a long wait. Quill pushed the doorbell again. There was a faint shuffling sound, and eventually, Connie herself opened the front door. The skin under her eyes was purple with fatigue. She looked shrunken; her tunic top hung loose on her large frame. There was a gray tinge to her magnificent mahogany skin. She smelled of grief. Wordlessly she backed away from the door, and Quill went in.

The living room was covered in wall-to-wall Berber carpet in a neutral beige. There was an absence of knickknacks and small tables. A wheelchair was placed in front of the TV set, which was on without sound. Barbara Weyerhauser sat curled in it, head resting to one side on the back, her painfully thin arms and wrists in an *S* position.

"Are you all right?" Quill asked Connie.

"For now."

"I'll just say hello to Barbara. Maybe we could talk a little?"

"Back porch."

Quill went to the wheelchair and kneeled down. Barbara rolled her head and smiled, making her "Hello" sound.

"It's good to see you again," said Quill. "Your mother told me you're at the adult center most days during the week. Do you like it?"

Barbara made her "yes" sound and Quill smiled. "I'd like to talk to your mother for a while. Do you mind if we go out on the back porch?"

Barbara moved her head side to side in agreement. One finger pressed her buzzer.

"We'll come if you call," said Quill. "I'll see you later."

She followed Connie to the back porch. A ramp ran from the decking to flowers in raised beds. "She likes the roses best," said Connie. "And the bees. Loves the bees."

"She told me she was sorry Mike had taken the bees' nest from under the gazebo the last time she was at the Inn," said Quill. "She said she'd never been stung."

"Only a matter of time, isn't it?"

"Meaning we're all destined to get stung? Maybe you're right. This seems to be one of those times for you."

"Looks like."

"Connie, what's really going on?"

The dimples Quill had seen before shadowed briefly on her cheeks. "You messing in the sheriff's investigations again?"

"Was he right about the embezzlement? About Dawn?"

Connie nodded slowly. "Yes, he was."

"Connie, were you involved?"

"Hard to say I wasn't."

Quill, shocked, made a movement of protest.

"Oh, not in the way you think. I knew about it, is all, I didn't take any of the money. Never took any of the money."

"How much of this have you told Myles?"

"All of it." She sighed, her eyes shadowed. "You want to hear? I'll tell you everything I told Sheriff McHale. Dawn was always a little crooked. A little sly. And Mr. Zabriskie . . ." She shook her head, the shadow of the dimples back. "Sometimes I don't think that man's elevator goes all the way to the top. Anyway, he was set on this leadless paint process for the orange-red oil-base paints. Hard to get that color, you know, without lead oxide, but it's dangerous to handle. And expensive. When New York decided to cut expenses through this empowerment training . . . you know, handing off decisions usually made by the big shots to employee teams, Hudson got all excited. Took it into his head that he could save on research, that the Bosses Club could come up with a way to get that color without using lead oxide. Well, we couldn't, of course."

"But you did."

"No, we didn't What we came up with was this scheme of Dawn's. We get the supplier to label the lead oxide *iron* oxide, which he did, because his markets for lead oxide were shrinking. Now. Lead oxide's expensive, upward of two thousand dollars a ton. But Dawn was smart. She got the supplier to accept eight hundred a ton, because it was crooked, you see. And she billed Paramount twelve hundred more a ton and took the difference."

"Hudson didn't notice?"

Connie laughed. "Not a thing. Then New York imposed new profit quotas, and Hudson got himself all of a dither and gave the Bosses Club an output to cut costs."

"An output?"

"You know, a job for the team to do. The way this stuff works, the boss isn't supposed to look at how the team decides to cut costs, just whether or not we did it. We kind of leaned on Dawn, then, to stop the double billing. Our jobs were at risk. Kay and I were the most vulnerable. Kay doesn't have much in the way of savings, and she's paying off some heavy medical bills for her husband."

"But Hudson never found out about the substitution?" said Quill.

"No, ma'am." Connie was empathetic. "Just loved the awards and the bonuses he got for running an efficient plant. And why should he ask? Things were going just fine."

"Until Dawn disappeared."

"That's right."

"And you don't know what happened to her?"

"Last I saw of Dawn Pennifarm, she was headed to the Qwik Freeze to do benchmarking." Her eyes shifted. Quill had a sudden conviction she was lying.

"Do you know the supplier for the lead?"

"Mr. Whitman. That crazy group of his is at the Inn."

"Do you know why he chose the Inn for his convention?"

"He was squawking pretty hard about Dawn upping the prices on him. Dawn just said, let him scream. She did mention that he was going to come up here to talk it over."

The Whitmans, Quill recalled, had arrived at the Inn on Tuesday. Which wasn't to say that Makepeace hadn't come into town earlier, shoved Dawn into the cold room at the Qwik Freeze, and dumped her body in the ball mill Monday night after the plant was closed. He was in the woods on a hike when Dot had been murdered, too.

"Connie, do you have any idea who's committing these murders?"

Connie looked at her, alarmed. "What murders? Sheriff McHale didn't say anything about murders. There's been a lot of talk in town about Rickie and Dawn. Do you mean Dot? We all thought that was a hunting accident."

"I think someone's being very clever," said Quill. "There are only two bodies, Connie, but four women are missing." She watched Connie closely.

Connie's hands twisted in her lap. "But Dawn's run off. And Kay's at her son's. And Sandy . . ." She shuddered. "And I get the money" she whispered. "I get the money. No. No. It can't be!" she burst out finally. "Who?!" Then with horror: "I'm a fool. Sitting here counting that extra money and being a fool. All the Bosses Club!" She half started out of her chair.

"Well, that's the question, isn't it," said Quill with the voice she'd used when Meg was little and had scared herself. "Let's be objective about this, Connie. Why would someone want the Bosses Club out of the way?"

"She was angry, that woman," said Connie jerkily. "Said she was going to find some way to take it away. Dawn said we'd sue her. Dawn said we'd call the papers, and those reporters for *A Current Affair*."

Quill held her breath and let it put softly. "You mean Helena Houndswood?"

"She was looking for the Hall on Monday. Asked at the post office, I guess. Asked who I was, and did I live in the big farmhouse down in the park."

"Peterson's," said Quill. "She's there now."

"Vern said I worked at the plant. This must have been, oh, about three-thirty on Monday, just at the shift change. Dawn was going home in that rusty old Buick of hers and saw her come out of the post office. So Dawn pulls over and starts asking her, did we win, and it wasn't just me that won that million, it was all of us. I guess there was a fuss. Ms. Houndswood sat in that old Buick of Dawn's and took on something fierce." Connie sighed heavily. "Dawn called me, soon as she got home. Said she told her off, good. Said not to worry, she'd made some kind of deal with Helena about the money. Not to worry? Of course, we worried. We knew Dawn's kind of deals. We were all just waiting to see what she was going to do. And Wednesday, when you came in to tell us that we'd won. Well!" She smiled a little. "You saw how we reacted. Relief, mostly. We were sure Ms. Houndswood could find some way to hold up that money."

"God," said Quill.

Connie grasped the sides of the lawn chair, her knuckles a pale cream. "You think she killed them? You think she killed them all? Do you think she's going to kill me?"

"God," Quill said again helplessly. "I don't know."

"I'll tell you one thing, I'm not stepping but of this house. I'm not going anywhere without Roosevelt. And I'm not letting anyone in."

"There's another possibility," said Quill. "We'll have to tell Myles all this, of course. But until he gets back . . . just let me ask you this: Did everyone from the Bosses Club join in the . . . um . . . scam?"

"What? Taking the money from the double billing, you mean? Everyone knew about it. Sandy took some once in a while, when things got tight. I don't know about Kay, or Dot. I'd say Kay wouldn't have understood. I'd guess Dot was in on it, but I don't know. It wasn't something we talked about, Quill. And it wasn't something we were proud of. When we had that output to reduce costs—nobody took a dime except Dawn." Her face set. "You may not believe me."

"Connie, if you knew about the embezzlement, why didn't you do something?"

"Your sheriff knows."

"Myles?"

Connie had been looking at the far end of the garden. She switched her gaze to Quill's face. Her eyes were terrible. "You tell me what happens to me and mine if I lose my job. You tell me what happens to people that blow the whistle. You tell me, Quill. Who's going to give me another job with health benefits to cover Barb? Where would we go? You tell me that."

Quill came back to the Inn to find Meg sitting by the fireplace dressed in a skirt and blouse. "You look great." She sniffed the air. "And you used my Andiamo."

"It smells better than my Blue Grass."

"It's also more expensive than your Blue Grass."

Quill moved restlessly from the counter to the sink and back again.

"What's the matter, Quillie?" Meg drew a sharp breath. "Connie didn't confess, did she?"

"Not to killing Dot. Or Sandy. Or Dawn. No. She confessed to being helpless. What are we *doing* here, Meg?"

"Waiting for Andy Bishop to come and tell us if there's a body in the paint can." She watched Quill with an air of concern. "You mean, running the Inn? Staying out of the action in New York. To give you a more sober answer, I'm getting better and better as a chef. But you?" She hesitated.

"What?"

"You're not painting. You haven't picked up a brush in three years. Not seriously, at least. And you're not deciding about Myles. I think what you're doing is taking care of me. Which is a pretty dumb way to spend your time when you could be working. Really working."

"I am really working. I'm working like Connie's working. That's worthwhile."

"Well that depends on your world view, I guess. And look at the results. She's in big trouble, isn't she?"

"She is," said Quill shortly, "but only because she was caught between two terrible choices when she did what she had to do."

"Am I interrupting something?" Andy Bishop came through the dining room door. His hair was freshly combed. Quill, touched, decided he had stopped by the men's room on his way in.

"Yes," said Meg.

Andy's face fell. Quill frowned at her sister. "Of course you're not. We're glad to see you. Have you had lunch? It's a little late, but we've got some pâté? Maybe some soup?"

"Sounds great," said Andy, his eye on Meg.

She ignored him, unfolding herself from the rocker. "Have a seat. I'll get you something. Quill? You want to make some coffee? I'll have caffe latte."

"Sure. Andy?"

"After the pâté, maybe." He sat at the counter, eyes still on Meg, and began to chat, in much the same way, Quill bet, that he eased a sulky child into accepting an injection. "So, what's up? Meg said you had some questions about blood. Let me tell you all I know about blood. I see your reception area is still blotted with that little accident you had a few days ago, Quill. Which reminds me." He got up from the counter and peeled the bandage at her temple back with gentle fingers. "You must have had a remarkable surgeon. Looks great." He pressed the bandage back into place and resumed his seat. "About your foyer wall. Your guy Mike's going to have to replace the sheetrock there. The blood's soaked into the wall, and serum protein is pretty resilient stuff. I can see by your expression, Meg, that you are absolutely fascinated. I can also see that you are puzzled. What, you are asking yourself, is serum protein? Well, it's part of blood, ladies, and courtesy of my course in Hematology one-oh-one, I can tell you that blood is made up of all kinds of interesting things. Plasma. Red blood cells White blood—"

"We think Dawn Pennifarm's been ground up and put in the paint can," said Meg.

"I beg your pardon?"

"I'll get the can," said Quill. She went to the storeroom for the box, and by the time she returned, Meg was sitting close to Andy at the counter.

He rubbed the paint between his thumb and forefinger, sniffed the contents of the can, and listened to Quill's summary of the events at the post office.

"Hm," he said.

"Do you think we've totally lost our minds?" said Meg defensively. "Is Doreen right? Do you think this is a rodent?"

"No," said Andy. "And serum protein would make those blotches on the post office, Quill, just like the blotches on your foyer wall, there. And there's too much of whatever it is to come from Vern's cut finger. There is absolutely blood in this paint. Have you talked to Myles—of course not. We're going to solve this ourselves, aren't we? I remember how envious I was last year when you two solved the History Days murder."

Meg flushed. Quill grinned; this guy, she thought, was in love, no question about it.

"I'll run a few tests at the clinic. Now, there's a problem. I'll be able to tell you if it's human blood, but . . ." He picked up one of the unopened cans of paint and read aloud, "Black iron oxide. Silicates. Two-four-five-six tetrachloro-Isopthalonitrile—betcha you didn't think I could pronounce that, did you? That's what medical school will do for a guy. Acrylic resin, glycols, and water. These babies are going to break down the identifying factors in the blood. So I'll be able to tell you what is in the can. But not who."

"There must be some way" Quill insisted.

"DNA typing. DNA strands survive practically anything. But then we'd have to have a sample of the victim's DNA to compare it to."

"How could we do that?" asked Meg. "I mean, if the body's in the paint can, how do we get a sample?"

"If it's a woman, there's, a bare possibility that she's had a pap smear recently. If that sample's still around, then we can use that. Have either of the purported victims been to the doctor recently?"

"We don't know," said Meg.

"Dawn Pennifarm must have," said Quill. "Her husband said she was pregnant. The employee records at Paramount might show us."

"And we have a way of getting those," said Meg with a rather mischievous smile.

"If it's breaking in to Paramount, like Quill and John broke into Peterson's warehouse last year, then I have a better way," said Andy. "I do the comp claims for Paramount, you know. Physician of record. Let me check the files, okay? I don't want you two padding around that plant at two in the morning, especially if this"— he tapped the paint can—"is what we think it is. Too dangerous."

"Don't go into the basement," said Meg.

"What? Never mind. If Dawn was pregnant, she must have gone to Pete Dubrovnick in Syracuse, he handles most of the obstetrics-gyn work for the employees. Let me check with him, and see if we can come up with a tissue sample. In the meantime, you have an empty spice jar or something? I'll just take a bit of this and let you know." He eased off the stool.

"You'd do that for us?" asked Meg. "No questions asked?"

"Well." He leaned over the counter. His lips brushed her cheek. "There's a price."

"I'll go find John, or something," said Quill, "while you guys discuss the price."

Quill withdrew to the dining room. Several of the staff were setting up for afternoon tea. She waved at Kathleen Kiddermeister and asked for John.

"Last time I saw him, he was headed for the office. Quill? Is Helena Houndswood going to eat here tonight? Everyone's asking for her."

"Did you check the reservations list?"

"Yes." Kathleen's face dropped "She's not on it."

"Then probably not."

"It's been so exciting having her around here."

"Yes," said Quill.

She found John absorbed in the calculator when she walked into her office. She sat on the couch facing the desk, guiltily aware she hadn't spared much time being fiscally responsible. "How's it look?"

"The cash situation?" He sat back and rubbed his eyes. "Not good. We're into the reserve line of credit. We're going to have a serious case of the cash shorts next week." He tossed the pencil he'd been using to punch the calculator keys onto the desktop. "No luck as far as Hudson giving us that check?"

"Not so far, but I haven't really tried," said Quill. "I'll give it another shot. But, surely with all this business we've booked, the bank will give us a loan?"

"Bankers loan you money when you don't need it. It's an oath they take when they buy their three-piece suits."

"What about Mark Jefferson at the Savings and Loan?"

"I talked to him. We need a total of fifteen thousand to carry us through July. It's too small an amount."

"Too small?"

"Yes. They hold our mortgage. If we were in serious danger of defaulting, they'd lend us the whole half million. But we're not in danger of defaulting. What we need is fifteen thousand to carry us over the hump of the next three weeks. The risk to the bank's mortgage is low; the risk involved in extending an unsecured loan to us of fifteen thousand is high—at least that's what their actuarial tables say."

"That makes no sense at all," said Quill, indignant.

"It does if you're a banker. You know the options: we may have to close down for a couple of weeks, recruit volunteers to staff the Inn, beg the suppliers to wait more than ninety days for payment for laundry and food stock. The bank knows they're first in line to be paid, Quill, if we go belly up. They're just as happy to let our suppliers take the risk, rather than them taking the risk for the suppliers. You see what I mean?"

"Let's picket," said Quill, who always regretted missing the sixties.

"Let's find another lender. Half the problem is that Hemlock Falls Savings and Loan is the only game in town. They can afford the hard line. This is my fault, Quill. I should have gone to Syracuse or Rochester for the mortgage. The banks there are larger, and more willing to absorb possible losses."

"I was the one who insisted that we use a local lender," said Quill. "You warned me. What do you want to do now?"

"Well, we're not as notorious as we were last year. I'll go into Syracuse tomorrow and talk to Chase. See what I can scare up."

"By the notoriety, you mean the murders?"

"That, and the business with the Board of Health."

"But you always told Meg—"

"You know Meg. The restaurant and hotel business is first and last built on reputation. If she'd known how worried I was over the temporary closure, we'd have had to put her on Prozac. The situation's dire, but not critical. Helena Houndswood's going to help us a lot. I know you don't like her, Quill, but her endorsement is going to tip the balance for any loan we might get. If you don't mind, I thought I'd stop down to her place tonight to see if I can use her name with the bank. Maybe get a written assurance that the show will be shot here."

"No," said Quill, "I don't mind."

He smiled slightly. "You do. I can tell. But that's the way the world works."

"John. If she were discredited or something. What would the chances of getting the loan be?"

"Poor to awful. Why?" He quirked an eyebrow. "You're not still on the gig about her knocking off the Bosses Club, are you?"

"Who, me?" said Quill.

CHAPTER 12

Quill went upstairs, took a shower, threw on a pair of shorts and a T-shirt, and sat on her balcony with her investigation book on her lap. Twilight came and deepened into night. Sounds of guests arriving, leaving, walking through the gardens drifted through the air. Her rooms were located over the kitchen; one end of her balcony formed the roof over the back entrance, and she heard the chatter of the *sous* chefs; Meg's voice raised in occasional outrage; bouts of laughter; the clink of pots and dishes. The sound of the falls wound through it all, and it was the best tranquilizer she knew, and it didn't work. Finally she tossed her pencil into the pot of dianthus near the French doors and called the sheriff's office: no,

Myles hadn't checked in yet, but a message could be gotten to him right away. No, Quill said, no message.

Quill was switching through television programs that seemed increasingly stupid when Meg tapped on her door and pushed it open. Her face was both somber and excited.

"Andy called. It's human."

"Oh, my God," said Quill. "Does he know who? Not Dawn!"

"Not yet. He's going over to talk to this Pete Dubrovnick tomorrow. He said Dawn had an amniocentesis; that'll give us the tissue sample we need to match the DNA. Unless it's Kay."

"I called Myles's office. He's not expected back until Sunday."

"He'll miss the Little Miss Hemlock Falls beauty contest," said Meg. "Poor him. But it gives us two days to solve the murders. I've figured it out, Quill. It's—"

"You haven't figured it out, Meg. You couldn't possibly. You don't know everything Connie told me this afternoon." She told her. Meg, curled up on one end of the davenport, clapped her hand over her mouth, and yelled "Jeez!"

"So I don't think we should break into the Paramount factory. Andy's going to get the information anyway. I think we should break into the Peterson farmhouse."

"Okay," said Meg readily. "What are we looking for?"

"Evidence. Connie said that Dawn had given Helena something or done something that would guarantee they got their million dollars."

"What kind of something?" asked Meg skeptically.

"Well, I don't know, do I? Maybe she had figured out some kind of blackmail. Maybe she was just putting off Dawn until she had time to kill her. I won't know until I look."

"So when are we going to do it?"

"She's supposed to be at some Chamber lunch tomorrow—"

"Not here!" Meg's eyes glittered dangerously. "There's nothing on the agenda sheet in the kitchen."

"No, down at the diner. I'll wait until she's out of the way, and then get in through a window or something. I'll bet she keeps a lot of files. Doreen said she had tons of paper and whatnot all over her room."

"And then what?" asked Meg. "What about Makepeace Whitman? Let's say that the story Dawn was going to give Helena was about pollution. If Dawn threatened to expose his substitution of lead oxide for iron oxide, he could be in real trouble with just about every government agency in the state. In the country."

"Makepeace is a prime suspect," said Quill "I think you should join FOFA tomorrow and follow him around on his hikes. It's Saturday, and you don't have to be in the kitchen until dinner."

"Trudge around Hemlock Falls wearing one of those stupid T-shirts?" said Meg.

"Just try to find out if he came into town earlier this week. Be subtle."

"Okay. I'll do it. I just hope they don't have any lectures on insects of North America. I hate stuff like that."

"I'll see you at breakfast, then."

"Sleep well, Quillie." Meg reached over and hugged her. "We'll talk about stuff when this is all over."

"What kind of stuff?"

"You know, stuff."

Quill went to bed and dreamed of clocks. Dozens of them, the sound of their ticking merging into the roar of a ball mill. In her dream she approached the clock face, a huge, frightening combination of digital numbers and thick black hands. The hands descended, second by second. She reached up to grab it, stop it . . . stop it, and woke up with a jerk. Her alarm was ringing. The sun was shining through the French doors. She showered and put on a pair of cotton jeans.

She stood on the balcony and brushed her hair, the early sunshine warm on her face and arms. It was a very Grieg-ish scene, with the pale violet-pink of dawn submerged under the rising tide of stronger morning light, the finches and the barn sparrows arguing mildly in the poplars. Even the chickens busy on the fresh-clipped lawn were pleasing to the eye.

Except the Inn didn't have any chickens.

Quill frowned and leaned over the railing. Three of them—hens, she guessed—were right below her on the lawn. The asphalt drive leading away from the back door to the rear parking lot was covered with suspicious-looking piles. The jerky movement of the tarragon in the breezeless air indicated the presence of several more chickens in the herb garden.

The back door slammed. There was a sliding, scraping thud, then a shout: "Hellfire!"

"Doreen!" Quill leaned over the rail. Her hair swung into her eyes, and she brushed it away. "Doreen, are you all right?"

"Durn things!" Doreen marched out on the lawn and peered up at her. Her bun was askew. Chicken manure smeared the side of her white apron. Her expression rivaled that of the monk who took such umbrage at the innocent Brother Lippi. "If the Friends hadn't taught me 'bout the sanctity of livin' creetures, I'd be getting me an ax," she said.

"Where did they come from?" asked Quill. "Oh. Of course, Helena Houndswood's gentleman farm."

"There's chicken shit all over the place!" Doreen tramped determinedly across the lawn, flapping her apron at the chickens. This occasioned a curiously lethargic panic, demonstrated by a tentative jerk forward with one clawed foot, a frantic look from side to side, several distressed clucks, and a resumption of the foot into its former position.

"We should catch them and return them," said Quill. "Get a box. I'll be right down."

She knotted her hair on the top of her head and briefly debated the best components of a chicken-catching outfit. Shorts and a T-shirt should offer fewer opportunities for chicken droppings, and she changed out of her jeans.

Shorts, however, offered more flesh to chicken beaks. "Jeez!" exclaimed Meg, who'd joined them in the hunt. "The little suckers are nasty!" She shoved the last hen into the wire milk case Doreen had unearthed from the storeroom and held a garbage can lid over the top. "We need a bunch of heavy boards, or something. They're going to wiggle—*Ow*!" She sucked the back of her hand and scowled at the crate. A flat black eye glittered balefully back.

Doreen, who'd thought ahead, had rummaged several thick planks from the garden shed. She slid them over the top of the crate with a tender regard for those birds who refused to duck. "There. Your legs look a treat. Better get iodine on 'em."

Quill looked down at her bare legs, peppered with beak marks.

Doreen hefted the crate. A chorus of indignant clucks and screeches assaulted them. "I'll get the pickup and take 'em on back to Peterson's. You got any messages for Ms. Houndswood?"

"No. Just make sure she's going to that Chamber meeting."

"Anything else? Doc Bishop find anything in that paint can?"

"Um," said Quill.

"Rats, right?" Doreen stumped, toward the parking lot and pickup truck, the chickens protesting fiercely at every step. Or maybe, being chickens, Quill thought, simply squawking for the heck of it. Myles had been right about them—stupid and mean. "Be back in a few minutes."

Meg suggested breakfast, and they retired to the kitchen.

"So, you're going to break into the farmhouse?" said Meg. She slapped a bowl of blueberries on the counter and reached for the heavy cream.

"Yep. And I figured out what to look for. I'm convinced those phone calls supposedly from Kay were phony. Helena made at least four phony calls. One to Sandy the day before, to lead us to believe that Kay was still alive, the second to Sandy's home, to get her out on the road so she could smack her with that rental car, the other to Connie. Helena's got that cellular phone, and the phone company keeps records of all the calls made on cellular phones. I'll get the number from the farmhouse, and we can get hold of the records."

"She wouldn't be that stupid," said Meg. She apportioned the berries into two bowls and handed Quill a spoon.

"This murderer is taking risks," said Quill. "Look at what happened to Dawn. Frozen to death, transported across the parking lot to Paramount in the dead of night, and tipped into the ball mill."

"So how would she know where to put the body?" asked Meg. "How many people know about the ball mills?"

"Brought them chickens back," said Doreen as she came in the back door. She pulled out a stool and sat down with them at the counter.

"That was fast," said Meg. "About the ball mills . . ."

"What?" said Quill, who didn't want to answer Meg's question, because it pointed to Connie as the murderer. "Weren't they her chickens?"

"They was her chickens, all right," said Doreen grimly. "The last of the herd."

"Flock," corrected Meg. "Wasn't she around? Out in the barn, I suppose, doing picturesque things with the cows."

"Out in the driveway," said Doreen. "Doing you're not goin' to believe what with that fancy Jeep."

"You mean the Range Rover?" said Meg. "It did seem kind of excessive to buy a brand-new Range Rover for her project. I mean, what farmer do you know that can afford a brand-new Range Rover?"

"What was she doing with the Range Rover?" asked Quill.

"I drove up the hill, carrying them chickens," said Doreen. "They was squalling fit to bust. Fit to wake the dead and pecking each other like you wouldn't believe. I said," Doreen pointed out with a consciously virtuous air, "a prayer over 'em. And there she was."

"Helena Houndswood?" asked Meg.

"In that there Jeep. Running back and forth over this big flat garbage bag."

"Over a garbage bag?" said Quill.

"Me, I thought she was recycling. She come up that little hill to the house gunnin' that Jeep—"

"Range Rover," said Meg.

"Like some Nazi tank driver. *Wham!* She'd hit the bag. Then she'd back up. All the way down that little hill. Then gunnin' back up and *Wham!* right over the garbage bag."

"Cans?" said Quill, confused, "she was flattening cans?"

"Chickens. Flattening them chickens. Or what was left of them."

"She ran over the chickens!" said Quill. "Why?"

"Well, I ast her that. Why she'd go and flatten one of God's innocent creatures with that there Rover. 'Innocent my ass!' she says. You look what they done to me. 'What they done?' I says."

Quill glanced under the table at her pecked and iodined legs. "Pecked her, I bet."

"Pecked her good. And she slipped and fell in the chicken poop like I done, and sprained her ankle all to golly. 'They stink and they're stoopid,' she says to me. 'And don't you go tellin' nobody. Chicken is not part of a beautiful life,' she says, and she whomps that ol' garbage bag in the Dumpster and stomps off. So I brung our chickens back."

"Uh, Doreen," said Quill. "I don't really want those chickens. Do you, Meg?"

"Nossir," said Meg. "Me, I think Helena Houndswood has the right idea."

"You watch your mouth, missy!" said Doreen. "Why do you want to go and punish one of God's innocent creetures?"

"What's this 'God's innocent creatures' stuff," complained Meg. "Did I miss something?"

"One of the Friends of Fresh Air lectures," said Quill glumly. "The 'Friends' extends to all living things, I guess."

"Including chickens?" Meg rolled her eyes.

"What I want you to do with them chickens is to let them run free on the grass, just as God made them. They deserve to enjoy the sunshine and the fresh air, like all of us."

"Doreen," said Meg, with winning candor, "I don't want those chickens. Except maybe to stew. You don't want those chickens. You fell flat on your whatsis this morning because of those chickens, and my goodness, what's going to happen with the guests? Those Friends of Fresh Air of yours will be slipping and sliding all over the *lawn*, for Pete's sake. No. No chickens."

"You refuse sanctuary to them chickens?"

"I refuse what?"

"Sanctuary," interrupted Quill. "You could take them to the church, Doreen."

"The church?" Meg shook her head back and forth, as if trying to clear it.

"Take the chickens to Harland Peterson's," said Quill. "You know, the farmer that sold them to Helena Houndswood in the first place. He'll put them back with their relatives."

"He'll cook them," said Doreen indignantly.

"Well, probably," said Quill. "I don't care what you do with them. Take them home with you, if you want. Just don't let them roam all over the lawn."

"I know what to do," said Doreen. She rose, adjusted her bun with grim determination. "I seen my duty, and I'm doin' it."

"Jeez," said Meg as Doreen stumped off. "Do you suppose Helena really squashed those chickens like that?"

"Doreen wouldn't make it up." Quill shuddered. "Now, if she could do that to chickens, Meg . . ."

"Oh, I don't know. Somebody told me once that chickens are so brainless that if they look up to see if it's raining, they'll drown because they forget to look down. No, that's turkeys. Whatever. I'm a cook, Quill, and one of the things I cook is chickens. So I don't see Helena's disposal of her chicken problem as a major character flaw. Actually, given the kind of person she is, it was a typical tidy solution. I mean, obviously, these chickens were going to embarrass her big time. It's a neat, tidy way to dispose of an annoyance without making a big deal of it."

"Sure," said Quill skeptically. "I'm going down there now. And you're going to join Doreen and the nature hike, right?"

"Oh, right. Well. Guess I better get going." She sat, unmoving. "Quill?"

"What?"

"It might not be Helena. It might be someone else altogether."

Quill said, searching through her purse for the keys to her Olds, "Who else could it be?"

"I don't know. But one thing that's struck me about this murder is the need to absolutely conceal the body or bodies from identification. I mean—why else go through this elaborate stuff? The murderer had to get Dawn or Kay or both of them to the Qwik Freeze, then take the frozen body out and over to the ball mill. All within a space of what—two to three hours in the dead of night and eluding the security guards. All this to obliterate the corpse. Think about it."

"What do you think?"

"I don't have an answer," said Meg. "I'm just raising the question."

"Some help you are."

"Why are you so upset? All I'm saying is just thi—"

"Stop," said Quill. "It's perfectly fine for you to help with this investigation, but if you're simply going to be an obstructionist, forget it."

"You don't know what to think about it, do you?" said Meg. "Ha. Some Hawkshaw. Me, I'm going to think about it, and when I've come up with the answer, I'll let you know. Deal?"

"I'll come up with the answer before you do," said Quill. "So sure. Deal."

"Quill?"

"What?!"

"Ask yourself what *really* happened to Kay Gondowski."

Quill drove the Olds to the Peterson farm, thinking about it. Why would there be a need to destroy the body? And what *had* happened to Kay Gondowski?

The old farmhouse looked like the cover of a very expensive coffee table book. Quill half expected to see letters across the velvety grass reading: HELENA HOUNDSWOOD PRESENTS: IT'S A BEAUTIFUL LIFE ON THE FARM, or whatever it was that she was going to call her next best-seller. The Range Rover wasn't in the driveway. The yard was conspicuous for its lack of chickens. Quill got out of the Olds, went to the front door, and plied the brass door knocker vigorously. No answer. She walked around the back of the house, passing by the Dumpster. A large curiously flattened green Hefty bag lay on top. Quill hesitated. Miss Marple would have looked in the bag. Miss Marple, however, didn't have a housekeeper whose word was as good as Doreen's.

In the back of the house Quill saw that the horse and the cow had been fed large armfuls of hay and were chewing away in their paddocks. The pig was there, too, gloriously smelly, but only, Quill figured, because it was too large to fit under the Range Rover. Quill went back to the house and peered into the ground-floor windows facing the red barn. The Peterson kitchen was gorgeous, with custom cherry cupboards, granite countertops, and pine flooring. Mrs. Peterson had ruthlessly modernized it some time before Norm's commitment to the state slammer for criminal activities. There was a stack of empty Lean Cuisine boxes in the sink and a teacup near the coffeemaker.

Gingerly, Quill tried the back door. It was locked. She tried the kitchen window next. It opened easily. Quill, her heart pounding, hoisted herself up and went inside.

The house smelled faintly of Giorgio. Quill poked through the trash in the kitchen waste basket: tea bags, coffee grounds, and remains of a tube of Retin-A. The living room was as neat and impersonal as a magazine ad, the braided rugs on the hardwood floors placed equidistant from the walls. Recent copies of *Publishers Weekly* and *W* lay on the coffee table.

The Peterson den had been converted into a temporary office. A laptop computer was open on the desk; a plastic file case, the sort that had a handle and could be carried, was open beside it. Quill, glancing around her with the furtiveness of a cat burglar, which, she thought, she was, gingerly flipped through the manila folders.

Helena was an organized woman, which didn't surprise Quill at all. Anyone who did twenty-seven television shows a year, published a book a year, and appeared at all the celebrity functions necessary to keep her in the media's eye had to be organized and fearsomely productive. There was a file on the china contest. Quill found biographical notes on Connie, Dot, Sandy, and Kay. They were short descriptions, rather acerbic, but otherwise unrevealing.

There was an outline for a book, simply labeled "Farm." She'd made an entry that morning: "Bag chickens," which made Quill grin and shake her head.

The file behind it was called "A Sharper Eye." Quill opened it to a series of faxes from someone named Max, who appeared to be Helena's agent. Helena's responses were on bond. At first perusal, Max came across as servile, obsequious, and fawning, agreeing to everything Helena suggested. Just, Quill thought, the sort of person she would have expected to be the actress's representative. As she read on, she realized Helena was begging him to find a credible alternative to her TV show. People, she complained, were not taking her seriously. Her audience share had dropped thirty-two percent in the past twelve months. And Max, in prose as oily as Göring's must have been to Hitler's, was telling her it was hopeless.

". . . even for someone as loved by the audience as you are, another investigative news show is not going to fly. *60 Minutes, 20/20, PRIMETIME* have carved up what small market there is . . ."

". . . Look at Julia. Eighty-three and still beloved. Forty-six is not the end of the world . . . (forty-six? Quill was astonished) . . . you're a fixture with your fans . . ."

"Fixture?" Helena had responded. "So's a toilet. I've run across an interesting problem here. Lot of resonance for the Greenpeace types. It's a hell of a story. Wallace is seventy-two, right? Unless the bastard's planning to die on the air, I want you to make some inquiries about my replacing him. This could be the feature that gives me an entrée."

That was the last fax. It was dated the day before. Quill reread the messages and found no clue as to what the story was that would "have a lot of resonance for the Greenpeace types." Whatever was going on had to be related to FOFA and Makepeace Whitman's substitution of lead oxide for iron oxide. Dawn said she'd fixed it, Connie had said. Dawn said the cash prize was in the bag, she'd made a trade. And here was confirmation. "Damn," said Quill, since Helena now had every possible motive to keep the Bosses Club alive. Quill closed the file, replaced it, and began thumbing through the correspondence file for the cellular phone bill. She found it for the prior month and copied the account number on a slip of paper. With any luck, she could figure out a way to get the record of calls made in the last week. John, she bet, would have an idea.

A squeal came from outside. Quill jumped. Her heart thudding painfully, she peered cautiously out the window. One of the pigs was digging in the lawn. She slipped quietly out the back door and into the car. The pig went "hrunh" and trotted toward her, eyes alight. Quill pulled out of the driveway and into the road.

"So much for being a burglar," she muttered aloud. Clearly, the next step was to confront Helena with the fact that she had evidence relating to a suspected homicide, and she had to cough up or suffer the consequences. Just as clearly, Helena would want to know how Quill had come by the information. Quill wondered what the penalty for breaking and entering was. So far, the only witness to her felony, if it was a felony, was the pig, and all things considered, she'd rather keep it that way. Maybe Meg would have some answers.

"Meg's still out with the FOFA people," said Dina when Quill got back to the Inn. "So's Doreen."

"Where's John?"

"Syracuse. He left this morning."

"Right. I forgot." Balked, Quill drummed her fingers on top of the reception desk. "Makepeace Whitman and his wife are on the hike, aren't they?"

"Yes," said Dina. "They left about an hour ago. They hike until teatime. Those guys are some hikers, Quill. But they never seem to get sweaty. They're the cleanest hikers I've ever seen."

"Would you hand me the master key, please?"

"Quill. You're not going to . . ."

"Going to what!" Guilt made Quill snappish, and she apologized. "Anyway, it's just a room check, to see how housekeeping's doing." Dina handed over the master key. Quill slipped it into her pocket and went upstairs. Great detectives, she was beginning to realize, had to cultivate character traits like nosiness and deception that made them less than desirable inn managers, much less prospective wives for sheriffs. Peter Wimsey was always plunged into guilt over the whole ethics thing, but kept determinedly on in the course of bringing criminals to justice; on the other hand, Harriet loved him anyway.

Makepeace Whitman's room didn't provide a single clue to prove his culpability in the environmental disaster Helena had alluded to in her fax. The only thing Quill discovered was that he and his wife traveled with remarkably few possessions and used a lot of towels. Quill relocked the door and went downstairs to her office, where she brooded for three hours, concluding only that it was unlikely Helena Houndswood was behind the killings, that Connie still had the best motive extant—and that she *really* wanted to find Kay Gondowski—prospective heir to a cool, clear million. When Meg banged into the office, she greeted her with a sigh of relief.

"So, how was it?"

Meg, in shorts and a grubby tank top, sank into the couch with a groan and untied her tennis shoes. "Awful."

"Awful?" She cast a critical eye over her sister. "How come you look like you've been rolling around in the Peterson barnyard, and they look so clean all the time?"

"They must take a lot of showers." Meg groaned. "Boy, my legs hurt. And I jog, Quill! Those people are fanatics. We tramped all the way down to the end of the gorge. And they're worse proselytizers than the Moonies at the airport. 'I wouldn't know what it was really like until I joined,' they said. 'My body wouldn't get the full benefit of the fresh air until I was a member.' Aaagh!" She shook herself like a puppy. "Spare me. And I didn't learn a damn thing about Makepeace Whitman's business. Just that he believes in benign use of the earth's resources, and his company turns rock quarries into parks and a whole *load* of baloney. This was *not* one of your better ideas. Next time *you* go on the endless tramp through the woods and listen to bozos going on and on and *on* about God's feathered friends. I tell you one thing, they were some kind of pissed off when Doreen got up to 'testify' and told them about Helena running over those chickens. They were ready to storm the Bastille, or, in her case, the Peterson farmhouse. Starving French peasants have nothing on them, I'll tell you. I hope you got something, because I'll tell you, I'm up the creek without a paddle." She glowered. "Stuck in a sinking canoe with crazies. And no life jacket. And no *food*! We walked for four hours without so much as a cookie. You better spill what you found fast, because I'm about to raid the refrigerator big time."

"I found something, but we're in the same canoe, so to speak. I'm not sure what to do next. The 'trade' that Dawn made with Helena to assure the Bosses Club win was a hot story on some kind of environmental disaster."

"So Helena's off the suspect list."

"I suppose so," said Quill with reluctance, "but I got the account number for the phone bill all the same."

The phone rang with one short, two long, that meant the call was for the office and not the reception desk. Quill picked it up.

"Quill? This is Andy Bishop. We're on the way to identifying the body in the paint can."

"Meg's here," said Quill. "I'm going to put you on the speaker phone." She punched the button and set the receiver in the cradle.

"Am I on? Are you there, Meg? I talked to Pete. He's sending the amniocentesis sample Dawn Pennifarm had taken over, so we can try and match the DNA. It's odd, though, a woman as young as Dawn having the test. Pete said it showed the fetus had a number of birth defects. I won't bother you with the medical jargon, but they're tetraogenic. That is, there's a strong probability the defects originated from environmental causes. And the results from the autopsy on Dot Vandermolen are back. She had a grade-three lung cancer. Are we moving along here?"

"Environmental?" Quill drew her breath in sharply. "Of course!

And the clocks! The timing's off! That's it! Could a long-term exposure to lead do that?"

"I'm not sure about the lung cancer, but the evidence is pretty clear about the fetal defect."

"That's a yes?"

"Yes."

"Then that's it. Thanks, Andy." She rang off.

"That's what?" demanded Meg.

"Hudson Zabriskie."

"*Hudson!?* The Bloater!? He didn't even *know* about the lead oxide!"

"Bull," said Quill, inelegantly. "He runs the factory. And I don't care how stupid everyone thinks he is. He's got the best motive in the world, Meg. His entire career would come to a screeching halt. He'd lose everything if Helena exposed him on TV. It fits, Meg. Dawn's pregnant, about to blow the whistle. He's not sure how many members of the Bosses Club know about it—so he picks them off one by one . . ."

"And he knows Connie's not about to testify against him because of her daughter—and even if she *did*, she genuinely doesn't believe he knows anything."

"I'll bet he would have tried for her in the end, solved," said Quill grimly.

"Solved but not proved," said Meg. "He's going to get away with it."

Quill, silent for a moment, said finally, "I guess we break into Paramount after all. I'll do it tomorrow. The factory's closed on Sunday. And Hudson will be at the beauty contest. He's a judge." With a frown, she flipped the scrap of paper carrying Helena Houndswood's cellular phone account number into the waste basket. "It's the dream about clocks, Meg. I broke into the wrong file. The proof we want is at Paramount."

CHAPTER 13

Quill and John piled out of the Inn van in the high-school parking lot. They'd had trouble finding a parking spot; most of the town had turned out for the preliminaries of the Little Miss Hemlock Falls Beauty contest, and the lot was jammed.

"There he is!" hissed Meg. She poked her elbow into Quill's ribs. Meg stopped, staring at Hudson, one foot up on the curb. Quill tried to look elaborately unconcerned. They both waved to Hudson, who waved back. Meg's socks were pale blue. The past three days she'd been heavily into the pastels: pink, pale yellow, and now this. Quill'd laid it to Andy Bishop's softening influence, but the colors could very well signal rumination. Perhaps even a swing to the contemplative.

"You think Hudson Zabriskie is capable of pushing Dawn Pennifarm into the Zero Room at the Qwik Freeze, hauling the body half a city block to Paramount, and dumping her into the ball mill?" asked John. He had taken the news that Quill was going to break into the paint factory very well. Chase Bank had extended a twenty-thousand-dollar loan. "It doesn't seem quite in character. I'd *much* prefer Helena as a suspect."

"So would Doreen," said Meg. "She thinks that anyone who could run over a flock of defenseless chickens is capable of anything."

The scabs on Quilt's ankles had forced Quill to temporarily give up her pantyhose since the assault by the survivors. She forebore any comment relating to poultry and character, but instead commented that they were obviously in a minority of two, given the excitement around them over the star's rumored presence at the beauty contest.

"Are you sure Helena's going to be here?" whispered Meg to John as they walked to the athletic field. The not-too-distant sound

Claudia Bishop

of tubas, trumpets, and drums heralded the approach of the Hemlock Falls High School Marching Band. "If she's not, Hudson probably won't stick around. You be careful!"

"Harvey said she definitely was going to show up when I borrowed the cellular thinggummy this morning. We can always ditch the plan if she doesn't, Meg. Look!"

"What?" shouted Meg, over the sound of the band.

Quill gestured to wait a minute. The band started a ragged march at the end of the football field, the crimson and purple uniforms bright flags against the green. Two cheerleaders carried a banner reading WE LOVE HELENA! The drum had been painted to read IT'S A BEAUTIFUL LIFE!! in a semicircle surrounding a fairly well-executed portrait of the actress. The drummer wielded the drumsticks with a youthful enthusiasm that had smeared the paint a bit.

Meg and Quill settled onto a front-row bleacher next to a family of Petersons whose first names Quill couldn't remember. John stood on the field, hands tucked into the back pockets of his chinos. Elmer Henry ascended the two shallow steps to the stage at the north end of the field and raised his hands for silence. The judges, Helena and Hudson among them, sat under an awning to his extreme left.

"You've got the phone?" Quill said. "Although they both look like they're settled in."

Meg patted her purse. "I checked the battery. Everything's fine. What did you tell Harvey we wanted it for?"

"I didn't have to justify it; he assumed we were 'improving field-Inn communications.'"

Meg held up her hand against the sun and scanned the field. "Do you see Myles anywhere?"

"No. He wasn't due back until this evening. Deputy Dave's over there."

"Good. Wave at him."

"Why should I wave at Dave Kiddermeister?"

"Alibi," hissed Meg. "We want everyone to see you here. Then they'll just make an assumption that you were here all along and not burglarizing Paramount."

"Meg! If I find what we're looking for, people will know I burglarized the paint factory. And Helena's house."

"And if you don't?"

"Good point." Quill, not precisely sure how to dress for a daylight burglary, had opted for light cotton trousers (for mobility) and a Lycra bodysuit (it wouldn't get caught on anything if she had to hide in a ball mill). The bodysuit was hot and she wriggled uncomfortably. "You'll ring the plant three short rings if anything happens?"

"Two rings, then I hang up, then I ring again once." She patted Quill's shoulder. "It'll be fine. You've done warehouse-type burglaries before, remember."

Quill had. She and John had broken into the Peterson warehouse to gather evidence for a crime the year before. That effort, to save John from a murder charge, had seemed less—*crooklike* was the word she wanted—than a deliberate break-in in broad daylight.

"Meg," she said.

"Shhh!" hissed the rather large female Peterson to her right.

"*Citizens of Hemlock Falls!*" boomed Elmer Henry, too close to the microphone. "Dang!" he said, and moved back two paces. "Citizens of Hemlock Falls! I welcome you to the first annual Little Miss Hemlock Falls Beauty Pageant!"

A roar of applause swept the football field.

"There's going to be more pageants? The Second Annual? The Third Annual?" muttered Meg. "Swell."

"*Shhh!*" hissed Mrs. Peterson.

"I still think we should have brought the signs," said Quill, worriedly scanning the line-up of little girls on the stage.

"I wanted to bring the signs to help establish an alibi," Meg pointed out. "You said nobody believes in protests anymore. You're right. Besides, we agreed it'd upset the little kids." She viewed the children onstage with misgiving.

Elmer, the microphone adjusted to his satisfaction, said, "Now, I know how anxious you folks are to get started, but first, there's a number of people I have to thank for today."

He turned and beamed on the children behind him, then addressed himself to his speech. The number of people Elmer needed to thank appeared to consist of the entire voting population of Hemlock Falls. The children twisted their hair, picked their noses, and made faces at various relatives offstage. "Hurry it *up*, bozo!" shouted a little girl in pink and white starched ruffles accompanied by a West Highland terrier. "It's hot!" The little girl scowled, adjusted the scraggy bow on her dog's collar, polished her patent-leather shoes with spit and forefinger, and scratched her back. Then, heat and boredom combining to ignition point, she punched the little girl next to her. The child on the opposite side, dressed in a miniature tuxedo, pulled the pink and white one's hair. A short but lively brawl ensued onstage, engaging most of the contestants except for the dog, who watched the proceedings with dignified curiosity.

"Prizes," shouted Elmer into the microphone, sublimely ignoring the melee in process behind him, "will be awarded by that star of stage, screen, and television . . . Miss Helena Houndswood!"

Applause swept the audience once more. The children straightened to abrupt attention. Helena, under the temporary awning set up on one corner of the stage, rose and flashed a brilliant smile. Hudson beamed proudly beside her.

"And now, without further ado . . . our first entry! Miss Merrilee Pasquale and her pet dog Star, singing, 'You Are My Lucky Star.'"

Shouts and wild hand clapping indicated the presence of Merrilee Pasquale's large family in the stands. Elmer held up his hands for silence "Ladies and gentlemen, I must ask you to hold your applause, please. Hold your applause until after each and every performance. Merrilee?"

Elmer stepped back. The pink and white girl who looked, Quill thought, about eight, skipped to the front of the stage, the terrier's leash clutched in one freckled fist. She stopped in front of the microphone and said with self-conscious sincerity, "This is my dog, Star. An' I'm singing this song because he is my lucky Star. He's the smartest, bestest dog there ever was." Star, who'd taken the opportunity to sit down, scratched energetically for fleas and succeeded in looking temporarily idiotic.

"Sweet," said Mrs. Peterson. "Isn't that sweet?"

"Oh, my God," muttered Meg, sliding down into her seat.

Merrilee waved an imperious hand and bellowed "Hit it!" The music intro to "You Are My Lucky Star" came over the loudspeaker. "Up, Star," said Merrilee, jerking the leash, "C'mon, boy."

Star rolled over, dreamily contemplating the clear June sky.

"C'mon!"

Star waved his paws and thought dog thoughts.

"Up!" Merrilee hauled up on the leash, and perhaps, thought Quill charitably, out of nervousness, elevated the dog into the air. Star, feet dangling, his tongue much pinker than the ruffles on Merrilee's dress, looked momentarily confused.

"Yeeww are my Luck-ee Star," sang Merrilee in a childish treble.

"Gaack," said Star, in response.

"Put the dog down, Merrilee!" shouted a frantic woman whose freckles signified a close, if not maternal, relationship to the child.

"I saaw you from afar . . ." Merrilee stopped, frowned, and said, "Wait, wait, wait, wait. I forgot. Start over."

"Put the dog *down*!"

"I fergot ta dance!" Merrilee abjured her parent, swinging the leash in admonition. Star, airborne, made a movement in mild protest.

The music intro played once more.

"Yeeww are my Luck-ee Star," shrilled Merrilee, dancing. Star, swinging in four/four time, rolled an exasperated eye skyward.

"Merrilee!" hollered Mrs. Pasquale.

Star, whose experience had apparently taught him not to hold his personal safety hostage to parental intervention, corkscrewed out of his collar and regained solid ground. Merrilee tapped on, patent-leather shoes twinkling in the sunlight. Star's ears flattened in a considering way. He elevated his hindquarters and extended his forepaws. Head cocked, muzzle to the ground, he regarded his mistress's shoes with a somewhat baleful eye.

". . . bee-cawse *yew* are my luck-ee . . . *Ow!* Leggo!"

Star struck the other shoe with the innate precision of any self-respecting terrier after a large black rodent.

"*Get away from me, you stupid dog!*" shrieked Merrilee. She flung herself on the stage and drummed her heels on the floor. "Aaooow!" Star howled, perhaps in a belated attempt to resume the performance.

"Next entry," said Elmer, stepping over the recumbent Merrilee with all the aplomb of Yeltsin resuming control of the Russian white house, "is Tiffany Peterson in a performance of 'New York, New York.'"

Mrs. Peterson applauded energetically. Hudson, with the other judges, sat on the stage in rapt attention. Quill gave Meg's hand a warning squeeze and slipped unobtrusively off the field.

She drove to the paint factory with the sense she was behind enemy lines, braking carefully at intersections, trying not to accelerate too aggressively. She rolled into the parking lot, her palms wet, and parked behind the Dumpsters at the rear of the building. In the strategy session the night before, John had suggested upper windows as the best bet for gaining entry into the locked building. Paramount wasn't air-conditioned, and in the warm summer air the upper windows would be open for ventilation.

Quill scanned the back of the building. He'd been right. She got back into the car and pulled it under the one closest to the back door. Getting out once she was inside would be no problem.

She climbed on the car roof and got her hands firmly over the sill. She swung back. Her tennis shoes took firm hold on the corrugated wall. She pushed herself up and over the ledge. She dangled half in, head down. Grasping the window frame, she hitched her legs up until she was sitting on the ledge. Then, her right hand tight on the window frame, the left on the ledge, she shifted herself around and dropped her leg, stomach to the wall. She eased herself straight, took a deep breath, and dropped to the floor.

She took a moment to catch her breath. Her knees and ankles hurt. The factory was quiet, the great ball mills shrouded. The scent of linseed oil hung in the air like a heavy drape. She picked her way carefully across the concrete to the round cardboard canisters that held the minerals used in mixing paint. The barrels were stacked on steel shelving that reached to the top of the fourteen-foot ceiling. She scanned the barrels. IRON OXIDE was the third rack up. A wheeled stepladder had been pushed to the side of the shelving. She rolled it across the floor, mounted, and pried the lid off a barrel that looked as though it had been opened before.

Iron oxide, Quill knew, was essentially rust. The mineral she was looking at was black, finely ground, and, when she picked up a handful, felt like the graphite used in pencils, soft and shiny. Quill would have bet her set of oils that she was looking at lead oxide.

The same lead oxide that OSHA had labeled a hazardous material. A mineral that caused birth defects, brain damage, and cancers to those who'd been exposed to it for years and years without protective clothing. She dropped a handful into the bread bag Meg had given her, then climbed down the stepladder.

The glycols next. She tucked the bread bag into her jeans pocket and pulled out an empty spice jar. The glycols were stacked in polyurethane vats with spouts on the bottom third, on shelves at right angles to the oxides. Quill filled the jar with a sample.

The last thing, she thought, was that dream about clocks. The budget requests were filed in the accountant's office. Quill searched methodically and found it.

Three days before Helena Houndswood had rolled into town on a Sunday, Hudson Zabriskie had requested funds for five new supervisors. Five supervisors he knew he was going to replace—because he was going to kill all of them.

The phone shrilled as loud as a rifle report. One ring, A pause. Then two. Meg's warning.

The office door opened. Quill whirled, the approved budget request in one hand.

Hudson Zabriskie. With a rifle.

"This," said Quill, "is just like one of those 'B' movies. You won't get away with this."

"I have four times before." He was in the backseat of her car, the deer rifle tucked between his knees, six inches from her head. Quill's hands were slippery on the wheel.

"You were using oil-based ingredients in some of the latex paints. Lead, kerosene. The whole operation exposed the employees to pollutants."

"Made a much better paint," said Hudson. "My own devising, actually. I know paint."

"A lot of the hazardous materials were mislabeled as glycols or iron oxide, both inert matter. It's been years since you've had an OSHA inspection, but you'd get one eventually, Hudson. How did you think you were going to get away with it?"

"Take a left here."

Quill turned and faced him. "Well?"

He jerked the rifle at her. "Keep your eyes on the road. We're still making oil-based. It's not illegal for another six years. If OSHA caught us unaware, we'd just say we made a mistake, that's all. In the labeling room. The QA function was the most brilliant stroke, I have to admit. I simply recalibrated the gauges."

"I don't understand."

"Let's say you have a clock mechanism. What it does is push the hands of the dial into a certain position, right? But what do you design on the face of the clock? If you don't put numbers on the face of the clock, if you put, for example, degrees Fahrenheit, you can turn a clock into a thermometer. I simply redid the gauges in the QA function so they read for, say, iron oxide, instead of lead. Or kerosene. OSHA never checks the gauges onsite. You send them off to NIST to be recalibrated. All you have to do is send the correct gauges and store them in the back room until you need to send them to NIST again. If we get nailed, we apologize, explain that the changeover from latex had been the week before, and we'd screwed up this one time. We'd get a fine. Be properly apologetic for the error. But I wouldn't go to jail. And New York wasn't about to fire me over an OSHA violation. My numbers are too good. And that's what New York cares about, numbers. Would they fire me over screw-ups? Well, never underestimate how much you can blame on the worker, Quill. Stop here."

They were in the granite quarry behind the Qwik Freeze. In the distance Quill could hear the sounds of the Hemlock Falls High School Marching Band playing "Oh, What a Beautiful Morning." She turned off the ignition.

The rifle nudged her skull. "You're going to get caught, Hudson. It's only a matter of time. I can't believe you've gotten away with it for as long as you have."

"Well, I had some cooperation. Sandy. Dawn. Kay. Appropriate bonuses at appropriate times keep a lot of people quiet."

"But Dawn didn't keep quiet, did she? Or wouldn't when she discovered her baby was—"

"Defective," said Hudson. "No. The stupid woman went into a major fit of hysteria. Threatened to blow the whistle. Without her, Sandy and Kay folded, too."

"And what about Connie?"

"Connie?" He raised his eyebrows.

"Did she know what was going on?"

"Well, she must have, mustn't she? But she needed the job. I had Dawn sound her out once about getting paid off. She said she didn't know what Dawn was talking about."

"So she just kept silent."

"She just kept silent." He slid back the rifle's bolt.

Quill turned around to face him. "So you killed them? All of them?"

"Ashes to ashes," said Hudson. "Or rather, paint to paint. Not Sandy and Dot, of course. Doesn't do to repeat yourself. Get out of the car, please."

"You're going to have to kill Helena Houndswood, too, Hudson."

"Helena Houndswood? Why should I?"

"Because Dawn told her what was going on. I found a file in her house, Hudson. She knows about the crimes at the paint factory, and she's already contacted her agent about arranging for the media to blow the whistle."

"You're missing the point, Quill. I haven't committed any crimes. They're violations! Do you understand me? And all that happens is you get fined for a violation. I won't go to jail. I won't serve time. I won't even lose my job. Paramount will pay the fine!"

"Then why did you kill four women? Dawn. Dot. Kay. Sandy."

"Why? Why? No witnesses! Do you know what the media does to people, Quill? Do you have any idea? You take perfectly good human beings, like me"—he gestured with his rifle and Quill, choking with fear, wondered if she'd have the nerve to struggle with him for it—"just trying to do a good job. Trying to adjust to the changes in all these regulations, and all these rules, and all of a sudden what you've done before has been legal, but when you do it now, it's not illegal. But it's going to be illegal, in the future. And where does that leave you? The media comes in, *20/20*, or *60 Minutes* or those guys and Dawn starts bawling about deformed babies and the public crucifies you. *Even when you haven't done anything wrong!* I was within the law. When I started in this business, I was one of the best! I was doing it right. And then the rules changed! Only they don't change now, so that there's no clear-cut line. They change in the future. So what the hell was I supposed to do? Give up my job? Where am I going to find a job in a town this size? At my age, where am I going to find a job in a town any size? So don't tell me I committed crimes. I didn't commit crimes. I committed violations. And you get fined for violations, and eventually New York tells you, 'No more oil-based paint,' and *then* you stop making oil-base because *then* it's a crime. And the quality's so bad with latex. So many customer complaints with latex. You know, Quill, more people are satisfied with paint that comes from my factory than anywhere else."

"You told me that," said Quill.

"So then here comes this little bitch," he said bitterly. "This mother, who'd been going along like everybody else, even that Connie turning a blind eye because she knows just like me that we're just committing violations, not crimes, and guess what? All of a sudden I'm going to be nailed up and hung out to dry. Dawn's going to tell the media that I knew. That I deformed her baby on purpose. And I'd have nothing," said Hudson bitterly. "Nothing. Now get out of the car."

Quill opened her door and slipped out of the driver's seat. Hudson, the rifle steadily held at the back of her neck, slid after her. He nudged her with the rifle barrel. Quill started up the heavily wooded slope to the Qwik Freeze, Hudson breathing heavily behind her. Casting desperately about for the sight of another human being, she saw nothing but trees, shrubs, and tall grass. The Qwik Freeze was built right into the hill. The likelihood of anyone coming on them was slim to none. She said, trying to hide the hopelessness in her voice, "Hudson, you can't get away with this for much longer."

"Sure I can. Where's the evidence? There's no evidence. There's no bodies."

"Dawn had an amniocentesis, Hudson. That leaves enough tissue to make a DNA match. They may never know what happened to Kay. Or to me. But they'll know what happened to Dawn."

"Rickie will get nailed for Dawn and Dot, too," said Hudson as though he hadn't heard her. "I made sure of that. And as for you—well, you're just going to disappear. You're going to go out in a Crimson Blaze of glory. There's *no proof.* None. Nothing links me to this. No one links me to this. Now that I took care of those interfering bitches. Stop here."

The utility door to the Qwik Freeze was barred and padlocked. Hudson braced the rifle on his left hip, the long barrel pointed slightly up, and pulled a slim file from his trousers pocket. "This always takes a minute," he said. "Don't move."

"Somebody will see us," said Quill, stepping toward him. "It's broad daylight."

"I said don't move!" Hudson swung the rifle directly at her.

Quill moved closer, slowly.

"Come on! Come on!" Hudson snapped.

Quill kept her eyes on his, ignoring the rifle barrel.

The middle of the rifle stock caught her shoulder. Quill sprang, shoved Hudson against the door, and grabbed with both hands, hanging on to the barrel, pushing herself against Hudson's thin chest in determined, frantic desperation so that he couldn't shoot. Crumpled against the metal utility door, Hudson started to cry.

The handle turned. The door opened inward. Hudson shouted, half-fell into the darkness beyond the door, and scrambled to his feet. Quill tightened her grip, the rifle steady in her hands. A familiar figure in gray stepped into the sunlight.

"Myles," said Quill. "It's about bloody time."

CHAPTER 14

"How do I look?" asked Quill.

"Without the rifle? Not half as exciting." Myles's grin broadened. "Just as ready to do battle, I hope."

"Very funny." Quill patted her hair tentatively; Dwight had spent a long time with the curling iron and the mousse, and it felt strange. "You should see what he's done with Connie. She looks magnificent."

"I spoke with her when I came in. She's sitting on the set. Said she's afraid to move."

"I know the feeling."

The two of them were alone in the conference room, which had been co-opted as a Green Room.

"I think I'm nervous."

"You look wonderful. But then, you always look wonderful."

Quill looked at him from under her lashes. "I look awful. You could scrape the makeup off my face with a palette knife. My hair feels like it's been glued. My mother always said the best man to marry is the man who thinks you look terrific when you look your worst."

His face changed. He took her hand. "And what do you think?"

"She was probably right."

"I don't want you to touch me!" shouted Meg, charging into the room. Dwight trotted behind her, dragging his wheeled cart. "This is the way I look when I cook, and this is the way I feel comfortable when I cook, and I don't want anything different!" She was wearing her usual chef's outfit: black leggings and sweatshirt. A yellow sweat band held her dark hair from her face.

Myles glanced at her feet. "Bright green?" he asked, his eyebrows raised.

"Could go either way," said John as he joined them. "That is, if you're trying to diagnose the sock color."

"You appear to be totally unflapped," said Quill with a touch of envy.

His eyes narrowed in a smile. "Has Helena settled on which parts of the Inn she'll show on television?"

"We've already taped the Shaker suite and the Provençal rooms," said Dwight, who'd been pulling various items from the drawers of his cart. "She's going to run them as leaders. We've set the remotes up near the hiking trails at the falls so Herself can talk about the Eden-like simplicity of the village. We'll go live from the foyer."

Quill took several deep breaths. "I don't think I'd be as nervous if we weren't going to be live. If I am nervous. Maybe I'm scared."

"What's the difference?" asked Myles, his hand warm and comforting in hers.

"Nervous is just . . . you know, nervous. Scared is like, I think I'll throw up if I have to do this."

"You'll be fine," said John. "I have confidence in you, Quill. Any woman who can wrench a rifle from a man who's killed four women and deliver him into the hands of the law isn't going to throw up being interviewed by Helena Houndswood."

Dwight tweaked a curl into place around Quill's cheek. He consulted the clipboard, then surveyed Meg with a thoughtful expression. "I must say you do clean up to advantage, dear."

"It's nowhere near time, is it?" said Quill in a panic. "I thought we were going on the air at ten o'clock. It's only nine-thirty!"

"Herself's a fiend on making sure everything's in place well before airtime," soothed Dwight. "Now. Tell me about your lovely murders. The gentleman in question's been hauled off to the pokey?" He drifted in Meg's direction, a vaguely purposeful look in his eye. Meg regarded him dubiously.

"He was arraigned on three counts of murder," said Myles. "We won't be able to prove the fourth."

"Sandy, Dawn, and Dot, and that nice Kay, what was her name? Gondowski?" Dwight took a comb from the breast pocket of his white linen blazer and began fiddling with Meg's hair. She protested. He put a firm hand on her shoulder and said, "Wait, ducky. It'll be painless, I assure you. That Kay. Never found her?"

"Zabriskie's not admitting to anything." Myles released Quill's hand and stretched his long legs out in front of him. "And we can't prove that the second body in the paint is Kay's. There's no DNA match."

"But you'll get him for the others. Right? He's in jail, isn't he?" Dwight shuddered dramatically. "Four murders! A serial killer. You got him on tissue samples, or something?" Dwight moved to the back of Meg's head. At Myles's uncommunicative grunt he wiggled his eyebrows suggestively and pointed to Meg. Meg twisted around to look at Dwight who firmly turned her around to face her sister. Quill, who liked very much what Dwight was doing to Meg's hair, picked up her cue and said, "Yes, Dwight. Myles, that is, Sheriff McHale, was able to confirm Dawn's death because her amniocentesis provided a tissue sample to match the DNA. We didn't have a tissue sample for Kay. But the analysis of the contents of the paint can last week showed two bodies. We just can't confirm it's Kay."

"And that third one, Sandy? She had wonderful cheekbones . . . I call that a crying shame." From somewhere in the depths of his jacket, he produced a small can of hair spray. Meg glowered, but remained still. Quill nodded encouragement to Myles.

"One fingerprint, on the trunk of the Willis Chevette, at least links him to it," said Myles. "And we found his hair and skin cell samples in the front seat of the rented Cortina. You know how that goes in court. We'll see. And we've got a minute blood sample from the suit he was wearing the day he allegedly shot Dot Vandermolen. Type AB, which matches hers."

"The way they let these bastards off . . ." Dwight spread matte makeup on Meg's face with quick strokes of his finger. "I ask you."

"Oh, I think we can prove premeditation," said Myles. "Something Ms. Quilliam discovered will make a difference there."

Quill blushed under Dwight's admiring glance. "Do tell, Sheriff," he said.

"The budget request. Zabriskie applied to have the five supervisor positions replaced the Friday before Helena Houndswood came to Hemlock Falls to announce the win."

"So he'd planned to get rid of them ahead of time," said Quill. "There's a lot to be said for the dream tactic in investigations."

"Won't he put up a defense that he was simply planning on firing them?" asked John.

"He could try," said Myles. "Except the payoff money he was giving Dawn and the others to assure silence about the lead oxide was in the form of bonuses for excellent performance. Pretty hard to justify firing your best workers for incompetence. And Connie Weyerhauser is going to testify about the intentional violations and the OSHA scam. So we've got him wrapped up pretty tightly."

"Well, I am just as impressed as all get-out." Dwight held Meg's chin firmly in one hand and began to apply eyeliner. "Did you suspect him from the beginning, Quill?"

"I didn't suspect him at all," said Quill ruefully. "I thought it was Makepeace Whitman."

Dwight turned and raised an astonished eyebrow. "I mean to say! I thought the poor fellow was just devoted to that wonderful environmental cause of his. I was talking about his group's dedication to that marvelous character you have rolling around here . . . the birdy-looking one? The older woman?"

"Doreen," said Quill. "I'm surprised she hasn't come to work yet. She seemed pretty interested in the show."

Meg sent her a significant glance. Quill, on whom the significance was lost, was bewildered.

Dwight fluffed Meg's hair and said chattily, "Doreen, that's it. She just couldn't say enough good things about him. Although I have to say I don't know exactly what the Friends of Fresh Air stand for, but it must be very, very important. He's a lovely, lovely man."

"That lovely, lovely man was dumping lead oxide on Paramount," said Meg tartly, "and submitting two sets of invoices to Paramount. He knew darn well what was going on. He's been arrested."

"I'll tell you," said Dwight, doing wonders with blusher and Meg's cheekbones, "I had a few moments when I really thought Herself might be behind this. Not that seeing her sent up the river on a murder rap would make me cry in my beer. But then, I'm clearly not a star in the amateur sleuth line, like you, Quill."

Quill was wearing an extremely pretty bronze print off-the-shoulder dress. She smoothed the silky material over her knees with a consciously innocent air. "I'll tell you something else, strictly *entre nous*," Dwight continued. "We're not sticking with this Beautiful Living crap forever, you know. No, the boss lady has plans. Think you'll be seeing some surprising things from her in the very near future. Investigative reporting. But *don't* say I told you! There!" He stepped back from Meg, and clapped his hands together with decisive delight.

John let loose a long low whistle. Myles nodded appreciatively.

"Just sit there for one little minute more, ducky. I'll be right back."

"You look terrific," said Quill.

Meg rolled her eyes.

"Now, for the *pièce de résistance*!" Dwight pulled the lowest drawer of his cart open and withdrew a tissue-wrapped package. "Here! I asked for this from downstate ages ago, and it just arrived last night. Try it." "It" was a chef's coat in a swirl of soft, cream-colored jersey. "Such a tacky design, essentially," Dwight fussed. He eased Meg into the coat. "Double breasted! Foul! But I asked for a few alterations and voilà!"

The high collar peaked attractively around Meg's face. The buttons were antiqued gold. The sleeves draped over a tight cuff. Meg moved her arms up and down experimentally. "Hey," she said.

"You look beautiful," said Quill. "Andy should see this. I thought he was going to be here?"

"I asked him not to come," said Meg. "I thought you'd be nervous."

"Me! Why should Andy make me nervous?"

"Well, he sure wouldn't make me nervous," said Meg nervously.

"Then I'll call him."

"Don't call him. If I want to call him, I'll call him."

"Don't you two ever quit?" Helena Houndswood swept into the room, trailed by her producer. She inspected Meg with a coldly critical eye, looked Quill up and down, and nodded sharply. "You'll both do. We're ready. Positions, please."

"Thank you so much, Dwight, darling," said Dwight to the air. "The transformation is simply astonishing."

"Check the cameras in the foyer," Helena said to the producer. "And I want the remotes over the falls and in the kitchen tested." She snapped her fingers at Meg. "You. Into position in the kitchen. And Sarah, you come with me. The rest of you stay out of the way." She swept out again.

Myles smiled. "Break a leg."

"We'll be on the front stairs," said John. "The whole staff. You'll do fine, both of you."

"What's this about Doreen, Meg?" Quill looked around the room, as though expecting the housekeeper to crawl out from under the table. "Gosh, I was sure she'd be here."

"Chop-chop!" said Dwight, snapping his fingers. "Places, ladies!"

"I meant to tell you about this earlier, but you were getting made over." Meg followed Quill into the hall. "She showed up early this morning. Asked for some time off."

"Well, you gave it to her, didn't you? I mean she works like a dog. If she wants to take a day off . . ."

"She didn't say 'a day.' She said some time. And when I asked her how much time, she said she wasn't sure. God and Nature needed her, she said. And then she muttered something about her feathered friends. I know she took those chickens home. You think she's maybe gone to feed them?"

"She took them to Dookie's church. After I explained the theory of sanctuary to her."

"You know what else? All the Friends of Fresh Air are back. They checked in this morning and went right out again."

Quill stopped at the entrance to the foyer. The area was clogged with hot white lights, cameras, and mysterious black boxes. Cables as thick as pythons snaked over every available inch of floor space. "They paid their bills, even Makepeace did, before he was arrested," said Quill absentmindedly. "And they were very quiet guests. Except for Myles arresting Makepeace, they were no trouble at all." She came to attention as what Meg was implying sank in. "Meg! Do you think she went off with them?!"

"Yep."

"She's never actually run off before," said Quill. "I mean, all of her enthusiasms have been local up until now."

"The Friends tour from place to place," Meg reminded her, "seeking out the pure and natural where they find it, and where they don't, saving the planet from man's horny-handed destruction."

"She couldn't leave us!" Quill, dismayed, forgot her nervousness about her first television appearance at the thought of life at the Inn without Doreen. "Meg, how could you let her go? Why didn't you come and get me?"

"She's a grown woman, Quill."

"Places!" shouted the producer.

Quill made a horrible face at Meg, then stepped carefully over the cables to the space cleared in front of the fireplace for the shoot. The cream leather couch had been replaced by three leather chairs. A low coffee table, covered with a damask cloth and set with the Bosses Club prizewinning dishes, stood in front of the chairs. Connie, magnificent in teal and violet, presided over the table. Quill sat next to her. "You match the china!" she whispered delightedly.

"They did a nice job," Connie said. "They're going to give me a place setting for twelve."

Quill picked up a coffee cup. The rose-breasted grosbeak stared at her with a gold-rimmed eye. "Will you keep it?"

"Barb likes it. So I guess I will. Myles arranged for her to watch. See her? She's over there."

Quill turned. The entrance to the dining room was filled with people. Barbara sat in her wheelchair with her father smiling proudly behind her. Kathleen Kiddermeister, Peter Hairston, and the rest of the waiters and waitresses crowded around them. She caught sight of Harvey Bozzel's thinning blond hair. A large space in the cluster of heads indicated the presence of Mayor Henry and Marge Schmidt. Myles had told her the dining room was filled with the Chamber members and every citizen of Hemlock Falls that could wangle standing room. Myles and John sat on the stairs, staring down at them. There was no sign of Doreen.

Quill twiddled her thumbs, suddenly nervous again. The minutes before airtime seemed endless. To distract herself, she turned to Connie. "Will you be staying on in Hemlock Falls?"

"Oh, yes. We've set aside the money for Barb, mostly, although we're going to take a few trips." She laughed. "And I've left Paramount, of course. A million dollars pays quite a bit of interest."

"All right." Helena sat in the third leather chair. "Five minutes. Follow my lead, the two of you. Answer the questions just as we rehearsed them. Ready!" The klieg lights snapped on. Quill squinted in the glare. Someone behind the bank of white lights began to count.

"Ten . . . nine . . . eight . . ."

Quill waved at Myles and John. Andy had joined them; from his smile, it looked as though Meg had relented and called him after all.

"Don't see Doreen up there," said Connie in a low voice.

"Meg said she left us, Connie. I just can't believe—"

"Quiet!" snapped Helena.

"Three . . . two . . . one . . . *And!*"

Helena bloomed. She stared into the little red eye of the camera directly in front of her and said in a low, musical voice, complete with upper-class vowels, "Welcome, America, to the beauty in your lives. I'm speaking to you today from a charming hideaway in upstate New York . . ."

Quill, frozen, realized she was in front of eighty million households. She was going to throw up.

". . . cobblestone, demonstrating the best of taste," Helena said.

"The camera's not on us," Connie whispered reassuringly. "See? They're on the remote." She pointed to Quill's left. A large TV screen showed the remote cameras panning the village. Helena had made good on her promise of golden retrievers and yuppie couples. Five or six blond, well-dressed men and women strolled down Main Street, dogs at their sides.

". . . the falls themselves create an environment reminiscent of those ducky little villages in the Cotswolds," Helena continued, "and the citizens of this village of elegance and discretion—"

"Whoop!" shouted Connie Weyerhauser suddenly, with a gust of laughter.

"My God!" screamed Helena.

"We have temporarily taken control of this remote station," announced the voice of Mrs. Whitman. She and the twenty or so members of the Friends of Fresh Air filled the remote monitor screen, edge to edge. "Our organization is here to bring an injustice to the attention of the people of the United States!"

"Turn off the goddam remote!" snarled Helena.

"I have to warn those viewers sensitive to violence that the contents of this garbage bag may affront you," said Mrs. Whitman with evangelical fervor.

Helena charged the remote monitor. Connie was laughing so hard that the leather chair vibrated. Quill, bemused, wondered why she hadn't figured it out before; the lack of luggage should have tipped her off. "They're nudists," she said, which, on later reflection, she decided was unnecessary, since eighty million viewers of Helena Houndswood's *It's a Beautiful Life* could see that for themselves. "Thank goodness, though, Connie. I was afraid Doreen had left town, and there she is, right next to that tall guy." She leaned forward, peering at the screen. "If I could see his head, I could tell which of the FOFA members it is. There. He's ducked a little bit. Good Lord! It's Dookie Shuttleworth!"